The Legend of the Rose

The Legend of the Rose

copyright © 2014 by Jack Braby

ISBN 978-0-9817244-7-8

Book design by Joy Troyer

Printed in the United States of America

Dyeing Arts Books
Kentfield, California
www.dyeingarts.com

The Legend of the Rose

by

Lois E. Taylor Braby

Author's Note

This tender tale, though fiction, is also true, for those who
have experienced the power of love know that:
Love can come quickly and without warning.
Love can bloom fully with great joy.
Love can be shattered in the face of misunderstanding or
tragedy or grief but, though lost, love can never be destroyed!

This tale is told by one who knows whereof she speaks,
"a Wonderer and a Wanderer."

Lois E. Taylor Braby

Introduction

This is a simple love story, yet, is love ever simple? And even more complex when shared between persons of uniquely different cultures and lifestyles! The story begins in Tokyo, Japan, and chronicles the lives of several young people who come together as friends.

The two main characters of the story are Ana Maria Gabrielli and Toshiburo Matsushita Yamamoto. Toshiburo is a young Japanese man, a Buddhist and a 'child of privilege,' who is destined to follow in the footsteps of his ancestry. He may choose, however, one of two pathways—the world of business as his own father, Tatsume Yamamoto, has done or the arena of diplomatic service as his great-grandfather Matsushita (the father of his dear grandmother and mentor, Sukiyama Matsushita Yamamoto). This gentleman was of high status in the Japanese government during the brilliant Meiji period. Toshiburo has been taught well the highest values of Japanese life—responsibility and honor to one's family! He has chosen the path of his great-grandfather Matsushita.

Ana Maria Gabrielli is an American woman, a 'child of poverty' from Italian, Catholic descent. Her family was immigrants to the Boston area in the 1920's. Her parents are deceased and her closest living relatives are her sister and family, Valentina and Roger Tristano and their children. Ana's background has taught her the importance of hard work and independence of spirit. She is a true Bostonian and her highest value is freedom!

Ana comes to Japan with her two Japanese friends from their stateside college days, Myuki Kitada and Mishima Matsumura, to pursue their professional goals as 'intercultural specialists.' Their shared concerns are to find ways to assist others in developing cultural sensitivity and international understanding for the purpose of peace within the world.

Thus, the story begins…and that eternal struggle continues between responsibility and freedom!

List of Main Characters

Ana Maria Gabrielli..................Intercultural Specialist, Tokyo Intercultural Center

Miyuki Kitada..........................Intercultural Specialist, Tokyo Intercultural Center

Mishima Matsumura.................Intercultural Specialist, Tokyo Intercultural Center

Ito Nishiyama...........................Director, Tokyo Intercultural Center

Yoko and Junichi Matsumura...Parents of Mishima

Kyoshi Satoyama......................Close friend of Mishima

Toshiburo Matsushita Yamamoto......Professor of Political Science, Tokyo University

Tatsume and Kumiko Yamamoto......Parents of Toshiburo

Sukiyama Yamamoto................Grandmother of Toshiburo

Sano Ishikawa..........................Companion to Toshiburo

Sachiko Matsuda.......................Toshiburo's promised wife

Masao Izaki..............................Hotel manager, Tokyo

Valentina and Roger Tristano...Ana's sister and husband, Boston

Mikoto Toshiburo Matsumura..Ana and Mishima's son

Suzannah Morgan Randolph.....Mikoto's special friend in Virginia

Dominic Donatelli ....Heart specialist for Toshiburo, Washington, D.C.

Yoshiko and Ishiro Yasutaka....Caretakers, Ana's Virginia home

Setting:

This story begins in Japan where Ana, Miyuki, and Mishima live and work at the Intercultural Center in Tokyo. The three young people are graduates of Georgetown University in Washington, D.C. and hold master's degrees in Anthropology/Intercultural Studies with Japanese cultural emphasis. Ito Nishiyama has hired the three friends to serve on staff as Intercultural Program Specialists.

Book One

The Land of Mirror, Sword, and Jewel

CHAPTER 1

"Thunder pounds 'gainst summer sky
like the throbbing beat of kodo drums
on a sultry August night,
both predicting storms to come.

There is no reason to fear the storm
that rips apart the sky or heart.
Calm will follow, hearts will heal.
Why then do I shudder so...at thunder's roll?"

--T. Yamamoto, Journal
The Night of O-bon

The hot, August night was filled with the sights and sounds of celebration as happy crowds milled through the streets of downtown Tokyo. It was the night of the annual O-bon[1] festival. Women in their bright, silk kimonos of red, orange, or pink and men in their black and gold silk or cool blue and white cotton created a maze of brilliant color as far as the eye could see. Scattered among this colorful throng were the Buddhist priests, dressed in gleaming white robes and carrying tall, bamboo poles with huge paper lanterns attached. Swaying above the crowds, the lanterns displayed special blessings written in bright red kanji[2] for those who were celebrated on this night.

Anxious shouts of sidewalk vendors echoed from every corner tempting the celebrants with their wares. Sweet and

---

*1 (O-bon) During the first weeks of August, the people of Japan pay homage to their ancestors who, according to Buddhist belief, revisit the earth at this time of year. Everywhere throughout the nation, lanterns are lit to guide the spirits home and anxious relatives prepare to greet the returning souls with lively 'bon-odori' (folk dances) and special foods. Thousands of Japanese citizens plan their annual vacations so they can return to the homes of their birth and share in the 'O-bon- holiday with their families.
*2 (kanji) Japanese language characters

pungent odors filled the air but the crowds were most often drawn to the smoking grills. Here they found their tasty favorites, tomorokoshi[3] and yaki-tori[4]. But the favorites for the children were not necessarily the foods. These little ones shouted with delight and crowded around the cages containing huge crickets and beetles, begging their parents for a new pet. Of course, most walked away with happy smiles and small cages filled with black, squirming 'monsters' which were chomping contentedly on crunchy, green leaves.

Like a backdrop for it all, the throbbing beat of exotic rhythms echoed from gigantic drums mounted on high, wooden platforms at various locations throughout the city. The famous Kodo drummers, dressed in loincloths and headbands, literally became one with their instruments. Their muscular bodies covered with sweat, they pounded out the cadence of the ancient celebration while energetic crowds responded to the frenzied beat by shouting and clapping. Many joined in circle dances, moving to the intoxicating rhythm of the drums.

Though it was apparent that Ana was an outsider, she was drawn into the spirit of the occasion and with her video camera attempted to record as much of the festival as possible. She was especially fascinated by the dancers with their colorful costumes and rhythmic movements. They, in turn, were willing subjects for the attention of the attractive, young Westerner and were pleasantly surprised when she thanked them in "near-perfect" Japanese for allowing her to film their dance.

Ana enjoyed every minute of this unique celebration and was perfectly comfortable being one of the few Westerners in the streets. She didn't even mind the children's stares or, at times, their obvious shock as she mingled with the crowds. These little ones loved to watch the *gaijin*[5] sample their special treats, waiting breathlessly to see if she would smile or frown at the tastes. They giggled shyly at her responses while their black eyes sparkled with pleasure. Now and then, the bravest of them would

*3 (tomorokoshi) sweet corn roasted over hot coals
*4 (yaki-tori) grilled chicken covered with soy sauce, served on bamboo sticks
*5 (gaijin) foreigner

point at her camera, laughing and striking silly poses. To their surprise and joy, Ana gladly filmed their antics. She found nothing so enchanting nor so beautiful as these Oriental children with their bright, dark eyes and silky black hair.

After walking many blocks through the city and spending several hours taping the festivities, Ana began looking for a place to rest and cool off. She was pushing through the crowd near one of the drum platforms when she felt someone grasp her arm. She turned, afraid that her camera was about to become the victim of a thief. Instead, she stumbled into the chest of a young Japanese man. He smiled and quickly reassured her.

"Please don't be upset! I noticed you watching the festivities and thought you might want to join me in the *bon odori*…the dance. Perhaps you'd like to know how the "natives" do it."

The young man was in Western dress and spoke perfect English with a hint of a British accent. Ana assumed by his courteous manner and language skills that he must be well-educated and, perhaps, a gentleman. She decided to take a chance and replied with enthusiasm, "I'd at least like to try! I've been watching the dancers all evening and would definitely appreciate a lesson from a 'native.'"

With no further comment, the young man took Ana's arm and led her toward one of the dance circles. They watched the dancers for a while as he carefully explained the movements: "Actually, it's very simple. We walk in a circle behind one another, take three steps forward, touch your hand to your elbow and raise your arm, then the other, and continue until the group has made a full circle. Then turn and go the other direction. We're not trying to keep up with the timing of the drums, just stay on a beat."

Then he issued the challenge, "Are you ready to try it?"

Though somewhat hesitant, Ana smiled and nodded her head, yes, buckled the camera into its case, threw it over her shoulder and they joined the dance. At first, the partners did fairly well and, moving to the rhythm of the dance, Ana felt the pounding beat of the drums vibrate through her whole body. She loved the sensation of sharing in this ancient celebration as if she were truly a part of it. After all, this is why she had come to this far-away land—to experience the culture as if it were her own and for these few moments, she did not feel like a foreigner. She felt as if she truly belonged here. But, to her dismay, the others in the circle had trouble keeping in step while eagerly watching to see what the *gaijin* would do.

Ana soon found herself turning on the wrong beat and bumping into nearly everyone until they were all laughing too hard to continue. Finally, her partner took Ana's arm and bowing courteously to the group explained in Japanese, "I think my partner and I should take a break now, so you can get back to the dance!"

As the pair turned to leave, the dancers laughed and waved at Ana, some thanking her in broken English for joining them. They were pleasantly surprised when she apologized for her clumsy behavior in their own language. Moving away from the circle, Ana turned to her partner, "I really must beg your pardon. I love the music and the rhythms, but I've never been much of a dancer. I guess I'd better stick to 'spectating.'"

The young man smiled warmly but kept a firm grip on Ana's arm, guiding her toward the sidewalk as he spoke. "You needn't apologize. At least you were willing to try and you did very well for a first time with the *bon-odori*. In fact, you did better than anyone in our group! They were so fascinated with the beautiful American they could barely keep in step. But now, I think we need a drink to cool off and rest a while. There's a place around the corner where we can enjoy the festival from the sidelines."

"I was about to do that when you stopped me. I honestly thought someone was trying to steal my camera or my bag. That's why I turned on you so quickly."

"I didn't mean to upset you, but I was having trouble catching up with you."

Before Ana could respond to this rather surprising statement, her partner had guided her through the crowd and around the corner to a quieter street. She began to feel uneasy, thinking to herself, 'Who is this young man and why am I letting him lead me through the streets of Tokyo?' She knew better. Through years of intercultural travel and living in large cities, Ana certainly had enough experience to be very careful about her choice of companions. Yet, in the excitement of the evening, she had let her guard down. But it was working again, now.

She stopped and pulled away from him.

"To be quite honest, I feel a bit uneasy right now. I'm not accustomed to going into strange bars with strange men."

The young man turned to her with a warm smile.

"Perhaps I *am* a stranger to you, but please be assured that I am not what one would describe as a *strange* man. And the bar is right here close to the street."

He pointed just ahead where Ana saw the door to the bar and the crowd gathered there. She was a bit more relaxed now due to his kind manner and replied hesitantly,

"Well…since we're here and I'm *very* thirsty!"

Ana was careful not to apologize for her hesitation. She wanted this young man to know that even though she was a *gaijin* in his homeland, she was *not* an 'easy mark.' Her partner seemed to understand her concerns and did not attempt to take her arm again. She relaxed then, glad that he had responded with courtesy rather than in the more aggressive manner she had experienced many times in the past in several different settings.

When the pair entered the crowded bar, they found a small table near the front where they could watch the festivities. After being seated, Ana's partner asked politely,

"As your kyuji[6] for the evening, what may I bring you from the bar?"

"Please…a very large coke with lots of ice. It's been a long, hot night and I'm dying of thirst!"

He seemed surprised at her request,

"You mean you won't try our famous Japanese beer? Unless you taste our Asahi or Kirin, you will miss an important part of this 'intercultural' experience."

She laughed and answered with a touch of sarcasm,

"No way! I've *had* that 'intercultural experience' and tonight I intend to make it home on my own two feet!"

Her partner replied with a courteous smile,

"Then we'll drink your American cokes…tonight."

Ana immediately caught the hidden message in his words, as if there might be *other* nights when they would share drinks

*6 (kyuji) waiter

together. But she decided to ignore his comment for the moment, relieved that he had chosen to join her in remaining sober. This seemed to be a positive sign of respect or of a very smooth approach to women. She wondered which.

The bar was so packed that it was a while before Ana's 'mystery escort' made his way back through the crowd. For the first time, she had a chance to look more carefully at the young man who had whisked her into the dance. He was rather tall and slender with light olive skin and silky, black hair worn in a longer, more casual style than most Japanese men she had met here. His appearance and manner gave the impression of one who was well-educated and refined. And she knew enough about clothes to recognize his silk trousers and French-style shirt as expensive. Ana had no doubts that this stranger, waiting on her with such grace and courtesy, was *not* an ordinary Japanese working man.

Within a few moments, Ana's *kyuji* set the tray down in the middle of the table, seated himself and made a statement that caused her to stare at him in surprise.

"I've decided to be totally honest with you. You should know that I've been following you all evening." He hesitated a moment, then continued with a teasing smile, "Does that disturb you?" He did not move his eyes from hers, waiting for an answer. She replied in the same manner,

"Only if you have some *ominous* purpose in doing so."

He was caught off guard by this unexpected response, wondering if she were teasing or had issued him an intentional insult. He asked with a slight smile,

"And what might you consider *ominous*?"

Ana leaned toward her evening host and replied in a way which left no doubt of her meaning.

"I hardly think I need explain that to you. From your Western dress and command of the English language, I assume that you've spent some time in that part of the world. And your smooth approach to women you meet along the street indicates that you know very well what I mean."

The young woman's pointed comments sobered her Japanese host. In fact, he was shocked at her harsh manner! He felt a sudden rush of anger fill his chest but instead of responding 'in kind,' the young man leaned back in his chair and slowly took a drink. After a moment or two of silence, he spoke in a calm, almost humble, manner,

"Perhaps you have misjudged me."

Ana looked away from him, gazing at the noisy crowd in the bar. Then she began to sip her drink as if she were alone. While her apparent dismissal was disturbing to her partner, it also presented him with a challenge which he decided was worth accepting. He took a deep breath and, with a reassuring smile, began to speak to his companion as if she had not insulted him,

"I have just returned to Japan after nearly eight years in *your* Western world. Perhaps I have become somewhat enculturated to the freedoms of life that I experienced there. I beg your pardon if you were insulted by my rather 'forward' approach. But, how else can two people meet in the midst of these crowded streets and the noise of such a celebration?"

Ana responded to his explanation with surprise,

"Eight years in the 'Western world'? What were you doing there all that time?"

He leaned toward her with a grave expression on his face, as if he were revealing a dark secret,

"I was being 'ed-u-cated'!"

Ana suddenly burst out laughing,

"Goodness…I hope it worked!"

When her partner responded, Ana noted a twinkle in his eye. The atmosphere eased between them,

"That is yet to be determined. All I can say is this: I am a very different person from the innocent, young boy who left Japan all those years ago."

"I did detect a slight British accent so assume that's where you've spent those years."

"Yes, in a private high school, then to Oxford for the rest of the time. That is where I learned much about the Western world…including the accent."

Ana commented with a sly smile,

"And…including ways to approach women."

Once again, the young woman's rather blunt remark surprised him, but he chose to respond in a positive manner as if he had not felt its sting,

13

"Perhaps that is one part of my education that I most enjoyed, the relaxed ways of sharing relationships with both men and women. I made many good friends there. It was a new and pleasant experience for me."

Try as she might, Ana could not resist a pointed comment,

"I believe that you have assimilated the Western culture very well!"

Her partner commented, pretending he hadn't understood her meaning,

"Thank you for the compliment. Do your kind words suggest that you are now open to our becoming friends?"

She replied with some hesitation,

"Well...perhaps."

The young man leaned forward with a warm smile,

"Then let me introduce myself. My name is Toshiburo Matsushita Yamamoto and I am a resident of Tokyo, Seijo prefecture. Please do not be formal. I am merely 'Toshi' to my friends, which I hope will include you. Since my return from England, I have been serving as a professor of international politics and foreign relations at Tokyo University. Because of the time I've spent in the West, I enjoy sharing with people from that part of the world. When I saw you here at the festival, I was intrigued with your comfort level as a '*gaijin*' in these crowded streets and very much alone. Then, I was pleasantly surprised when I heard you speaking Japanese, so I assumed that you have lived here for some time or are an excellent student of our language."

Toshi stopped and smiled warmly at the young woman across the table from him,

"Now it's your turn."

Ana was still a bit hesitant to trust the intentions of this polite stranger so chose to keep her response as simple as possible,

"Well, I am definitely impressed with your credentials, Yamamoto-san! As for me, there is very little to say. I've been in and out of Japan over the past few years and have tried to learn your language though I find it *very* difficult. So, I thank you for the compliment. However, I'm fully aware of my lack of skill."

Ana was becoming very nervous in this young man's presence. From certain past experiences, she had developed a

14

suspicious attitude toward male strangers. She was not blind
when she looked in the mirror. Her long, curly, black hair, dark
eyes, and ready smile had invited trouble for her many times.
And, no matter how he presented himself, Ana saw no evidence
that 'Yamamoto-san' was any different from others she had met
on so many occasions. She decided to find a casual and,
hopefully, polite way to make her exit.

Ana jumped as Toshi's hand touched hers. She looked up to
his smile and question,

"Excuse me, I'm still here. Where are you?"

Ana looked at her watch and smiled,

"Oh, I'm sorry. I was just thinking that I need to get back to
my friends. We've made plans to meet later this
evening…and…it seems that it is now *later*!"

Of course, she had no plans at all and Ana had the distinct
impression that her Japanese partner knew she was making an
excuse to leave. He frowned and looked somewhat hurt as he
asked,

"Where are you staying in the city?"

She replied without thinking,

"I'm at the Imperial."

Then quickly catching herself, she began to tell further lies
without knowing why,

"But I've promised to meet my friends at the Otani a bit later
so I should be going as soon as we finish our drinks."

Though it was obvious to Toshi that this elusive young
Westerner planned to leave without a hint of who she was or how
he might contact her, he was determined to keep trying,

"Then perhaps I can walk with you to the Imperial and we
can visit there, in a quieter setting, until it's time to join your
friends."

At this suggestion, Ana heard a familiar warning from her
inner voice, 'Okay, Gabrelli, you're dealing with a professional.
He even knows when you're lying. Get yourself out of this…and
do it now!"

She reacted to his suggestion with obvious hostility,

"If you think I would invite you to my hotel room, you're
quite mistaken!"

Toshi was shocked at the implication this young woman had drawn from his suggestion and quickly attempted to calm her fears,

"Please forgive me if I have given you the wrong impression. The Imperial has a very nice coffee bar where we can visit in more pleasant surroundings." He paused a moment, then continued with a teasing smile,

"And, I'm quite certain that they also have security guards should one of us become unmanageable. It's just that…I would enjoy hearing more about your experiences here in Japan and share my own from the West. We seem to have many things in common. And, besides, you *do* owe me a drink."

Toshi's pleasant manner calmed Ana's initial fears. She was no longer afraid in the same way, but the inner warning now was to 'go with care.' She addressed her Japanese dance partner in a polite, yet formal, manner,

"And, I do thank you, Yamamoto-san, for the dance, the drinks, and our pleasant conversation."

Ana rose to leave, but Toshi caught her arm. He hadn't expected the sudden dismissal,

"Please, at least tell me your name. Perhaps we could meet at another time and in a more agreeable setting."

Ana had already told him where she was staying and was certain that this persistent stranger was resourceful enough to discover who she was, even with that small bit of information. But she conceded a part of her name, using his own phrase,

"My friends call me 'Ana.' And now, Yamamoto-san, I bid you goodnight!"

Toshi immediately dropped his hand from her arm. He heard the rising anger in her voice, but more than that, he saw a hint of fear in her eyes. He did not intend to give this intriguing young woman reason to be afraid, but neither did he intend to let her go so easily. 'Ana' could be found and, no matter what it demanded of him, he would find her.

When she fled from Toshi's presence, Ana did not stop to look back for many blocks. When she did, of course, he was nowhere in sight. Even then she couldn't rest. She hurried to the hotel and quickly took an elevator to her room, fumbling with the key until the door finally opened. Once inside the safety of her room, Ana slammed the door and double-locked it, then fell down on the bed and began to laugh at her ridiculous behavior.

In the midst of her laughter, Ana recalled a poem she had read during her college studies entitled, "The Hound of Heaven."[7] Now she wondered if *her* 'nemesis' would come striding through the double-locked door and stand facing her after all.

She whispered to herself in the darkness of her safe haven,

"He's a man, not a phantom, and he has no power over me. Remember your resolves, Ana: No complications, no *romantic* relationships. Now keep them!"

Much later that night, Ana found herself staring out the window at the lights of the never-ending megalopolis surrounding her. She heard her own voice whispering in the silence,

"Why did you come now? Out of all these masses of people, why did you step forward and take my hand as if I were lost and needed to be found?"

Sometime, in the early morning hours, she fell asleep.

After Ana had disappeared into the crowd, Toshi sat in the bar for a while nursing a drink and his disappointment. He realized that this young American woman may have been misleading him when she mentioned staying at the Imperial Hotel. However, he also recalled that Ana had rather suspiciously remembered her 'date' with friends at the Otani. No doubt, she had intended to throw him off the track.

Toshi could not explain his immediate 'sense of connection' with this mysterious stranger from the West. These kinds of things did not happen to Toshiburo Matsushita Yamamoto. He was not one who followed sudden urges nor was he given to behavior that was not carefully calculated. The truth was that every step of his life had been planned for him from the moment of his birth even far into the future. And he was a dutiful who willingly followed the dictates of his family. Presently, he was

*7 "The Hound of Heaven" poem by Francis Thompson from *Anthology: The Golden Book of Catholic Poetry*. Ed. Alfred Noyes. Philadelphia: J.B. Lippincott. 1946.

being groomed to serve his country in a position related to the field of international politics.

During his academic career, Toshi had distinguished himself in the areas of negotiation and problem solving. His present role as a professor at Tokyo University had been chosen for him to allow further experience before moving into the arena of political power. Even now, Toshi served as a consultant on international issues with the Japanese diplomatic corps, assigned to both the United States and Great Britain, and he fully expected an embassy appointment within the next few months.

Though he was a partner in a marriage contract, the agreement had been made between the two families. He and his future bride had met on only two occasions, once when they were very young and once when he had returned to Japan to begin his professorship three years ago. Sachiko Matsuda was much younger than he and was presently attending a college of fine arts in Paris. When she graduated, and when he received the governmental appointment, they would be expected to announce their wedding date.

In spite of these family obligations, Toshi had never denied himself the pleasures of life or of love. His heart was easily touched; therefore, it had been broken many times, even as he had broken the hearts of others. In his personal philosophy, there was no reason to fear the pain of brokenness. Indeed, he welcomed it for he was fully aware that the experience of loving another brought knowledge of oneself and of life's ultimate meaning.

And, because of who he was, his willingness to accept what life offered and to live with the results, Toshiburo Yamamoto chose to pursue this young woman whose dark eyes and intense manner had stolen his heart in a moment. There was something in Ana's presence that he could not resist. Yet, he was hesitant, as well, for she was different from other Western women he had known. Though he was certain that she had felt the connection between them, she ran from it. Ana was afraid…and that was what concerned him most and caused his hesitation.

As he walked toward the hotel, Toshi continued to examine his heart and his intentions. What had Ana seen in him that caused her to be afraid? Did she instinctively know that if she allowed it, he would offer his love to her wholly and completely, yet, one day, would surely walk away from her? Was Ana so fearful of the 'bitterness of endings' that she refused to taste the 'sweetness of beginnings'? Didn't she realize that there is, for each person, the promise of a love that will last beyond this moment...even to eternity? There was no reason to weigh the cost nor to consider the consequences. Toshiburo Yamamoto had no recourse but to pursue the promise he had glimpsed beyond the fear in Ana's eyes.

Much later that evening, when Toshi arrived at the Imperial Hotel, he went directly to the desk clerk and asked for the room number of the young American woman who was staying there for a few days. He explained to the clerk that he had lost her '*meishi*'[8] and could only remember that her first name was 'Ana.' He made up a sad tale of having to contact her for an important business appointment.

The desk clerk was very considerate of his plight,

"Oh yes, that would be Ms. Ana Maria Gabrelli. She is the only Western woman registered alone here this week. They usually stay at the smaller hotels. If you wish to call her, the room number is 712."

Toshi thanked the clerk graciously and made sure that he had Ana's name spelled according to the hotel records. Then he walked into the flower shop and ordered a special arrangement to be delivered early the next morning. He intended to offer the flowers to Ana as a token of friendship and, if she thought it necessary, his "Thank you for a pleasant evening at the 'O-bon' festival...and farewell!"

The card he attached to the gift was more difficult to write. Toshi wanted to express his feelings in a way that would encourage Ana to consider a possible relationship between them. He chose the words carefully, slipped the card and his meishi into an envelope and handed it to the florist,

"Would you please deliver these flowers early tomorrow morning? I plan to meet Ms. Gabrelli for breakfast and would like for her to receive them before I arrive, about 8:30."

*8 (meishi) business card

19

As Toshi left the hotel, he knew that he had done everything in his power to reach Ana. Perhaps she would understand that this was a special moment for them. Perhaps she would not be afraid to grasp it, to share the joy in it, and, when it was over, to savor the memory. Whatever followed would be in her hands…and tomorrow he would be here to discover what that decision was to be.

CHAPTER 2

"Petals white as snow.
Pure crystals in the moonlight.
Shine like Ana's eyes."
　　　　--T. Yamamoto, Journal
　　　　The Night of O-bon

Ana heard a quiet knock on the door waking her from a sound sleep. She jumped out of bed, somewhat disoriented, grabbed her robe, and stumbled to the door. Without opening it, she asked,

"What is it?" A hotel employee replied in broken English,

"Excuse, please. I have message for you."

She whispered to herself, "What now? Who would be crazy enough to wake me at this hour of the morning? It must be from Miyuki changing our plans for today."

Ana mumbled an answer,

"Just slip it under the door, please." The young man hesitated a moment, then stammered,

"A...a...I have flowers for you."

There was only one person Ana knew who would be sending her flowers at eight o'clock on Sunday morning. And that person was not Miyuki. It could only be her midnight 'nemesis,' Toshiburo Yamamoto. She spoke her thoughts out loud,

"Oh no, he must have a detective agency on his payroll. Am I the only Western woman alone in this hotel today? Just my luck, I am!"

Ana finally got the locks unhooked and opened the door barely enough to see a very embarrassed young man in hotel uniform. He apologized profusely,

"Please, so sorry to wake you. The gentleman left note to deliver them this morning. He said 'early.' So sorry, please."

Ana opened the door to receive the flowers and set them quickly on the windowsill. She grabbed her purse to offer the young man a tip, but he refused,

"Oh no, no! Gentleman paid extra tip already. Everything taken care of, okay."

Ana tried to thank him, but he was out of sight by the time she got her head out the door. She turned back to look at the flowers sitting in the early sunlight. There were four large, white chrysanthemums arranged with great care in a lovely gold-leafed bowl. She walked slowly to the windowsill and opened the card attached to the flowers. The message was written in an artistic script. Ana read it aloud,

"Petals white as snow
 Pure crystals in the moonlight
 Shine like Ana's eyes."

The card was signed, 'T. Yamamoto,' and his meishi was enclosed. Ana touched the soft, white petals of the chrysanthemums, so symbolic of the 'pure spirit' of the samurai. She couldn't deny the depth of feeling expressed through his simple words, the flowing script and the beauty of the flowers.

Her heart was pounding as she whispered,

"What am I to do? You have worked your magic well, Yamamoto-san."

Ana could almost feel the piercing touch of an ancient samurai sword against her heart. She knew there was only one choice of action and that was to run. But there were two choices of direction. Would she run away from him…or toward him? She laid down on the bed, stretched out on her back and stared at the ceiling. Why had she come to this place? She recalled that it was not in search of a love affair. She had become fascinated by the culture of this tiny, compact isle.

As a student at Georgetown University in the States, Ana had become close friends with Mishima Matsamura and Miyuki Kitada, both from the Tokyo area. All three were involved in the Intercultural Club on campus and enrolled in the same classes in anthropology and intercultural studies. Ana's Japanese friends had convinced her to take a year's study in Japan to learn the basics of the language and to gain a broader understanding of the culture. That experience had been the beginning of her great love for this tiny nation and its people and, as a result, she chose to continue graduate work in Japanese Studies. Since that time, she had returned several times for further cultural study and had come to feel more at home here than in her own country.

Ana was fascinated by the ancient beauties of this land, but also found the Japanese lifestyle allowed her great freedom. She was never afraid to wander the streets of the huge cities, day or night, alone. She had found the people here receptive and friendly to the 'gaijin,' which was a totally new experience for a young woman from inner city Boston. And she could jump on a fast train or subway and go anywhere she chose with little difficulty and minimal cost.

Finally, Ana's love for this country had directed her career path. After completing a Master's degree in anthropology with concentration in Japan Studies, she accepted a position at the Intercultural Education Exchange Center (IEEC) in Washington, D.C. and three years ago, transferred to the Tokyo office. She had just returned from several months of administrative training at the D.C. office to enter a new position as co-director of the Tokyo Center.

When Ana had returned to the States for the training sessions, her financial situation made it necessary to give up her precious Tokyo apartment. So, once again, she was searching for an apartment in the city. Lying on the bed in her hotel room, Ana wondered why she was so hesitant to accept the offer of friendship from an attractive, well-educated Japanese gentleman. Hadn't she chosen to become 'engulfed' in the Japanese culture? She began to wonder just how deep that commitment really went and why she was suddenly afraid.

Ana jumped up from the bed and stared at herself in the mirror, lecturing to the image there,

"So, Ana Maria Gabrelli, what's the problem? Why not take the opportunity for a new adventure? You're a free woman and certainly have the option to get out anytime. What can be wrong with a little excitement and perhaps even a bit of romance? Who knows when the next offer might come…maybe never!"

Ana looked at the flowers and thought of her night in the city and of Toshiburo Yamamoto. She finally admitted that she was intrigued by this persistent stranger who had followed her through the holiday crowd. Ana had chosen her direction. She would not walk away from him. At least, not yet.

The meishi with Yamamoto's name, business address, and telephone number was on the table beside the flowers. Since it was Sunday, she could not call his office, so she chose to write a 'Thank You' note to put in the mail. Ana wrote as simply as

Toshi had done, but with much less depth of meaning, and not in the poetic 'haiku' style,

"The lovely chrysanthemums are a pleasant reminder of an evening celebration and the bon-odori. Thank you for sharing a few moments with a stranger from the West."

She signed the card with her full name and enclosed her 'meishi,' certain that the words could not be construed to carry any hidden meaning, one way or the other. Sighing with relief when the note was ready to mail, she began to prepare for the Sunday activities with her friends.

Nearly an hour later, Ana was ready to grab a quick breakfast when the telephone rang. She knew it would be Miyuki, so she picked up the phone and spoke without offering a greeting,

"Yuki, I'm just going down for breakfast. What time do you want to leave?"

There was silence on the other end of the line, then a masculine voice spoke rather hesitantly,

"I'd be very happy to join you for breakfast. However, this is not 'Yuki.' This is your midnight 'bon-odori' partner. I had hoped we might spend some time together today. Perhaps share an early breakfast and do some sight-seeing. It's a beautiful morning!"

She could barely stammer a reply,

"I...I beg your pardon, Yamamoto-san, for answering so rudely. I...was expecting to hear from my friend, Miyuki. We've made some plans to do some traveling today...but perhaps you and I could share a quick breakfast before I leave."

Toshi's disappointment was apparent in his voice,

"I'm sorry we didn't make arrangements last night. However, I would be happy to join you for breakfast. I came by the hotel this morning with the intention of visiting with you, so I'll meet you here in the lobby whenever you're ready."

"Fine, I'll be down in just a few minutes."

When Ana hung up the phone, she had to sit down on the bed for a moment. Toshi had surprised her and she felt strangely excited and confused. She realized that her reactions were more like those of a high school girl than a mature young woman of the world. She began pacing the room and talking to herself,

"Okay, okay, get a grip, Ana. Don't make this something more than it is. Just remember, you're in control…so get controlled!"

She took several deep breaths, picked up her purse, and started for the door. On the way out, she grabbed her 'Thank You' note off the desk. Once again, she reminded herself,

"This is my choice."

When Ana stepped off the elevator, her eyes were drawn immediately to Toshi. He was standing near one of the large, comfortable sofas in the lobby coffee bar, holding a cup in his hand. As their eyes met, she smiled and lifted her hand in greeting. He set the cup down and walked toward her with a slight smile,

"I'm happy to see you this morning, Ms. Gabrelli, and thank you very much for sharing a few moments with me before your busy day."

Ana was surprised by his pleasant mood, not knowing what to expect after the way she had treated him the night before. She returned the smile as she spoke,

"Good morning, Yamamoto-san. I hadn't expected to see you today."

Toshi couldn't refrain from a teasing response,

"Judging from the chase you led me last night, I must assume that you hadn't expected to ever see me again!"

Ana laughed and picked up quickly on his comment,

"I might as well have invited you to walk home with me. You discovered all my secrets anyway. Are you sure you're not involved in some 'undercover' work for your government on the side?"

"Absolutely not! I work only for myself to search out hiding places of mysterious Western women."

Without a second thought, Ana turned his comments back against him,

"And I would imagine that you've had great success in your exploits, judging from your skillful approach to *this* Western woman last night."

"My dear Ms. Gabrelli, you persist in misunderstanding my motives. You choose to measure me by the standards of that

25

strange 'world of the West' from which you come. I fear that you have much to learn about the Japanese mind."

Toshi had unwittingly thrown down the 'gauntlet' between him and this fiery Italian-American, and she was not about to ignore the challenge. Ana smiled in a sly, sarcastic way, giving the distinguished, Japanese gentleman evidence of her cultural knowledge without mercy,

"I'm quite certain that I understand the mind of the Japanese man well enough to know that you fit the mold perfectly. You see a Western woman who sparks your interest, you follow her to the hotel and send her a beautiful bouquet…astonishing her with your sentimental haiku. Then you casually awaken her with an invitation for breakfast. I can also predict what your next step will be, where it will lead, and where it all will end. You are mistaken, Yamamoto-san. I know your 'Japanese mind' only too well!"

Toshi stared at Ana, shocked at the harshness of her reproach. This beautiful young woman with such clear and intelligent eyes had accused him of the lowest possible motives for pursuing her. He could not refrain from responding in kind,

"How little you know of this Oriental world, Ms. Gabrelli. You see everything here through a Western haze. You imagine that you understand my actions. But, I must contradict you. What you think you see…is not what is…nor is it anywhere close to my reality. What you have described is that which you may have experienced with men in another world. What do they call it there in the West…the 'chase'…the 'conquest'? Perhaps when you have been here longer and have become more closely acquainted with the true Japanese mind, you will understand how deeply you have insulted me. You have taken a very special moment and labeled it as a meaningless flirtation! Tell me, Ms. Gabrelli, what right have you to place me in the same category as your Western male friends?"

The antagonism between these two strangers had moved out of control. Ana, it seemed, had crushed Toshi's spirit with her insults and Toshi had read, only too well, from whence those insults had derived. Though ashamed of her sarcastic comments, Ana was livid with anger at his attack and replied accordingly,

"How dare you accuse me of insulting you? *You* have insulted *me*! You have no right to step into my life and rip it apart with your 'all-knowing Oriental wisdom'!"

Ana turned to leave, but Toshi caught her arm and drew her down beside him on the hotel sofa. His grip was so strong that she couldn't move but was forced to listen as he spoke in an unusually calm manner,

"You think you know so much about the Oriental mind...well, Ms. Gabrelli, let me tell you what I know of you. I see depth and intelligence in your eyes. I see openness and warmth in your smile. And, I see you in a great capacity to give love and receive it. I have seen in one glance more of who you are than you know of yourself!"

Ana tried to pull away, but Toshi did not release her. She turned to face him, offering him the full benefit of her hot Italian temper,

"How can you be so arrogant as to think that you know more of me than I know of myself? You know nothing of my life journey, nor would you ever want to know! Be assured, Yamamoto-san, I know very well who I am and where I have been and where I do not want to go!"

Toshi did not back away from her anger but replied calmly, hoping to defuse the tension that had come between them,

"Then, surely you've learned on that journey that there is no value to life without relationships. When we allow others into our lives, there may be joy or there may be sorrow. Aren't these just two sides of the same experience? One cannot exist without the other. To deny oneself the joy of loving because one fears that the outcome might be painful is to deny the reason for life itself. Is that what you choose, Ms. Gabrelli, a life so filled with fear that you deny the very purpose for your existence?"

Ana was quieted by his words and the manner in which they were spoken. She was finally able to respond with more careful thought,

"I understand what you're saying and I would certainly prefer a world where happiness is a natural part of life, where there is comfort and safety rather than sorrow or fear. But I, for one, don't need the depths to appreciate the heights, so...if I can't have one without the other, I choose to have neither. It's fine with me to live a peaceful, stable existence with no shocks or surprises. If that means I sacrifice 'joy,' then so be it. That's my choice. I guess my personal description of joy is just plain, old contentment with no 'soaring heights' nor 'despairing depths.' So, professor, what do you think…would that be acceptable to you?"

Ana intended to mock him, but to her surprise Toshi leaned close to her and placed his mouth against her ear, whispering as if they were lovers,

"No, that is not acceptable to me, nor will it be to you. For if I am certain of anything, I am certain of this, Ms. Gabrelli, until you have experienced the joy of loving another with your whole heart and soul, you will never be content!"

Toshi's words struck too close to Ana's inner fears. She pulled away from him, expressing her anger in a mocking tone,

"Oh, tell me about it, Yamamoto-san, you who have obviously experienced the joy of loving so many with you 'whole heart and soul.' Of what are you trying to convince me? That I should be the next one you choose to share the joy of your 'sweet love' with the certain promise that one day I shall taste the sorrow of your 'fond farewell?' I think not!"

Toshi realized, too late, that he had overstepped all the boundaries of courtesy. He had allowed himself to be drawn into an emotional confrontation when it was not possible for this young woman to understand his words or his feelings. He attempted to calm her anger with a humble apology,

"Forgive me, Ms. Gabrelli. I have no right to speak to you in such a personal way. We hardly know each other and I have presumed to have answers for the deep questions of your life. The truth is, I barely have answers for my own. Please, can we make a truce…and start again?"

To Toshi's surprise, Ana burst out laughing,

"What in the world are we doing, anyway? You're so right, Yamamoto-san. We're strangers acting as if we were 'sweethearts locked in a lover's quarrel!' I accept the truce. Now, let's eat our breakfast in peace and get on with our separate lives."

Ana gave Toshi a bright smile that was obviously intended to be a 'shut down' before complete dismissal. He was upset by her uncompromising attitude but knew they could not continue their heated exchange. In order to leave the door open for some future relationship, Toshi chose to back away, though he had no intention of letting her go easily. He was certain that Ana had felt some attraction to him or she would not have reacted to his words with such strong emotion.

Toshi calmly returned Ana's smile and stood to guide her into the hotel dining room where they ordered breakfast. As they ate together, he attempted to become better acquainted with the young woman sitting across from him,

"Ms. Gabrelli, tell me, what is your purpose for coming to this strange world of the East? What fascination does this world hold for you that has brought you so far from your own?"

Ana was relieved by Toshi's apparent desire to create a more relaxed atmosphere between them and responded with the same casual manner,

"Actually, I began that fascination in the States when I met several classmates at Georgetown University who are from the Tokyo area. We became friends and through them I was encouraged to begin an in-depth study of this 'strange world of the East.' The result has been that I completed a master's degree in anthropology with a concentration in Japan Studies. Through the past several years I've lived and studied here and am now working at the Tokyo office of the Intercultural Education Exchange Center. My role there is to plan and direct workshops for college students, business personnel, diplomats, and anyone else who is interested in learning about various other cultures beyond their own."

"You've chosen a very interesting profession. To open the doors of intercultural understanding between people and among cultures is, indeed, a challenge."

"Thank you for the kind words, professor. However, it appears that I'm not doing so well at 'opening doors of understanding' between one Japanese gentleman and myself. Perhaps I should attend one of my own seminars as a student."

Toshi smiled, recognizing her honest desire to bring peace between them,

"I'm sure that intercultural understanding can be more easily achieved in a classroom setting where personal feelings are less involved."

"In the last few minutes, I've blown my cover completely. I'm not at all the 'expert' I envisioned myself to be. In fact, I feel very much a novice on the personal level, no matter how impressive I may be on paper or in the lecture hall. I would like to beg your pardon."

Toshi was surprised at the unexpected apology and responded with kindness,

"You need not beg anything of me, Ms. Gabrelli. We've just been expressing our thoughts and feeling to one another. We come from very different backgrounds and certainly from different experiences. It's only natural that we have differing opinions about life and its meaning. Isn't that what you teach your students? The challenge is to discover those important ways that our differing minds can agree, is it not?"

Ana bent her head to avoid his steady gaze,

"Yes, that *is* the challenge, to be sure. But it's possible there are no ways that '*our*' differing minds can agree."

When she looked up, Toshi was smiling,

"You give up too easily, Ms. Gabrelli. I don't intend to let this be our final struggle with East-West 'world views.' If you and I can't come to a treaty of peace, then how can either of us claim expertise in our professions of intercultural compromise and understanding?

Ana appreciated his question, but she chose not to address it. The time had come to bring an end to this conversation and get on with the day's plans. All that she needed or wanted to say to Toshiburo Yamamoto had been said except a last 'thank you and goodbye.'

"My friends will be coming soon, so I must thank you for our evening together, the challenging discussion over breakfast and, of course, my gracious thanks for the lovely flowers. Forgive me for not mentioning your gift earlier…it seems that we became engrossed in more important matters."

They both laughed as Ana handed Toshi her 'Thank You' note and got up to leave. He took the note from her, then stood and bowed graciously,

"And I must thank you for sharing your precious time with me. I have valued each moment and am quite certain that we will meet again, Ms. Gabrelli."

Ana smiled and answered in the only way she could to let this courteous gentleman know that she did not wish to continue their emotionally-charged relationship,

"Goodbye, Yamamoto-san."

She turned and left the restaurant without looking back.

Toshi felt the blow of Ana's firm dismissal and knew that if anything were to follow between them, once again, it would be up to him. Though put off for the moment, he was not discouraged. Never in his life had he met a woman who had so quickly touched his heart nor so aggressively challenged his mind. He would not soon forget the night of the 'O-bon' festival, nor would he let Ana Maria Gabrelli do so. They would meet again. He would see to it.

CHAPTER 3

"The festival... 'samurai'
In ancient battle stance;
Clash of sword on sword
Brings instant pain
In memory...
The clash of heart-on-heart"
　　　　-T. Yamamoto, Journal
　　　　The Samurai Festival-Nikko

Ana left Toshi and dashed up to her room to prepare for the day with friends, anxious to relax and be herself with those who knew her from inside out. The tension between her and Yamamoto had not only angered her but had worn her out as well. In some ways, Ana found him to be the 'typical Japanese man,' speaking words that seemed to mean one thing but meant another. And in other ways he portrayed the 'typical American male,' telling her what she did and did not feel or should and should not do. The only thing they seemed to agree on was that they disagreed on nearly everything.

When she entered the hotel room, Ana slammed the door shut and released her 'pent-up' emotions on the empty space. She shouted out loud and didn't care who heard,

"Who does he think he is—the philosopher of all philosophers, the guru of all gurus, the...the...Buddha's gift to 'gaijin' women? If I were afraid of life, I surely wouldn't be here. I came to this place for the challenge and excitement of a different world, to expand my personal and professional horizons. I'm strong and ready for new experiences, but that doesn't make me stupid. I'm smart enough to be very careful of when and with whom I share those experiences!"

Ana ripped off her good clothes and flung them on hangers, changing into khaki shorts, matching shirt and walking shoes. She was ready for the busy day ahead with friends who knew and respected her. When the telephone rang, Ana answered Miyuki's question without hesitation,

"I'm ready...be right down!"

She grabbed the camera case and looked around the room to see if she had remembered everything. Suddenly, her eyes were drawn to a ray of sunlight streaming across the pure, white petals of the flowers on the window sill. Ana caught her breath at their beauty as if she had seen an omen of her future. She muttered on the way out the door,

"Oh, god, what's happening to me?"

Miyuki and Mishima were excited about the trip and anxious that Ana see and understand everything along the way. They both loved sharing their Japanese culture with their American friend because they sensed her deep appreciation of their homeland, its beauties and traditions. And Ana, in turn, appreciated their willingness to share it. Without their detailed explanations of the many festivals, the art, the ancient architecture, and the unique traditions of Japan, she would only have a bare understanding of all that she had seen and experienced. These good friends were excellent cultural guides and, beyond that, they had great fun together.

On this beautiful Sunday morning, the travelers drove along the hairpin curves through the mountains toward Nikko. Mishima and Miyuki were talking a 'mile a minute,' explaining the many sights to their 'captive Westerner' and Ana was trying to keep her enthusiasm alive on the journey. For she knew that, even as her Japanese friends shared their culture with her, they were revisiting its value to themselves.

After a while, Ana's head began to ache. She realized that the very light breakfast she had with Toshi was not fit for a busy day of travel and sightseeing. And the bumper-to-bumper traffic made her nervous as well. She understood the traveler's desires to get out of the city into the beauty of the countryside. And she knew that the excitement of the many festivals were always a drawing card for city dwellers. But today she longed for peace and quiet and sleep.

Finally, they arrived at their destination, found a place to park, and walked to the site of the 'Samurai Festival.' Ana regained some energy during the colorful presentations. The elaborate costuming of the samurai warriors, their excellent skills in horseback riding, the mock duels by sword, and *yabusame* (archery on horseback) were breathtaking.

33

Ana recorded the enactments on her video camera and tried her best to maintain a mood of enthusiasm for the benefit of her hosts knowing their desire to share this bit of Japanese culture with her. Yet, try as she might, she could not keep her usual upbeat attitude and, in fact, the samurai's clashing of weapons only served to remind her of the clash of ideas and emotions that she had felt with Yamamoto. She couldn't seem to shake the intense anger that he had called up within her, nor could she understand why it mattered to her what a stranger off the street said or felt about anything at all.

After a while, Miyuki realized that something was going on with Ana and finally approached her,

"What's wrong, Ana? Are you sick? Do you want to rest a while or go back to Tokyo? I can tell you're not feeling well."

Miyuki was genuinely concerned about her friend for it was obvious that Ana had lost her usual vibrant interest in everything that was happening around her. But Ana tried to cover her exhaustion,

"Maybe I just need to eat something and rest a while. I was out late last night for the O-bon festival and walked all over downtown Tokyo. I took some wonderful camera shots, but in the process totally wore myself out! But let's not leave yet. I'll get my energy back soon."

Mishima came over to find out how Ana was feeling. He had also noticed that she had lost her usual spark and when Ana's spark was gone that meant the party was pretty much over. He volunteered to help,

"Why don't I get us some lunch and we'll take a break. Wait here while I get a blanket from the car and then I'll bring the food and drinks. Be right back."

They took their lunch break with sandwiches and Cokes. Then Miyuki and Mishima went back to the festivities while Ana rested. She laid down and immediately fell sound asleep. Miyuki finally woke her at 5 o'clock. Ana couldn't believe she had slept so long, nearly three hours, but was relieved to feel almost normal again. Still, there were shadows lingering in her mind from the disturbing confrontation with the illustrious Professor Yamamoto.

Ana knew her friends were disappointed and apologized that she hadn't been able to enjoy the day they had planned especially for her. But they were understanding and assured her that they had enjoyed every minute of the festival and only wished she could have shared it with them. They promised to bring her back on another weekend and when Mishima suggested they head back to the city, Ana did not protest.

On the drive toward Tokyo, Ana offered to buy dinner when they were ready to stop. They agreed to find some small place where they could relax and enjoy the view. And they did just that, finally coming across a tiny mountainside inn overlooking the highway. The setting gave them a chance to relax, enjoy the beauty of the scene below, and share a leisurely meal.

Though she wanted to talk to her friends about the O-bon experience, Ana was wise enough to know that Mishima would not appreciate it. Nor was she distant enough from her own emotions to tell the tale objectively to Miyuki. Perhaps tomorrow, when her life returned to its normal pace, she could think more clearly. Perhaps then she would understand more about herself and her confused emotions as well. The day ended with the three friends laughing and singing together in the car, a bit louder than usual from a little too much 'Asahi.'

Ana returned to the hotel late that evening, relaxed and recovered from her weekend 'fiasco.' As she undressed in the dark, she looked down at the city from the seventh-floor window. The lighted grounds of the Imperial Palace fully displayed the beauty of the impressive structure. Her thoughts turned to the history of this small island that she had come to claim as her 'special place.'

Today, at Nikko, she had witnessed a portion of that history. She recalled the colorful drama that portrayed the life of the ancient samurai and, once again, was reminded of Yamamoto. He was the 'new samurai,' the educated, professional Japanese man who had used his words against her similarly to the way that the Nikko warriors had wielded their swords and arrows against one another in mock battle.

For some reason, Ana felt wounded, but didn't know why. Her final thoughts before sleep were merely questions: 'Why did we meet...this 'new samurai' and I? Of what am I afraid and why do I resist him so?' She whispered the answer to her own question. 'I know why.' Ana's sleep was a long time coming and was restless.

Toshi's Sunday was even more troubled than Ana's. When he left her after their breakfast confrontation, his mind was reeling from the impact of her last words to him,

"Goodbye, Yamamoto-san!"

He did not miss her clear intention to wound him by those words of dismissal. And she had done so. Ana had also accused him of treating her like a future conquest of meaningless love. The harshness of her insinuations had shocked him. He could not understand how she could so quickly accuse him of that which he had never, nor would ever, enter his mind.

Why couldn't he tell her 'goodbye' and move on as she so clearly wanted him to do? But as much as he realized the wisdom in that, there was no way he could do it. For he remembered too well Ana's wide, dark eyes and the shining silk of her black hair in the city lights. Toshi could still feel the touch of her hand in his and the motion of her body as he guided her through the steps of the bon-odori. She had responded to him in one moment and had resisted him in the next. Toshi was willing to accept every challenge this beautiful Westerner offered him, as long as she allowed him some presence in her life. If the time came when that was no longer possible, he would recognize it and would turn away without protest.

After breakfast with Ana at the hotel, Toshi had returned by subway and train to his house in Seijo. Because of his station in life, Toshiburo Yamamoto was fortunate to live in a home protected from the surrounding city by high wood and stucco walls. His private entrance was a thick steel gate that opened automatically with a special combination.

Upon entering this gate, Toshi was transported into an ancient, though thoroughly modernized, world. The park around his home included an expanse of carefully-trimmed grounds with trees of every kind, gardens with unique rock formations and exotic plants. Well-stocked fish ponds were placed throughout the area and tiny streams came flowing down from the steep hillsides behind the estate. And hidden within this natural beauty were a tea house, a small building for 'moon-viewing,' and a private Shinto shrine.

In the center of it all stood the large, oblong residence. Though it was as ancient as the grounds, the home had been remodeled to include every available comfort under the guise of living in the 'old way.' All the main rooms in the house were 'tatami' (woven floor matting) except the kitchen and all opened onto an inner porch which surrounded a beautiful garden of rock, tiny evergreens, and flowers.

The formal living areas displayed precious works of art from past eras of the nation's history, including *byobu* (folding screens), 'kakemono' (hanging scrolls), and *yakimono* (pottery). Huge *chochin* (rice-paper lanterns) hung from the wood-beamed ceilings of each room, yet they contained electric lighting.

The simplicity of the lovely home was the choice of its resident. Upon Toshi's return to Japan, after completing his academic study abroad, his father had given him the option of living in the ancient Seijo estate or their modern city residence in Shibya prefecture. Toshi had chosen Seijo as the 'home of his heart.' Toshi's parents remained at the original Yamamoto estate in the mountains near Kyoto. Here they lived in a large, modern home near his grandmother, Sukiyama Matsushita Yamamoto, who was 90 years old, yet still quite alert and active.

All of the family financial and political power had come through Sukiyama's heritage. The financial power was traced through her father-in-law, a major financier during the Meiji Restoration period and the political power had come through her own father, Ishiro Matsushita, a distinguished member of the first diplomatic mission to Great Britain during this same era of Japanese history. Toshi's grandmother was, indeed, the "family treasure." However, to him, she was a treasure apart from her financial or political power. The power of her love had sustained Toshi at every stage of his life.

The estate holdings of the Yamamoto family, in their size and beauty, spoke of the eminence accorded them in Japanese society. Though very distant cousins of the Emperor, they were still considered 'of the Imperial line.' This meant power and privilege as well as an accompanying sense of responsibility. Toshiburo Matsushita Yamamoto had been taught from

37

childhood to respect this heritage and to prepare for whatever it should require of him.

Though Toshi had spent several years in the Western world and fully enjoyed the lifestyle there, his heart always longed for the ancient beauty of Japan. For this reason, he chose to live in this peaceful, traditional setting rather than the modern showplace in the city. Though he was sometimes lonely, he was a man who appreciated solitude. He could always find others with whom to share good times, if that were his desire, but in his private life he was very much his own man.

Today, as Toshi returned to his home, he was thankful for the quiet comfort found within its walls. Here, in this special place, he could reflect on the experiences of the last few hours without interruption from the outside world. As soon as he arrived, Toshi chose to enjoy the burning, hot waters of the Japanese bath and a deep, relaxing massage offered by his companion and friend, Sano Ishikawa. Ishikawa, as he was called at his own request, had come to live with the Yamamoto family when he was fifteen years old and had become a part, but not a part, of the family.

Sano Ishikawa had been 'contracted for life' to be a companion to Toshi, the only child of the Yamamoto family. Because of a serious heart ailment with which their son was born, Tatsume and Kumiko Yamamoto had invited Ishikawa to their home when their son was only five years old. The young man was well-known for his unique skill in the 'healing arts' which he had learned from his own grandfather in far north Japan. When Ishikawa examined Toshi and studied his medical history, he was confident that the skills he possessed would be effective in treating the child's illness.

The strong, stoic Ishikawa had saved the life of the five-year-old Yamamoto child and agreed to remain as his companion for as long as Toshi should live. Though Ishikawa was ten years older than his charge, through their years together they had become, by necessity, inseparable. Wherever Toshi went, Ishikawa was there to preserve his life and strength. And the child who was destined to die before his sixth birthday was still able to live a fairly normal life at age thirty. Even from childhood, Toshi knew that he was the dependent one and never failed to give his utmost respect and honor to his elder guardian.

Ishikawa had always refused to reveal the methods or the medicinal remedies he used in the treatment of his patient, and Toshi had long ago made a solemn oath that he would never speak of those things to anyone. He had learned as a child to accept the counsel of his companion and never to question his methods of healing. While Ishikawa did not at any time forget his accepted role in the Yamamoto household, Toshi refused to treat him as a contracted servant or less than himself in social position. Strong ties of love had developed between the two men, and they had become much closer to brothers than friends.

Today, as Toshi returned to his home from the difficult breakfast confrontation with Ana Maria Gabrelli, he continued to struggle with his own questions: 'What is it about this dark-eyed Western stranger, as fearful as a watchful doe in an open meadow, that has captivated me so? And why is she so fearful? What experiences has she suffered that would cause her to turn away from one who can be trusted and loved without fear? Surely he would never intentionally hurt her…or would he?'

For a moment he considered the possibility that perhaps those penetrating black eyes of Ana's had seen more than he could reveal to himself. Perhaps she could see that if they were to become lovers, the affair could only be of short duration. And if she saw these things, wouldn't she be the more insightful of the two? But Toshi refused to follow that train of thought. He had become too involved emotionally and could not look into the future. Because of his own history, his philosophy of life could only deal with the present. And for the present, Toshiburo Yamamoto had fallen in love with Ana Maria Gabrelli and he was determined to discover if she could love him in return.

Finally, Toshi spoke aloud the questions that would plague him as he continued to struggle with what to do about Ana,

"Why doesn't she understand that the sweetness of true love is the most precious gift that life can offer…no matter what the duration? Isn't one moment of joy enough for you, Ana?"

Much later that night, after all was quiet and the moon shed its light across the beautiful grounds of the Yamamoto estate, a solitary figure stood on the porch viewing the peaceful scene. Looking to the sky, he spoke in a reverent whisper,

"I have experienced the power that dwells in your brilliant rays. That power has touched my life and I could not live without its presence. But now I understand what I have never known before. There is a power in this amazing universe that cannot be seen, but can only be felt within the heart. And for the first time in my life I have felt that unseen power in a most burdensome way. Wise spirits of the night, tell me…how shall I live without the presence of Ana?"

CHAPTER 4

"A wanderer, searching for a quiet, solitary place
Where rest is found and scent of flower and pine
Fills the clear night air
At last, the gift received
That one, sweet spot...my home!"
            --Ana Gabrelli, Journal
            First Night in Seijo Home

Several weeks after the trip to Nikko, Mishima approached Ana at the end of their working day,

"Ana, please have dinner with me tonight. I've got an interesting proposition for you. We can stop at a place near your hotel and I'll explain it. You're going to be very happy."

She laughed and responded quickly,

"For heaven's sake, Mishi, what a way to 'proposition' a Western woman. Why don't you just come out and ask the 'big question?'"

Ana laughed as she teased her friend. He blushed and replied quickly,

"No, no, I don't mean anything sinister. You're crazy! It's about a place for you to live."

Ana brightened,

"What is it? Where is it? Tell me now! I can hardly wait to get out of that hotel. See if Yuki wants to come with us, too. We'll make a party out of the evening."

Mishima hesitated a moment, then, realizing the hope of being alone with Ana was useless, waved and answered,

"I'll get her and meet you downstairs in the lobby. We'll talk about the place at dinner."

Ana was excited about the prospect of a move. She hurried to lock her office, grab her jacket and purse, and meet her friends. When they had decided where to eat, Mishima offered a suggestion,

"Wait a minute and I'll call my friend so he can meet us for dinner. It's his place that's available so he can tell you all about it while we're eating. I think you're going to like it, Ana."

Mishima called his friend, Kyoshi Satoyama, and 'Sato' agreed to meet them at a small restaurant near the Imperial Hotel.

41

The place was on the Ginza (world-famous Tokyo shopping area) and its specialty was *ton-katsu*, a delicious, deep-fried pork cutlet served over white rice and covered with a tangy sauce. This was always a favorite quick meal for the downtown working crowd.

They were seated and had drinks ordered before Mishima's friend arrived. When he came to their table, Ana saw a handsome, young Japanese man dressed neatly in the 'businessman's uniform,' a dark blue suit and tie with light blue shirt. He had a ready smile and bright, flashing eyes that seemed to be laughing at the world.

Mishima introduced his friend to Ana and Miyuki, instructing them to please call him "Sato" rather than Kyoshi. Sato wasted no time but proceeded immediately to tell Ana about his house. He leaned toward her and began to talk excitedly,

"I'm so happy to know that you might be interested in my house. Mishi says you want a quiet place away from so much city noise. When I heard this, I was even happier, because I want a place *in* the city noise…and *away* from the quiet!"

Sato laughed loudly and raised his glass to Ana, then drained it. She could see that this young man loved his precious Asahi a whole lot! Probably a bit too much, she concluded. But Sato went on with his sales pitch,

"You see, I'm living in a small house on my grandparents' property. My sister lived there for a while and then she got married so my parents begged me to please stay to watch over the elderly folks. As you can tell," he raised his glass for another long drink, "I like to have good times and not worry so much. But I am a good son, so I will do what my parents wish. Now, I am happy to know that you might take my place. If you like my little house, all you would have to do is just see that my grandparents are okay and if they need to call my parents or anything like that. They have a housemaid during the day and a caretaker for the property. So they just like to know someone is there, close by, if an emergency comes. Do you think you might be interested in my house? It is very nice, even if it is very small."

Sato looked intently at Ana, waiting breathlessly for her answer. He was not disappointed. She liked what she heard so far and was anxious to see if it was as perfect as Sato described,

"I think I'm very interested! Tell me what station it's closest to, how much I will have to pay, and when I can see it."

He answered with a huge smile,

"We can go right away! It's just a few walking blocks from Seijo Station on the Odakyu line, very east to get to downtown Tokyo. As soon as we finish dinner, we can all go there to meet my grandparents and to see the house, okay? When we go through it, I'll tell you everything about it."

Ana looked at Mishima and Miyuki. They both nodded their heads 'yes,' and they agreed to do just that. Ana was a bit put off by Sato. She could see that he was a typical, young Japanese businessman who would drink his way home every night. But he was only one among millions. It was a way of life for most of them, a way to relieve the stress of long, intense working days.

Though she understood that his drinking habits were fairly normal in this society, she had an uneasy feeling that Sato might accidentally, or not so accidentally, stumble into his little house again some night. If she decided to rent the place, Ana would find a way to make sure that Sato did not keep his key.

The group enjoyed the ton-katsu together, then made their way to the Satoyama home. As they approached the train station, Ana recalled staying in the Seijo area during her college exchange program. This prefecture included many beautiful homes, both traditional and modern, Japanese and Western. She remembered walking through the streets and enjoying large, open, landscaped yards next to the high wood-stucco walls, and a mixture of Christian churches with shrines and temples. She had loved the area for its intercultural atmosphere.

Walking from the station, Ana also remembered the little ice cream shop where she had spent many a hot, muggy summer evening. And she pointed out to Mishima and Miyuki the British-style restaurant, "Bertrum's," known for its 'proper' pot roast. Ana felt comfortable and almost 'at home' again. She began to relax, hoping that the little house would be as nice as the area around it.

Suddenly Sato announced in a proud…and loud…voice, "Here's my place!"

They stood in front of a high wooden fence. Sato took out a key to unlock a small door in the fence and they entered the 'old

43

world' of Japan. He pointed to the large house on the right-hand side of the rocky path where they stood.

"This is where my grandparents live. We should go in and speak to them now. I know they will like you very much, Ana."

He was all smiles and high energy and just a bit 'tipsy.' Ana gave Mishima a slightly worried look as she turned to make sure her friends were still with her. She put her hand on Mishima's shoulder and whispered in his ear,

"How well do you know this guy? Is this going to be a legitimate deal?" They both laughed, but Ana was serious.

Sato led the way into the large, beautiful Japanese home. They left their street shoes in the *genkan* (entry way) in exchange for the *uwabaki* (house slippers). Then they entered the large tatami room, bowing and offering greetings to Satoyama's grandparents.

Ana was well-known as a softie when it came to children or the older generation and, indeed, her heart melted when the grandparents came forward to greet her. They were both very small in stature and quite elderly. Though wrinkled and slightly bent from age, their faces were alight with warmth and welcome. When Ana responded to their greetings in Japanese, they became very excited and could hardly contain their pleasure.

Soon everyone in the room was exchanging bows and laughing together. The grandparents insisted that their guests sit down and share a cup of tea and sweet bean cakes before they go out to look at the little house. This took quite some time but was necessary to show respect for their elderly hosts.

"You will love this, Ana, I know you will. Just wait. Mishima says you like things old-style Japanese. This house is just for you."

Sato was bubbling over with excitement as he led his friends out to the little house. He could tell that Ana had met with his grandparents' full approval. Now, if she felt the same about them and the house, he would be set free!

A small, rock pathway led around the grandparents' residence and past a row of tall evergreens. Behind the trees, Ana saw a tiny house huddled on the edge of the hillside with the city lights flickering like stars in the darkness beyond. Sato pointed to the hillside,

"Look, can you believe this view? You can see far across the city."

Mishima laughed and commented,

"Sato, you're a great real estate agent. You'd better put up your sign and begin a new career!"

Ana responded to Sato's excitement,

"It's truly a wonder, Sato."

Miyuki turned to Ana,

"This looks too good to be true."

Everyone was excited and somewhat apprehensive as Sato unlocked the door to the house and stepped in, turning on the porch and entry lights. With a huge smile, he beckoned to them,

"Come this way and straight into the kitchen."

He guided them through the tiny genkan where they exchanged their shoes for the uwabaki. Then they stepped into a very small kitchen area. It was like a narrow hallway with the cupboards, sink, a tiny refrigerator, and table-top stove along one wall. Behind a divider was a tiny washer-dryer combination. A bathroom with a shower, more like a closet, was at the far end of the kitchen.

Sato continued his sales pitch,

"Everything works, I promise you! Of course, I don't use it much. I just sleep here and make tea and rice once in a while. But it's all good, very good. You can try anything. Here, try the stove or the washer."

He started turning on everything until they all burst out laughing and Mishima suggested he get a job selling housewares along with his new real estate business. From the kitchen, their 'guide' led them into the large, square tatami room that served as living room, bedroom, and dining room, all in one.

"Do you like it, Ana?" Sato was so anxious that Ana love everything, he continued his sales pitch, "The room is very large. You can have guests here and still have space. I know you'll love the closets! You women have so many things to hide away."

He ran to the huge sliding doors that matched the walls. Besides space for hanging clothes, she saw there were large shelves to store belongings, including the futon.

Ana was very happy with the appearance of things. Not only was everything handy, it was immaculately clean. No doubt,

Sato had spent very little time in this place. Ana responded positively to his excitement,

"I'll have to say, Sato, this is a wonderful place. There must be something wrong with it; it's too perfect!"

Sato, so excited by her positive response, ran quickly to the outside wall of the living room and began to slide open the wide *shoji* doors (heavy, rice-paper sliding doors), then the glass doors, then the screens to reveal the beauty spot of the house. Ana was amazed at what she saw there, hidden behind this tiny place.

They stepped onto a porch that spanned the width of the house with a rock pathway stretching around a small Japanese garden. In the center of the garden was a tiny fish pond with a variety of small fish of many shapes and colors. A few plum and cherry trees were planted near the back of the garden, mixed with evergreens that had been trimmed to differing shapes. Flowering azalea bushes lined the pathway.

Miyuki walked over to Ana and whispered,

"My god, Ana, this is something else! If you don't want it, I'll move in tomorrow. Is this a dream home...or what?"

The young women stood together looking out at the garden and the lights sparkling across the hillsides. Ana whispered,

"I believe that I have found my home at last!"

Even Sato recognized the importance of this moment. He remained silent as he watched Ana and Miyuki whispering together. Ana broke the spell that had touched them all,

"Okay, Sato, now tell me the bad news. How much is the rent and what will *really* be expected of me should I choose to live here?"

Sato nearly jumped for joy at her response but contained his excitement,

"This is the absolute truth, Ana...the rent is moderate and I promise that the only needs my grandparents have is that a kind, trustworthy person live close by should there ever be an emergency. You will have my telephone number and that of my parents in Kyoto should anything serious come up. And my grandparents don't mind a party, either, once in a while. It's just that I want to party *every* night and that disturbs their quiet lifestyle. My friends get wild like me, you know, and I need my freedom. When I live near my grandparents, I feel like a tight

46

rope is wrapped around my neck! Mishima will understand how it can be for a Japanese man."

Sato looked at Mishima and they both laughed. Mishima responded by slapping his friend on the back,

"We all know how it can be for *you*, Sato!" He knew his friend only too well.

Since Mishima had picked up on Ana's apprehension regarding Sato, he asked the question that she most wanted to ask,

"By the way, friend, you won't be forgetting the way to your new apartment some night, will you, and suddenly turn up in Ana's kitchen?"

Sato roared with laughter. "You know me too well, Mishi!"

Then Sato turned to Ana and bowed, addressing her with exaggerated courtesy,

"Ana, I promise that I will give you the *only* key to this place, except my grandparents', of course. And, if I should ever turn up in your kitchen without invitation, you can buzz my grandmother's house and she will lash me with her sharp tongue. She may be tiny and wrinkled, but she is still a *tiger* when angry!

Seriously, Ana, I will be good. And this is my key to prove it. Would you like to keep it? And, by the way, I won't need anything here except my electronic stuff. Everything is yours to use, if you want it—the sofa, the tables and chairs, the futon. I'm buying new things for my apartment and it will save me moving everything to my grandparents' upstairs rooms. If you move later, just leave these things here for the next tenant, okay? Is that helpful to you? Does that encourage you to rent my little house?"

Sato was holding up his key chain with an excited look on his face. Ana was quiet for a moment. She looked at Mishima, who nodded his head, 'yes,' and then Miyuki, who whispered,

"If you don't take it, I will!"

Ana smiled at Sato and grabbed his key.

"You've convinced me…and I love your little house! I want to move in as soon as possible. I'm so anxious to get out of that hotel room! Now, what do I need to do?"

Everyone cheered Ana's decision and they all began talking at once about ways they could help her move and when and what needed to be done. Ana and Sato immediately went to talk with the grandparents who were very happy as Ana signed the rental

47

agreement and gave them her first month's rent. Beginning on Sunday, the little house would be hers. When Miyuki and Mishima came back to the grandparents' house, Sato poured them each a cup of *amakuchi* (sweet) sake for a toast to Ana's good luck and to the relief and happiness of Sato and his grandparents.

On the way home, the friends planned the move and talked about having a housewarming party as soon as Ana could get everything arranged the way she wanted it. When they dropped Sato off at his new apartment, he bowed low to Ana and said joyfully,

"Ana, thank you for my freedom!"

They all laughed and Ana responded with thanks and a warning,

"And thank you, Sato, for my beautiful new home. But, remember, *obaa-san tora* (grandmother tiger) will be watching over me!"

Sato accepted Ana's thanks, and her warning, with joyful laughter. On their way back to the city, the three friends stopped at a small bar near the Imperial Hotel to share a final toast for Ana's good fortune. Later that night when Ana walked into her hotel room, she jumped on the bed and laughed out loud with joy, shouting into the emptiness,

"I'm going to have a home! My first home of all time and I love it. Thank you, Sato, and have a happy time with your friends drinking, drinking, drinking, drinking, while I sit in my quiet garden enjoying the sweet scent of flowers…all alone!"

Saturday was moving day for Ana. Her friends gladly offered their help, knowing how much she wanted to get out of the hotel and settled in her own place. The move wasn't a major undertaking since Ana's list of possessions included only her clothes, a stereo, and a small television set, plus a few boxes of personal belongings stored with Miyuki. She had learned to travel light in Japan.

While Ana and Miyuki shopped for the usual household needs, Sato and Mishima arranged the furniture in her living room. They put Ana's television set and stereo in the closet then wired the stereo speakers and set them beside her couch. If she wanted to watch television she could set it out on the floor and is she wanted music it would come through the speakers. This saved precious space in her living area.

By the end of the day, Ana's new home was exactly as she wanted it...cozy and comfortable. The four friends celebrated with wine and sushi the women brought back from their shopping trip. Their toasts were for Ana's happiness in Sato's tiny house so, of course, they had to offer a special toast of 'thanks' to their wild friend, as well.

The first night in her new home was like a dream for Ana. After everyone had gone, she turned off the inside lights and lit the garden lanterns from a gas jet in the kitchen. Each lantern had a separate control so one or all could be lit and she could choose a soft or bright light, whatever her mood. She pulled the futon out of the closet and placed it in front of the sofa using the soft pillows to lean against as she sat looking out into the garden. The sounds she heard were foreign to her ear...the croaking of frogs, the chirping of crickets, and the soft whispering of the evergreens moving in the breeze that came across the hillside.

Ana's heart was overflowing with joy for the gifts that nature offered her and for the simple beauty of this tiny Japanese home. She felt that she had received a great blessing and in such an unusual way. She could hardly imagine being forever grateful to the "wild and crazy" Sato. That prospect was a bit frightening, but she was fairly certain that she could handle it.

When Ana slept that night, the first night in her little house, her dreams were filled with images of a garden path and evergreens swaying gracefully in the evening breeze. And there, floating on her tiny pond, were three, pure, white chrysanthemums sparkling like crystal in the moonlight!

CHAPTER 5

"Why now, in this far-off land
Am I caught in that 'sweet mystery'
That moment when two lives touch
And both seem to know
That it was meant to be so?
How did it begin? How will it end?
And why am I so afraid?"
                    --Ana Gabrelli, Journal

For the next few weeks, Ana basked in the pleasures of her little house. After work, she was anxious to return to her private space and relax in its peaceful atmosphere. Miyuki understood Ana's need to be alone for a while after the months of living out of suitcases in the hotel, but Mishima began to feel the loss of their time together. He had been in love with Ana since their first meeting at the Georgetown University Intercultural Club nearly ten years ago.

Mishima had been surprised to find this beautiful Italian-American woman from Boston interested in the tiny far eastern islands of Japan. But he found her to be friendly, honest, and fun-loving, yet sensitive to other's feelings. He had often wondered what she had seen in him, a shy, young student from the far-off isle of Japan, that had brought him the gift of her friendship. During their college years, both Mishima and Miyuki had become frequent visitors in the Boston home of Ana's sister, Valentina. Ana's parents were deceased and her sister was her only family. 'Val,' her husband, Roger Tristano, and their three children had become the "American family" for both Miyuki and Mishima.

The three friends became a constant trio during these years and when they chose their career directions, it seemed natural that they would go together. At times, Mishima wondered if Ana knew how often she had broken his heart. He was certain that she had never even considered such a thing, for Ana trusted his friendship. She would have no reason to know how many tears he had shed for loving her.

Now, Mishima was worried about their relationship. Though he was happy that Ana had a nice place to live, he missed their after-work gatherings and, so far, she had not invited either him or Miyuki to visit her there. Sometimes at night when he was thinking of her, Mishima wondered, *'Who have you invited to your little house, Ana? Will it ever be Mishima?'* He was certain that it would never be as he desired it. But when his heart became heavy and tears for Ana fell from his eyes, he told himself,

"I may never be her lover, but we will always love each other as friends and that will be enough for me."

Mishima was determined that the love Ana offered him as a friend would be enough, for without that, his life would be as dry and brittle as the tiny, sun-dried creatures he had discovered as a child along the rocky shores of the Japan Sea. Yes, Ana's friendship was enough, and more than enough, to bring joy to Mishima's heart.

Ana's days were filled with the challenge of an exciting profession, the pleasure of sharing with good friends, and the added joy of quiet evenings in her tiny, Japanese home. On one of those evenings, several weeks after the night of *O-bon*, she opened her personal journal and wrote what she had decided would be the final entry under the title, "Toshiburo Yamamoto,"

"I'll always remember one special night…the surprise of a stranger touching my arm, our struggle with the oduri *and each other. I will remember waking to the beauty of white chrysanthemums and a sweet* haiku*. Perhaps another time we shall meet, perhaps not."*

Ana uttered a sigh as she completed the entry and closed the journal. She did not have the courage to do more than that, and it was evident that Yamamoto had accepted her words of dismissal exactly as she had meant them at the time…a 'final farewell.' So, these few paragraphs joined entries of other near-romances that were scattered throughout the pages of Ana's journal. She had always stopped short of in-depth relationships that might involve a commitment of the heart, for Ana's highest value was her independent spirit. She intended to keep it intact!

Much later in the evening, Ana walked out onto the porch and sat quietly viewing the peaceful garden and her one bright, orange carp swimming in the tiny pond. 'Well,' she thought, 'my life is almost perfect. One can hardly expect to have it all.'

On that same evening in another part of the city, Toshiburo Yamamoto was preparing to leave his office after a long day at the University when his thoughts turned to Ana. Suddenly, he found himself picking up the telephone and dialing a number he had written on his desk pad. He decided to make one last attempt to penetrate the heart of this unique, Western woman. When the hotel desk clerk answered the telephone, Toshi asked for Ana by her full name and felt a sudden shock as the clerk replied,

"Ms. Gabrelli no longer resides here, sir. I'm very sorry, but I have no forwarding address or telephone number."

Toshi was silent for a moment, then answered the clerk with a polite "Thank you" and hung up. He remembered that he had Ana's meishi so could call her office and try to make contact in that way. But he knew that he had waited too long, thinking she would not continue to haunt him. How wrong he was! As he drove home that night, he was a bit more reckless than usual.

Disturbing thoughts crept into his mind. *What if Ana has returned to the States? Many things can happen in a few weeks' time. If I've lost contact with her, I have only myself to blame. Even while I was expressing my true feelings to her, I knew it was wrong to do so. Now, should we have an opportunity to meet again, I must approach this volatile, young woman with care. Otherwise, it will do me no good to renew the relationship, only to tear it apart again with conflict.*

Before retiring for the night, Toshi found Ana's meishi, still inside the infamous 'Thank You' card that had said nothing and meant nothing except confusion to his heart. Now, it was the key to Ana.

The next morning, Toshi drove into the city early to avoid the rush-hour traffic. He knew the area near the Intercultural Education Exchange Center, so he was able to find it without any problem, even finding a parking space within walking distance of the building. After a leisurely breakfast at a small hotel nearby, Toshi slowly walked to the telephone booth, dialed the IEEC number, and asked for "Ms. Ana Maria Gabrelli." There was a pause on the line. After what seemed like hours, the answer came.

"This is Ana Gabrelli. May I help you?"

Toshi felt a sudden stirring in his chest at the sound of her voice but was able to reply calmly,

"Ms. Gabrelli, this is Toshiburo Yamamoto, your dance partner at the O-bon Festival, if you recall. I've tried to contact you at the hotel, but discovered that you no longer reside there. I hope you've found a suitable place to live."

Ana was somewhat stunned at his greeting. After her recent thoughts about Toshi, it seemed ironic that she would suddenly hear his voice. She answered in a warm, friendly manner,

"I'm surprised to hear from you, Yamamoto-san! How could I forget the infamous 'night of O-bon' and our amazing performance in the oduri circle? And, yes, I *have* found a very nice place to live. It seems so strange to hear from you, since I've been thinking about you recently."

Toshi was somewhat shocked at her pleasant reply and felt freer to share with her,

"I appreciate your thoughts, Ana. Perhaps that's what has given me the courage to contact you after our rather disturbing 'farewell' a few weeks ago. I've wanted many times to apologize for my behavior toward you the last time we were together. I surely overstepped the boundaries of courtesy and want you to know how very sorry I am. But there is another reason I'm calling. I've been thinking about the intercultural programs you mentioned that are available at the Center and I would like to talk with you about them. Would it be possible for us to visit this morning about some ideas I have in this regard? Do you have time now, before I begin my day at the University?"

Ana was trying to follow Toshi's conversation. He had moved from the personal to the professional so quickly that she couldn't decide which direction he was most interested in pursuing. All she could do was to try and find out,

"Well…of course. Do you know where our office is located?"

"Yes. Actually, I had breakfast as a nearby hotel hoping that we could get together this morning. I can be at your office in just a few moments…and thank you for giving me this time, Ana."

Toshi was surprised by Ana's positive attitude. He walked the three blocks slowly to give himself time to consider the best way to approach her. He hoped that she would be open to renew a relationship between them, whether personal or professional. He would accept whichever she chose.

A short time later, Toshi was escorted into the very plush office of Ms. Ana Maria Gabrelli, Co-Director of the Intercultural Education Exchange Center, Tokyo Office. He was duly impressed. And even more impressed with her gracious welcome.

Ana greeted him with a warm smile, a slight bow, and an extended hand,

"I'm happy to see you, Yamamoto-san."

He reached out to take her hand while bowing politely. Ana felt a heart beat in the palm of her hand and wondered whose it was. She quickly pulled her hand away and motioned for Toshi to take a chair then she began speaking to him as if they were close friends,

"It's been a while since we met, so I'd like to catch you up on some major changes in my life. The most wonderful thing has happened...at least, it's wonderful for me!"

Toshi was more than surprised by Ana's warm greeting and was drawn into her mood. He responded with a smile and a question,

"What has happened that makes you so happy, Ms. Gabrelli? Please, tell me your good news."

"Well...it is actually...a miracle! Just out of the blue, a friend of mine was offered a house to rent, but he's happy in his city apartment and didn't want to move, so...he asked if I would be interested and, of course, I said 'yes'! When we went to see it, I was a bit skeptical because the young man who has been living there is quite a 'wild' man. As it turned out, everything was perfect and I am now the happy resident of a very nice, private house. It's small, but has everything I would ever want in a home. By that I mean, it's a traditional Japanese house overlooking the city with a little garden and pond. I even have my own pet carp!"

Ana laughed as she continued. "The only requirement, besides rent, of course, is to watch over the elderly grandparents who live in the big house on the front of the property. Can you believe such good fortune? I'm so happy I can hardly contain myself!"

Toshi smiled at Ana's enthusiastic description of her new home,

"Congratulations on your miracle, Ana! It sounds like something you've wanted very much. Tell me, where is your new home located?"

"It's close to Seijo Station on the Odakyu line. But, I don't want to tell you anymore about it, now. Instead, I'd like you to come see it. I'm planning a housewarming party this Saturday night. Would you like to join us?"

Before Toshi could answer, Ana apologized for her excitement,

"I don't mean to overwhelm you with my good news. We do have more important things to discuss. We'd better get to that."

Toshi responded with a warm smile,

"Please don't apologize for your happiness, Ana! I'm happy for you and feel honored by your invitation. I wouldn't want to miss celebrating such a momentous event."

Ana laughed,

"It IS momentous for me! I've never had such a private place before and it's a very nice little house. I'll draw you a map. It's only a few blocks from Seijo Station and quite easy to find."

She proceeded to draw the map for him. He was surprised that he knew exactly where it was located,

"We're practically neighbors! I live very near this area and am acquainted with the shopping streets of Seijo. There are some very nice restaurants in that area."

"Yes, the house is just a few blocks from there. We'll also have lanterns hanging on the outside walls of the big house, so you can't miss it. Just come in the lighted door there and follow the rock pathway as far back as you can go…and you will find my place! I think you'll enjoy meeting my friends, too. Some of them are a bit crazy, but I'm sure you're used to that, being with college students every day."

"I will also be *most* anxious to meet your 'wild' landlord and thank him for making Ms. Gabrelli so happy."

Ana wondered if there were some hidden meanings behind Toshi's statement. If so, she knew what he was implying. She chose to ignore it, however, for she had some concerns about Sato herself. She quickly changed the subject,

"Well, now that we've discussed all my good news, what is it you'd like us to do for you, Toshi, in regard to our intercultural programs."

He paused a moment to redirect his thoughts from the personal to the professional,

"My responsibility is to help my students understand the politics of diplomacy. But I can't begin to prepare them in my classroom to actually meet people, face-to-face, and see them as persons with very different views of the world. That's where I could use your help. What can you do for these young students who hope for professions in world affairs?"

Ana responded with enthusiasm,

"We have a team of intercultural specialists who represent several areas of the world. Their purpose is to simulate 'real-life' experiences where the students learn to appreciate the differences among people and ways to relate to those differences. Our main goals are to challenge students to understand the cultural uniqueness of others and to seek for more in-depth intercultural experiences themselves."

Toshi liked what he heard,

"What you're suggesting sounds like the very thing these young people need at this point in their education. I'm quite interested in participating in this type of program, if possible. What do you need from me to develop such a learning plan?"

"We can provide a study of four separate cultural areas. It works like this…you divide the classes into two main groups and allow each group to choose two areas they want to study over a two-week period. Though the experience seems short, it's intensive and provides an excellent introduction to the 'real life' of another world. We call it 'cultural immersion.' We're talking about relating on personal levels such as family, education, and social life. Politics is up to you!"

"What you're telling me is exactly what I want to hear. If we decide to use your program, then I'll need to give you the dates, times, and places where we will be meeting?"

"That's about it! We'll provide the cultural specialists and everything that goes with the study. So your students choose which areas of the world they want to explore."

"This could be a very challenging experience for my students in more ways than one. Some may find they're not so excited about international service, after all."

"We've both been through that, I'm sure, and the struggle of living in a very different world from our own! I'll never fully understand Japan, its people, or its culture, but I certainly welcome any help anyone can give me along the way. That's all we can do for your students, give them a few valuable 'road signs' as a foundation to more in-depth understanding when they're in the actual setting."

Toshi responded with enthusiasm as he stood to leave,

"Ana, I'm definitely interested in what you're doing here and look forward to sharing this learning experience with my students and with your colleagues. I'll call you with the necessary information within the next few days."

Ana stood and offered her hand with a warm smile,

"I'm glad that you called and I'm very happy that you'll be at my party!"

Toshi gripped her hand in response to her kindness,

"It's been much too long since we met, Ana. I hope that your invitation to the housewarming party means that you've forgiven my discourteous behavior in the past."

He did not release her hand but seemed to be waiting for a sign of a new beginning for their relationship. Ana offered it willingly.

"This seems like a good time to start over as friends, especially if we're going to be working together during the next few weeks. So…until Saturday night?"

"Thank you, Ana, for a 'new beginning,' and, yes, I will be most happy to join you Saturday night!"

Toshi smiled and bowed politely then turned and left the office.

A short time later, Miyuki dropped by Ana's office to check on some seminar information. She found Ana leaning against the desk, staring out the window with a pensive look on her face. Miyuki asked, somewhat worried about interrupting her friend's thoughts,

"Are you all right?"

Ana answered with a sigh and a frown,

57

"I was until a few minutes ago."

Miyuki had seen the gentleman leaving Ana's office and quickly put two and two together. She walked over and put her arm around Ana,

"Why fight it? Don't you know you'll never win that battle?"

"I can't allow myself to get involved, Yuki. And yet, I've just walked headlong into it as if it were inevitable."

"So this is the 'mystery man' who's been haunting your life. I knew that day when we were at Nikko that something had happened. You haven't been the same person since the night of the O-bon Festival. And he's the reason, isn't he?"

Ana avoided Miyuki's question,

"I'm not good at endings; they frighten me."

There was silence between the two women for a few moments. Then, without warning, Miyuki grabbed her friend's shoulders and shook her,

"Hey! Wake up and be part of the real world, Ana! You're not a wizard. You don't know what's around the corner, so why not do what the rest of us do? We accept life as it comes, we enjoy it, and when the joy's over, it's over, and we take the consequences. Stop analyzing *everything* until it's too late to do *anything*. You're going to go right on missing all the good parts of this crazy life we have the good fortune to live!"

Ana was surprised by her friend's outburst, but before she could respond, Miyuki looked straight into her eyes and spoke in a voice filled with emotion,

"Listen to me and remember what I'm saying. I learned a little poem a long time ago and I've never forgotten it. These words have given me the freedom to take a risk for love whenever it's offered and *never* to regret it:

> *"Spend all you have for loveliness,*
> *Buy it and never count the cost;*
> *For one white, singing hour of peach,*
> *Count many a year of strife well-lost*
> *And for a breath of ecstasy,*
> *Give all you have been or could be."*
> --Sara Teasdale, "Barter" (1917)

"And that, my friend, is the best and last advice I can offer you on this tender subject!"

Miyuki left the room, her own tears welling up from her empty heart. Ana was touched by her friend's poetic words and, for the first time in her life, felt an emptiness from within that needed to be filled. The sensation frightened her for she recognized it as a yearning to love and to be loved by another. But Ana was most afraid for she knew, but did not want to know, who that other was. Now, she was anxious for the day to end so she could return to the silence of her little house and ponder the stirrings within her heart.

Later that night, Ana sat on the porch of her little house watching the stars and the city lights flickering beyond the tops of the evergreens. She couldn't explain why she felt so close to this stranger she had met on the festival night in a Tokyo street. What did she know about him? Only that he had been educated in the West. He was obviously intelligent enough to be a professor at Tokyo University and to be concerned with the intercultural education of his students. But what of his character? Toshiburo Yamamoto seemed refined in manner. And though they had been frustrated with each other in their moments of confrontation, he had remained polite and kind.

Ana could find no reason to turn away from him, except the memories that haunted her from the past and her overriding fear of ultimate loss. As Ana stood and looked at the dark sky and the stars breaking through that darkness, she was reminded of those memories that haunted her and had kept her from ever allowing herself to experience the joy of loving another. Though she had seen the joys of love expressed in the lives of others, she found it nearly impossible to overcome the fears within her own heart. Ana was not afraid of life, nor of caring for others in many ways, yet she was fearful of 'giving herself' to another in a relationship that would demand her whole heart. She was intent on finding fulfillment in her profession and joy with her friends and, yet, in her quiet, private moments she could not deny a longing for something beyond.

Ana finally admitted to herself, *'I want to listen to Yuki. I want to conquer my fears, for it is true that this persistent stranger has touched my heart and I feel alive in a way that I've never felt before. If I don't risk this beginning, the relationship is ended already and there will be nothing left but the question, "What if...?" I don't want to live the rest of my life with those words echoing through my mind and heart.'*

Ana had issued the invitation to this 'new samurai' who seemed to know more of her than she knew of herself. Perhaps they *could* experience that "one white, singing hour of peace." Perhaps they *could* share that "sweet breath of ecstasy." For the first time in her life, though with hesitation, Ana allowed herself the dream.

CHAPTER 6

"One moment in time two lives touch.
Can love breach the barriers of culture?
Can love calm the fears in the heart?
Only by 'risk' come the answers.
How much am I willing to risk?
Yet, how much am I willing to lose?"
--Ana Gabrelli, Journal

A few days before Ana's housewarming, she visited with Sato's grandparents so they would be aware of the upcoming celebration. The Satoyamas were so happy to have Ana living in their little house, they quickly assured her that whatever noise was made would not disturb them in the least. To show her appreciation, Ana took them a gift of French wine so they could feel a part of the Saturday activities. They graciously accepted her kindness, promising to enjoy the wine as if they were her special guests.

The party night finally arrived. Sato volunteered to bring the food and drink to Ana's house in his van, though everyone at the office had contributed to the costs. There were many small boxes of delicious foods, both Japanese and Western style and, of course, plenty of drinks. Ana provided the coffee and tea.

The guests came by train and car bringing their favorite music and small gifts for Ana's new home. Her office friends were a truly international group from many nations of the world. Presently, Ana was the only one at IEEC from the United States, though all of her colleagues were fluent in English. They were good friends who respected one another in their professional roles and enjoyed their informal times together.

Toshi had planned to slip into the party quietly, but the gift he brought drew everyone's immediate attention. When he handed the magnum of fine French champagne to the hostess, claps and cheers filled the air. Ana realized that this party was obviously going to be a rowdy celebration. She was glad that she had warned the grandparents. So the 'official' party began with the pouring of the champagne and a toast to Ana for 'ten thousand years of happiness' in her new home. Everyone shouted their 'banzais,' begging to hear why in the world she was living in a tiny hillside house next to Sato's grandparents. She was teased mercilessly with many questions about where Sato slept when he came stumbling in at midnight, forgetting that he had moved. This was a favorite storyline and, of course, Sato loved every minute of it.

After Ana opened the presents and offered a gracious thanks to her friends, the 'karaoke' contest began. Most everyone adjourned to the porch and garden area to play their wild tapes and pretend they were famous musical stars. Later in the evening, the food was served and the guests moved into small groups to eat and talk together. Ana was the very busy hostess, making sure everyone had drinks and food and places to sit. She hadn't spent much more than a moment with Toshi except to thank him for the wonderful gift he'd brought to the party and to help him pour it into the many glasses.

From time to time, Ana noticed that the Japanese guests seemed very anxious to meet 'Yamamoto-san' and, when introduced, displayed obvious deference toward him by bowing as if to one of high status. This surprised Ana and caused her to wonder what they knew about this gentleman that she did not. Perhaps it was the expensive champagne that had impressed them or the fact that he was a professor at one of the most prestigious universities in Japan.

On the other hand, Ana noticed that Toshi seemed to relate more comfortably with her Western guests. She wondered if his educational background and language fluency were the major factors in that regard or perhaps he was interested in sharing some of the experiences he had enjoyed in their respective countries. All in all, she was glad that her friends had welcomed him and seemed to appreciate his warm, open personality. And Toshi appeared to be having a good time becoming acquainted with them as well. He was not, in the least, hesitant to engage any of them in conversation.

At one point in the evening, Ana caught the arm of her co-director at IEEC, Ito Nishiyama,

"Ito, tell me something. As you might have heard or noticed tonight, I've recently become acquainted with Toshiburo Yamamoto, a professor at Tokyo University. Do you happen to know him? Is there anything, in particular, that I should know about his background?"

Ito looked surprised and responded with a smile,

"Why, Ana, I thought he must be a very good friend of yours to bring such a gift to your house party! You did invite him here, didn't you?"

"Yes, of course, but I first met him in an informal setting and since we've been together on just a few occasions, I know very little about him personally."

Ito leaned over and spoke to her very slowly and clearly,

"In case you're not aware, Toshiburo Yamamoto is a well-known member of the Imperial House. Though he is only a distant cousin of the Emperor, his family is recognized as one of high status in Japan and holds both financial and political power. Of course, you wouldn't know this by meeting him socially. I've met him at several gatherings and have found him to be a very pleasant and down-to-earth young man. I understand, however, that he may soon be accepting a high diplomatic post and perhaps even serve Japan as an ambassador in the future. Since he's been educated in both the United States and Great Britain, he's well-prepared for either appointment. I consider it quite an honor for us to be working with him and his students at the university. This will surely bring the Center some added prestige and could open other doors for our programs. Congratulations on your good work!"

Ito noticed that as he spoke, Ana's face had turned pale and she appeared to be ill. He quickly took the champagne glass from her hand and held her arm steady,

"What is it? You don't look well at all. Perhaps you've had your champagne limit, Ana. Please sit down here and I'll get you something to counteract the alcohol."

He guided Ana to the sofa, then brought her two small sandwiches and a glass of tea,

"Here, eat these slowly and drink the tea. You'll feel better in a minute. I think you've overdone on your party."

Ito was concerned about Ana's sudden weakness. After she had eaten the sandwiches and drank a few sips of tea, he whispered to her,

"Let's go outside for a while. I think the cool air and the quiet will help you revive."

He put his arm around Ana to steady her as they went out the kitchen door to the front of the house. There, they sat down on a small stone bench among the evergreens where it was quiet and cool. After resting for a few moments and sipping the cold tea, Ana's strength returned, but the headache continued.

"Thanks, Ito. I had a quick flash of pain in my head that knocked me for a loop. I need an aspirin desperately. Would you mind? They're in the cupboard right above the kitchen sink."

Ito found the aspirin and returned. Ana quickly swallowed four small tablets with the tea and breathed deeply,

"I'll be okay, now, and thanks for saving my 'face.' I nearly fell on it!"

"Why don't you stay out here a while longer and relax. It's quiet and if anyone asks, I'll tell them you're taking a break, okay?"

"Okay, but I'll be back in a few minutes."

"If you're not, I'll come check on you." Ito appeared to be very concerned. Before he went inside, Ana pleaded,

"Please don't say anything to anyone else. I don't want to dampen the party."

After Ito left, Ana leaned back against the bench and tried to stop some surprise tears that seemed to come of their own accord into her eyes. She asked herself,

'What now? Just as I was about to grab the proverbial 'brass ring.' What now? Why did I ask the question of Ito? If it were so important to me, why not trust Toshi enough to ask him about his own background? And why would it be important?'

The cool air helped Ana restore her balance and think more clearly. She finally asked the only questions that needed to be answered, *'Does it matter what our pasts have been or what our future might be? Isn't who we are at this moment all that really counts?'*

Ana felt the emptiness in her heart and knew that she wanted it filled. As she prepared to return to the party, she whispered into the darkness,

"I want that 'one white, singing hour of peace'!"

Toshi had noticed Ana leaving the party with Nishiyama and was surprised. He hadn't had time to do more than greet the hostess and share the champagne toast with her before they were both drawn into the activities of the evening. Though he found Ana's friends to be of diverse backgrounds, he discovered that most were very concerned with the process of developing positive relations among the nations of the world. Toshi was enjoying their conversations and, at the same time, trying to determine what roles they played at the IEEC office, and, in particular, their relationships to the hostess of the evening.

But Toshi had two questions now: Were Ana and her co-director involved intimately? And, if so, why would Ana seem so anxious to renew their relationship by inviting him to her home if there was someone else in her personal life? He was confused by what was happening but chose to relax and enjoy the party. Toshi knew that he would not leave tonight before he and Ana had discussed the direction of their relationship. He was determined on that issue.

The party livened as the group devoured more food and a lot more drink. Then Sato held up his guitar and asked if anyone could play. By that time, Toshi had just enough to drink that he was ready to risk getting more involved in the action and, to his own surprise, volunteered to 'do the honors.' While a student at Harvard, he had acquired some musical skills, though now he played just for himself or for close friends. But tonight he was relaxed and in the mood to add to the entertainment of the evening. Sato handed Toshi the instrument, they got everything plugged in and the guitarist began to play some favorite music from his college days. To his surprise, nearly everyone knew the songs he chose and sang along with him. The major 'jazz and blues' session began.

When Ana came back into the house, most of the crowd were on the porch, clapping, singing, and moving to the rhythm of "The San Francisco Bay Blues." She could hardly believe her eyes when she walked out to join them. There was Toshi, dressed elegantly in his olive green, silk trousers, and white knit shirt, entertaining the party with an amazingly-skilled guitar. He had definitely become the 'star' of the show. This was a side of

Yamamoto that surprised Ana completely and pleasantly. So he was a man of many faces and varied talents.

After a little more jazz and blues, Toshi ended his concert with an old folk song, "The First Time Ever I Saw Your Face." Ana watched him closely as he sang the opening verse. But when his eyes met hers, she turned away. The words brought to mind the tender haiku he had sent her with the chrysanthemums on the morning after O-bon. *"Petals, white as snow, pure crystal in the moonlight, shine like Ana's eyes."* She knew this 'gentle samurai' was making love to her through the words of the song and the movement in her heart confirmed Ana's desire to follow Miyuki's wise counsel.

Toshi bowed in feigned reverence to the many claps and cheers as he handed the guitar back to Sato. He came directly to Ana, taking her hand and guiding her down the porch steps to a quieter corner of the garden. They were both laughing and, of course, Ana couldn't help but comment on his performance,

"What a surprise you are, Yamamoto-san, and such amazing talent! You know everyone's favorite music. Here I thought you were such a serious scholar and gentleman. I've heard it said that one should watch out for the quiet types; they occasionally revert to erratic behaviors."

Toshi wiped his brow with his handkerchief as he answered,

"I found that the beautiful hostess was ignoring me, so I had to do something to get her attention."

"I'm sorry, but I was in great demand keeping the glasses filled. And, besides, you seemed to be doing fine without me. Am I right?"

Toshi turned to her and whispered,

"I could never do fine without you, Ana. Surely you know that by now."

Ana felt those 'ever-present fears' welling up inside her heart and quickly changed the mood,

"We'd better get back to the group. I think the party is winding down and I need to finish my hostess duties."

Toshi gave up and let her go. He walked slowly back to the porch and visited a while with Nishiyama as the guests prepared to leave. But when Miyuki volunteered her, Sato, and Mishima to stay and help with the cleanup, he stepped in.

"I'll be glad to assist the hostess with the cleanup duties. You go ahead with the others. I'm sure the two of us can handle it."

Miyuki gave Toshi a friendly smile,

"Thanks, 'guitar-man,' for one wild and crazy evening…and for the cleanup!"

Sato shook Toshi's hand and offered his guitar 'anytime,' but Mishima stood by silently, fully aware of the direction the evening had taken. As Miyuki started toward the door, she drew Ana aside and whispered,

"Go for that 'white, singing hour,' woman! If I had the chance, I wouldn't waste a minute!"

The women laughed in their separate plights. Then Miyuki yelled at Sato and Mishima,

"Let's get out of here before they change their minds about the cleanup!"

The three friends were the final guests to leave. Suddenly, the little house was quiet. Ana and Toshi looked at the mess, looked at each other, and started laughing. Then Toshi headed for the kitchen and called back to Ana,

"I want you to know that I am a truly multi-talented, modern man who is quite capable of doing housework. You bring 'em and I'll wash 'em!"

"Well, I'm impressed! Did you work as a dishwasher at that London 'dive' where you played guitar? What a guy!"

Together, the pair slowly but surely put everything back in order and Toshi helped Ana pull out the futon to arrange the 'party room' for her night's sleep. It was nearly 2 a.m. when the little house was neat again and all was quiet. Ana turned off the inside lights and dimmed the garden lanterns, while Toshi poured them each a final glass of champagne. They walked out to sit on the porch and relax in the peaceful atmosphere. After a while, it seemed as if the garden sounds became a love song to them and the fragrance of azalea and pine were love's sweet incense. Both felt as if nature was drawing them together at this special moment for a special purpose, though they did not touch. They sat in the stillness until Ana broke the silence with a whisper,

"What do you want from me, Yamamoto?"

Toshi's heart turned over at her surprising question. When he was finally able to answer, he could barely speak above the pounding in his chest,

"I want your heart, Ana, but I ask nothing more than you're willing to give."

Toshi had no idea where Ana was leading him. He waited for her response not knowing how to proceed. She gave it, in her most cutting 'Gabrelli' way,

"I can't give you my heart, Yamamoto. That is a gift that can only be shared with one who is deserving of it."

Toshi felt as if Ana had struck him. He turned to look at her, wondering if she might be teasing, but there was no gentle light in her eyes. Ana knew that her honesty had hit its mark and that he was wounded by it. But to her surprise, he did not respond with anger but with humility,

"Perhaps you're right about me, Ana, and more than likely, you are. But who is ever deserving of another's love? If love were shared only with those who deserved it, what a cold, barren world this would be!"

Toshi set his glass down on the step and rose, preparing to leave. Ana stood quickly and took his hand, stopping him with a question,

"How does one love another when there is no future in it?"

He looked at her, wondering if she were still trying to trap him into further confrontation. But what he saw in her eyes was neither anger nor defiance. What he saw there melted his heart and broke it all at once. For in that one, quick glance he knew that Ana Maria Gabrelli surely loved him, whether or not she would ever acknowledge it to herself or to him. He chose to answer his question in the only way he knew,

"I believe that when one loves another truly, the future has no meaning. Its power is lost in the present."

For a few moments there was silence between them. Then Ana whispered,

"If the present is all there is, then teach me about loving, Yamamoto-san. I have no knowledge of its power."

Toshi knew only too well the risk to his own fragile heart as well as to hers, but could respond in no other way,

"I will teach you all I know, Ana, and then you must teach me."

She smiled and led him into the house where, for a time their expressions of love bridged the ideological distance and the intercultural difference between them. There was an abandon in those first moments of intimacy which spoke of a purely physical desire; yet, there was a sweetness, as well, which spoke of a promise between them that could never be broken. And for these reasons, they offered their love to one another and shed their tears together without shame.

It was still dark when Toshi woke. The shoji doors were open and the garden lanterns shed their light across the room. He looked down at the woman sleeping peacefully beside him. Though he had spoken words of love to many women, he knew for a certainty that this was the only one who would ever claim his heart. Ana's invitation had taken him by complete surprise. Toshi didn't want to think it was the champagne that had weakened her resistance to his open advances, but neither could he explain her sudden emotional response.

Tonight, in their most intimate moments, he had declared his love for Ana, but she had not spoken the words he longed to hear. He had been warned that she would not give her heart to the undeserving, and Toshi knew that as much as he desired that gift, he did not deserve it. But he also knew what she did not. Ana had already given it. As he watched this beautiful American woman in the flickering light from the garden lanterns, Toshi could not resist touching her long, dark curls. When he put his face against their softness, Ana stirred and opened her eyes. He whispered,

"I'm sorry, Ana, I didn't mean to wake you. Your hair was shining in the light. I had to touch it."

She smiled and drew him close to her again. In that instant, Toshi caught his breath in sudden pain as if a knife had been thrust into his heart. Ana sensed the movement and asked,

"What is it, Toshi?"

He answered quickly,

"It's nothing, Ana."

How could he say, 'You're breaking my heart, sweet Ana'? Toshi felt the pain of the struggle facing him now. For the 'way

69

of the samurai' was to taste the pleasures of love, but never to deny the higher power of *on*, that bond of obligation ingrained so deeply in the Japanese soul. Toshiburo Yamamoto had been taught well. He knew the power of that bond. And because of that knowledge, he would never know peace again.

The instant he had touched Ana's hand and led her into the *bon-odori* circle, her spirit had wrapped itself around his heart and would never let him go. He could not curse the gods for the 'gift of Ana.' Indeed, he would offer prayers of homage to them though the gift would cost him dearly. And for these reasons, Toshi felt his heart breaking even as Ana offered him that which he most desired, her tender love.

Toshi woke late to find the bed empty beside him. He called to her,

"Ana, where are you?"

She walked up the porch steps, opened the screen door, and came in to him. Her face was bright with smiles,

"So, 'guitar-man,' do you know where you are this morning?"

Toshi moaned and covered his face with a pillow.

"Ohhh, I can see now that I should never have let you see my 'wild, seamy side.' Will I ever live it down?"

Ana laughed as she sat down beside them,

"You're right, of course. You will no longer be our distinguished professor. Sorry, but you must suffer for your weakness of character…and your amazing talent. But there are rewards, too. People will be calling to hire you for parties all over the city! There's no limit to where your musical talent might lead you."

Toshi took Ana's arm and pulled her toward him. With his mouth against her silky hair, he whispered,

"I love you, Ana Maria Gabrelli. Thank you for sharing your love with this undeserving heart."

Ana felt Toshi's words grip her own heart like a vice. How could she say she loved him in return? What did she know of love? She had never experienced it. Toshi had touched a response within her that no man had touched before. She had never allowed anyone so close to her and she couldn't explain why she had done so now. She was as surprised as he. Perhaps it was the evening—the excitement and fun, the champagne, his wild guitar and gentle sweetness.

How could she explain her feelings when she wasn't certain at all what they were? Ana had allowed herself 'one white, singing hour.' Perhaps that was all she needed or wanted. Tonight, in their most intimate moments, Toshi had declared that he would love only Ana for the rest of his life. But now, in the morning light, she had too many questions. Not about their night together, for that had been her choice, but about the words he had whispered to her. She found herself questioning those words.

Ana recalled what Ito had told her about Toshi's relationship with the Imperial House. Why hadn't Toshi been open about these things from the beginning? Ana knew that she cared for this gentle man, or she would never have invited him to stay with her. Yet, she found herself moving away from him emotionally, rebuilding the walls of protection around her heart for fear of that which could break it. She chose to retreat to her place of safety, giving Toshi a quick 'good morning' kiss and a word of farewell,

"Thank you, for the champagne, the great music, and a beautiful evening together. Now, it's time to move. I've got an assignment to finish up today. I'll fix us some fruit and tea, that's my usual breakfast."

Toshi released her, sensing the sudden change of mood.

"No, it's late and I have weekend duties, as well. But tell me when we can see each other again, just the two of us."

He paused for a response which did not come, then added quietly,

"I promise that whatever you suggest will be on your terms."

Ana was relieved that Toshi had given her the power to define their future relationship. For this she was grateful and felt freer to consider that future,

"Call me at my office Monday, sometime before 3 o'clock. We'll be planning the seminars, so we might have things pretty well together. Maybe we can have dinner sometime next week and finish up with everything…okay?"

Toshi gave Ana a questioning look. A sudden thought crossed his mind: *'Perhaps I am, after all, just one of a string of Ana's lovers!'* But even if that were so, he could not deny what he knew to be true. He was only sorry that she could not accept that truth for herself. Later, when Ana walked with him to the door, Toshi promised to call her the next day. Then he kissed her gently and whispered,

"Do you know how much I love you, Gabrelli?"

Ana returned his kiss as she whispered a reply,

"Yes, I know how much you love me, Yamamoto."

After he was gone, she shut the door and leaned against it, speaking into the silence,

"You love me…just enough to taste the sweetness of a moment then smile and walk away."

She slid to the floor and began to cry, the kind of sobs that shook her whole body. She remembered with a sudden shock the last time she had cried like this. She recalled the scene and the reason for it. It was long ago, when she was merely a child, but it seemed as if it were just a moment ago. A Catholic nun was standing beside her. Ana could see the heavy, brown shoes and the long black skirt. As she raised her eyes, she noticed the shiny, gold cross swaying against the darkness of the Sister's skirt. It was like a sign that even in darkness there was light.

Sister Mary Elizabeth knelt down and pulled the child close, surrounding her with softness and strength,

"It's all right to cry, Ana Maria, but tell me, why such tears?"

The child thought of the words her mother had spoken to her,

'I love you, Ana Maria, don't be afraid. I'll take care of you.'
But she had been left without a mother's care. The child remembered her father's assurance,

"You needn't be afraid, Ana Maria, I will be here to protect you." But the father had left her without protection.

The child answered the Sister's question in the midst of her tears,

"Everything frightens me, now. There is no safe place. I'm afraid of the darkness and of being alone."

The good Sister saw before her a little girl whose mother had died of a terrible illness and whose father had chosen to take his own life rather than face that sorrow. The Sister knew that Ana's older sister, Valentina, was doing the best she could to be both mother and father to the child while working and going to night school. And Sister Mary Elizabeth also knew that it was time to save a lonely and frightened little girl. She put her arms around Ana and spoke softly,

"You no longer need to be afraid, Ana Maria. Would you like to come here with us where you will be safe?"

Those words quieted the fearful child.

"Yes, please let me stay here. I want to be here where I won't be alone and afraid!"

Arrangements were made within a few days for the ten-year-old child, Ana Maria Gabrelli, to become a resident student of St. Mary's Convent School for Girls in South Boston. Ana completed her education through high school from behind those safe iron gates. And she would always be thankful for it. As she recalled those traumatic moments in her life, Ana felt a great love for the woman who led her through such a difficult time. Sister Mary Elizabeth had not only protected Ana, but had given a frightened child the gift of strength and self-assurance which would carry her into an exciting and fulfilling life. But the good Sister could not erase the child's inner fears. Only Ana could do that.

Last night, Ana had gone beyond those fears. For the first time since childhood, she had opened her heart to another and that one, she was certain, would break it as those she had loved before had done. Nishiyama's words to her at the party were like a prophecy of the future. Toshi's 'path' had already been set and she knew, only too well, that path would not include her. Once again, she would be left alone with nothing but empty promises. Ana spoke aloud to the empty house,

"So, Miyuki, your little poem will become the story of my life. I will give everything for that 'one, white, singing hour of peace; that one sweet breath of ecstasy.' And what will I receive in return? Once again…I shall be left with the gifts of loneliness and tears!"

The tears Ana shed now were not for the past nor for the present. They were shed for what was yet to come. And that future, 'the years of strife well-lost,' was the price Ana would pay for loving this 'sweet samurai.' Whether or not it was worth the cost did not matter. She had already chosen to pay it. Only her tears could offer solace now, and the bittersweet joy of memory.

When Toshi returned to his home, he walked out onto the porch overlooking the gardens of the Yamamoto estate. Empowered by the beauty surrounding him, he reflected on his life. All had been harmony for him. Outside of the ill health that plagued him, he was privileged beyond most and was wise enough to appreciate those privileges. But suddenly a beautiful Westerner had walked across his pathway and disrupted his near-perfect existence. Toshi believed that the gods had destined them to meet, for there were lessons they must learn from each other. Already, he had learned the meaning of patience as he dealt with Ana's quick temper and depth of emotion. But that which he most needed to learn from her was the power of love.

Even when Ana fought against him, turned away from him, tried in every way to discourage him, Toshi could feel her love drawing them together. She refused to acknowledge its presence in her heart, but tonight he had seen it in her eyes and felt it in her touch. That love was his blessing and his curse, for it offered him life and joy. Yet, Toshi knew that he could not fulfill its demands and, thus, would never know the extent of its promise. And this knowledge was breaking an already-broken heart.

Toshi whispered his joy and his fear to the garden's emptiness,

"Thank you, Ana, for the gift you have given this unworthy heart and for whatever time we are allowed. I beg your forgiveness for the loss that either of us may suffer, but, you see, even though I know what's ahead, I cannot turn away. I love you, Gabrelli, far too much…and I fear for both our hearts!"

CHAPTER 7

"Two cultures meet, experiencing
The challenge and joy of 'difference'
Yet, difference melts at Fuji's feet.
Her beauty captures both their hearts."
--Ana and Toshiburo at Fuji

Ana wasn't anxious to walk into her office on Monday morning. She knew Miyuki would be there waiting to ask all kinds of questions so she decided to visit with her friend early in the day and get the issue settled. And she was right. At 8:30 a.m. Miyuki strolled quietly into Ana's office, sat down in front of her desk and asked the question,

"Well? Do you have anything to share with me today?" They both burst out laughing as Ana replied with her own question,

"How much can you handle?"

Miyuki's eyes widened in mock surprise,

"Take me to lunch and give me the minute-by-minute report! My life is dull and boring, I need excitement and I'm tired of reading novels. I want some real live experiences to assure me that love is not dead in this cold, cynical world."

"Okay for lunch, but not necessarily 'okay' for telling everything. I wouldn't want to send you into an emotional relapse. I'm afraid you'd grab Sato and make the biggest mistake of your life."

Miyuki reacted quickly to such a suggestion,

"Oh no! Don't even mention Sato. We had to shove him out of the car Saturday night, he was so crazy drunk. It took Mishi and me both to drag him into his apartment and dump him on the floor. What a maniac!"

Ana ended their conversation abruptly,

"Back to business, friend. We're planning the seminars for Toshi's classes today, so let's meet with Ito and Mishi and get our calendars set. This is kind of a big deal, you know. Ito's very happy about being invited to Tokyo University. It could mean some real opportunities with the other universities, as well. We just might help create some major intercultural sensitivity

among the students in this area. At least, the challenge is there.
I'll check with Ito right away for a time to meet, then I'll let you
know about us. We have to get the seminars planned before
Toshi calls at 3 o'clock today."

"Okay, let's do it then. And you and I 'alone' for lunch,
remember?"

Ana laughed and waved Miyuki out of her office.

The four colleagues met at 11 o'clock to begin their planning
session. They all gave input on parts of the program they felt
would be most valuable for the students, then Ito assigned the
different responsibilities. Using ideas from former seminars they
had presented, an outline was completed that seemed the most
effective approach for Toshi's student group. Unfortunately for
Miyuki, they worked until noon when Ito suggested they
complete the project over a 'working lunch.' Miyuki was
grumpy, but finally agreed. The group walked to a nearby sushi
bar and finished their planning with a delicious lunch together.

In between the sushi and their work, they laughed and joked
about the wild evening at Ana's place. They finally decided to
open a 'disco' at her house on Saturday nights. Toshi could play
and sing, while Sato tended bar. On the way back to the office,
Miyuki frowned at Ana and whispered,

"When?"

"Okay, okay, come to my house tonight and stay over. We'll
talk all night if you want. I'd better get this over with before I
forget the whole evening."

Miyuki laughed,

"Sure, sure, as if you could ever forget the first wild night of
your life. I'll come by your office after work and we'll make a
night of it. And don't make any other appointments. I'm not
letting you off the hook this time."

When they returned to the office, Ana found a message to call
Toshi. She looked over her notes from the luncheon meeting so
she could report their decisions to him, then dialed the number.
She was anxious to let him know the progress they were making
and was fine until she heard his voice,

"Toshiburo Yamamoto speaking."

Ana felt something going on in her chest and had to swallow
a couple of times before she answered in a casual, upbeat way,

"Hi, Toshi, this is Ana reporting back to confirm the dates and other information for our workshops. Do you have any news at this point?"

"Yes, we've checked calendars here and it seems that anytime within the next four weeks will work out very well. The students are excited about the idea and have even chosen the cultures they want to study. The four are Australia, Germany, Indonesia, and the United States. Also, our classes meet each day for two-hour slots both morning and afternoon."

"Sounds like we're on track. If it's okay with you, we'll begin two weeks from today. That will give us time to complete all the arrangements and get materials together."

"Is there any background you want me to present to the students or other information for your planning?"

"The only other things are to finalize our technology needs and the layout of your classrooms. I'll have to check with the cultural specialists to find out what kind of space they want for their groups. I guess everything is falling into place."

"Then let's change the subject a moment. When can you and I get together for some private, personal time?"

Ana wasn't prepared for the question and hesitated,

"I…I'm not sure. Not during the week, though. Things are too busy here right now. What do you have in mind?"

Toshi chose to ignore Ana's 'all business' approach,

"Go with me to the mountains this weekend. Fuji will be beautiful and I know a very nice place to spend a day or two. We could leave Friday night and be back Sunday."

There was dead silence on the other end of the line. He broke it with a gentle plea,

"Will you please come with me, Ana?"

She could see the usual warning lights flashing in her mind and a voice shouting, *'Watch out…hang on…these are deep waters…keep your head, Ana!'* And in the next instant, a tiny voice from inside her heart whispering, *'Remember, love is a gift…accept it…enjoy it…and savor the moment.'*

She chose to listen to her heart,

"That sounds great! I'd love to get away for a weekend, but could we leave on Saturday morning instead? Friday is going to be so busy here and I'd like to be relaxed so I can enjoy the beauty of the mountains, especially Fuji."

Toshi breathed a sigh of relief,

"I was afraid you were going to say 'no.' I promise you the trip will be beautiful, Ana, and I'll love sharing it with you. It's okay to go Saturday morning, but we should start early, probably by 7 o'clock. Is that all right?"

"I'll be ready and look forward to it with pleasure. So, I'll see you early Saturday morning unless either of us has a change of plans."

"We're set, then. I'll make the reservations and be at your house Saturday morning at seven sharp! And thanks for all the work you and your colleagues have done for the seminars. I appreciate your help in creating a broader intercultural sensitivity among these young people and, of course, I'll also enjoy becoming acquainted with you in a professional setting."

Ana laughed.

"Thanks, professor. I guess there are some perks to our labors now and then. So...goodbye for now."

"Sayonara, Gabrelli."

Toshi felt a letdown after hanging up the telephone. He couldn't understand Ana's response, or, rather, the lack of it. She had seemed suddenly distant as if nothing had occurred between them. Though disturbed, he decided to put aside his concerns until they could be together on the weekend.

Miyuki and Ana were late finishing their work at the office, so they stopped at a small restaurant near Shinjuku Station for one of their 'quickie' meals of *okonomi-yaki* and green tea. They each poured the mixture of beaten eggs, chopped cabbage, and spices on the hot griddle in the center of the table. When it was cooked to their taste they covered it with their favorite toppings and savored every bite. Of course, the conversation quickly turned to the topic of men, women, and the meaning of love.

"Well?" Miyuki put the pressure on Ana to tell all

"Well...yes. I did take your advice, Yuki. I decided to put away my fears, relax, and enjoy the evening. And, I'll have to admit, with the help of music, champagne, moonlight, and those sweet-scented flowers in Grandmother Satoyama's garden, well, how could a hot-blooded Italian resist such a moment?"

"And…so…what?" Miyuki refused to let her off the hook.

"So...what do you think? He kissed me and I kissed him back. It was very nice."

"Oh sure! I know you only too well, Ana. Here's what I think. As soon as we were out of sight you shoved him right out the door. I've seen you do that too many times. It's just a natural response for you. Are you ever going to loosen up and let a man close to you? You will promise, won't you, to let me know the minute you really do fall in love? I want to gloat and say things like, 'I told you it could happen, even to you' or 'welcome to the human race, at last'!"

"Hey, don't give up on me yet, Yuki. I'm honestly working on the 'human' thing."

"I don't believe you let him close enough to kiss you and if he did, you certainly didn't kiss him back!"

Ana was laughing at Miyuki's disbelief and thinking to herself, *'I'll never tell Yuki the truth; she wouldn't believe me if I did.'* But she decided to tease her friend further,

"Now just a minute! I may not tell everything, but I don't tell outright fibs. I honestly initiated a 'goodnight' kiss on my very own. So…what do you think of that?"

"You must have been very drunk, if you did. I'm going to ask Toshi the next time I see him and find out what really happened."

"Oh, now you're overstepping the boundaries of a perfect friendship. Don't you dare say a word to him about this or you will surely die…and I'm serious about that!"

The friends went to Ana's house and spent the rest of the evening laughing and teasing each other about their many escapades and their different ways of approaching life and love. Just before they went to sleep, Miyuki concluded,

"You are doomed to a life of cold-hearted loneliness, Ana Gabrelli!"

Ana laughed at Miyuki and whispered into the darkness,

"Good night, Yuki. Oh, by the way, I forgot to mention that Toshi and I are going to the mountains for the weekend."

Miyuki jumped up quickly and threw a pillow at Ana,

"You're no friend of mine. You're purposely holding out on me and I don't know what to believe about anything you tell me!"

"I suggest you believe everything I tell you from now on. It's very possible that it will be true."

They ended their evening with laughter and a major pillow fight. Miyuki won.

The friends were sound asleep when the phone rang. Ana jumped up quickly and grabbed it to keep from disturbing Miyuki. She answered in a near-whisper,

"This is Ana Gabrelli."

"Ana, I'm sorry if I woke you. It's Toshi. I just needed to hear your voice, to talk a while. I was late getting home and haven't been able to relax…"

"Are you okay? You sound concerned."

"I was worried, I guess, after our visit today. There seemed to be some distance between us that I hadn't expected. Everything was on such a professional level. I felt that you were moving away from me as if we were mere acquaintances."

Ana felt a sudden pounding in her chest. He was coming too close to the truth, but she couldn't talk to him now with Miyuki beside her,

"Yuki's here. She's staying overnight with me. I think we should wait and talk this weekend when we'll have time to spend together."

Before Toshi could reply, Miyuki rolled over and asked, "Is that Toshi on the phone?"

Ana was afraid to answer and started to tell her 'no,' but Miyuki jumped up and grabbed the phone from Ana's hand. Toshi heard Ana scream and someone laughing. Then Miyuki came on the line, speaking in an exaggerated 'sugar-coated' style,

"Hello, Toshi, I'm so glad you called. I have a very important question to ask you. Ana and I have been having a rather in-depth discussion about life and love and, since I know her so well, I just have to ask you this one question: Now, please tell the truth. Did my long-time friend…you know that 'wild Italian,' Ana Maria Gabrelli, at any time during your evening together actually…kiss you?"

Toshi laughed at her craziness,

"What are you women doing over there? Drinking *sake* and telling all your secrets?"

Miyuki wouldn't give up.

"It's just one question, that's all. Did Ana really kiss you goodnight?"

"Miyuki, if your best friend won't tell you what you want to know, you can count on it, my lips are sealed. I'm sorry, but you're on your own!"

Miyuki made a face at Ana and handed her the phone. Ana glared at her troublesome friend as she spoke,

"Yuki is trying to torture information out of me about our 'after-party' celebration. I did reveal to her that I willingly offered you a 'goodnight' kiss.' And since she knows that type of behavior is against my normal standards she refuses to believe me."

Toshi laughed and asked her, unbelieving,

"Are you serious, Ana? Is sharing a simple kiss against your 'normal' standards? What about the rest of the evening?"

Ana answered in a whisper,

"Now you know how powerful you are."

Toshi was nearly speechless, not expecting her unusual revelation,

"You take my breath away, Gabrelli. I will never know what to expect from you."

She answered with her goodnight,

"Surely you know by now that you can always expect the unexpected! Goodnight, Yamamoto-san."

"Goodnight, Gabrelli. I love you…far too much."

Toshi knew that Ana wouldn't tell him that she loved him and she didn't. But he also knew that words weren't necessary for she had shared her truth with him in many other ways and that was all he needed.

Saturday morning the sun rose to promise a beautiful day for the travelers as they drove out of Tokyo into the mountains. Though Ana had been on this trip once before, it was like a new experience with Toshi there to explain the sights along the way.

The touch of ancient Japanese civilization was still evident all around them. The mountainsides were decorated with large, beautiful farm homes as reminders of another era of time. Their manicured grounds and plush gardens echoed the artistry on ancient Japanese screens found in the great museums of the world. The many rows of neatly-planted tea bushes, mulberry trees for silk production, and layered rice fields in the flat lands seemed to have been painted there, too perfect to be real.

As they drove higher into the mountains, they looked down to see lakes scattered like shiny pieces of broken glass among the deep valleys below. At lunch time, the travelers stopped at a small wayside inn and sat next to a huge window where they could enjoy a spectacular view of the mountain scenery. Ana was overwhelmed by the beauty surrounding them,

"Why does all this look so different from anything I've seen before? Is it just because I know this is Japan that everything appears to be uniquely Japanese?"

Toshi was quiet for a few moments as he considered her question.

"I'm certain that every country in the world has its own special aura, its unique 'spirit.' It seems so, at least, when one is traveling. The Oriental countries might resemble each other to travelers from the West, as Western countries appear alike in many ways to those of us from the East. Yet, I believe there are special differences in every cultural setting that a perceptive traveler can discover. That's what makes travel so exciting, to experience those differences."

"I never tire of it, that 'specialness.' I realize that even though there are certain parts of life that all people share, we may do so in such different ways and for different reasons. That's what excites me about life, as you suggested."

Toshi leaned toward Ana and looked directly into her eyes as he asked,

"Is that what excites us about each other, Ana? That we are so different from one another? We come from different cultures with differing values and even different patterns of thought. You look at life out of those wide, Italian-American eyes and I see life through this narrow Japanese view. Is that 'difference' between us what has drawn us together?"

Toshi didn't take his eyes from hers and, with a slight smile that to Ana always seemed to bear a touch of the cynical, waited for an answer to his question. At first, she thought he might be pulling her into one of their usual confrontations, as if this were a game of mental chess. It took her back a moment. He seemed to be changing the atmosphere between them.

But Ana kept her gaze steady as she answered truthfully,

"I can only speak for myself, Toshi. And from my 'wide, Italian-American' view, the answer is 'no.' I've never thought of others as simple products of a culture when I'm relating with them personally. I evaluate people by how they treat me and others and themselves. Though I recognize many cultural differences between you and me, those differences are of no value to me at an intimate level. Whether you believe it or not, I look at you as a sensitive, intelligent person, separate and apart from your cultural heritage. And no matter what your background, if you evidence those personal qualities, that is all that matters to me. So, what about you, Tosh?"

He leaned back in his chair and hesitated, somewhat afraid to reveal his thoughts to her. But he spoke them, even at the risk of rejection,

"I'd be foolish to deny it, Ana. Your physical attributes were my first, most powerful attraction to you. Perhaps it's because you're so different from what I know. That difference is what caused me to follow you in the *O-bon* crowd. And I have found your vibrancy enthralling. That, too, is uniquely different from the manner in which Japanese men and women generally approach personal relationships. To be perfectly honest, I'd never seen anyone so beautiful and that's why I followed you, but that's not why I love you. I fully agree with what you said in this regard. I love you, Ana, because of who you are, no matter how you came to be that person."

Ana was touched by Toshi's honesty and asked her own 'loaded' question,

"Do you think, then, that it wasn't destiny that brought us together, but our difference?"

Toshi was quick to reply,

"This much I know, Ana. If 'you' had been 'you' in a Japanese face, how could I have found you in the crowd? That's the argument for difference. But I must give destiny its due. Why were you walking there in front of me? So, isn't it destiny, after all, that we are different and because of that difference I saw you, separate and apart from all the others around us."

Ana burst out laughing at his answer,

83

"You are unbelievable! There is no way to get around you. Do you practice these intellectual exercises with your students in the classroom every day? I give up. Let's get back on the road so I can take in all this wonderfully 'different' scenery from your Japanese countryside and enjoy the fact that 'destiny' has made this visit possible!"

Toshi laughed and when he leaned over to kiss her, she did not pull away. They enjoyed a tender moment, both fully aware that whether 'destiny' or 'difference,' it did not matter why they met, only that they had met and neither would ever be the same person again.

Soon after lunch, Ana saw the sight that would forever be imprinted in her memory. As they came down into the low lands closer to the hotel where they were to stay, the clouds that had come over the sky during the afternoon suddenly parted. There before them stood the mountain that all Japanese worship as their gracious protector. Fujiyama, in all her glory, filled the sky. Ana gasped at its sudden appearance while Toshi quickly pulled the car into a turnoff. They got out and stood together in silence, transfixed by the beauty before them. After a while, Toshi spoke with an attitude of deep reverence,

"She is our spirit…our power and our strength. We worship her because she always watches over us. She will never fail us."

They stood quietly for some time. Then Ana whispered as if she were standing in a holy temple,

"I've never seen her before, but never like this."

Toshi was surprised at her statement,

"You didn't mention that you'd been to our great mountain before. When were you here, Ana?"

"It was the first time I came to Japan, several years ago. I'd been here for a while and was very tired and discouraged. Somehow, I believed that if I came to this holy mountain my spirit would be healed. So I came with a tour group just to see her, to take some of her strength, but she was covered with clouds and rain. On the way back to Tokyo that day, the sun finally came out. I turned to see if Fuji might show me her face, after all. She offered me one quick glimpse, as if she were teasing me with her power. But that glimpse was not enough to heal my broken spirit. I felt somehow betrayed, to have come so far…from the other side of the world and not to have seen her like this, in all her glory."

Ana felt the tears coming down her cheeks, partly because of the joy of this moment and partly from the pain of that former time. Toshi was touched by her experience with the mountain and put his arms around her to offer comfort. She appreciated his strength and his kindness,

"Thank you for bringing me here for this glorious sight. I needed this to quiet those voices from the past."

They stood a long time, drinking in the power and beauty of the mountain. Then Toshi asked,

"Why was your spirit broken when you came here on that rainy day, Ana?"

She hesitated,

"Perhaps this isn't a good time to talk about sadness. It's in the past and this is so beautiful."

"The best time to speak of sadness is when it comes to one's mind. But if it would hurt you to speak of it, then you must not do so."

Ana was quiet for a while, considering Toshi's words, then replied,

"Perhaps now, in Fuji's presence, the pain of that memory could finally be healed. But I feel hesitant to speak of such a personal matter in your presence; I don't want to ruin this moment for you."

"Nothing could ruin this moment for me except to know there is sadness in it for you."

With the beautiful mountain before her and the strength of Toshi's arms around her, Ana told the story. She knew there would be no better time to share it,

"Japan, for me had been warm and sweet from the first moment I set foot on this tiny island. She welcomed me with an open heart, yet when I longed for healing, it didn't come. I believe that if I hadn't looked back that day and seen that one, brief glimpse of Fuji's face, I would never have returned."

"How was it that we couldn't heal your broken spirit? How could we refuse you, Ana?"

"When I most needed help, there was none to be found. It was no one's fault but my own. There was someone who had promised warmth, but refused to give it. Someone who betrayed my trust and left me helpless at a difficult moment."

"Was this person…someone you loved?"

"He offered me a promise of love. I didn't ask for his promise, nor did I expect it. But he gave it, and when I needed him most, he wasn't there. He was to call, but he didn't call. He was to be there to meet me, but he didn't come. I'd been in Japan for several months and, at the time, was very tired from intensive study and travel. I was staying alone in a house in Seijo. The owners were in the States and I was caring for their home in return for a place to live.

My schedule was heavy, getting across the city, meeting people, conducting studies and interviews without language proficiency. You can imagine my struggles. In the midst of this, my physical strength failed me. I became very ill and, in fact, totally helpless. Each time I tried to leave the house, I just passed out on the floor. It was a very strange illness. I tried calling my Japanese friends, but it was during the *O-bon* holiday and not one person I knew was at home.

The time came and passed that my friend was to be in Tokyo. I remember lying on the floor beside the telephone, praying that his call would come. But it didn't. I don't even know how I recovered, except just to wear out the illness, whatever it was. It was nearly two weeks before I had the strength to walk to the Seijo shopping area for some nourishing food. I had been living on tea and a bit of rice, when I could keep it down.

The final blow came when I was strong enough to make the trip to the Imperial Hotel where I had a reservation for two days rest before I was to leave for the States. There was a message for me there. Just….'*Sorry, I left a bit early. See you in the States.*' I don't know how I lived through it."

Toshi whispered the question,

"Did you ever see him again?"

"Yes…back in the States. There was no choice in that. He was my major professor for Japanese studies. He laughed and said, 'Maybe we'll meet on the Ginza one day.' I walked away without a word."

"Did he break your heart, Ana?"

She was silent for a moment,

"In a way he did, yes. I had great respect for him until that moment and perhaps could have loved him. Unfortunately, my life history has included betrayal by those who seem to be most trustworthy. In each instance, I've suffered the kind of pain that lingers somewhere inside and surfaces at odd moments. Because of these kinds of experiences, I'm quite wary of promises made to me, especially by those I want to trust."

Toshi heard Ana's warning clearly. He longed to offer her a trustworthy heart, but instead hid his own fears behind rhetorical questions,

"How does one control the heart? How does one keep from suffering heartache? Is there a way except to turn the heart to stone?"

"I suppose the only way is to search as much as possible for the joys of life. Just try to live it and let the chips fall where they may. You know, '*l'chaim*!'"

Toshi tightened his arms around Ana, wanting to let her know that he understood her suffering, but he knew that he could promise nothing else,

"I'm sorry, Ana, that Japan was cruel to you, that no one was there when you most needed help. And even, that Fuji refused to heal your broken spirit."

Ana grabbed his hand and squeezed it,

"Hey, I recovered and I'm here with you and Fuji. That should be all the healing I'll ever need. Now, let's go to the lodge and enjoy our weekend with the mighty mountain!"

CHAPTER 8

"Fuji…majestic mountain,
Nippon's sacred treasure
Your memory lifts me
To the heights where once I stood
And touched your face"

Fuji…moving shadow on
The face of Kawaguchi
Bringing life, hope, joy
Reflecting that which is
And which is yet to be."

Fuji…sturdy sentinel,
Born of earth's eruptive heat
Dark and craggy surface
Standing as protector
Of this tiny isle."

Fuji…eternal spirit,
How I long for thee.
Your beauty unsurpassed,
Your power…your majesty
Have transfixed me!"
--Ana Maria Gabrelli, Journal

Toshi drove down into the valley to their destination, the Fujiview Lodge. As they came closer, Ana saw a lovely wood and stone structure built in the British style of the 1930's. The architecture reminded her of an old estate, with turrets and peaked roofs. She saw balconies and special benches placed around the building where people could view the great mountain at any time of day or night. There were also large windows for viewing from the inside. Fujiview was surrounded with beautifully-landscaped grounds and gardens covering the rolling hills. Ana could see part of a golf course in the back of the lodge, as well as a swimming pool, and beyond that appeared to be a large lake. Fujiyama hovered over it all, gigantic and faithful, always there to remind the visitors of her power.

Ana could hardly believe they were going to stay here,

"This is such a beautiful place, Toshi. I just assumed we'd stop at a small mountainside inn. I'm not sure I'll fit into this kind of elegance."

He answered with a teasing smile,

"Oh, I think we can fit you into it, Ana. You'll just add your own beauty to this magnificent scene. As far as I know, there is no special requirement to enter here, except to be in love with Fuji."

As they came around the circle drive to the front door, white-gloved assistants hurried to the car, bowing and offering help with their luggage. In the red-carpeted entry of the lodge, they were surrounded with gracious helpers. And, within a few moments of their arrival, an impressive-looking gentleman welcomed 'Yamamoto-san' and his guest with deep bows and promises of excellent service.

Ana was amused at the 'hustle and bustle' to care for their every need and was well aware that this kind of service was not available to ordinary tourists just off the road. It was all she could do to keep a straight face as they were directed to a private elevator. She noted that it was designed for just one stop at the top floor. This seemed to be a very private and secure arrangement, obviously for 'special guests' only. Ana was certain that Toshiburo Yamamoto had used the amenities of the lovely place on many occasions.

They stepped out of the elevator into the entry hall of a beautiful and spacious suite. Ana had never seen such luxury in all of her life. Her only travel experience, up to this point, had been economy rate. And she recalled the many times in Tokyo when she had stayed in 'businessmen's hotels' with rooms so small that she took one step in the door and one step into bed.

Glancing around the living area, Ana could see that the glass doors on the front and side of the suite gave a direct view of Mt. Fuji and the beautiful grounds of the hotel. These doors opened onto a balcony where guests could walk outside and look directly into the mountain's face.

The décor of the suite included beautiful art work, overstuffed furniture and plush carpeting. It was more than elegant. Ana reminded herself that this Japanese gentleman with whom she was traveling was, no doubt, used to luxury. This might even be a step down from his normal lifestyle. After all, it was just a hotel, not a castle in the countryside where he had, no doubt, been born and raised.

After their helpful assistants had left the room, Ana knew that she was in danger of creating havoc. But, try as she might, she could not resist a teasing comment,

"Well, dear samurai, sir, I have a strong suspicion that you have been here before since everyone seems to know you so well. Could it be that this is one of your very special 'love hotels'?"

Toshi laughed at Ana's pointed question but, realizing it was dangerous territory, offered only a casual response that told her little,

"I have been here, yet. They do know me, yes. And more than that I refuse to reveal. You'll have to use your own vivid imagination about the rest!"

Without giving her time to respond, Toshi purposely changed the subject,

"What do you think of this, Ana?"

He pointed to the scene framed by the huge side window. They were looking into the face of Fuji as if it were a painting across the wall. Ana was speechless at its beauty. She dropped into one of the soft chairs facing the window while Toshi sat down on the other side of the room at some distance from her. For a while they were both silent. She was the first to speak,

"It's so beautiful. I feel as if I were in an airplane flying right into Fuji's face. I could never imagine being in such a place as this. This is a wonderful gift, Toshi. Thank you so much!"

Toshi did not respond, but walked to the dining area and poured them each a glass of wine. He handed a glass to Ana and sat down again. They enjoyed the wine and the scene before them in silence. Toshi appreciated these peaceful moments with Ana, but he knew she was restless and began to worry about the decision to bring her here.

As much as he loved this woman, he did not want to open his life to her. Ana was too perceptive, watching and evaluating everything he said or did. Eventually, she would touch on the subjects that would separate them, but he did not want to face that separation, not yet. All he wanted was to share his love with this beautiful Western woman until it was no longer possible. For these few hours together, Toshi promised himself that he would do everything in his power to keep the atmosphere between them a gentle and loving one.

Ana was the one who broke the silence with her disturbing questions. She wanted Toshi to share with her openly, to trust her with the knowledge that she had already received from someone else. She chose to approach the subject carefully, since he had already refused to address her casual insinuations earlier,

"There's something I'd like to ask you, Toshi. Our entry to the hotel has brought several questions to mind. Who, may I ask, are you, anyway? What should I know about you? Are you some great war lord, a boss of the *Yakuza*, or perhaps a favored prince of the realm? I thought you were just an ordinary guy I met on the street one night who plays a mean guitar. But somehow the obvious deference being given to you, not only here, but in other places we've been together, indicates that perhaps I'm traveling with someone who has a bit more power and privilege than a mere professor at Tokyo University or a Harvard man. What is the truth about you, Toshiburo Yamamoto? Who are you, anyway?"

Since Toshi was fairly certain Ana's questions were coming, he had prepared his answers. He could only hope to satisfy or silence her,

"I want you to know that I'm not just a 'guy' you met on the street one night. I'm the one who fell in love with Gabrelli the moment she flashed those huge, black eyes and that brilliant smile…at everyone but him! But, yes, you're right. I do enjoy a bit of luxury now and then. We deserve the best, don't we? Who knows when we might have an opportunity like this again?"

Ana smiled, her questions still unanswered.

"I suppose you've saved your professor's salary for weeks to splurge on this amazing trip. Oh, Yamamoto-san, I urge you to be careful. Those who weave tangled webs are often caught in them."

She chose to drop the questions for now. He was not going to open his life to her and she knew, very well, why. And what did it matter at this moment, anyway? Ana convinced herself to enjoy the beauty of the mountain, the luxury Toshi had provided for her, and the precious moments they could share without conflict. The truth would all be told soon enough.

After the travelers had relaxed with the wine and the beauty of the mountain, they decided to hike around the area and take some photographs while the sun was high and bright. The hotel assistants had placed their belongings in separate bedrooms, Ana's in the Western-style room near the living area. Before they left, Toshi asked Ana about their evening meal,

"Shall we make reservations for dinner in the lodge dining room with the rest of the travelers, or would you rather have our private dinner here in the suite?"

"I don't think I'll feel like dressing for the dining room after walking over the hills for the next three or four hours. Why not eat on the balcony? Surely with your influence here, we could have a simple meal served in the mountain air and the moonlight. How about it?"

"That sounds like a fitting ending to a beautiful day. I'll let the staff know what we want and I'm sure they'll do their best to please."

Toshi winked at Ana, knowing she would not be able to resist comment, and he was right. She added her note of sarcasm,

"Yes, I agree. They will want very much to please a most important guest."

But he was ready for her,

"If they are a discriminating staff, they'll know that to please Ana Maria Gabrelli will be the most important challenge of their career."

"Ah, yes, the Gabrelli name is of great value here, I'm sure. By the way, do you think I could reserve this beautiful suite for a weekend later in the summer?"

Toshi gripped her arm and led her to the elevator,

"Let's get this outside before we do serious damage to something, namely, each other!"

As soon as they were on the elevator, he pulled Ana close and pleaded,

"Please, Ana, we must be good to each other. These few moments together can be a beautiful experience for us, or it can be the end of us. We're not ready for an ending, and certainly not here surrounded by the power of Fuji."

Ana knew what she had been doing and also knew to stop,

"I'm sorry, Toshi. I'm having trouble putting some of my old baggage away. I promise to try harder to soak up the beauty around me and to enjoy the moment."

"Tomorrows come too soon, Ana, but today is ours, to do with as we please. We must make this a precious memory!"

"I promise. I'll do my very best!" She smiled and gave him a quick kiss before the elevator door opened.

Toshi stopped at the manager's desk to arrange for their balcony dinner, then the pair headed toward the hotel park. As they walked through the lobby, they were stopped on several occasions by guests who were acquainted with Toshi. Each time, Ana noted the special courtesy shown to him. Toshi, in turn, introduced her very graciously to several acquaintances as, 'Ms. Ana Maria Gabrelli, Director of Intercultural Relations at the Intercultural Education Exchange Center in Tokyo.' They always seemed duly impressed and responded with deep bows of respect.

The couple spent the rest of the afternoon hiking over the several miles of the hotel park. Ana took some excellent photographs of the area and of Fuji's magnificence. The bright sun and clear, blue sky made a perfect frame for the mountain. At one point, they stood on a spot just beyond the beautiful Lake Kawaguchi. There they could see Fuji, the lodge and the mountain's reflection in the water all at once. Here Ana took her most exciting photograph, a perfect reflection of Fuji in the still waters of the lake. She was ecstatic,

"What an unbelievable scene! This photo will be a treasure. Who knows, I may even become famous. I can't believe we were at the right place at just the right time…that's hardly ever happened to me!"

They stopped there and sat down to enjoy the beauty around them. Both were entranced as they watched the mountain's reflection moving across the waters of the lake. After a while, Ana became aware that Toshi's mood had changed. He seemed to be struggling with some inner conflict. She intruded into his private space with a question,

"What deep thoughts are going through your mind, professor? You appear to be suddenly solemn and serious in the midst of all this beauty."

Toshi's gaze did not leave the water. Ana wondered if he'd even heard the question, but she waited for a response. Finally, he spoke in a voice filled with emotion.

"The first time I came here, I was just a small child. I saw this identical scene, the mountain and the mountain on the water. In my childish way, I couldn't understand how the mountain's face could be floating on the water and still be standing there in front of me.

My grandmother was with me at the time. She tried to explain it by telling me that what was in front of my eyes was the physical form of Fujiyama, and what was on the water was her spirit. She said that we are all created in the same way. We each have a physical form and a spiritual form.

I remember thinking that when I died, I wanted my ashes scattered across Lake Kawaguchi for then my spirit would always be present with the spirit of the mountain. I even thought that people who stopped here would be able to see my reflection with Fuji's on the water. I considered it a noble wish to, at last, be one with our sacred mountain."

Ana was deeply touched by the thoughts of a small child in the midst of this beauty. She could find no way to communicate her feelings at such a moment. Toshi finally broke the silence with a bare whisper,

"I've never changed that wish. I've taken steps to see that my childish wish will be honored. There is no other place I would want to be when I enter the eternal world. My spirit could never find rest in any other place."

Ana felt a sudden movement in her chest, like the wings of a tiny bird. It frightened her for a moment. She had been taught in her strong Italian Catholic faith to believe in signs. She found it hard now to shake those childhood teachings. She broke the solemn spell that had come over them,

"Let's hike on up the hillside and look down on this amazing scene." She grabbed Toshi's hand and helped him to his feet.

Ana wanted to move away from the haunted waters of Lake Kawaguchi.

The hikers climbed to the highest point among the more rugged hills surrounding the hotel. There they sat until twilight, watching the sun go down and the shadow of the great mountain become less vivid with each moment. Then the moon rose above them, shining its silver light over their world. They were silenced in the face of such beauty.

Toshi finally broke the silence,

"I've never experienced such a moment. The majesty of the natural world is all around us. It seems that we're enfolded in it and our love for each other is a part of it, Ana. This is a perfect moment."

She replied in a mere whisper, "Yes, it is perfect."

Neither could resist an emotional response to the beauty surrounding them. They offered their love to one another without reservation. Much later, when the moon was high to light their pathway, they walked arm-in-arm toward the lodge. There were no words spoken between them. Fujiyama had silenced them with her power.

When the couple arrived at the lodge, the dinner hour was nearly over. They entered the front door and went up the private elevator so they would not disturb the late diners and those who were enjoying the game rooms. In their suite, the hikers found a lovely meal arranged for them on the balcony facing the mountain. The night was warm and the moonlight still allowed them a view of Fuji, though a mere silhouette.

They both showered and changed into the only evening clothes available, silk kimonos provided as a gift by the hotel. Ana's was white with gold and red flower patterns. Toshi's was the masculine version, black with gold dragons. Ana found a gold iris in the artificial flower arrangement on her dresser, so she pulled her hair back on one side and wrapped the wire stem around it to add a little spark to her evening costume.

Toshi had obviously called the servers while she was changing, for when Ana walked into the living room, two young men were lighting the tall candelabra on the balcony. Their dinner was arranged on a *kotatsu* with white and gold china, black and gold *hashi* (chopsticks), and what Ana assumed were gold-plated knives, forks, and spoons. She couldn't imagine anyone actually eating with real gold dinnerware.

One of the young men left the suite, while the other remained behind to serve the meal. When the food arrived by elevator, he carefully prepared the table for their dinner. Ana didn't know exactly what to do, so she sat down in one of the soft chairs at the far end of the living room to watch what would happen next. This was another world for her. Even as an intercultural specialist, she had not yet experienced the life of the 'rich and famous Japanese samurai.' She decided to watch and enjoy and try very hard to be discreet with her comments.

Toshi finally came into the living room to greet his dinner partner. He walked toward her with a bright smile and graciously extended his hand,

"It appears that our dinner is served, Ms. Gabrelli. And, may I add, you look stunning in that gown."

Ana smiled and played the game,

"Thank you for your gracious compliment, Yamamoto-san. This is, no doubt, a Tokyo original." She gave him her hand and a slight bow as they went to their formal balcony dinner.

Toshi helped Ana get comfortable on the *zaisu* (soft, floor chair), then sat down opposite her. She leaned toward him and smiled,

"I can't imagine any dining room with a more elegant setting or a more courteous and handsome host." Then she added in a whisper, "But I like your gown better than mine. I'm definitely a 'gold dragon' person!"

Toshi laughed and took her hand,

"Ana Maria, you are the most beautiful woman I have ever met and I would be most happy to serve as your 'courteous host' for the rest of my life. However, I'm not sure about the 'handsome' part. I can only promise to do my best in that regard!"

A sudden rush of tears came to Ana's eyes as she responded to his sweet words,

"If what you say could only be so, I would be the happiest of women for the rest of *my* life."

Toshi felt a sudden pain strike his heart at her words, realizing that Ana surely loved him as he loved her, and that he could not fulfill the words he had just spoken. He looked away from her tears, motioning their server to move ahead with dinner.

The spell was broken as their meal was served. But before they began, Toshi raised his wine glass to Ana's and offered a toast for the evening,

"To our night together with the majestic mountain. May this moment live in our hearts forever."

Every morsel of their delicious meal was a true joy. Ana could not remember eating anything, anywhere, that matched it. The small, thick Kobe beefsteaks literally melted in their mouths. Added to that delicacy were fresh, sliced cucumber and tomatoes, steamed rice covered with ginger sauce, and tiny broiled shrimp. The dessert of sweet cheesecake was topped with tangy pomegranate sauce and served with hot, green tea. With their final glass of wine, they were served huge strawberries to be dipped in either chocolate sauce or heavy, sweet cream.

Neither of them could refuse any part of their candlelight dinner. They ate slowly, savoring every morsel and enjoying the relaxing evening together. When they could eat no more, Ana and Toshi thanked the server for providing such an elegant setting and for his gracious assistance. Then they went into the living room and sat down while the remnants of their mountainside meal were cleared away.

When the server had gone and all was quiet, the mountain only a dark shadow in the sky, Ana rose from her chair and walked toward Toshi. He stood to embrace her. As they held each other close, she whispered, "Thank you, Yamamoto-san, for a perfect day and a perfect evening and a perfect moonlight meal."

But then she pulled away from him and walked toward her bedroom. Toshi reacted to her apparent dismissal,

"Ana, there is only one way to make this evening perfect."

Though his words touched her heart, she did not turn back. Ana longed to share her love with Toshi, but she also needed to be alone. She wanted to savor the beauty of their day together, to hold it and pretend there was a future in it. But something inside her heart had cracked when he had so carelessly said, *'I would be most happy to serve as your host for the rest of my life.'*

Ana could not fathom the reason that he would speak such words to her when he knew there was no truth in them. She knew, only too well, that Toshiburo Yamamoto had no intention of spending the rest of his life with Ana Maria Gabrelli. After this beautiful day together, their closeness to the power of nature, their expressions of love, he might as well have struck her as speak such lies.

Yet, Ana was not ready to tell him openly that she knew all there was to know. She wanted him to care enough to tell her himself. Perhaps she could live with his pretense for a while. And what did it matter, anyway? She loved him and that was all there was to it. But she chose to speak from her head, instead of her heart.

"Then, perhaps, this day will be 'almost' perfect."

Ana left him with the hope that Toshi would have the courage to face his own truth and to help her face it as well, for it wasn't the truth that hurt her as much as the lie.

CHAPTER 9

"Let the truth finally be spoken.
What is the meaning of the love we have expressed?
Is it only for a moment...a game between two travelers?
Met by chance upon life's pathway?
Tell me, Toshiburo, the secrets of your heart...
I have shared all of mine with you!"
--Ana and Toshiburo, at Fuji

Toshi was stunned by Ana's words. If there were ever a time when they needed to be together, it was now. Their day with Fuji had been perfect. He could find no flaw in it. Throughout this whole day, Ana had expressed her deep feelings for him in so many ways. Her love had been reflected in her eyes, in her touch, in her understanding of the power of Fuji, and even in her gentle 'goodnight' kiss. Yet, she had walked away from him as if these moments meant nothing.

Questions began to plague Toshi's mind. Why had Ana created a wall between them on such a night as this? Was she different than he had believed? Was she, after all, like so many Western women he had known who merely enjoyed love as a 'game'? Perhaps he had read more into her responses than ever existed in her heart.

Toshi found that it took all of his inner strength to keep from shouting at her, 'Why are you doing this to us? Why are you denying the love we have already expressed to each other?' But he cared for her too much. If he had hurt her in some way, he must wait for an explanation. Perhaps tomorrow he would have the courage to approach Ana with his questions.

But for now, Toshi chose the only way he knew to face his disappointment. He grabbed a glass and a bottle of wine from the living room cabinet and went out on the balcony to sit with Fuji. Though he couldn't sleep, he hoped that the mountain's presence and the warm Bordeaux would calm his spirit.

Dawn was just breaking when Ana heard the knock on her bedroom door. She hadn't slept well and answered in a groggy voice,

"What is it? Have I slept too late?"

Toshi answered, his own words somewhat slurred from the sleepless night and the alcohol,

"It's...early and I'm sorry to wake you, Ana, but we need to talk. Will you come out here, or shall I come in there?"

"My god, Toshi, are you drunk? I'm not even sure where I am, let alone able to put two words together! Can't we wait until after breakfast?"

"First, I have been drinking, but I'm not drunk. And second, we have to talk. I've been awake all night and we've got to get some things clear between us...now, Ana, please!"

Ana didn't feel like facing this issue at such an hour, but knew that they might as well be done with it. She forced her eyes open and answered,

"Come in, then, the door isn't locked."

She sat up in bed as Toshi came in. He walked over and sat down on the floor, leaning against the glass doors to the balcony. Ana could see a bare outline of the mountain behind him. Her heart was pounding with apprehension as she waited for him to speak, not knowing what was coming.

"Ana, can you give me some reason why you've shut me out at a time when we've been so close? I don't understand what's in your mind or your heart. Just a few days ago, you offered your love to me freely. I didn't ask. I would never have asked to stay with you, but you issued the invitation.

And now, after everything here has been so perfect...the beauty of the mountain, our moments together at the lake, the balcony dinner...you turn away from me as if there were nothing between us at all, as if we were strangers who had just met. For god's sake, Ana, we're far from being strangers! Tell me why you turn away from me now."

Toshi's words and the emotion with which they were spoken cracked the fragile wall around Ana's heart. She couldn't look at him, but pulled her knees close to her chest and leaned against them, covering her face with her hands. She could barely whisper her answer,

"You seem to be so perceptive, Toshi, as if you could read my mind. You seem to know what to say to touch my heart. Why don't you understand now without my having to speak the words?"

100

Toshi had no idea what she was thinking. He leaned his head back against the window and shut his eyes as he answered,

"I honestly don't know what's happening with us, Ana. Yesterday, I was certain that we could love each other, that everything was good between us. But when you walked away from me last night, I was totally confused. Talk to me, Ana. If there is something I've done to hurt you, please tell me."

Ana sighed at his total lack of understanding. It was obvious that he could not read her heart, after all. She was quiet a moment, then began to speak, knowing that her words would crack all the barriers of safety between them. Her voice shook with fear of the loss that their truth, finally spoken, must surely bring.

"Don't you know...that I'm afraid of you, Yamamoto-san?"

Ana's words came as a shock to Toshi. He stared at her, unbelieving.

"What are you saying, Ana? Surely you know that I love you. What reason would you have to be afraid of me? I would never purposely hurt you!"

Ana shook her head and sighed as she answered,

"You already have and you don't even know how much. Your words to me at dinner last night...so lightly spoken, so artificial. You thought you were paying me a compliment. In the midst of all this beauty, you spoke the very words that would hurt me most!"

Toshi was too stunned to even attempt a reply. He merely stared at her in disbelief. She turned to look directly at him as she continued,

"I believe that you love me, Toshi, and that you would never purposely hurt me. But I know other things, as well. I know that there is a past that determines who we are and where we are to go with our future. And that's what I fear.

Don't you think it's time for honesty between us? I know, only too well, what your past has been and what your future is to be. You haven't been fair with me in this relationship. I couldn't believe that you would utter such a lie: 'I would be most happy to serve as your courteous host for the rest of my life!'

What is this game you play with me, Yamamoto-san, soon to be Ambassador, soon to be the husband of another woman? I'm

101

afraid of my love for you and of your lies to me! Do you wonder that I turn away from you? How casually and with such charm and grace...you use me!"

Ana slid down in the bed and covered her face with her arms, trying to control her emotions. She didn't want to cry. She wanted to be strong enough to confront her nemesis with his guild. She heard him utter a deep sigh, but he did not speak.

Toshi was completely undone. Now he understood everything. The comments Ana had made as they came in the hotel yesterday, all the little things she mentioned to him and her question, 'Who are you, anyway?' Ana had hoped that he would be honest with her. And he had failed every test. He was ashamed and could barely speak,

"I have no excuses...no words...but I understand so many things now."

Toshi stood up and slowly walked onto the balcony into the early morning air. He needed to gain control of his emotions and put his thoughts together in some coherent manner. The pain he suffered now was beyond anything he had ever known. It was the pain of his own guilt, the guilt of hurting the one he most treasured, and of doing it willfully.

All that Ana had said was true. There was no way to free himself from it. Certainly, he had done everything in his power to win her heart. But he was not playing a game, as she believed. Whatever he had done, was done out of love. Toshi knew that the only thing he could do now was to be totally honest. She must know the truth. But how could he ever expect Ana to believe that his love for her was a part of that truth?

While Toshi struggled with how to approach the woman he loved with the knowledge of their inevitable parting, Ana was experiencing an unusual response to their confrontation. Instead of the rush of sorrow that she had expected when she faced Toshi with his lies, she felt an exhilarating sense of freedom, as if a burden had been lifted from her shoulders. She no longer had to play games with him.

From this moment on, there would be no lies, no cover-ups. Everything between them would be in the open. She could care for him, being fully aware of the limits of their relationship. And Ana Maria Gabrelli would face those limits on her own terms.

The sun was up and shining against the face of the great mountain when Toshi returned to face Ana. When he walked into the living room from the balcony, breakfast was set on the dining table and Ana was waiting for him. Toshi stood as if frozen, not knowing what she expected him to do. To his surprise, Ana walked over and put her arms around him,

"Talk to me, Tosh. Tell me what's in your heart. I've shared mine with you."

He held her carefully, afraid to show his true feelings, but afraid to speak of them,

"I fully accept the guilt for what I've done. There's no way I can expect you to forgive me for keeping the truth from you, for hurting you as I've done. But, it was not a game, Ana. I only wanted to be with you as long as possible. For a while, I even pretended that there might be a way for us. But my life is not my own. My only hope now is that you will believe in the love we've shared, that you will believe that I will never forsake that love, even though I must follow another path."

Ana kept her arms around him as she asked, "Then you feel there is no way, except our parting?"

Toshi pulled away from her, wondering if she could still love him after all that had happened between them. His voice shook with deep emotion,

"Ana, as much as I love you, I cannot change the past, nor can I promise you the future. All I can give you is this moment. If you want that of me, then it's yours, but it's all I have to offer you."

Toshi was shocked at her response.

"When I finally gathered the courage to face you with your pretense and lies, I forgave you, Toshi. I know that we have no future, but perhaps we can share whatever present is left to us."

"But, what of the fears, Ana? How shall we live with them, knowing that which will come too soon upon us? Those fears can destroy us. We may hurt each other too much."

"I'm sure we'll hurt each other, Toshi. That's inevitable. But perhaps we can share our love in between the difficult times. It's worth a try, isn't it?"

She waited for his answer. Toshi could barely whisper it,

"We come from such different worlds, you and I. But if you can still love me after what I've done to us, I promise that I will do everything in my power to soothe your fears."

"And I promise to help you with yours."

For Toshi and Ana there was, after all, only the present moment. They had both known the truth, separately, but now they could face that knowledge with their combined strength and love. And in this present, the past had no relevance, nor did the future exist. They offered their love to each other with the urgency of those who know the value of one precious moment.

It was nearly noon before Ana and Toshi headed back to Tokyo. They stopped along the way for a late lunch and, after some nourishment, both began to recover from their restless night. Ana watched the scenes rushing by as they returned to the city and thought to herself, '*Is this how fast time goes? One minute you're on top of the mountain, and the next you're in the valley?*'

Only a short time later, they drove in to Seijo. Toshi grabbed Ana's bag and put his arm around her as they walked to her little house. They lingered a while at the door, enjoying a final moment together. Then Ana pulled away and stepped inside.

"Thanks, Toshi, for the beautiful parts of this weekend. No matter what happens to us, I won't forget Fujiyama and Kawaguchi and…your sweet love."

Toshi whispered in reply, "I don't know how you can still care for me, Ana, but I am thankful that you do."

Ana stumbled into the house and fell on the soft chair in her living room, dropping everything on the floor. She was tired, confused, sad, and happy, all at once. She had made a commitment to love this 'sweet samurai' despite the loss she would face. Ana was not fooling herself. She had consciously stepped into deep waters, knowing that those waters could very well pull her into an undertow of sorrow.

Much later that night, she walked out onto the porch with a cup of hot tea to relax and reflect on the events of the weekend. In the midst of the peaceful setting, a rush of night wind came across the valley through the evergreens. As it touched her face, Ana felt a sudden chill. She whispered the truth that hung like a cloud over her future,

"I've chosen to love you, Yamamoto, on my own and with my eyes wide open. But I know who you are. You are my *kamikaze*, the spirit wind that has moved across my heart with the promise of warmth and love…but will finally leave it cold and broken."

Ana shook herself from the disturbing thoughts that had come with the wind. She was worn out from the weekend and fell into bed fully expecting to sleep through the night. But, for the first time, her little house seemed bare and lonely.

Toshi was awakened by Ishikawa's voice,

"Toshiburo, there's a telephone call for you. I'm sorry to disturb you so late, but I think it's important."

Toshi shook himself awake,

"Who is it, Ishikawa? Who's calling so late?"

Ishikawa smiled at his friend,

"She didn't tell me her name, only that she needed to talk with you. I hesitated asking."

Toshi knew immediately that it was Ana. He sat up and took the phone, answering somewhat hesitantly,

"This is Toshiburo Yamamoto speaking." He was relieved to hear Ana's voice.

"Hi, Tosh. I'm sorry to call you so late. When I got home, I was so tired that I went to bed too early and couldn't sleep. I guess I just wanted to hear your voice to make sure you're still there."

Toshi laughed at her sweetness.

"I'm still here, Ana, and you didn't disturb me. In fact, I feel honored that you would want to hear my voice in the middle of the night. What can I say to ease your mind and help you sleep?"

"Don't you know any bedtime stories or songs your grandmother sang to put you to sleep at night?"

"I'm not good at either of those things. But, if you need someone to drive away the 'haunting spirits of the night,' I can do that very well. I can bring my guitar and come there to lull you to sleep with my love songs…or you could come here with me, if you wish."

Ana laughed. "No, I just wanted to…"

Toshi interrupted her,

"I love you, Gabrelli, don't let your worries disturb your sleep. There's nothing wrong with loving someone and wanting them close. That's what life is about. Tell me, Ana, tell me why you offered me your heart, even when you knew I didn't deserve such a gift?"

There was a long silence before she could answer,

"I guess…I wanted to love you before you went away. I wanted to know everything there was to know about loving you."

"But what made you love me, Ana? What was it that drew you to me?"

"You challenge my mind every moment and will never let me rest. But, at the same time, you have a gentle nature and you're always kind. Is that kindness just the 'culture of courtesy' that you've been taught so well? Or is that really who you are? I often wonder."

"Were you wondering tonight, why you should love me?"

"Yes, and why we should even have met as we did. Just there, on the street, among those thousands of people."

"Our meeting and our love were written in the stars. It's our destiny, Ana. There was no other reason that we should have met. Our worlds are too far apart. We don't think the same thoughts. We have conflicting views of nearly everything. We found each other. The gods brought us together and nothing will ever separate us!"

"Toshi, you know that's not true! We're already destined to part."

"There's nothing that can break us apart, Ana. Our spirits live inside each other and will never, never leave their chosen places. Even if you were a million miles away, you would still be with me."

Ana began laughing at him. "Your words make me love you even more. You speak a language that has no connection with anything I've ever known or with any system of reality from my pragmatic world. Even though I don't believe what you say, you make me want to believe. But now, I think it's time for me to ponder your philosophical meanderings until I slip into oblivion. Goodnight, Yamamoto-san. And thanks for your late night 'love songs!'"

"So, you will be able to sleep without my loving presence?"

"Didn't you just tell me that your presence is always with me? I'll do fine."

"Gabrelli, you win the point again! I hope you will remember in the future to concede as graciously as I."

"You know very well that I shall never be as gracious as you. That is what I love about you: you're not afraid to 'concede with kindness.' Good night, Toshi, and thank you for our beautiful weekend with Fuji and Kawaguchi. It was almost perfect. If that is all we were ever to have, it would be enough."

"Goodnight, sweet Ana. You know I love you, far too much."

"Yes, I know that. I know it now, for certain."

After she hung up, Ana slept well, assured that Toshi's love would be with her always, even in their parting. But Toshi realized that his sleepless nights had just begun. The impact of his coming loss drove him to the quiet shrine by the hillside. There, he begged the gods he worshipped for wisdom and direction. He begged them for the strength to follow whatever path that destiny would require of him. And, if there were no other way, for the strength to leave the one he loved with his whole heart and soul.

CHAPTER 10

"The struggle begins:
How to be true to one's destiny,
Yet, how to be true to one's heart.
There is no answer to relieve the mind.
Whichever choice...comes the pain!"
        --T. Yamamoto, Journal

During the week after their trip to Mt. Fuji, Toshi and Ana returned to their separate responsibilities. They talked by telephone each day in preparation for the seminars that were to begin the next Monday. Both continued to express their deep feelings for each other, but Ana was not emotionally able to renew their close relationship. Toshi carried a heavy burden of responsibility for hurting Ana, realizing that the cultural differences between them, which in so many ways had drawn them together, had now become the chasm that would separate them.

In Ana's Western world, honesty in relationships and the freedom to make life choices on one's own were of the highest value. In Toshi's Japanese culture, courtesy to others and obligation to one's family and country came before all else. He recognized that they were both, in a very real sense, products of their enculturation. How could either change those ingrained patterns of thought and behavior?

At one moment, Toshi was certain that he could turn his back on both family and country to be with the woman he loved. Yet, in the next moment, a knife struck his heart as he considered denying the expectations that had been place upon him since childhood.

As he struggled with these decisions, Toshi sensed a desperate need to visit with his grandmother, Sukiyama Matsushita Yamamoto. She was the one member of his family who had understood him better than any others. Though she seemed ancient at nearly 90 years old, and sometimes feeble, her mind was neither. "Suki-ma," Toshi's childhood name for his grandmother, seemed always to recognize truth in every situation.

She had guided him throughout his life to make wise decisions. He was certain that she could help him now.

Toshi decide that as soon as the Intercultural Seminars were completed, he would visit his grandmother to ask for her wisdom. With that in mind, he called her immediately knowing that she would need time to prepare for his visit. He respected her constant plea, "Do not surprise me. I must prepare for each moment beforehand."

When Toshi made the request to his grandmother, she reviewed her calendar carefully, for she had many dates to remember. Sukiyama was very happy at the prospect of seeing her 'precious grandson' for she took great joy in offering her gifts of wisdom to those she especially loved. They arranged to meet in two weeks on the Saturday morning following the last seminar session. Toshi breathed a sigh of relief for the possibility of, at the very least, sharing his heart with someone who knew him from the 'inside out.'

On Monday morning, Toshi was relaxed as he entered his University office in preparation for the Intercultural Seminars. The IEEC teams were to take charge of his classes for the next two weeks. And though Toshi looked forward to being with Ana and working with the group leaders, he was somewhat worried about facing both Mishima and Miyuki. He wasn't certain how much they knew about the relationship between him and Ana at this point. But he was prepared to do whatever was necessary to create a professional and accepting atmosphere among them all.

Within the hour, the seminar leaders and students had arrived. Toshi greeted the team leaders and introduced them to his students with gratitude for their willingness to assist in this important learning process. Ana's co-director, Ito Nishiyama, responded warmly to the introductions and thanked Toshi for the opportunity to share their expertise with the young people.

Mishima was brisk and barely courteous to Toshi, but related well with the students. He introduced the team member representing the cultural areas and the program got underway. As the groups made their ways to their respective locations, Ana caught Toshi's eye and gave him a quick smile and a wink that touched his heart He thought to himself, *'Perhaps we'll be all right for a while.'*

Since Nishiyama was in the role of observer for the program, he and Toshi had time to become better acquainted. During one of the morning breaks, Ito came over to visit with Toshi for a moment. He was very courteous, but had a twinkle in his eye as he spoke,

"Professor Yamamoto, I feel that I know you somewhat from the party at Ana's house and also from mutual friends at the Department of State. I must say that with your musical talents you could certainly do well in an appointment to the British or American embassy."

Toshi appeared very serious as he replied to Nishiyama's comment,

"That's probably the best reason anyone would consider me for such a post. I could entertain at the embassy parties. I understand that relaxing the 'foreigner' is an excellent way to win one's point in negotiation!"

They laughed together and Nishiyama responded,

"Well spoken! And do you, then, maintain a continued desire to enter the service at the embassy, perhaps in Britain or America?"

Toshi was taken by surprise at Nishiyama's very personal question. It seemed out of character for such a distinguished gentleman. Toshi knew to answer carefully, for he had the distinct impression that his answer would be shared with others,

"My family has instilled in me the desire to serve my country. I have always felt that I could do this best through education and training in other cultures. My academic background seems to have provided me with a broader understanding of the world and its many complicated issues than if I had studied in Japan during those years.

But, the fact is, I enjoy teaching here at the University and would be quite satisfied to remain in this position. I love the give and take of the academic setting and enjoy working with young people. Though I am the professor, I am also a learner with them. For that reason, I feel certain of learning many new things during these two intensive weeks of intercultural study. I appreciate this opportunity very much."

Toshi had carefully guided the conversation away from his personal life and to Nishiyama's arena, the seminars and their value to the group. He did not want to speak with a stranger about such private matters as his own future.

As yet, Toshi was not aware of any contact made with his family by the embassy staff, or by anyone of stature regarding a diplomatic appointment. Though it was known that he was being considered for such a post, he also knew that when the decision was made it would come through the proper channels. Nishiyama's statements caused Toshi to be careful of every word he spoke to Ana's colleagues. He felt as if they were providing protection against his intrusion into the life of their close friend.

During the lunch break, Toshi invited the staff members to dine in the luxurious university faculty lounge. They walked from the classroom through a beautiful garden area to a traditional Japanese structure. The building was set on a grassy hillside surrounded by plants and flowers. At the bottom of the hill was a small lake. Once inside the lounge, the visitors were directed to a private room with huge windows looking out on a restful scene. Here they were served a very tasty meal and treated as important guests of the university.

The location and presentation of the meal also indicated the status accorded Professor Yamamoto. This was well-observed by the IEEC staff, and much appreciated. During lunch, Ana chose to sit with her colleagues at the far end of the table from Toshi. Though he did not like being at a distance from her, Toshi knew it was best for their relations within the group.

For the rest of the seminar sessions, meals would be served in the student building with special menus related to each culture being studied. In this way, the students would become acquainted not only with the different foods of each area, but with the customs related to serving and sharing the meal.

The seminar leaders were excited by the positive response of the students in their sessions and, whenever there was a break, they sought out the professor to let him know how things were going. Toshi enjoyed being in the observer role for a change. At the conclusion of the first day's sessions, the group leaders gathered with Toshi to discuss any questions or concerns they might have. The professor expressed his appreciation for the in-depth content of the sessions and congratulated the leadership team on their expertise. He assured them that he would be more than happy to recommend continuing the program and also expanding it to other area universities.

As the group prepared to leave for the day, Ana walked over to visit with Toshi a moment,

"This has been a very productive day, and a tiring one! I'm beat and I'm sure you are, too. You've had the fun of following us around, entertaining us for a fabulous lunch, and worrying about all the arrangements. Thanks so much, Toshi. If you're going to be home, I'll call you later tonight."

As she turned to leave, she slipped her hand in his and gave it a quick squeeze. Toshi glanced up to see Mishima watching them. He gripped her hand as he responded,

"I'll be at home and please call me, Ana. We need to have a moment, at least, to talk alone."

Ana turned to join the group as they headed back to the office. Toshi noticed that when they went out the door, Ana had taken Mishima's arm. He heard Mishima say to her,

"Let's stop for a drink, I think we all deserve it!"

Toshi was uncomfortable with the thought that perhaps Ana and Mishima were redefining their relationship. He feared that Ana may have made some decision in that regard and that he would not be privy to it. Yet, he also knew that there was no reason why he should be.

Much later that night, Toshi was surprised when Ana actually called him.

"I get to see you all day, Tosh, but I'm missing you. When can we get together? Can't we just take a walk around the campus or have a private moment during the break?"

"Surely, we can arrange that. Let's work on it tomorrow. But you'll have to take charge. I feel intimidated by your colleagues. I feel as if they are guarding you from me. Have I become paranoid, or is that really happening?"

"Don't worry about my 'guards.' They have no power over me. They just want to keep me safe. All they really know is that I care about you, and I guess, they knew that was a 'bust' before I did!"

Toshi was quieted by her words and the flippant manner in which they were spoken. She quickly apologized. "I'm sorry, Tosh, please forgive me. I'm trying to keep up the charade of 'everything is okay,' but it isn't okay at all! We need to be together."

"We'll get together tomorrow during the lunch hour. At least we can walk around campus for a few minutes. Meet me then and we'll try to avoid the group."

Toshi also wanted to ask what was happening between her and Mishima, but he knew that was not his prerogative to do so. How could he expect things to be the same, now? They would never be the same again. Whatever she wanted from him, he would give, but he could ask nothing of her.

In his most unselfish moments, Toshi had to admit that Ana's future would best be served by the one who would love and care for her no matter what the demands. Toshi knew that Mishima would always be there for Ana. He would be the one who would sacrifice his own life, give up everything, if she would ask. And Mishima would never expect Ana to return his love in equal measure.

As much as it hurt, Toshi knew that he was not the one who could do those things for her. He had given away his right to her love when he put his loyalties to family and country above his loyalty and love for Ana.

Later that night, before Toshi could sleep, he walked out to the hillside shrine. He knelt and place his forehead against the stone floor before the altar, praying to whatever gods might be present there.

"Please give me the strength to love Ana enough to let her go…to the one who will give his whole heart to her. Give me the strength to let her go with Mishima!"

The next day, during the group lunch hour, since Ana was not in charge of a group session, she found Toshi.

"Hey, let's take that walk around campus now. Show me the sights."

He took Ana's hand and led her along the winding pathways around the lake. They enjoyed the beauty and being together. As they came near the library, Toshi found a quiet alcove where they could talk in privacy. Ana spoke first,

"Toshi, you have to tell me what you expect from me."

He was surprised at her direct question and hesitated to express his real feelings. He tried to think of the words that would let her know of his deference to her wishes,

"I have no right to any expectations now. I want to love you and be with you, but how can I ask for that?"

"You can ask for anything you wish. We can't just be like this, so separate when we've been so close. We have to be together, Toshi."

He looked at Ana, trying to decide if she were serious,

"Then let's plan something for next weekend, after the seminars are completed. I have an appointment Saturday morning with my grandmother in Kyoto, but I can be back early. Why don't we have dinner downtown and go to the Tokyo Concert Hall for a real evening out? The Moscow Symphony will be here with Tchaikovsky. If you would like to go, I can get reservations with no problem."

Ana was excited about the idea of a 'fancy dress' occasion with Toshi,

"I'd love it! Since I've been back in Tokyo, I haven't had time for much music appreciation. It sounds like fun to get dressed up and celebrate something like the successful completion of the seminars…and the Moscow Symphony! What could be more exciting than that?"

Ana hesitated a moment, then added,

"And just perhaps, at the end of our evening, you'll give me a guided tour of your very private, mountain home. I'd love to visit the place that is so special to you."

Toshi looked at Ana in surprise. Her casual implication took his breath away. He found it difficult to believe that this amazing woman could still love him, and especially, now. Ana smiled at him, awaiting a response. He returned the smile and, on impulse, leaned over and ruffled her thick, dark hair as he kissed her. Then he whispered,

"It would be an honor to share my 'mountain home' with you. You are a crazy woman to still love me, Gabrelli, but I thank the gods that you do!"

They enjoyed being close for a few moments. As they walked onto the path to return to the group, Toshi felt warmth returning to his cold heart.

During the lunch break, Mishima had received directions to the library from one of his seminar students. He needed to find some information that had come up in his group regarding Japanese-Indonesian relations. Strolling through the stacks, he happened to glance out the window at the beautiful scene across campus. The green hillside, the bright-colored flower gardens, and neatly trimmed evergreens were restful to his spirit.

But his eyes caught another scene that caused him to gasp out loud. Very close to the library window where he stood was a small alcove with a stone bench among the trees and bushes. He saw Ana and Professor Yamamoto standing close together, talking and laughing.

Even as Mishima watched, Yamamoto reached out and touched Ana's hair, then drew her close and kissed her. She did not resist him, but, more than that, she responded to him with a passion that spoke clearly to the shocked observer. The distinguished professor and soon-to-be Japanese diplomat, was Ana's lover!

There was no doubt in his mind now. What Mishima feared most had already happened. Ana, the innocent, who had waited patiently all her adult life for that one special love, had fallen prey to the well-calculated advances of a handsome, intelligent, man-of-the-world. And Mishima was also certain that this man of noble and powerful birth would break Ana's heart and leave her shattered.

Mishima felt his tears fall as he considered the disastrous results of Ana's decision to finally give away her precious heart. He was certain that Yamamoto had no intentions whatever beyond sharing a sweet love affair with a beautiful, exciting American woman. Ana's lifelong friend and the one who had loved her secretly since they met as freshmen in college, felt his heart breaking all the way through.

So Ana had chosen not to listen to his warnings. She had chosen her lover and it was not, nor would it ever be, Mishima. He stood silent for a long time, trying to restore some calm to his mind in order to return to the classroom, for there he would have to face the woman he loved and the man she had chosen to love. All the strength he could muster would be required for him to walk into that room.

The seminars were completed on Friday morning of the second week and the student evaluations were excellent. They had all expressed the value of intensive intercultural training and suggested that the programs be included each term as a structured part of the course.

Toshi expressed his thanks to the seminar leaders and staff by inviting them, with the students, to a final luncheon together in the faculty dining room. There the leaders were given special gifts from their student groups and the students received certificates of completion from their leaders. At the end of the meal, the students all stood and together shouted an energetic 'banzai!' cheer to the IEEC team. Afterwards, everyone enjoyed visiting and saying their final goodbyes, before going their separate ways.

When the students had finally left Toshi's office, Ana walked in, shut the door, and put her arms around him.

"Are we all set for the weekend festivities?"

Toshi responded to her warmth with a smile and a kiss.

"Everything is arranged, we're set! I'm doing down tonight and stay at a place close to Kyoto. I don't want to see anyone there except my grandmother, so I'm hoping to avoid a visit with my parents. That would take too long. I'll be back early Saturday afternoon, at least by 4 o'clock. But if I don't call you by then, something may have prevented me from being on time. So I'm giving you the dinner reservations and concert tickets, just in case."

He handed her an envelope.

"If I should be delayed for any reason, I'll meet you at the Otani dining room by 7 o'clock, for certain."

Ana took the envelope and put it carefully in her handbag, then turned to Toshi, and in a more serious manner,

"What do you expect from your visit, Toshi? How can your grandmother help you?"

He hesitated, then answered thoughtfully,

"Perhaps she will offer me a different path. Perhaps she can show me a way I haven't considered, some way to relieve my struggle. Perhaps she can only comfort me as she did when I was a child and used to run to her for wise counsel. I guess, more than anything, I need to be assured of her constant love."

Ana recognized from his solemn mood how difficult his decision had become. As Toshi spoke of his grandmother, Ana was aware of the depth of love he had for this woman. She gave him a kiss on the cheek and turned to leave. Toshi held her arm a moment as he asked,

"We'll be together tomorrow night?"

Ana replied with a bright smile and a 'thumbs-up.'

"Yes!"

He breathed a sigh of relief and let her go.

CHAPTER 11

"Sukiyama...tiny, wrinkled 'obaa-san'
Waiting patiently for time to pass
That she might join her dear ones
In the land of tengoku
Where spirits dwell in peace and joy
Remembering days gone by.
Sukiyama...touching all with kindness,
  Loving 'obaa-san.'
            --T. Yamamoto, Journal
            Visit to family home

   Grandmother Sukiyama Matsushita Yamamoto was a tiny,
frail woman of nearly 90 years whose beauty still shone through
her bright, dark eyes and alert manner. She had been of noble
birth, so she was not bent from the physical burdens as so many
grandmothers of her day had been. Sukiyama was strong in her
opinions, and wise, for she had experienced much of life: love
and hate, fear and joy. She had suffered with her beloved nation
through the agonies of wars, defeats, humiliation, and had
rejoiced with the excitement of victories, restoration, and growth.
   Sukiyama lived with her house staff on the huge, original
Yamamoto family estate joining land with the estate of her only
son, Tatsume Yamamoto, who was Toshiburo's father. Here she
spent her days in the study of art and classical literature of both
east and west, learning languages of the world, and keeping alert
to the social and political struggles throughout the globe.
   Though Sukiyama's home was traditional in design, it was
filled with modern technology which kept her in tune with each
day's events. She missed nothing and found great joy in being
well-informed of the news from every corner of the world.
   Toshi especially loved his grandmother, Suki-ma. When he
was a little child, he could not say her name properly, so his
childhood name for her had become his special greeting. She
would never let him change it when he grew older. Sukiyama
had prepared Toshi for the world he would inherit by teaching
him to look outside of his small island nation for wisdom. She
challenged him always to study and to learn, to be open to all

people, and to care for others as if they were as important as himself.

Sukiyama's father, Toshi's great grandfather Matsushita, had been an ambassador to Great Britain many years ago, beginning during the brilliant Meiji Restoration period. Sukiyama had always dreamed of her grandson following in his footsteps. Her son, Tatsume Yamamoto, had chosen the world of banking and finance as his own father had taught him. Tatsume had done well in his profession, investing the family fortunes and nearly tripling the wealth that he had inherited.

Toshi's mother, Kumiko Yamamoto, did not love Sukiyama. There had always been struggles between them, for Sukiyama was strong and led the family as Japanese tradition dictated. The mother of the eldest son, in this case the only son, held power over the daughter-in-law in all things regarding the family. Kumiko had hoped that Sukiyama would not live so long, for she had been denied her place in the family power structure and always gave her husband trouble for deferring to his mother. She particularly resented Toshi's special love for his grandmother.

Because of this family tension, when Toshi came to see his grandmother he tried to avoid visiting his own parents. He did not have close relations with his father or mother. As their only son, they held a tight rein on his life and often caused him problems when they felt he might be turning from the traditional ways.

Toshi had been particularly careful on this fast trip that no message went to his parents' home of his visit to Sukiyama. He could not risk a long visit or any confrontation with his parents that would cause him to be late for the special evening with Ana.

Early Saturday morning, Toshi's grandmother welcomed him with smiles and pats and kisses. She had given up, long ago, on the structured lifestyle of family expectations. She no longer kept her stiff, polite approach to greeting and conversation with those closest to her. Toshi had to nearly kneel to give his grandmother a warm embrace and she laughed at him, but loved it.

"Toshi, Toshi, come have tea and cake and we'll talk about everything in your heart. Come, come here...sit!"

119

Sukiyama led him to a quiet, sunny corner of her home where they could look out of the large windows into the garden. Toshi sat on the floor cushion opposite her while servants brought tea and sweet bean cakes for them.

"Now tell my, why are you suddenly coming to see your aged grandmother?"

"I don't know how to tell you, Suki-ma."

"There is only one reason you would travel on a busy day to see your Suki-ma. I know it. You have an unhappy face today. There is no reason for your unhappiness, except one. There is love in your life. Tell me now about the affairs of your heart. I may be old and frail, but I have good memories and I know what love is!"

Her words cut through all the preliminary explanations.

Toshi replied simply, "She's American, of Italian heritage and a strong Catholic."

"Ah, say no more. I know why you came. I know very well what you want from me. For the young lovers there is only one purpose in life. They always answer the same when asked, 'What do you want from life?' They always say with beaming, innocent smiles and damp, glowing eyes, 'We only want happiness!' Ah, yes, happiness. That is what you want, Toshi. And what will bring you happiness?"

Toshi shook his head at her wisdom and smiled,

"You've caught me, Suki-ma. That's why I came. I don't know what will bring happiness to my life, except to be free to love Ana Maria Gabrelli."

Sukiyama leaned back from him with feigned astonishment.

"So, it's Ana Maria Gabrelli that you love. And happiness will come when you are free of all restraints and expectations and nooses of tradition tied around your neck. Is that it, Toshi?"

Toshi felt a sudden anger at his grandmother's sarcastic words. He answered her question with a note of desperation,

"I didn't expect your harshness or mockery, Suki-ma. I came to you because I'm confused and torn between the desire for freedom and the burden of responsibility. I need your help, not your scorn!"

Sukiyama leaned forward and patted Toshi's hand gently, then, holding it in her tiny, wrinkled palm, she asked,

120

"Is loving everything to you?"

"Loving Ana is everything to me. I can't even envision myself leaving her for the dry, harshness of a loveless marriage. Or even for the opportunity to walk in my great-grandfather's footsteps. Can it be possible that I am destined to break away from my family's expectations? Perhaps, after all, that is my destiny."

Toshi felt Sukiyama's grip on his hand tighten as she answered,

"If you choose it, then that will be your destiny."

He looked squarely at his grandmother and replied with shock at her words,

"What do you mean, Suki-ma? Are you telling me that I am free to choose my own pathway?"

"That is up to you. Are you free to choose it?"

"I don't understand you! I've always followed the path set for me by my parents. I have thought that is what a good son must do. Even when I did not enjoy it, I did it because I was taught to obey and to be responsible to their wishes for me."

"Is that what you believed? Did you go against your inner voice, your own strong desires, to obey them?"

"N-no, I don't think that I did. I love learning. I love travel and they encouraged my search for knowledge, even my travel throughout the world. They set my feet on a path that I probably would have chosen for myself. But I felt that they had chosen it for me."

"How wise your parents were to recognize your gifts and offer you opportunity to fulfill them. Were they not?"

Sukiyama held her grandson's hand against her heart and continued to speak,

"Toshi, Toshi, why do you struggle so? Your life is your own and your choices belong to you. But you are only as free as you allow yourself to be."

Toshi looked pleadingly at his grandmother and whispered his supplication,

"Tell me what to do, Suki-ma, I cannot choose. It is too hard, I cannot do it."

She felt his internal struggle and answered quietly, with a faraway look in her eyes,

"Ah, yes, the choice, to take the road of the heart or to follow the direction that the mind tells us is best. That ancient struggle that all of us everywhere in the world must make. And each one must make it for themselves. Certainly, I could make your choice for you. But, then it would be my choice, not yours. And I cannot see into the secret corners of your heart. I cannot hear the voices that echo there."

"But, surely, you can give me some kind of help, some wise counsel to guide my decisions!"

Sukiyama became very serious as she responded to his plea,

"I can only say this. Whatever you choose you must live by it with strength and courage and see it to the end. If you choose to go with your love, then give your life fully to savor the joys of that choice and never look back. If you choose to follow the pathway that you feel your family has set for you, then follow it with the same passion that you would have given to the one you love.

The only difference is this. In the first case, you have only a vision of what might have been had you chosen the way of your family. There is no certainty in that vision. But in the second, you have a precious gift to take with you, certainty of your love is forever with you in memory. That memory will be present with you and will fill your heart with warmth, even in the cold places of life."

Sukiyama's last sentence was spoken in a trembling whisper. Toshi looked up at her. Her eyes were shut and she held her hand close against her heart. He took her tiny, wrinkled hand in his and held it tight. Then he asked her quietly, so as not to injure the spirit of her words,

"Tell me, Suki-ma, what is the memory that you hold in your heart?"

With her eyes still shut, she smiled and replied to his question,

"I have no regrets, Toshi. I have the blessing of remembrance."

Then Sukiyama pulled her hand away from his and pointed to a beautiful teak chest near the window.

"There, in the bottom shelf. Bring me the shiny, red box."

Toshi rose and very carefully opened the chest. He lifted the red box from its place and handed it to her. He knew it was precious. Sukiyama smiled and gently stroked the smooth surface. Then, reaching to her neck, she pulled out a slender gold chain with a key attached. Very carefully, she undid the chain and slid the key off, then unlocked the box and lifted out its contents, one by one.

Toshi was visibly shaken. He knew that his grandmother was going to open her heart to him, as he was certain that she had never done to another living soul. Tears of apprehension filled his eyes. Sukiyama smiled and handed him a small, faded photograph. He saw a beautiful, tiny Japanese doll with bright, dark eyes and a sweet, shy smile. He smiled at the beauty,

"I see excitement and joy in these beautiful eyes. Is this you, Suki-ma?"

She answered with pride, "Yes, that is me on my thirteenth birthday." Then she handed him another photograph and, in a breathless voice, said, "And here is my samurai."

Toshi saw a serious, but very handsome, young boy in the formal clothing of a long-ago samurai, sitting stiffly with a sword hung across his waist and head shorn in the old style. He asked carefully,

"Was he your lover, Suki-ma?"

"Ah, yes, we loved each other. Even though we were so young, we knew it was forever. But, you see, I was promised to another. Only once, we met in a hidden place. Up the mountainside, behind the old family house. There is a beautiful grove of trees there and, long ago, a small Shinto shrine was built among the trees. We met there. It was a secret liaison, exciting and romantic.

He was my first love, my only love. He cut off his topknot and gave it to me. Each night of my life, he comes to me with comfort and strength to help me follow life's pathway. He is my strong, tender memory."

Tears fell from Sukiyama's eyes. She dabbed them with her soft, white handkerchief as she stroked the black, silken hair of her lover. Toshi put his arms around his tiny grandmother to let her share this heartache with him. He kissed her cheek and her hands to comfort her and himself. Then he asked,

"Oh, Suki-ma, you know my heart better than me. You've lived your memory every day of your life. Is this what I must do, as well? Touch the fragments of my lover's hair each night and weep for the joy of past memories?"

Suddenly Sukiyama's tears stopped. She jerked her hands away from Toshi. Sitting up as straight as her tiny body would allow, she spoke with pride and strength,

"It was my choice! I could have gone with him. He begged me to go. But I chose to stay. We each have our pathways to follow. I cannot choose yours. I did not choose his. He said, 'Farewell' to me and went his way."

"Did you meet again, ever?"

"No, we did not meet again." Sukiyama hesitated a moment, then very slowly continued her narrative,

"Yet, I saw his face once more in my life."

She reached over and touched Toshi's cheek with a trembling hand,

"When they brought you to me for a grandmother's blessing and placed you in my arms. His face was imprinted upon yours. That is why you have always been my most precious child. You see, Toshi, your father was his son and mine."

Sukiyama buried her face in Toshi's hands and wept once more. Toshi spoke in a shocked whisper,

"My god, Suki-ma! Why do you tell me this, now? This is your secret and it is too painful for me. I cannot bear it!"

Sukiyama suddenly controlled her tears and wiped her face with her handkerchief. Then, holding her head high, she spoke to him in a stern, strong voice.

"There is no disgrace in loving, Toshi. And if there were, then it is mine to bear, not yours!"

"But, Suki-ma, how could you endure the pain of losing him, even by your own choice?"

"All things are present when we walk in the pathway of our memories. He has never been lost to me."

Toshi pulled back and looked deep into his grandmother's beautiful, dark eyes. He searched them for a trace of the suffering that might belie her declaration. They were clear and bright. She smiled lovingly at him, than patted his cheek and spoke,

"Thank you for coming to me today and sharing your heart. I have trusted you with a most precious secret. I have never told your father. You must never do so. He is different from you and would not understand.

I needed to tell you, Toshi, so you would know that choices are what life is made of and when we make them with an open heart and a clear mind, we will always have the strength to live by them, no matter the price."

Toshi knew he must take leave of Sukiyama. His heart was broken for her. He knelt down, placing his strong arms around her fragile body and whispered,

"Suki-ma, there is no one alive that I love more than you. I respect your wisdom. You have given me a great gift today, to know that I am a child of your dearest love, that one who loved you enough to share the gift of himself with you. And to know that you were strong enough to make the choice that you believed in your heart was best, no matter what it cost you in tears."

Sukiyama touched Toshi's cheek and kissed him goodbye.

"Yes, you are his gift to me. He was a noble and gentle boy, like you. Now go, Toshiburo Matsushita Yamamoto, to make your own decisions and live by them. Leave me to my sweet memories; there I find my peace."

Before Toshi left Sukiyama, a telephone call came for him. He hoped it was not one of his parents, for he was in no mood to deal with family encounters after such an intense morning with his grandmother. She had given Toshi much to think about, and he needed the quiet time on his trip back to consider her words and his own feelings.

The voice on the telephone confirmed Toshi's worst fears. Tatsume Yamamoto demanded that his son come to the house after he completed his visit with Sukiyama. It seemed that his father had important matters to discuss that could not wait and would best be shared in person. Toshi reluctantly agreed, but let his father know that he had an important appointment in Tokyo and must leave as soon as possible.

For some reason, which Toshi had never understood, there had always been an uncomfortable distance between him and his parents. He had been a quiet, contemplative child, and he felt that his parents had never understood, nor accepted, his solemn nature. As Toshi recalled, the only time that he had received

125

positive response from them was related to his outstanding achievement in academics during his school years.

These academic skills had served him well when he attended college. He had been accepted at Harvard for his bachelor's degree, and later at Oxford for a master's and doctorate. Toshi had graduated from both universities with distinction. He appreciated his parents' support in these achievements, yet he had never received outward expressions of their parental love.

As a small child, Toshi had often dreamed of running away or of being adopted by loving, ordinary parents. Without the warm affection that had been offered him from his grandmother and from Ishikawa, Toshi believed that he could not have lived through his childhood. There were times when he even though that the illness he suffered was a result of never experiencing a connection of love with his own parents.

The immense wealth of the Yamamoto family had also been a burden for Toshi in many ways. Expectations were place on him to follow in the footsteps of his father, yet the financial world held no interest for him. Only Sukiyama's intervention had saved him to an academic career. She had convinced his parents that, with his ability and interest in politics, their son could very well serve his country and bring honor to the family as a diplomat.

In his private heart, however, Toshi wanted to be exactly who he was: a professor of international politics and foreign relations. He loved teaching, relating with students, and challenging their mind as he had been challenged through his own years of study. Toshi's personal dream was to teach at either Harvard or Oxford. But he had laid that dream to rest long ago, realizing that teaching was not a prestige position worthy of the son of the powerful financial tycoon, Tatsume Yamamoto.

Now, with trepidation, Toshi went to face whatever important matters his father intended to discuss with him. He offered secret prayers in his heart that those matters did not include an embassy appointment, for that would mean an end to his relationship with Ana, or an end to his role as a dutiful son.

CHAPTER 12

"I weep...to know that this strong, stoic man
Has felt the sweetness of love deep within his heart.
I weep...to know that he has trade the joy of love's
Fulfillment for the harsh, cold world of power.
I weep...for fear that I shall do the same!"

The modern world had invaded the Yamamoto estate. When Toshi arrived at the entry to his parents' home, he used an automatic code to open the heavy, steel gates. Though the house had the appearance of a traditional Japanese home, this was merely a façade, for inside the doors was a purely Westernized world.

Kumiko Yamamoto was a lover of all things French. Not only did she speak the language with perfection and had diligently taught it to her son, but the décor of their home was entirely French provincial. As a connoisseur of the arts, Kumiko had acquired many original works from past and present Western artists. These pieces, both paintings and sculptures, were found in every corner of the house.

Toshi recalled that, as a child, he had never been comfortable in his own home. He had always felt that he was living in an art museum where everything was precious, except the persons living there. In his childish way, he had come to hate his mother's treasures. However, as he grew older, he realized the value of those things which his mother had loved more than her own son, for when he visited Europe and the great museums there, he finally understood something of his mother's heart.

This was the world that had surrounded Toshi all of his life. Only through his grandmother had he discovered the beauty of the traditional Japanese lifestyle. In Sukiyama's home he had found love and peace in an atmosphere of simplicity. He could never replace that simplicity with the ornate.

As Toshi got out of the car, he saw his father standing on the porch of the house waiting for him. Tatsume Yamamoto was not as tall as his son and was built strong and square. He presented a stern, solid appearance as different from Toshiburo Yamamoto as could be possible.

Father and son faced each other, bowing in formal greeting. Toshi was careful to give deference to his father, bowing a bit lower than him. Tatsume led the way into the house. After they had entered the library, which served as the home office for his father, a servant offered them each a cup of *sake* and left the room. The men faced each other, one stern and serious, the other apprehensive.

Tatsume did not wait for casual conversation. He raised his cup and touched it against Toshi's. They swallowed the rice wine quickly, sharing the traditional toast, then Tatsume looked directly at Toshi and began to speak in a manner which felt harsh and cold to his son.

"This trip to your family is very timely, in light of what I have to say to you. I have received information which indicates that within the next few weeks you will be offered the post of Assistant to the Ambassador for the United States. This means that you must be prepared to make a change in your lifestyle. Not only will you be required to leave your professorship at the university, but you will go to this honorable position in the manner which is expected of a diplomat from this nation, with your wife by your side. For these reasons, your mother and I are moving ahead quickly with the final arrangements for your marriage. We are presently completing the contracts to be presented to the family of your promised bride.

Toshiburo, your future has come upon you! I know that you will distinguish yourself and bring honor to our family and to our nation in this grave responsibility!"

Tatsume bowed low to Toshi, as if his son already held the position of 'distinguished diplomat.' Toshi noted that there were tears in his father's eyes. He had never witnessed this side of Tatsume Yamamoto. Toshi was in shock. He had not come expecting to hear such words. Though he feared the results of responding to his father's dictatorial statements, Toshi could not restrain his reaction,

"Are you telling me that within the next few weeks I will be offered a diplomatic post, be expected to resign from the university, and complete the arrangements for a marriage? I'm not sure I understand. Do I have no choice in these matters? Am

I not involved in this planning? Am I simply to perform at your command?"

Tatsume's face turned white and his lips drew tightly together. Toshi's discourteous words had blinded him with sudden anger. Tatsume shouted his reply,

"You have been in the world of the West too long! You have learned too much from that world. You have forsaken the sacred traditions that have kept this nation strong and think only of yourself.

You are weak, Toshiburo, and unworthy of the great honor that has come to you. I am ashamed of my own son!"

Tatsume walked away from his son in an attempt to gain control of his emotions. Toshi's response had shocked him as much as his own words had shocked his son. The silence between them moved Tatsume to offer Toshi further reproach,

"Do you not know that I am well aware of your activities in Tokyo? I am aware of your casual lifestyle, your liberal political attitudes, and of your love affairs. I even know about the Western woman you are seeing!

Do you think a man of my station in this society would turn his only son into the world with no knowledge of his actions? Does the phrase 'responsibility to family and country' mean nothing to you?

You have been raised from childhood to offer your skills and abilities to this nation. All that you have done has prepared you for this moment. And now, you tell me that you will throw those years of preparation away...as if they were nothing?"

Toshi stared out the window at the landscaped grounds of his childhood home. He was surrounded by opulence and beauty, yet felt as if it would choke him. He wanted nothing more than to turn his back on this place forever. He wanted to fly to Ana and enjoy the simplicity of her tiny house that was filled with the joy of loving. What he would have accepted without question only a few months ago, now seemed to be a sentence of emotional death.

Toshi replied calmly to his father's rebukes,

"I am in love with this Western woman, father. I know that is difficult for you to understand. As far as I know, your greatest love has been for the material things of this world, surely not for persons...not for your wife, not for your son!"

Toshi heard his father gasp, but he was afraid to turn around to face Tatsume. The room was quiet as father and son stood separated from each other by a space which it seemed neither could bridge. Toshi feared for what would come next. He even had a childish thought that his father might strike him. What came was not a blow, but words that he would never have expected to hear from his father. Tatsume Yamamoto was speaking from his heart,

"Toshiburo Matsushita Yamamoto, how you dishonor me. You stand before me smugly thinking that you are a 'new' Japanese man, a modern, educated man who can quote the poetry of the masters and who has discovered that love holds a greater power than responsibility.

You look down on me for who I am and what I have become. Do you really think that I do not know the meaning of love? Do you really believe that I am so stone-cold that I could not love my own precious son? How you break my heart with such words. Every day of your life, I have had the terrible fear that you would not live to see the next sunrise. I have experienced in my own body the pain that you have suffered. And now, you strike me with words that I do not deserve.

And as strange as it may seem to you, Toshiburo, even this cold heart is haunted by the sweetness of a lover's song. Even I can weep at the scent of wisteria n a soft, spring breeze. But because of my deeper love for family and country, I have been able to put aside my personal desires. All that I have done, that you reject as useless and materialistic, have been because of that love. It has been for you, Toshiburo. All that I have accomplished and all that I have sacrificed…has been for you!"

The room was absent of sound, as if father and son were standing in a tunnel. Toshi could barely breathe. When he finally turned to face his father, he saw those harsh, stubborn features melt into the softness of sorrow. He saw tears falling from his father's eyes. Toshi walked to him and, in an unprecedented move, the son comforted the father. Tatsume held tightly to his son, then released him as he spoke a final word,

"The choice belongs to you, Toshiburo. You must believe me, now. No matter what you choose, even if it is against all my desires, I will love you. You will always be my precious son!"

130

Tatsume Yamamoto turned quickly and left the room. Toshi fell into the nearest chair and sat quietly, gathering his thoughts and trying to find the wisdom and strength to face the most important decision that he would ever make. Yet, somehow, he knew that it had already been made long ago by his sweet, frail, Suki-ma, and by the strong, stubborn Tatsume. Today, in a strange, unprecedented encounter, Toshi had discovered that he was, after all, his father's son.

For the first time in his life, Toshiburo Yamamoto understood the true meaning of that dreaded word, 'obligation.' It was not the harsh emptiness that he had always imagined; it was grounded in the power of love. There were no further questions in Toshi's mind. He had only to calm the stirrings of his heart and gather the strength to speak his farewells to that one who would haunt his own dreams for the rest of his life.

When Toshi left his father's home, he was certain that he could be in Tokyo for the special evening with Ana. Though he was troubled and his mind couldn't rest, he had made the decision and knew that he must face the results of that choice. He must tell Ana that their relationship would soon end. Toshi was nearly overcome with the grief that prospect called up within him, yet he knew that he must not delay the truth. Tonight, he must be honest with her. He must clarify their future.

As he considered Ana's response to his decision, Toshi thought to himself, *'Ana is an anthropologist who has studied Japanese culture and lived in it for years. She understands the importance of obligation to family and country. Surely she, of all people, would be prepared for what I must tell her.'*

Though he was hardly prepared to consider life without the woman he loved, Toshi knew that if he were to fulfill his chosen path with honor, he must be clear in his direction and strong enough to follow it. Perhaps the one most surprising element in this whole situation had been that both his grandmother and his father had left the door open for him to follow a different path.

That, in itself, had come as a shock. And though his father had berated him for his weakness, Tatsume Yamamoto had finally admitted the depth of his love for his son. Perhaps this surprising revelation had given Toshi the strength to make his choice. It seemed that when he had been offered the 'freedom to choose,' he saw his way very clearly….that there was no choice.

The decision had been made and he had made it. Toshi's family had not made it for him. Perhaps the years of diligent study and preparation; perhaps his personal concern for the improvement of relations among the countries of the world; perhaps even that which drew him so easily to love a woman who was so different from himself were the factors that made it impossible for him to refuse the call to serve his country. Toshi knew that he could not let anything deter him from fulfilling the choice he had made, not even his love for Ana.

The rain began as Toshi and the many other weekend travelers drove into the mountains on the way north to Tokyo. Suddenly, it became a major storm with torrents of water rolling onto the road and wind blowing against the cars. Toshi realized that he must stop as soon as possible. Though his car was safe, the blinding rain made it impossible to see where he was going. Finally, he and many other travelers left the highway at the nearest inn.

Toshi was more than upset at the delay this would cause him and paced the lobby of the inn, watching the storm. He was only three hours from Tokyo, but it was nearly 4 o'clock. He tried to make a call to Ana, but the storm ahead had been violent enough to break communication lines between the inn and Tokyo. Toshi pleaded with the manager, who was entirely helpless,

"There must be some other way to get through to Tokyo, to contact the people waiting for everyone here. What can we do?"

Everyone was upset, and Toshi knew that his attitude did not help himself, nor anyone else. Realizing that he hadn't eaten all day, he went into the dining room and tried to relax over a hot meal. There, the travelers commiserated with each other. They all had tales of terrible problems facing them if they did not get to Tokyo soon or, at least, be able to make a phone call. Toshi could hardly believe any of them would face the trauma he was now destined to experience. Ana would never believe this excuse. He cursed himself for not leaving earlier. He could have seen his father at another time.

By seven o'clock in the evening, the storm began to slow down, but the inn's radio report warned travelers to stay off the roads to Tokyo, for the rain and wind had simply moved ahead of them. If they drove into the storm, there might not be a safe place for them to stop. It was then that Toshi asked for a room, purchased a bottle of scotch in the bar, and went upstairs to forget everything. There was nothing he could do. He had missed this most important evening with Ana.

The ringing telephone jerked Toshi from a sound sleep. He jumped up, but was so disoriented that he didn't know where he was, nor could he find the telephone. He finally got his bearings and heard the manager's voice on the other end of the line,

"You may make your calls now, but there have been several accidents on the road to Tokyo, so the highway is still closed. I'm so sorry, but there is nothing that any of us can do but wait."

Toshi immediately put a call through to Ana. He let the telephone ring for what seemed like hours, but she did not answer. When he checked his watch, he saw that it was 2 o'clock in the morning. Either Ana was not at home, or she was so angry that she wouldn't pick up the phone. He couldn't blame her for either.

Toshi woke Sunday morning at 7 o'clock. From the manager's report, everything was returning to normal on the roads. He showered and grabbed a quick breakfast in the hotel dining room, then prepared for the trip back to Tokyo. Before leaving the hotel room, he tried once more to call Ana.

A sleepy voice answered, "Hullo."

"Ana, this is Toshi. I'm sorry to wake you. I don't know if you heard or not, but the mountain road to Tokyo was blocked last night due to a heavy wind and rain storm…"

His explanation was rudely interrupted by an angry voice that he realized was not Ana's.

"You jerk! Leave us alone. We just wrote you off the program…and don't call again! If you want to see Ana, make an appointment at her office, like everyone else. Good night and goodbye!"

Toshi knew the voice was Miyuki's. He had all kinds of visions of what had occurred the night before when he had neither shown up, nor called. He realized now that he'd better do exactly as Miyuki had suggested. He would try to see Ana at her office in the morning. Perhaps she would be somewhat cooled off by then.

Toshi also hoped that Ana might see the report of the storm in the news and realize that he was not making up excuses. Whatever her feelings, he had to face her with the reason for his absence and, beyond that, with the final decision that had been made for his future.

CHAPTER 13

"The joy of expectation, awaiting the promise of a new dimension of love. The anger of betrayal, as questions linger in the heart."
                    --Toshi does not appear

Ana was excited about the special evening she and Toshi had planned. After work on Friday, she asked Miyuki to go with her to pick out a formal dress for the occasion. Neither young woman was used to 'dressing up.' They had always had simple tastes and chose to stay within their budgets, no matter what the occasion. And, beyond that, they had little opportunity to attend fancy-dress gatherings. Miyuki was happy to help with the shopping and offer her opinions. Besides, she loved looking at beautiful things, whether or not she could take them home with her.

The two women took a cab to the Ginza and began their search. Running through the major department stores rather quickly, they found a tiny dress shop that displayed imported fashions from such places as London, Paris, and New York. They looked at each other and smiled. Miyuki grabbed Ana and dragged her inside.

"I think this could be it!"

One outfit caught Ana's eye and Miyuki's approval. It was a very dressy, black silk pantsuit with a sprinkling of black sequins. The top was designed with a straight neckline trimmed in black satin and long, loose black chiffon sleeves. The wide-legged pants were black chiffon over black silk. Against Ana's olive skin and dark hair, the suit was stunning.

Miyuki moaned, "O god, Ana, I don't know why I ever let you talk me into shopping with you. You ruin everything. I keep thinking I'll look like you when I try something on and then I see the mirror, and it's just me!"

Miyuki bemoaned Ana's beauty, though she was, herself, a beautiful woman. Ana grabbed her arm,

"Stop whining, oh self-defacing one! Grab that gorgeous white thing over there and put it on. Let's pretend we're going to Cinderella's ball."

Miyuki gladly put on the white dress and even felt good when she saw herself in the mirror. The dress was a tight-fitting crepe, with a V-neckline and long, fitted sleeves.

"Wow, what a classy woman! White is your color, Yuki. Buy it! We'll think of something to do with these things. We could have an office party and demand formal dress. How about that?"

Ana laughed while she complimented her friend on her classic Oriental beauty. Miyuki was finally convinced,

"Hey, you're right, I am beautiful. Funny, I never noticed it before. Maybe we do need to have a party and show off our classy selves. I'm gonna buy this thing right now!"

Miyuki proceeded to buy the dress before her practical side could take control. After they had their dresses in tow, they found shoes, jewelry, and purses to match each outfit. They were both ready for a big evening, even though Miyuki wasn't sure just when she'd be having hers.

It was nearly 8 o'clock when the women finished their shopping. Since they were downtown, they decided to see a movie and have a late supper on the Ginza. Miyuki suggested they call Mishima and Sato to join them for a group night, since the men always seemed to know where all the good eating places were. Ana was a bit hesitant, but didn't want to spoil Miyuki's evening. She had noticed that Miyuki and Sato were becoming rather close friends. Ana wasn't sure how Mishima would feel to be with her now, even as friends, but she put those concerns out of her mind. After all, they could ask and it would be his choice.

Miyuki made the call and they arranged to meet them at the hotel near the IEEC office. That made it easy for the women to take a cab back to the office and leave their 'finery' in a safe place before they went to dinner. It was just a short walk to the hotel where they would meet their evening escorts.

Though most Japanese businessmen worked on Saturday, Friday was the final work day for the IEEC group. They were ready to relax after their busy week with the Intercultural seminars. And, of course, Sato was always ready to celebrate any possible occasion. The foursome set out to visit several downtown bars for drinks. Then they headed for a bit classier restaurant for a late dinner and some live music.

Mishima was in good spirits, so they all relaxed and enjoyed being together. They danced, switching partners from time to time, and no mention was made of Toshi. Tonight was just for them, and it felt good to Ana. Everything was fine until about midnight when Sato began to get crazy and was going beyond his drinking limit, into the obnoxious stage. At least the three of them decided that the party was over. Sato was forced to go along with the majority.

Mishima drove the women to the office to pick up their purchases and then out to Seijo. Of course, Sato entertained them with his antics along the way. When they got to Ana's place, Miyuki jumped out quickly to avoid Sato's drunken advances,

"Goodnight, Sato, I'm staying all night with Ana. Had a great time, see you later!"

Mishima walked the women to the door while Sato slumped in the back seat of the car. After Miyuki hurried into the house, Ana turned to Mishima and gave him a hug and a friendly kiss on the cheek,

"Thanks, Mishi, for a fun time. You're a great friend!"

Ana didn't know why she kissed Mishima. Perhaps it was the wine and the good time they had all shared together. But she knew it wasn't fair to him, even though she had carefully included the 'friend' part.

"And thanks to you, Ana. You know I love you."

Ana pulled away from him and replied, "I know, Mishi. And you're very special to me. We'll always love each other." She turned quickly and disappeared inside.

All day Saturday. Ana was very nervous. She was relieved that Miyuki had stayed overnight to help keep her calm. Still, she was worried about Toshi's visit to his grandmother. From all that she knew of Japanese culture, family loyalty would have the strongest pull on Toshi's final decision. She only hoped that someone there would help him find peace with whatever he chose to do with his future.

But Ana was also making her own decisions. If Toshi decided to follow the path chosen for him by his family, she would leave Japan before his wedding day. If he chose to follow his heart, they would go together and start a new life in the States. Ana's worst fear was that tonight would be their last time together. But, if that were so and they were forced to part, she had promised herself that she would not go alone. Because of this personal decision, Ana was certain that she could face whatever the outcome of Toshi's visit to his family.

Of course, it was far too early when Ana began to prepare for the evening. She tried on her new clothes, washed her hair, and arranged it in several different ways. Nothing seemed right. Then she couldn't decide whether the new or her old jewelry looked best with the black sequins. All in all, Ana spent a useless day and, when it was close to 4 o'clock, she became very anxious to hear from Toshi.

Miyuki teased her friend as if she were the mother and her daughter was preparing for that first big date. To Ana, it actually seemed to be just that, her first 'dress-up and go out on the town' date with Yamamoto-san, or, for that matter, with anyone. But the telephone did not ring.

By 4:30 p.m., Ana was beyond being nervous. Her inner fears were beginning to dampen the excitement of this special evening,

"Okay, Yuki, this is not looking good. And if this is an indication of what's to come, I suggest you get on your new duds and prepare to spend an exciting evening with your best friend. And, what the heck, I've got the reservations for dinner and the concert tickets. We've both got the outfits to kill. Let's go for it!"

"You're crazy! He'll be here. He wouldn't miss this for anything. You know that. Hey, it's a major dress-up affair. That phone is going to ring and everything will be great!"

But the telephone did not ring. At 5 o'clock Ana was beyond impatient and had entered the dangerous stage of anger. She looked at her friend and said with determination, "This is it, babe, we're going to town!"

Ana grabbed Miyuki's new clothes and helped her into them. The two women dressed, did their hair, put on their jewelry, and, finally, looked with surprise at the amazing results. One beautiful Italian-American woman, wearing a black-sequined pantsuit with her long, black curls pulled back with sequined combs; and one stunning Japanese woman, wearing a clinging, white dress with matching shawl and her straight, black hair drawn tightly back into a heavy roll, were well-prepared to take Tokyo by storm.

Ana Maria Gabrelli and Miyuki Kitada were ready for whatever was out there. And, in their mood of anger mixed with anxiety, any man who got in their way would be in grave danger. Ana paid for a cab to take them to Seijo Station, but they didn't have enough money between them to take a cab all the way downtown, so they decided to head into the crowds and 'seize the moment.'

The women relished the many astonished stares as they climbed onto the trains and subway that took them to their destination. And they also enjoyed giving especially haughty glares to the many Japanese businessmen who could not avoid looking at these beautiful women, no matter how hard they tried. All the way to the hotel, Ana still had hopes that there would be a message from Toshi when they arrived at the restaurant. For a fleeting moment, she even entertained the thought that he would be there himself.

When they walked into the lobby of the Otani Towers restaurant, they drew more rave reviews with pleasant looks from everyone. But there was no message and there was no Yamamoto. Ana kept her emotions intact as she handed the reservation envelope to the gentleman who greeted them. He received it with a smile, but when he opened and read it, everything changed. He bowed very graciously to the young women and led them into a private reception room.

"Please enjoy our champagne for just one moment. Everything has been arranged for your pleasure. And will your friend, Yamamoto-san be with you tonight?"

Ana and Miyuki exchanged cool glances, pretending they were 'very important people.' Ana chose to answer,

"We are so sorry that he has been detained. It will only be the two of us, I'm afraid."

"Yes, yes, we are very sorry that he could not be with you. Everything will be as he requested. We sincerely wish to please you." He bowed several more times as he left them.

Within a few moments, another gentleman entered the room. He was a very handsome Japanese man with pure, white hair and a pleasant countenance. He spoke to them in perfect English,

"Good evening to you, I am Masao Izaki, manager of this restaurant. I understand that you are close friends of Toshiburo Yamamoto and that he will not be able to be here tonight. I am most happy to greet you on behalf of the Hotel Otani, but am sorry to miss my friend, Yamamoto-san!"

Ana introduced herself and Miyuki to the manager. They both offered their gracious thanks for his kindness. Then Izaki introduced the women to Taiko Isu, their waiter for the evening. The young man left to make preparations to serve their dinner, and, to Ana's surprise, the manager escorted the women through a hallway into a beautiful, private room overlooking the city lights of Tokyo. Next to the window was a lovely dining table with two soft chairs. Against the wall on the other side of the room was a soft, low couch and two lamps. It was a very cozy setting. Izaki bowed to them.

"If there is anything further I can do to bring you comfort and pleasure tonight, please let me know. Your waiter will contact me immediately if you have requests of any kind that he cannot supply."

They all bowed to one another and Izaki left them. Their cheerful waiter entered,

"Please, you must call me Taiko and I will do my best to serve you. You may ask for whatever you wish and I will see that it is done. Please enjoy the champagne. Your meal will be served now."

After carefully seating both women and pouring them each a glass of champagne, Taiko left the room. Miyuki looked at Ana,

"Well, what can I say? Yamamoto-san certainly knows how to entertain his guests!"

Ana responded, "I totally agree. It's just that he forgets to come with them!"

Her eyes surveyed the beautiful table, set with glassware, china, and silver as if for royalty. She did not miss the centerpiece, a gold-leafed bowl filled with white chrysanthemums. Ana touched the flower tips and thought of the first bouquet she had received from Toshi. It seemed like years ago, yet it was only a few months. She blinked to stop the tears that wanted very much to come.

Miyuki remained silent while Ana pulled herself together. Miyuki's own heart was hurting for her dear friend. She knew that Ana loved this man who seemed to be so carelessly using her, and she was intent on lifting Ana's spirits in any way she could. She began to lighten the atmosphere,

"If my mother could see me now! At the top of the tower, for goodness sake. And a guest of a very wealthy...a...will it be acceptable to say...'jerk'? I'm sorry, Ana, but that's the way I see it, tonight."

"You may be very correct with that in-depth analysis. The very first night we met, I tried to lose him in the crowd. I should have followed those initial instincts. I believe they may have been the right ones, after all."

From then on, the women chose to savor the moment. They were both amazed at the gracious service offered them, and often, throughout the very elegant, many-course meal they broke into laughter. Taiko and his assistants were so serious and so intent on giving perfection.

Miyuki commented as the servers left the room,

"Little do they know they are serving a street kid from the slums of South Boston and a penniless foreign-exchange student! Oh, how I wish I had the nerve to do something crazy, like ask them what all these utensils and saucers are doing here. Or eat something fancy with my hands and ask them what in the world it is. Shall I?"

Miyuki's eyes lit up with mischief while waiting for Ana's answer.

"Go ahead and liven up their lives! Or we could pretend we're hookers and go out in the dining room and hustle some ultra-rich businessmen."

"That's it! I like that one best. We could call this a 'participant observation study of the culture of the Hotel Otani upper-class dining room.' Then we could present a paper on our experiences at the next international anthropological society convention."

Ana responded as they laughed together, "What makes us so smart? Or perhaps, not so smart, after all, right?"

Miyuki refused to let Ana get serious again,

"Hey, we are astute anthropologists. We are brainy people. Now let's do what we came to do, get drunk and storm the concert!"

The women raised their glasses to the 'uselessness and insensitivity of men' and the 'intelligence and power of women.' When they finished their drinks, they gave each other a meaningful glance and smashed the very expensive champagne glasses against the outside wall of the private dining room.

Taiko came running into the room, "Oh, so sorry, so sorry, did your dish break or your glass?"

Ana frowned, as if very concerned, and answered,

"Those glasses just slipped off the table. They must have been too close to the edge, or perhaps something was on the table that caused it."

Both she and Miyuki looked very serious and apologized profusely. Then Taiko apologized profusely for the slick table and the thin glasses. In the end, everyone smiled at everyone else. And Ana and Miyuki rose, picked up their belongings, walked through their private hallway and out of the hotel to a waiting taxi.

By this time, the women were giddy from too much wine, the complete craziness of the evening and their exciting plots to 'draw and quarter' every many who looked askance at them. By the time they arrived at the concert hall, they had calmed down enough to regain some composure. There, they were rewarded with balcony seats that made it possible for them to see and hear every moment of the concert perfectly. They both cried at the tender and triumphant music of Tchaikovsky performed by the visiting Moscow Symphony Orchestra. Several hours later, they left the concert hall arm-in-arm and still in tears.

Miyuki recognized the risk of letting Ana end this night with tears in her eyes, for she was afraid that her friend would never stop crying. She suggested that they end the evening with a final celebration.

"Okay, we're downtown, dressed up, had our fancy food and our heartrending music. Now, I say we're ready to celebrate all this good stuff. Let's go back to the Otani and make them sit up and take notice of us, one last time!"

Ana threw back her head in laughter,

"Yuki, you are something else. You never give up! But, you're right. When will we have another chance like this? And all of it on someone else's tab! Let's go!"

They took the first cab open and headed for their final fling. When the women arrived at the hotel, Ana asked the doorman if she could speak with Izaki. Within moments, he was facing her with a pleasant smile,

"What may I do for you, Ms.Gabrelli?"

"Izaki-san, I am so sorry to ask this of you, but my friend and I were treated with such kindness here tonight, we wanted to stop back for a drink or two after the concert. Would you approve of accepting Toshiburo Yamamoto's name as our host for a few drinks and a cab to our home? I can assure you of his thanks for your kindness."

Izaki bowed again and seemed very happy to assist her,

"Of course, this is no problem at all, Ms. Gabrelli. And, I beg your pardon, that you even felt it necessary to make this request. Anything in Yamamoto's name is available to you here, without question. We are at your service!"

Ana remained very serious at great effort,

"Thank you so much, Izaki-san. You are so kind."

Izaki handed her a card and wrote a note on the back that would assure her every possible kindness on request.

Ana and Miyuki walked sedately from his presence to the bar on the lower level of the hotel where the music was wild and all the customers wilder. There they ordered exotic drinks and flirted mercilessly with every man in the place. They had great fun rejecting every offer of 'companionship' in very unladylike ways.

At last, to avoid the obvious fate awaiting them should they walk into the street alone, Ana gave Izaki's special card to the bartender. He raised his eyebrows, smiled, and picked up the telephone to call a driver. Within a few minutes, a uniformed taxi driver arrived on the scene and the bartender directed him to kindly escort the young women to their home. Many despairing eyes watched as two of the most beautiful and captivating women they would ever see walked with their driver to a private hotel taxi and disappeared from the scene.

All the way home, Ana and Miyuki laughed at the slick way they had escaped their bar companions. But, most of all, they enjoyed thinking of the day Toshi would receive the bill for their wild evening out. The taxi alone would cost him a fortune. They loved that final 'kick' and dedicated the evening to all the men in their lives who had "so crassly messed us over!"

The women fell into bed at Ana's place at 3 o'clock on Sunday morning. But before dropping off to sleep, they both swore on an invisible stack of Bibles and other famous scriptures that they would never reveal to a living soul what a fun-filled evening they had spent together. Of course, neither had any intention of keeping the vow, and both anxiously awaited an opportunity to tell everyone they knew about their 'wild night on Tokyo town!'

Miyuki didn't know what time it was when she answered Toshi's Sunday morning call. After she hung up, she was so angry that she didn't even bother to look at the clock. And she made another decision, she would not tell Ana that he had called. Then she swore at all men who had so many fine excuses for breaking women's hearts and felt so much better that she turned over and went sound asleep.

CHAPTER 14

"A time of sweetness, a confession of love, yet foretelling of sorrow to come; no promise of tomorrows to share. Is one moment enough? Yet, it must be!"
--Ana and Toshiburo

Toshi was awake early Monday morning, ate breakfast, and prepared for his visit with Ana. He intended to be at her office as early as possible, for he was aware, from his few words with Miyuki on Sunday morning, that the situation was as serious as he had imagined.

On the way to the IEEC office, Toshi rehearsed ways to approach Ana with an apology and, beyond that, how he could mention the subject of their future relationship. After trying everything he could imagine, Toshi realized that he had no idea what to say. He desperately wanted a very stiff drink to bolster his courage and to clear his mind, but he decided against that as an option.

When the receptionist called Ana to announce "Toshiburo Yamamoto," Ana's stomach tightened. Miyuki had finally told her about the Sunday morning call. So Ana had been warned that Toshi might try to contact her in some way. However, she hadn't expected him to come to the office, and certainly not first thing on Monday morning. She was suddenly very nervous.

Toshi walked into Ana's office looking pale and tired. She motioned to the soft chairs by the window and they sat down facing each other. Ana spoke first,

"You look like you've had a rough trip."

Toshi wanted her to know just how rough it was,

"I don't know if you've heard or not, but I was one of several hundred travelers caught in the storm Saturday on our way back to Tokyo. We all had to stay at whatever wayside inn we could find for the night. About 2 o'clock Sunday morning, the telephone service was finally restored, and that's when I tried to call you. There was no answer, but I did speak to Miyuki later Sunday morning."

Toshi paused for any comments Ana might make, but she didn't offer any, so he continued,

"It was a rough trip, but even more so when I think about our plans for the evening. All I could do was sit in a room just a few hours away, unable even to contact you. In order to make it through the night, I had to drink myself into a stupor."

When Toshi finished speaking, he put a hand to his head as if he were in pain. Ana noticed his hand shaking and realized how upset he really was. She decided to help ease his tension by making light of the whole situation,

"Well, at least, Miyuki was glad you didn't show! She was my escort for the evening and, I must admit, we made quite a pair. She met some exciting men at the Otani bar and actually has a date for next Saturday night."

He looked at her and asked carefully,

"Then you were able to enjoy the evening with your friend?"

She returned his gaze, answering with her usual sarcasm,

"Well, let's put it this way. For an evening with such a disappointing beginning, it certainly had one heck of an exciting ending! What can I say? We made the best of it! We dressed to kill and became the belles of several bars! I might warn you, by the way, not to be surprised the next time you go to the Otani dining room if they watch you very carefully in case you should break a glass or two.

And then, there is that thing about the bill for the evening. I beg your pardon, Yamamoto-san, we weren't planning on being out past train time and were a bit worried that our behavior in the bar might lend itself to being accosted on the street. I don't often drink beyond my limit, so I'm not sure what I said to those guys. They seemed to think we were going home with them. And since we weren't walking too steadily by then, I used your name to charge a taxi to Seijo.

Miyuki and I owe a great debt to Izaki-san for his kind assurance in granting us credit on your good name. At least, we were able to make it home safely. All in all, I'd call it quite an eventful evening!"

Ana had succeeded in rendering Toshi speechless. He had picked up every sarcastic note in her extensive description of their Saturday night party and knew that he mustn't let her bait

146

him into an emotional exchange of any kind. That trap would erase all hopes of salvaging their relationship and would only hurt them both. Instead, he smiled and replied,

"You women certainly know how to have a party! Frankly, I have no idea how much the taxi will cost, but I'll be very happy to pay it and any damages from broken glass that might be added to my bill." He paused, then added quietly, afraid to meet her steady gaze, "I don't know what else to say, Ana. There was nothing I could do. I had hoped it would be a special evening for us."

Recognizing that his total helplessness in the situation, Ana pulled back from her ridiculous attack,

"Actually, Toshi, the dinner was lovely and the concert, well, what can I say about the Moscow Symphony Orchestra? It was beautiful…beyond words! I'm only sorry that you and I couldn't have shared it together."

Her kind words brought some peace to Toshi's mind and he sighed in relief.

"Thank you, Ana, I appreciate the sentiment. I'm so sorry that our plans were ruined by such a simple thing as rain. I was entirely miserable, knowing how upset you would be without an explanation. What can I do to make this up to you…how can we put this behind us and move on?"

Ana looked out the window as she asked, "Perhaps you have a suggestion?"

Toshi struggled for words, but could find none, so Ana took the lead,

"The let me make the plans this time. Just be at my house at 8 o'clock on Friday night. Bring some wine and I'll take care of everything else. I think we both need a few days to recover from the weekend fiasco, don't you?"

Toshi was relieved that Ana recognized their need to be together, yet was apprehensive about what she had in mind. The invitation was given without her usual smile. Ana rose and walked toward the desk, keeping her back to him as if she were dismissing a client.

Toshi stood, but did not move toward the door.

"I don't want to leave you like this with such a distance between us."

When she turned to face him, Toshi saw the familiar flash in her eyes. This was not the time to attempt a reconciliation with Ana. He chose to accept her dismissal with, at least, a hope of reconciliation. He smiled and bowed politely,

"Thank you for seeing me today, Ana, and for your kind invitation. I promise that I will not miss our Friday night dinner."

Ana responded quickly, "And if it rains, I'll expect you to swim over...no excuses!"

They both laughed and, much relieved, Toshi stepped toward Ana to kiss her lightly on the cheek. But she did not respond as he hoped she would. He left her then with too many words unspoken.

Ana found herself trembling as Toshi shut the door behind him. She sat down in the soft chair by the window and took several deep breaths to ease the fluttering movement in her chest. He had volunteered no information about the visit with his family. That could mean only one thing. Their future was being determined by those who could not comprehend the depth of their love for each other. Yet how could she expect them to understand, for she couldn't even explain it to herself.

Over and over, Ana asked herself, *'What is it about such a man as Toshiburo Yamamoto that has drawn me to him and bound our hearts together? Didn't I try hard enough to resist his advances? If only I had been stronger. But why should I fight against loving him? My life had been barren of love.'*

Ana recalled the many times during her college years that she had tried to fall in love. She had longed to experience that which so many of her friends had shared. To find 'one true love' seemed to be everyone's goal in life...a love that would lead to a joy-filled wedding, to sweet children, and to an exciting and happy life with one special person.

But Ana had never 'fallen in love,' nor had she even known anyone with whom she wanted to share such deep emotion, until a few short months ago. In that space of time, her whole life had changed. Now she understood it all, but didn't understand any of it. Her life had been filled with the joy of study and teaching and friendships. Then, a stranger had touched her arm in a crowd and everything changed in an instant.

Suddenly, she felt the need to be part of another person's life. And now, when everything should have been perfect, the opportunity to experience this special love would be cut short. Yet, hadn't she heard it said so often, "A lifetime can be lived in a moment"? Ana made a personal vow that in the few short moments left to them, she and this 'sweet samurai' would share a 'lifetime' of love.

The next few days seemed to stretch into eternity for both Ana and Toshi. Toshi spent most of his time worried about how to tell Ana, openly and honestly, that his decision had been made and his future determined. How could he tell her that, of his own accord, he would accept the path that his family had set for him? How could he tell Ana that he had chosen to leave his heart in her hands and go, with empty heart, into the future? Toshi could only hope, though he did not dare expect, that Ana would choose to fill that emptiness with her love.

When Friday afternoon arrived, Ana left the office early to prepare for the special evening with Toshi. She had not mentioned this liaison to either Miyuki or Mishima. Mishima would never understand it. She was certain that he was aware of Toshi's expected embassy appointment since Ito had known and there was nothing secret about it. And, of course, after the concert night fiasco, she was afraid to even mention Toshi's name to Miyuki.

But Ana chose to put everyone out of her mind, except the one she loved and went to great pains to create a perfect setting for their evening together. The meal she prepared was simple, but elegant. Their dinner would begin with small bowls of fresh fruit over champagne ice, followed by shrimp and vegetable tempura served with flavored rice and small plates of colorful fish cakes. The dessert would be chocolate mousse served with thin, sweet wafers. She would serve hot tea with the meal, and Toshi would bring the dinner wine.

Friday evening was warm and the sky clear, so Ana arranged the *kotatsu* and *zaisu* on the porch by the garden. To add to the atmosphere, she placed candles and a bowl of bright, pink azaleas on a stand next to the table. To Ana's surprise, Grandmother Satoyama offered her a touch of elegance for the special dinner.

She loaned Ana a beautiful, linen scarf to lay across the *kotatsu* and two settings of china, silver, and crystal.

Looking over the arrangements, so carefully prepared for the evening, Ana still felt that something was missing. Suddenly, she knew what it was. She went to the closet and pulled out her box of personal treasures. There she found a precious memento from her past. Ana had no second thoughts. She wrapped the gift with gold foil and a wide, black velvet hair ribbon.

Placing the gift box beside the candles on the stand, Ana was assured that its contents would reveal, more than words, her true feelings for Toshiburo Yamamoto. Everything was prepared for this special night. Ana took a final look around then dressed for the evening in the black-sequined outfit that she had worn on the night of the concert.

Ana chose to pretend that this night was a new beginning, though she knew in her heart that it would more likely be the beginning of the end for this tender, but turbulent, relationship. But, in spite of her inner fears, Ana felt prepared for whatever lay ahead and promised herself that this would be a moment reserved only for happiness.

At exactly 8 o'clock, Ana greeted Toshi at the door. He handed her the wine and she offered him a warm kiss in return. They held each other close for a moment, then Toshi stepped back to survey the beauty before his eyes. In a hushed voice, he commented on Ana's outfit,

"My god, Ana! Is this what I missed the night of the symphony?"

She whirled around to reveal the full effect of the very expensive and very classy Paris fashion,

"What do you think? Is it worthy of Tchaikovsky?"

Toshi smiled and shook his head in amazement,

"By all means! It's better that I wasn't with you. I'm not worthy of sharing the presence of either that great artist or of 'Gabrelli's' beauty! I see now why you had such trouble escaping from the hotel."

Ana repaid the compliments with an even warmer kiss, then led him into the house.

"You're the guest tonight, Toshi. Just relax in the living room while I prepare our dinner table. There's music on the stereo, whatever you like. Actually, you should have brought your guitar and serenaded the hostess."

He laughed at her suggestion. "Perhaps another night, when we're left with no other choices."

"Oh, don't downplay your amazing talents. I thought you were great!"

Toshi ignored her compliment and turned on the stereo to some soft music, then he sat down on the couch to watch Ana. He was very nervous, but tried to appear relaxed. He had no idea what to expect from Ana tonight, but hoped that their time together would make up for last weekend's disaster. Finally, he jumped up to help,

"Sorry, Ana, but I can't just sit here and watch you work as if you were my servant. Tell me something I can do."

"Okay, okay. Come and pour the wine. Our dinner's almost ready."

Together they brought the food and wine to the table. Ana turned out the house lights, leaving only the garden lanterns and the candles to light their special meal. The setting was simple and demanded neither servants nor structured courtesies of the high-ranking society to which Toshi was accustomed. He loved the relaxed atmosphere of this little place and he loved the woman who sat across from him. For one sweet moment, a rush of happiness filled Toshi's heart and he could not resist expressing it.

"Ana Maria Gabrelli, you are the most beautiful woman I have ever known, and I love you with all my heart!"

Toshi reached over and took her hand in his, pressing her palm against his lips. Ana could see him struggling with emotion as he whispered to her,

"I pray the gods will be gentle with us."

Ana's eyes filled with tears at his words, and she quietly added, "And may we be gentle with one another."

Toshi released her hand and lifted his glass, making a toast to the words they had just spoken. They relaxed then and enjoyed every moment and each morsel of the delicious meal. It did seem as if the gods were smiling on them through the quiet garden sounds, the sweet fragrance of the evening air, and finally, the moon rising above the trees to shine over them.

After they finished dinner and cleared off the table, they returned to the porch to sit quietly, side by side, sipping the wine. Toshi broke the silence with a whisper,

"Everything here is so beautiful and peaceful. Perhaps the gods have chosen to bless us after all."

"I hope our time together may be peaceful. I promise to try."

They both laughed, fully aware of Ana's struggles to control her hot, Italian temper. Toshi replied, "And I promise to make it as easy as possible for you to do so. I'll do my best, Ana."

Once again, they made a toast to pledge their promises to each other. Then Ana set her glass down and picked up the gift she had prepared for Toshi,

"There's something very special I want to give you, Toshi." Ana placed the gift box in his hands and spoke in a trembling voice, "I hope you will accept this gift as a token of my love for you."

Toshi was overwhelmed and held the gift with care,

"This is too beautiful to open. I don't know what to say but...thank you, thank you, Ana."

Toshi opened the gift slowly, folding the paper and the ribbon together as if he planned to keep them forever. Then he picked up the small, black velvet box and very carefully lifted the lid. There he saw a beautiful, elegantly-carved gold watch with a heavy gold chain lying against a black velvet cloth. He touched the watch lightly with his fingertips, but didn't lift it from the box. He was overwhelmed and could barely whisper his thanks,

"My god, Ana, this is much too beautiful for me! How can I accept such a gift? Now, of all times, when I least deserve it?"

Ana ignored his words and told him about the watch,

"This watch belonged to my grandfather, Santino Gabrelli. It was passed down to him from his grandfather. 'Papa Santino' was my special friend. I knew he loved me because he was always kind and told me many stories about our ancestors in Italy. He died when I was only five years old, but before his death, he secretly gave me this watch and made me promise never to tell anyone in the family. I loved him very much. Now, I want you to have it as a token of my Italian heritage and of my love for you."

Toshi looked up and started to speak,

"Ana, this gift is far too precious for me. I can't accept this now. It should belong to…" She knew what he was going to say and held up her hand to silence him, "No, Toshi, this gift is for you. You and my grandfather are precious to me, and I have loved you both for your tenderness of heart."

Toshi struggled to control the conflicting emotions that this beautiful gift and Ana's sweet words had stirred within him. But he knew that he must not refuse even that which he did not deserve, for it had been offered as a token of love. Holding the gift in his hand, Toshi carefully lifted the watch from its case and opened it to read the inscription written in Italian,

"To be honorable is to be successful."

They were quiet for a moment, then Toshi whispered,

"I don't know how to thank you, Ana. I will treasure this gift and promise that I will attempt in every way to be worthy of it. And someday, when I am old and my time is gone, I shall return it to you for your eldest son. But tonight, I am ashamed. I've come to you, not only undeserving, but empty-handed."

Ana smiled to lighten the serious moment,

"You didn't come completely empty-handed. Let's drink one last glass of your sweet wine." Ana reached over and took his hand. "Then share your love with me, Toshi, and that will be the most precious gift you could ever give."

The atmosphere of the evening had been as perfect as Ana's dinner setting. The lovers put aside their fears and wisely refrained from discussing the future. They chose to share these few precious moments with peace between them.

The hour was late when Ana woke the next morning. The *shoji* doors were open and she saw that Toshi was dressed and sitting on the porch enjoying the beauty of the garden. Ana lay still, watching him. She not only loved this modern-day samurai for his gentle spirit, but admired him for his intelligence. He seemed to be thinking constantly, yet seldom spoke.

Ana knew that Toshiburo Yamamoto was an honorable man, for she had never seen him make use of his status or wealth to seek power over others, least of all, herself. This touched her deeply as one who believed in the equal value of all persons. And she knew that most of those in his social class would enjoy receiving deference from others, and would even demand it. This was the man she loved. His intelligence and tenderness had stolen her heart, and now was breaking it.

Toshi turned to look at Ana, sensing that she was awake. He smiled and spoke, "It's morning, or should I say, almost afternoon. Are you going to get up now and join me in your garden?"

Ana stretched and smiled back at him, but didn't answer.

"What are you thinking, Ana?"

"I shall never reveal my thoughts to you."

"So, I must try to guess them?"

They began the game of words which neither could resist, but which always led to trouble. Ana responded to his question.

"You can never guess them!"

Toshi laughed and accepted the challenge. He came to sit down beside her and whispered against her ear,

"You're thinking of how much you love me. You're thinking that you'll never find another as gentle or as passionate as I."

He paused and his voice broke as he continued, "But you are wrong, Ana. You will find another. You will find love and all the blessings of life that you deserve."

Ana felt a heavy sadness come over her like a shadow bringing darkness where light had been. He had guessed her thoughts, as he always did. He had spoken them as if he had read them on a page. She pulled him down against her and held him close. She wasn't ready to lose him. She would never be ready. Perhaps she would find another, but there would never be a love like this for her. Ana tried to control her tears, but they came of their own accord.

Toshi put his arms around her and pleaded,

"Forgive me, Ana. I know we mustn't do this. It's too hard on both of us. We mustn't spoil the joy we've shared these last few hours. It's my fault; I'm sorry."

"It's okay, Tosh. When I'm sad, I have to cry. There's nothing wrong with that. We can't always control our hearts or they'll burst open."

"We're no different, Ana. If I should release my emotions now, I would drown in my tears. I don't dare open those flood gates."

Toshi pulled away from her and walked out into the garden. He stood perfectly still, staring across the valley to the mountains beyond, attempting to gain the control that was so essential to his life. Ana followed him. Her heart was pounding as she felt everything coming apart too quickly, but she couldn't stop. She had to know the truth and she had to have it now. Their moments of peace were ended with her questions,

"Why don't you speak the words that have to be spoken? Why do you avoid the confrontation that has to come? You walk in a mist, Toshi. Nothing is clearly defined or openly stated with you. What does it mean in your language to say you love me? What does it mean when you tell me I'll find another? What are you saying to me? Tell me in words I can understand. What is going to happen to us?"

When he refused to respond, Ana pleaded, "For god's sake, Toshi, at least be merciful enough to be honest with me now. What are the decisions that were made in the Kyoto mountains?"

Toshi felt the heaviness of Ana's spirit and it nearly crushed him. She had begged him for truth. He could do nothing but honor her request. He did not turn around. He was unable to face her. Toshi answered all of her questions with unusual calm,

"I will receive the Letter of Appointment from the embassy within the next few weeks and my family is planning the marriage that has been arranged for many years. I beg your forgiveness, Ana, but I am not able to break the chains of responsibility to my family and my country.

Certainly, I know that I am unworthy of the love you have shared with me. But you knew, didn't you? You knew from the beginning what I refused to believe…that I could not fulfill my promises to you. You knew that I was not worthy of your love. Yet you offered it to me willingly. I thought I was the perceptive one who could read 'Gabrelli' like a book. But you knew my heart better than I.

I thought I could love you for a while and then walk away content with the taste of your sweetness. But now, my selfishness and my foolishness have broken both our hearts."

There was silence for a moment as Toshi struggled with the final truth that had to be spoken. He turned to face her, hoping that she could understand what this decision had cost him,

"Ana, I have no words to express the sorrow that burdens my soul at this moment. Perhaps if I were an ancient samurai, I would pierce my heart with my sword and be released. But I am a modern samurai who has chosen to lock that sorrow deep inside his heart and do what must be done!"

Ana felt the shock of his words go through her own heart as if his ceremonial sword had, indeed, pierced it. The decisions were made. Now, it was certain. She must face her future without this gentle man who had pursued her with all his passion and finally taught her, so well, how to love him.

Toshi turned to Ana and put his arms around her as they each let their tears speak for their shared sorrow. Ana finally pulled away from his embrace and spoke quietly, but firmly,

"I will never forgive you, Toshi, for the choices you've made. You must live with them, as well as I. But I will forgive you for your innocence, thinking that you could love me for just a little while, then walk away. Don't you know the power of 'Gabrelli's' heart? Once you've touched it, you will never be free again. You belong to me, Toshi, and even though you leave me, I will never let you go!"

Ana spoke her final words firmly, without tears,

"Go home, Yamamoto. Leave me alone now!"

Toshi turned immediately from Ana's rebuke and left her to think her own thoughts. He knew that he should not attempt to comfort her, for he had given away whatever power he might have had in their relationship. He had ended everything between them with a sentence. And he knew, only too well, the truth of her final words to him. There would never be room in his heart for another; it would forever be filled with Ana.

After Toshi left, Ana sat on the porch steps hoping against hope that the beauty of the garden and the silent hills beyond would calm her spirit. But her anger mixed with sorrow continued to plague her. She whispered into the silence,

"What is the truth about your love, Toshi? You promised so much to me, yet all that is left is the echo of your sweet words. Those words are hollow without your presence, and it seems that your presence is promised elsewhere."

Several times during that night, Ana almost called Toshi. She wanted him to hear her bitter thoughts. She wanted to turn her pain over to the one who caused it. Yet each time she recalled that loving him had been her own choice. She reminded herself of her knowledge of Japanese culture. She knew very well his struggles and the power of obligation which permeated the total life of each citizen of this island culture.

Ana's academic training had convinced her that it was, in fact, this very concept that had kept Japan united and strong through its total history, else it could so easily have been swallowed up by its larger and stronger neighbors. She was, after all, forced to respect Toshi for the great love and loyalty which he had given his family and the nation of his birth. But that knowledge could not bring Ana peace of mind, nor could it heal her heart.

So, thus, the lovers parted, their physical desires fully met, yet their emotional needs untouched. For one, the need for the fulfillment of a promise made. For the other, the need for forgiveness for breaking that promise and both their hearts.

CHAPTER 15

Amongst the beauties of man and nature peace is restored,
purpose is renewed.

Let me hide at least a petal in the sleeve of my flower-
viewing robe that I may remember the spring.
        --from The Makioka Sisters by Junichiro Tanizaki

Over the next few weeks, Ana felt herself slipping into a spiral of depression. She could see no future now, except the shadowy pathway of loneliness. She wept without reason and could hardly finish a day at work without snapping at the colleagues she most respected.

Finally, she had the courage to talk to Ito and let him know that she was not feeling well and needed a few days' rest and recovery. He understood, as the situation was known by more people than Ana imagined. Because of his family status, Ito was among those who were informed of embassy appointments and the public life of the powerful families in Japan. And that included the Yamamoto family.

Ito cared very much for Ana and respected her privacy as well. He responded as a good friend to her request,

"Ana, if there is anything I can do, please let me know. I realize that you've been burning candles at both ends with so much responsibility here. Take whatever time you need; just let me know when you'll be back."

"I'll only need a few days, Ito. I'm thinking of taking a short trip and probably be back sometime next week. But if I should need more time, I'll let you know. I'm sure you're aware of what's happening in my personal life."

"We're friends, Ana. I understand what you're going through and assure you of my confidence. Now, enjoy your trip and please take care."

Ana called Miyuki and Mishima to let them know that she was taking a break from work and would be back the next week. They both quizzed her and Miyuki even offered to be a partner on her trip, but Ana graciously declined the offer. She had told no one, not even Miyuki, about the confrontation with Toshi. She knew that everything would be public soon, and she wanted to be ready for that moment.

Ana assured her friend, "Yuki, I just need to be alone for a while and do some serious thinking about my future. But I'll call you as soon as I get back. Don't worry, I'll be okay!"

The thought crossed Ana's mind to leave a message for Toshi to let him know she would be out of town for a while. Ana knew that whatever occurred between them now would be her choice. He had given up all power in the relationship by his decision to end it. But she wasn't ready to hear his voice and quickly dismissed the thought.

The journey Ana planned was short but familiar. One other time in her life, during her cultural studies in Japan, she had found healing in this special place. She arranged a week-long stay at the Miyako Hotel in Kyoto. It was a quiet, but lovely, old hotel set among the steep hills in the eastern part of the city.

At the Miyako, Ana could stay in Japanese-style rooms with access to the beautiful, landscaped gardens surrounding the hotel. She was also within walking distance of many ancient temples and shrines of the old city. Kyoto offered her the gifts of comfort, quietness, and beauty. She needed all of these now to restore her strength and to plan the next steps in her life.

Entering the lobby of the old hotel, Ana found little changed from her visit several years earlier. The carpet in the lobby was new, but she was glad to see they had kept the same elegant design with large, gold-crown insignias placed at intervals across the expanse of French blue plush. The scene was impressive and the white-gloved assistants were courteous and anxious to meet her every need.

After checking in, Ana was guided to her quarters by one of the young assistants. Her suite included a sitting room and a small bedroom with attached Japanese bath. The *shoji* doors from her sitting room opened onto a private patio with a small garden for her personal enjoyment. From there, a rock pathway led to the larger gardens that stretched around the hillsides behind the hotel. The assistant explained the services available to her, then smiled graciously and left Ana to her solitude.

As soon as she was alone, she found some quiet music on the stereo, unpacked her things and prepared to enjoy this place of beauty. She spent a long time in the deep, hot waters of the bath and, as her body relaxed, Ana felt a calming spirit moving over her. Just being in this quiet, lovely place encouraged her search for the peace of mind she so desperately needed.

After the bath, Ana slipped into the soft, cotton kimono provided by the hotel and opened the patio doors to let the cool air from the garden flow through the rooms. Then she relaxed in a soft, low chair with her feet on a matching footstool and breathed in the scent of the ancient pines that stood, like sentinels, along the garden path outsider her rooms. She sighed and spoke aloud to herself, "I'm so glad I came to this beautiful, old place. This is, indeed, a blessing!"

Ana made the conscious choice to clear her mind of everything but her present surroundings. For a while, she walked in the small, patio garden until it entered the larger path, then she returned to her temporary home. Later in the evening, she ordered a light meal to be served in her rooms. With soft music as background and the scent of flowers and pine on the evening breeze, Ana chose to think of nothing but the pleasures of this quiet setting for the next few hours. Tomorrow she would enter the outside world.

To her own surprise, she slept through the night. This was a first for her since the painful scene with Toshi a few weeks ago. She gave herself permission to lounge in bed and move slowly to greet the day. After a breakfast of eggs, fruit, and tea, Ana decided to renew her acquaintance with two of her favorite places in Kyoto: the Kyomizu (Buddhist) Temple and the Heian (Shinto) Shrine.

In the past when she had taken this journey, Ana would have donned her backpack and walking shoes and set off on foot to enjoy the beauties of the ancient city. But today she chose to accept the offer of a hotel limousine. This was a new and very pleasant experience. Although she felt somewhat like a stereotypical 'rich tourist' looking out through the tinted windows of the fancy car, Ana knew that it was important to conserve her own precious energy. At the entrance to Kyomizu, Ana and the driver arranged a time to meet for the short trip to the Heian Shrine. Then she turned and walked through the temple gates with the other sightseers.

Upon entering the grounds of this huge Buddhist temple, Ana stopped to offer a silent word of thanks to the ancient craftsmen who possessed the artistry and skill to design such a wonder. The amazing structure was created entirely of wood, including the huge nails that held it together. And, as strange as it might seem to a visiting Westerner, the gigantic temple clings to the mountainside as sturdily as the day it was constructed, presumably in the eighth century. Kyomizu is considered the oldest building in the city of Kyoto.

Though Ana was one among many tourists visiting the temple, she felt very much alone, as if this were her private place. Walking slowly through each room, she used her eyes like a camera, as the anthropologist is taught to do. She attempted to record in her memory every piece and part of every room. And, beyond that which she could see, Ana wanted to remember the comforting spirit of this place.

In one large tatami room, she stood in reverence before a sacred altar, offering silent prayers to whatever god or gods were present. Ana needed peace of mind and direction for her future, and she felt an inner assurance that both would be found in this ancient city among these sacred treasures. After her silent meditations, she walked out onto the large, open platform to an awe-inspiring view of the entire Kyoto valley, including the city and the hills beyond.

Ana stood entrance, surrounded by the beauty which had come to her as a gift. She realized how much she loved this country, its unique culture, and its people, and how deeply Japan had become imbedded in her heart. She wondered why it had been so. What was it about this land so far from her own, and even farther from the land of her family heritage, that had captivated her?

Perhaps it was the amazing difference she found here, as Toshi had suggested. Nothing in this country matched, or even related to, anything Ana had ever known. Everything here was a mystery to her. Perhaps it was this fascination with mystery that continued to draw her into the spirit of Japan, for she knew, from the beginning of this journey, that if she lived here for a lifetime, she would never comprehend its totality. She would always be looking from the outside in.

But today Ana's thoughts were disturbed by the certainty that she would be leaving these precious islands and, most likely, would never return. These thoughts burdened her spirit as she walked out of the temple and across a small bridge to the steep hillside pathway. There she paused with other visitors to lift a wooden dipper to her lips and partake of the sacred 'waters of blessing' flowing from the rocky stream. She felt the need of that blessing.

As Ana continued along the pathway toward the entrance, she glanced back one last time at the intricate underpinnings of the ancient temple and whispered a heart-felt "Sayonara" to Kyomizu. When she arrived at the outside gate, the Miyako limousine was waiting, as arranged. After a short rest over a light lunch, they drove on to the Heian Shrine.

Though Ana was enthralled with Kyomizu and its amazing structure, she had found her 'true spirit' in the gardens of Heian. Here, in this place, nature was the gift. As she walked beneath the huge, red *torii* (gate to the Shinto shrine), Ana wondered if the beauties she had discovered here in the past would still be as she remembered them.

Because this was a weekday, the gardens were not crowded with sightseers and for this, Ana was grateful. She was able to keep a distance between herself and the other visitors as she came near the inner part of the gardens. There, once again, she found her special place. Walking along the narrow pathway through a heavy growth of shrubbery and trees, she came upon a small pond. Pink and white water lilies floated on its surface and slender, purple iris clustered along its edge. Trees protected the pond from the outside world, creating a sense of privacy to those who came for silent meditation. Here, Ana had often come in the past to re-center her life. She had come once more with that need.

Ana found a quiet spot on the far side of the pond where few visitors walked. There she sat on a small cement bench and looked across the water at the beauties surrounding her. With joy, Ana renewed her acquaintance with a special plum tree which, in the past, she had claimed as her kindred spirit. During her former visits to Heian, Ana recalled watching the leaves of this plum tree blossom in early spring, turn green for summer, change slowly to its multicolored dress for fall, and drop away in the short winter. The plum tree, in its simple beauty, had often reminded her that life is change and in this natural metamorphosis, there is nothing to be feared.

Today the white spring blossoms were covering the limbs of the small trees. Its unique beauty was there as a gift for Ana's pleasure. As she sat viewing the natural beauty before her eyes, she recalled visiting here with a friend, a Zen Buddhist priest from the Sho Ku Kuji monastery in Kyoto. She had asked him, "What is so special about this plum tree that I love it so?"

He had replied simply, "Plum tree is plum tree."

At the time, she had not asked for further explanation, fearing that she would not understand his words. But she had often thought of his statement. To her, it had come to mean that each living thing is special and has its own purpose and place in the scheme of things, even this tiny plum tree…even Ana.

Ana sat for a while with 'plum tree,' contemplating the future. The tree's pure white blossoms were especially bright against the evergreens behind it. They seemed to shine for Ana and lift her spirits with their beauty. After a while, she stood and bowed slightly to 'plum tree' in thanks for its reminder that there is purpose in her life that had yet to be realized.

Walking away from the sheltered pond, Ana directed her steps toward the main park and the bridge that spanned the lake. As she stood there looking out across the water, she saw a mass of color. Huge pink and white cherry blossoms could be seen in every corner of the park. Some trees were so loaded with the fragile blooms that the limbs had to be supported with bamboo frames, lest they break under their precious burden. It was nearly time for *Sakura Matsuri*, the Cherry Blossom Festival, and the streets of Kyoto would soon be filled with joyful celebration for one of Japan's most revered treasures.

As Ana strolled among these gifts of nature, she found herself covered with a shower of soft, sweet-smelling petals. She moved slowly beneath the heavy-laden branches toward the exit. There she turned to offer a final farewell to Heian's beauty. Just at that moment, a slight breeze moved through the park, creating the illusion that Japan's famed 'weeping cherry trees' were shedding flowery tears. Ana thought to herself, *'Perhaps they are weeping for me.'*

Ana felt renewed strength flowing through her body, as if she had received a transfusion of power from the blessings of this beautiful setting. It was then that she recalled the words of Junichiro Tanizaki from his novel, The Makioka Sisters. She whispered the words aloud, not caring who might hear her:

"Let me hide at least a petal in the sleeves of my flower-viewing robe that I may remember the spring."

Ana turned and walked under the giant red-orange *torii* and away from the beautiful shrine. Her heart was filled with both the joy and the sorrow of this day.

To Ana's surprise, her driver was waiting just outside the gate. She lifted her hand in greeting. He smiled and opened the car door for her. In an unusual gesture of concern, he touched her hand as he helped her into the car. He had seen the tears in her eyes and understood the tender spirit found among the beauties of Heian. The young man's kindness was the final blessing of Ana's day and brought to mind the touch of another's hand upon her arm one summer night, not so long ago.

Much later that evening, after a restful bath and a light dinner in her room, Ana walked out onto the garden terrace to sit in the quiet evening. She was suddenly filled with a sense of joy, as if she were the most fortunate person in the world. She began to recount the amazing life she had led…the good friends, the study, the travel, and the profession that she loved. All had been part of her life plan. All except the love affair. That had never been included in her plans, nor even in her dreams. That had come as a surprise. After everything came Yamamoto, the sweetest gift of all.

In the midst of these contemplations, Ana began to ask herself important questions. She spoke them aloud,

"What do you want to happen now? What is the dream that led you to this far-off land? What is the challenge that will lead you into the future?"

Though she knew the answers to these questions, she hadn't had the courage to pursue them in the past. But it was time to do so now. Ana went to the next room and found paper and pen in the desk drawer. She returned to the terrace and began to write.

Just as she had written plans for each part of her life, tonight she wrote a plan for "Ana's Future." Step by step, that future unfolded:

Professional Life Plan

1. Transfer to IEEC in the D.C. area
2. Return to the United States soon
3. Complete the Ph.D. program in Cultural Anthropology/Japanese Studies at Georgetown
4. Obtain a teaching position at an Eastern seaboard university, pref. Georgetown

Personal Life Plan

1. Let Toshi know of my plan
2. Talk to Ito to arrange transfer
3. If all works out as expected, talk to Mishima

When Ana finished writing, she felt as if a huge burden had been lifted from her shoulders. She was filled with new-found energy. Looking back on her life, Ana realized that she had been moving in the direction of her professional goal all along. Now, Toshi's decision had given her the push to fulfill it. As hard as it might be for them both, Ana knew that she could let him go. She had found direction for her life and there was excitement it in.

In the quiet of the evening, Ana spoke the words of challenge that had been a mystery to her in the past,

"Plum tree is plum tree."

The meaning of those words were suddenly clear to her mind.

"And, 'Ana is Ana.' It is now time to be Ana!"

She whispered her thanks to 'plum tree' for sharing its beauty, and thanks to the Zen priest for sharing his wisdom, and thanks to Yamamoto for sharing his love. Through each of them, her life had been enriched.

■■

Toshi heard the telephone ring in the living room and waited for Ishikawa to answer it. Somehow he knew it was Ana. Few people would call his residence at this late hour and she had often done so in the past. He waited with both hope and fear that he was right. Ishikawa came to the door of the porch overlooking the inner gardens of the house where Toshi was resting in a futile attempt to find some peace of mind.

Ishikawa touched his arm and spoke quietly, "The telephone is for you, Toshiburo. It is Ana."

Ishikawa knew of Toshi's emotional struggles and felt them in his own heart as well. He had been fully aware of the deep love between Toshi and Ana. As a companion to Toshiburo Yamamoto for many years, Ishikawa knew that his good friend was suffering. He prayed that there might be peace between these young lovers before they were destined to follow separate paths. His greatest concern was to protect his friend from further pain.

Toshi stood and walked slowly toward the living room. He and Ishikawa exchanged sympathetic glances as Toshi picked up the telephone and sat down in a soft chair close by. He took a deep breath and answered hesitantly, fearing what might follow,

"Ana..." He started to ask a question, but was interrupted.

"Wait, Toshi, please. I'm sorry for calling you so late. I'm spending a few days in Kyoto. I guess you could call it a rest and recovery program and something has happened to me here that I want to share with you. But I don't want to disturb your rest. Perhaps I should call you tomorrow at a special time."

"I'm very much awake and very glad to hear your voice, Ana. Please tell me whatever you wish. You sound as if you have good news."

Ana's voice had seemed filled with energy. He hoped that it was positive energy and that she had, indeed, called with good news. Though he couldn't imagine anything good coming out of their shared sorrow.

Ana began to speak, slowly and precisely, as if she were reading a dramatic script,

"I didn't call to apologize, Toshi. I've done that over and over again, and it would only be a waste of time and energy. Tonight, I'm sitting in a beautiful room at the Old Miyako Hotel in Kyoto. It's quiet and peaceful here. I don't mean to hurt you, but I need to be honest about everything now. Who else can I talk to, but you? Do you have the patience to listen?"

"Please, talk to me, Ana. I'll try my best to listen and to understand what you want to tell me, even if it takes all night."

They both laughed at his words and became more relaxed, as if they were having a normal conversation. Ana continued,

"I promise not to keep you up all night, but I want to tell you about an experience I've had today. I guess you'd call it my spiritual journey. I've walked in some old paths and visited some places that were very important to me during troubled times in the past.

This whole day has been an exercise in remembering where 'Gabrelli' has been, and where she needs to go. I've even recalled the goals I set for myself long before I first came to Japan. You know, the reason I came here in the first place was to experience this culture and to know its people from the inside out. And, I guess, in more ways than I could have imagined, I've fulfilled that goal. But coming here was to be the background of a future which had been a special dream for a long time, and I find that I still desire.

Though there has been some joy and challenge in the position at the Center, it has never been enough—not enough joy, not enough challenge. I need more. And now, with the situation between us, it's time to get on with my life and my future."

Ana paused to ask, "Are you asleep yet, Tosh?"

"I'm wide awake, listening to every word and will be here for as long as you need me. So please don't hesitate to share everything you're thinking and feeling."

"Okay, here's the rest. Sitting here in this quiet place and revisiting the past, it came to me that sometimes people don't recognize the gifts life offers them along the way. Today, as I've remembered some special gifts that Japan has given me, there's something you need to know. I have no idea what

167

will happen in our future or how much more we may hurt each other, but I want you to know this important truth: Of all the gifts that I have been so fortunate to receive from this country which I love…Yamamoto is the most precious."

Ana stopped speaking as she tried to control the tears that suddenly filled her eyes. Toshi was afraid to speak. Her sweetness had silenced him. Finally, she continued,

"You were the surprise that I didn't expect, nor plan, nor ever envision coming to me. Because you surprised me, I didn't know how to respond. I slipped off-center for a while, but 'Gabrelli' is back, and she appreciates all that you've shared with her and wants to return the gift before taking her final leave."

Ana's words touched Toshi's heart, but the pain struck him hard at hearing the words, "final leave." He hadn't been prepared for that. He had expected that she would be nearby, at least until he had received the embassy appointment. He even thought that they might see each other, if only as friends, from time to time. But, of course, he knew those expectations were unrealistic.

He was finally able to respond to her tenderness,

"Thank you, Ana, for your sweet words. I hope that you will remember the good times we've shared and forget the pain we may have caused each other. I'm sure that we're both aware that the love between us will extend far beyond this short moment in time. I know that we will always be a constant presence for each other.

I'll send you my love every day for the rest of my life, across whatever distance there is between us. And your sweet words allow me to hope that you will do the same for me."

Then Ana asked the question that Toshi would never have thought she would consider,

"Please be honest with me now, Tosh. Can we be together one last time? When I return from Kyoto, can we do that? Just to say 'goodbye'?"

He was quiet for a moment, then answered hesitantly,

"Our hearts are fragile, Ana. More than anything, I want to be with you and, at least, part with a loving farewell. But

168

how can we keep from hurting each other further? I don't want to hurt you, Ana. I cannot bear your tears!"

There was a space of silence between them, but Ana broke it with her plea,

"We need to close this chapter of our lives with kindness or there will always be an empty space in our hearts. Can you trust me this one last time, Tosh?"

They both laughed at her question, knowing how difficult it was for her to keep the peace.

"Ana, your gift to me tonight will surely give me the strength to live with whatever is ahead for us. If you can risk one last moment, I will trust that we can say farewell in peace."

"Then I'll call you when I get back and we'll arrange a time to meet. You can set the ground rules and I will do my very best to follow them. And thanks for your patience tonight with my intensive monologue."

As Ana said her goodnight, her voice betrayed the sorrow in her heart in spite of the attempts she had made to be upbeat in their conversation,

"Goodnight, Yamamoto-san, soon to be the "Honorable Ambassador." I do, and always will, love and respect you."

"And goodnight to you, Gabrelli. Be assured that what is left of my heart is yours always. No one else will ever lay claim to it."

Toshi felt a certain relief after hearing from Ana, yet her words were like a sharp sword. She had told him what he longed to hear, that she loved him and would always hold him close to her heart, but she had also foretold the clear ending of their relationship. There was excitement in her voice as she spoke of new beginnings. Though Toshi did not want Ana to suffer further, neither did he want to lose her.

He knew that if she were anyone else but Ana Maria Gabrelli, their relationship would not end. They would remain lovers, even after his marriage, and would always be together. But he would never suggest such an idea to Ana. He loved and respected her too much to ever speak of it.

After Toshi hung up the telephone, Ishikawa watched him carefully. He understood his friend's love for this young woman. Ana had become a powerful presence in their lives. Though Ishikawa thought of himself as a mere shadow in Toshi's life, standing close to protect and care for him, he had been gifted with a sensitive spirit. He knew Ana only as a voice on the telephone, but from the few words that she had spoken to him, he knew that she surely loved Toshiburo Yamamoto.

Ishikawa felt Ana's sorrow, even as he felt the sorrow of his dear friend, and he longed for some way to heal the hearts of both young lovers, but he knew that this was not within his power. He recognized Ana's free spirit, and, at the same time, understood only too well the obligations which Toshi was destined to fulfill. Ishikawa knew this pathway well, for it was his own. Long ago, as a very young man, he had chosen it for himself and would follow it to his death, in spite of the sacrifice he had made to do so. He knew that Toshiburo Yamamoto would do the same.

Ana hung up the telephone with a smile and a sigh of mixed relief and sadness. She was at peace with herself and the intense pain of loss that had plagued her was somewhat eased. Though the parting was yet to come, she knew it was inevitable and did not intend to delay it. Ana was ready for the next step in her life.

When morning came, Ana's energy was high. She chose not to linger in Kyoto. Here, she had found the key to her future. Her only hesitation was that she had not taken the time to contact her friend at the Zen monastery. Yet Ana felt his presence with her beside the quiet pond at Heian, and the memory of his words had brought clarity to her mind.

When Ana checked out of the hotel, she thanked the manager and the assistants for their courtesy and apologized for leaving sooner than she had planned. They all bowed many times as Ana left. This lovely, old place had, once again, brought comfort and peace to her spirit. She would always remember the restful and thoughtful moments she had spent here.

With a few days of vacation left, Ana returned to Tokyo. She was anxious to move ahead with her plans and, after unpacking and resting a few hours, she called Ito. They arranged to meet for lunch the next day at a place where Ana was certain none of her co-workers would be likely to see them. She was not ready to discuss her recent journey with her closest friends.

"You've aroused my curiosity, Ana. Can you tell me the topic of our luncheon meeting? Should I prepare for some shock or a pleasant surprise?"

"I can't tell you now what the topic is, and please don't mention our meeting to anyone else at this point. I'll take care of the newscasting after we've talked, okay?"

The next day, Ana dressed casually for the lunch with Ito. She had chosen a traditional Japanese restaurant where they would have privacy and need not hurry their discussion. Since they would be eating in the traditional, Japanese style, she wore slacks and slip-on shoes so she would be perfectly comfortable for these difficult moments with her friend and co-worker.

Ana was shown to a private corner of the restaurant, and was waiting when Ito arrived exactly on time. He bowed graciously as he greeted her, then seated himself. She wasted no time getting to the point of the meeting.

"Since I'm buying lunch, I've taken the liberty of ordering for both of us. I think you'll enjoy everything."

The attendant poured their tea and brought them various appetizers. But Ito was more concerned with the topic of their luncheon meeting and blurted out with a half-smile, "Tell me why I'm here, and do it now!"

Ana did not hesitate to satisfy his curiosity,

"Well, this is it, Ito. I'm leaving Japan."

Ito's mouth dropped open and he quickly replied, "I don't want to hear that, Ana! That's not what I came to hear. What's going on?"

Ana laughed at his shock,

"Surely you know that I've had plans to move on sooner or later. It's just that right now, with what's happening in my personal life, sooner is better."

"Of course, I know that you would have goals beyond this position. You're bright and energetic. You could very well set your sights as high as you like and meet them without any problem. But, Ana, what will we do without you? Tell me that!"

"I want to go back to graduate school and finish my doctorate. I'd just barely started when this position came up and I needed the money and experience here. I knew this would help me in my research, and it has. But it's time to move on."

"What do you want from me, Ana? How can I help you?"

"First of all, could you find out about any openings at IEEC in the D.C. area? I want to leave as soon as possible."

"Certainly, I can fax your credentials this afternoon and they'll get back with us right away, I'm sure. You know there are always positions there of one sort or another and they know you well. Whatever you want, Ana, I'll do my best to help. By the way, have you mentioned these plans to anyone in the office?"

"No, this is the first hint I've given that my tour in Japan will be shorter than I had expected. They say timing is everything, don't they? I feel an urgency in this choice."

Their conversation slowed while the meal was set before them. After a while, Ito looked directly at Ana and asked, "What about Yamamoto?"

Ana returned his gaze, a bit taken aback by his unusual entry into her private life. She answered thoughtfully,

"I think you and I both know the answer to that question. There's no future in that relationship. We each have different goals and responsibilities to fulfill. You know more about that, in Toshi's regard, than I. I'm the outsider in this culture."

"I understand what you're saying, Ana. And, yes, I do know more about the circumstances of Yamamoto's life, but remember, if you should change your mind, there's always a place for you here. I intend to be at IEEC until they close us down or kick me out!"

They finished their lunch and talked of other things for a while. Then Ana returned to the subject. "Ito, please don't tell anyone, yet. Let me share the news with our colleagues, okay?"

"Of course. I'll keep our conversation confidential and start working on your job search today. As much as I don't want you to leave us, I know you're in a hurry and will respect that. Do you have any idea how dull life will be without our resident 'wild Italian'?"

They laughed together, toasted Ana's future, and Ito finally gave Ana an out-of-character hug as they rose to leave the restaurant. He offered one last comment with a hint of tears in his eyes,

"I will miss you more than you will ever know!"

Ito turned quickly and left without waiting for her reply. Ana took a deep breath. Everything was moving faster than she had expected. It was true, after all. She would be leaving Japan and this time she would not return. Ana had given all that she had for that "one white, singing hour of peace…that sweet breath of ecstasy." There was no more to give, nor further reason to stay. The love affair was over so much sooner than she had ever imagined, and now she must prepare to pay the price.

CHAPTER 16

"Transfixed by beauty, a mountain view, the calm of peace and the 'cha-na-yu.' Yet, the pain of loss is such a mystery for it cannot be soothed by nature's hand, nor a cup of tea!"
--Friends together at Toshi's home

Over the next few weeks, Ana was very busy. Ito had made all the contacts as she requested. The Washington, D.C. office had excellent references for Ana from her former employment there, as well as from Nishiyama, and were happy to know that she was returning. Among their three job offers, Ana chose to accept a part-time position that would give her enough money for expenses, plus the time to complete her doctorate. Within the next few weeks, she would be back in D.C. and beginning a new chapter in her life journey.

Tonight, as Ana looked around at her little house and the beauty of the garden, she felt a heaviness of spirit. This part of her life would soon be over. When weighed against all the years before, these last few months in Japan held an amazingly high value for her. Within this short space of time, she had experienced both her greatest joy and her deepest sorrow. Ana knew to thank Yamamoto for the joy and to accept responsibility for the sorrow. She had invited him into her heart with the full knowledge that he could not remain there.

Now, most of her belongings were packed and ready to mail to her sister, Val, in Boston. Ana had just finished stacking them in the closet, when the telephone interrupted her contemplations. She didn't feel like talking to anyone and hesitated answering, but finally gave in.

"This is Ana Gabrelli."

She heard Toshi's voice,

"I'm glad you're home tonight, Ana. My classes are canceled tomorrow, so I...wondered if we could spend a few hours together, if you're free. Ishikawa and I would like to invite you to join us for lunch and a walking tour of the Yamamoto estate here in Seijo. The gardens are beautiful right now and Ishikawa would very much like to meet you face-to-face before you depart for your new adventures. Would you have some free time today?"

Ana's heart did a quick flip. She had promised herself never to enter the gates of Toshi's home where he would live with his promised bride. Yet, she had always wanted to see the Yamamoto estate, and especially to meet his friend. Though she knew Ishikawa only as a kind voice on the telephone, he had become an important part of her life. To Ana's own surprise, she answered calmly,

"Of course, I would love to see your home and finally meet Ishikawa."

"Wonderful! I'll pick you up about 9 o'clock tomorrow morning. By the way, wear your walking shoes and comfortable clothes; this place is very much like a park."

"And I'll bring my camera to record our tour. Thanks for the invitation, Toshi. I'll enjoy the break."

Ana was glad she had accepted Toshi's invitation. She knew it was foolish to let her fears destroy her own pleasure. Time would move swiftly and these last few moments with Yamamoto were precious.

Friday morning dawned with bright, sunny skies. It looked like the perfect day to enjoy the beauties of the ancient Yamamoto estate. As she dressed in her khaki shorts and hiking boots, Ana found herself becoming nervous at the prospect of being with Toshi again. She had planned that they would not be together until just before she left Japan, to say their final 'goodbyes.' But his call had interrupted those plans and, in some ways, put her on guard. Ana wondered if his purpose for the day went beyond the pleasures of sharing the natural beauty of his home. Perhaps he had expectations which she could not fulfill.

Toshi arrived exactly at 9 o'clock, dressed casually in jeans and a white, knit shirt. Ana was waiting for him on the steps of her house and found it natural to open her arms and offer him a warm kiss of greeting. They enjoyed their closeness for a moment, then walked to the car with their arms around each other. His tenderness touched Ana's heart, as it always did. They spoke of the beauty of the day and, wisely, did not mention Kyoto or the future.

As they drove close to the high, wood and stucco gates of the estate, Toshi pressed the automatic opener in his car and they slowly entered the world of old Japan. Ana was amazed at the beauty and immensity of the grounds and the ancient home that appeared among the huge, old evergreens. The shrubbery and lawn were neatly trimmed and flowers of many kinds were blooming at various locations across the expansive lawns.

They drove along the far side of the house among the tall pines. Here the cars were kept in a large garage built in the same traditional style as the house. Toshi parked the car and they walked along a graveled path among flowers and small, twisted evergreens to his home.

Ishikawa was waiting anxiously to meet the young woman who had made such an impact on his friend's life. When the pair stepped onto the shiny, wooden porch, Toshi introduced Ana to Ishikawa as his 'companion and friend, Sano Ishikawa.'

Ana saw before her a strongly-built Japanese man, not quite as tall as Toshi, with thick gray hair, mustache, and beard. He appeared stern, but his eyes were gentle and betrayed a slight twinkle as he bowed very low to her and spoke,

"Welcome to the Yamamoto estate, Ms. Gabrelli. I am so happy that, at last, you have chosen to grace us with your presence. I have looked forward to this meeting for some time."

Ana smiled at his warmth and knew immediately that he was her friend. She bowed in return.

"I'm very happy to meet you, at last! Though I feel as if I know you quite well from the kind words Toshi has spoken of you and from our short visits on the telephone."

Toshi addressed a question to Ishikawa,

"What have you planned for us today, my friend? I think we're ready for the tour."

Ishikawa smiled at Ana as he answered, "We'll walk for a while through the gardens, then visit the family shrine on our way to the tea house. When we arrive there, it will be my pleasure to perform *cha-no-yu* (tea ceremony) for you. Then we'll share a light lunch and hike along the hilltops for a fine view of the surrounding area. And when we return, I would like to guide you through the family home to see the Yamamoto treasures that are kept there."

Ana was amazed at the well-planned tour for the day. Toshi laughed and took her hand,

"You're in for the tour of your life, Ana. Get your camera ready to roll; Ishikawa is an expert guide!"

Ana did as she was told, for Ishikawa had already turned to lead them onto the rocky path around the estate park. This was the first time she had ever visited a Japanese park without the crowds to mar its beauty. Now and then, they stopped at various points where Ishikawa explained the unusual tree formations or the types of exotic flowers they were viewing.

She could hardly imagine a family living here and wondered where the children had played and how many servants it took to keep these grounds in such perfect shape. She knew that they were walking along the pathway where many very rich and powerful people had walked in ancient times, as well as this very day. Ana made good use of the camera.

Ishikawa led them closer to the steep hillsides and across a tiny bridge that spanned a flowing stream. There, almost hidden among a grove of slender, bamboo trees, was a small Shinto shrine. The stream surrounded the shrine and only by stepping carefully on the huge flat rocks could they enter it.

Toshi moved ahead of them into the tiny building. He lit the incense on the altar, then bowed his head and with one hand pulled the scented smoke towards him. He bowed again, very low, with folded hands pressed against his forehead. When he stepped back across the rocks to stand beside Ana, Ishikawa entered the shrine. Ana bowed in respect while her companions offered reverence in their special ways, but she did not follow their example, nor did they encourage her to do so.

As they walked away from the shrine, Toshi spoke in a whisper to Ana, "I've spent much time in this sacred place lately."

Ana smiled and asked, "Did you find comfort here?"

"Very little, I'm afraid. Perhaps some peace of mind."

Neither spoke further of what lay heavy upon their hearts, and the hikers moved along a trail that led them up the steep hillsides. The higher they went, the more awesome the scene became. Soon, they could see the total expanse of the estate below them. Ana noticed a group of small ancient structures built very close to the hills. Toshi explained that these were former homes of servants in the days when walls were necessary for protection. These structures were no longer in use. He mentioned that at some time in the future, the estate would be turned over to the Commissioner of National Treasures, and these buildings would be restored as part of Japanese history.

"And when might that be?" she asked of Toshi.

He laughed, "I hope it will be far in the future! Though most Japanese want to live in modern ways, I have chosen to live in the traditional style. These surroundings offer me peace and solitude. I would not want to be in any other setting. So, hopefully, as long as I live, this home will be available to me."

"This would be a beautiful public park, but a shame to think of it ever being trampled by thousands of visitors."

"That would break my heart, but some day it will probably happen. After all, my father is the official owner; he kindly grants me the privilege of living here."

As they walked higher up the pathway, they came to another ancient structure. It was a small tea house built in a cove near the top of the hills. Ishikawa led them into the center room and invited them to be seated on the soft *zabuton*. Then, he proceeded to open the *shoji* doors to reveal a broad view of the world around and below them. Ana caught her breath at the beauty, and she was suddenly overwhelmed with tears.

She couldn't help whispering, "My god, what a blessing it must have been to live in this place!" She reached over to touch Toshi's hand and added, "I guess I should say, what a blessing this must be for *you*…to live in it!"

He grasped her hand as their eyes met, "There is only one blessing I treasure above it."

Ana looked away from him to the scene below. Toshi released her hand and bowed his head as Ishikawa prepared the utensils for *cha no yu*. She followed his example. Ana was certain now that to end this day in peace would require all the strength that she could summon from within.

Ishikawa began the tea ceremony. Ana was aware of the importance of this ceremony in the lives of the ancient samurai. In those early times, it was valued as a discipline of the spirit, an inner journey, to guide the participants to a deeper enlightenment of mind and spirit. And, in sharing the *chawan* (tea bowl), a sense of community was formed among those who partook, which continues to be the essence of *cha no yu*.

The tea ceremony, as performed in modern times, is as much an art form as it had been a spiritual journey for the samurai of long ago. Today, Ana chose to view the ceremony as the ancients had done. She needed whatever inner strength she could gain from the beauty and discipline of this ancient ceremony to face what lay ahead for her.

The ceremony began. Ishikawa's preparations were like a 'ballet of the hands.' He caressed the utensils, just barely touching and holding them in the ways required of the ceremony. His concentration was perfect, no flick of the eyelash, no change of expression, no break in the rhythm of the movements. At last, he placed the *chawan* in the palm of one hand and moved it in three perfectly circular motions with the other hand. Carefully, with an attitude of deep reverence, he offered it to Ana.

Ana took the *chawan* and put it to her lips, sipping the thick *matcha* (green tea) until the cup was empty, then returning it to Ishikawa. He placed her cup beside the utensils, washed it carefully in a bowl of water, and prepared it for Toshi. Ana remained with her head bowed, while Toshi drank the *matcha* and returned the *chawan* to Ishikawa. Ana remained with her head bowed while Toshi drank the *matcha* and returned the *chawan* to Ishikawa. Once more, Ishikawa prepared the *chawan* and partook of the *matcha* himself.

Ana felt something happening deep inside her soul. That 'inner self' was changing, though she could neither define, nor describe what that change was, nor what it meant. She only knew that nothing would ever be the same for her again. Ana did not even know if that were good or bad. All she knew was that she was filled with a powerful sense of connection with these two samurai with whom she had shared this ancient ceremony. They were a part of her, who she had become, here in this place. Ana knew that no matter what happened to any one of them from this moment, there would be no way they could be separated...even though they must part.

Ishikawa rose with perfect movements to conclude the ceremony. Toshi stood and gave Ana his hand. Her knees had

179

trouble straightening after being so long in one position, and she stumbled against him.

"I'm sorry, it's been a while since I've knelt in reverence for any purpose."

Toshi smiled and steadied her, but he said nothing. Ana saw that he had been touched by the ceremony which they had shared, for his eyes were filled with tears.

The three walked in silence from the tea house toward a smaller structure along the same path. Again, they entered a simple, but lovely, tatami room. Ishikawa slid the large, wooden coverings back to reveal a huge wall of open space. From this opening, one could see the sky and only a bit of the mountain. Several zabuton were arranged in front of the 'window wall.'

Toshi explained the use of this building,

"This is the place for 'moon viewing,' another important part of our ancient culture. My ancestors knelt here to view the full moon and gain strength from its beauty. As we contemplate the beauty of the moon, we find meaning for our lives. There is power in the natural world that can enlighten our minds and heal our souls. I have found it to be so."

Ana watched Toshi as he spoke, though he did not look at her, but looked past her toward the blue sky, as if he were addressing it.

She was moved to add her own hope, "I pray that might be so...for myself, as well."

Ana didn't wait for Toshi to acknowledge her comment, but turned and began to take the photos she wanted in order to record this beautiful experience on the Yamamoto estate. While Ana shot photographs, Ishikawa and Toshi arranged a light lunch for them. A house servant had brought box lunches to the building for the hikers to enjoy as they rested from their mountain walk.

The three friends sat down on the zabuton to share a lunch of cucumber sandwiches, sushi, and fruit. There was also a Thermos of cold, black tea, and sweet cake for a light dessert. They were hungry from their excursion and enjoyed every morsel.

While they were resting, Ishikawa asked a question of Ana,

"What do you think of this ancient estate?"

"It's very beautiful, indeed. You have everything here, like a world set apart. I would imagine that those who lived here in ancient times hardly left these walls. What more could one want than this?"

Though the question had been addressed to Ishikawa, Toshi answered it in a way that surprised her,

"Walls are built for two purposes: to keep persons in or to keep them out. Those inside often feel confined rather than blessed, even though they may be safe and well-cared for. Perhaps, that thing inside the human soul that searches for the beyond is what caused those who lived within this walled estate to build structures with wide, open windows to see the sky. They could come here to dream of what might be out there on the other side of these walls."

Ana responded to his thoughts,

"I agree that sometimes walls offer needed safety. And, yes, it seems to be our human nature that there will always come a time when one wants to go beyond them. Maybe it's because of our need to break through our inner walls of confinement that we are more willing to risk breaking through physical barriers.

I've never really thought of it before, but perhaps that's why I came here so far from my own home, far across the walls of land and sea that separate us."

Toshi watched Ana carefully as she spoke, wondering what was hidden beneath her words. He asked the question,

"What inner walls of confinement have you known, Ana, that would cause you to risk the unknown…to come far from your Western world to this strange, far eastern isle?"

Ana moved quickly away from their serious mood and laughed,

"I suppose we all have inner walls where we hide our deepest fears that can never be revealed. We can often challenge the big things like oceans and mountains and cultural barriers, yet shudder at a 'whisper on the wind.' Those whispers are the truths that we hide from ourselves as well as from others."

Ana didn't want him to probe any deeper into the land of her inner fears. She suggested a change of direction,

"I think we should adjourn this philosophical discussion and move on with our tour."

Ana smiled at Toshi in an attempt to lighten his mood, but found him still solemn and serious. Ishikawa gathered the luncheon things and put them in a box by the door. Then he left his young friends alone.

Toshi turned to Ana. "What hurts me most, Ana, is that you don't trust me with your heart. You hide your truth behind the safety of your inner walls, just at the moment when we should be closest. And we will leave each other with so much unspoken between us.

Sometimes I think that if, for just one moment, you would give me that trust, I could live with what's ahead. But perhaps, after all, I don't deserve it. And that is the truth for which I will suffer a lifetime."

Ana could hardly bear the heaviness of heart that was evident in Toshi's words and his countenance. She leaned over and kissed him. For a few moments, they enjoyed the sweetness of their love, then she pulled away.

"There is only one truth you ever need to know about me, Toshi. I have loved you and will never love anyone the way I have loved you…and that is the only truth I know to tell you."

"If that is so, Ana, then you're right…that is all the truth I will ever need to know."

Toshi smiled and shook off his dark mood that had come over him during his exchange with Ana. He consciously chose to recover the positive atmosphere that had been with them during the morning. They both relaxed and enjoyed the journey down the hillside pathways, stopping now and then to view the beauty below from different perspectives. Several times, Ana asked Ishikawa to take photos of her and Toshi as mementoes of the day; and, in turn, Toshi took several of her and Ishikawa.

They had stopped to rest a moment on their way down the pathway to the estate, when Ishikawa suddenly turned to Ana and spoke in a hoarse whisper,

"You will be missed."

Toshi was leaning against a large rock along the path when he heard his friend speak. He watched Ana for her response. The intensity in Ishikawa's voice had touched and surprised her. She felt as if she might faint from sudden weakness and glanced toward Toshi with a question in her eyes. He turned away, looking instead toward the distant horizon.

Ana faced Ishikawa and took a deep breath, attempting some coherent response,

"I won't have to miss you, Ishikawa. I'll take your spirit with me, the spirit of *cha no yu*. I'll remember it always."

To Ana's own surprise, she felt drawn to go to Ishikawa and take his hand. He held her hand gently in his huge, square fingers and barely touched it to his cheek. She felt tears against her fingers, but before she could speak, Ishikawa released her hand and turned away to go down the mountain path. Ana looked at Toshi, wondering what she should do. Though he was watching her intently, he did not move, nor did he speak. She left him to his own thoughts and followed Ishikawa.

When she came closer to the house, Ana noticed some commotion on the porch. Ishikawa was greeting a gentleman with many bows of obvious deference. She was afraid to go further without Toshi's presence, so chose to wait for him. Ana had a sudden thought: '*Perhaps this is the father of Toshi's promised bride. That would be a perfect ending to this beautiful day!*' Ana shuddered at the possibility. But whomever the visitor was, he finally went into the house with Ishikawa.

Nearly fifteen minutes later, Toshi reached the place where Ana had stopped to wait for him.

"I'm sorry, Ana. I didn't mean to ignore your feelings. I was just surprised and very touched by your exchange with Ishikawa. You are important to him, more than you could know. He and I are so much a part of each other, that what I feel, he feels, and what I suffer, he suffers.

He has never in his life expressed such feelings. He will be struggling with his own shame for speaking so openly to you, and knowing that, in doing so, he has spoken my heart as well. I need to be with him for a few moments. Will you wait for me?"

"I really think you should take me home, Toshi. Our day together has been so perfect. I don't want it to end a different way. You have a visitor who appears to be very important. I saw Ishikawa bowing many times to him as they entered the house. Please Toshi, take me home now or let Ishikawa do it!"

"No, no, Ana, he won't be able to face you now. I'll take you, but first let me find out who's here. You can come in with me, it's all right. After all, it is my home!"

183

Ana moved quickly away from Toshi. There was no way she could be convinced to enter his house. She called back to him, "I won't come in the house, but I'll wait for you in the car. I'll be okay."

Toshi hesitated, but knew the futility of further discussion. He went into the house, leaving Ana to her own devices. She opened the car door and sat down inside.

The trip around the estate and up along the steep hillsides had been a beautiful experience in many ways. Yet, it had also been physically tiring and emotionally draining. Ana had used all of her physical energy to make the climb and all of her emotional energy to remain calm in Toshi's presence throughout the day. She pulled the lever to drop the front seat back, laid down against the soft beige leather of his Mercedes sports car and went sound asleep.

Someone was calling her name form a far distance. At first, she couldn't make out the words, but Ana felt her arm shaking. Finally, she struggled to open her eyes. Toshi was kneeling beside the car door trying to wake her. She smiled at him and stretched,

"I'm sorry. I just sat down and drifted off into another world. This car is so comfortable, and I was so tired. Can we go now? I need to get home and recover from all this exercise. I'm not used to walking up and down hills all day long!"

Toshi protested, "But, Ana, there's someone here I would like you to meet and who wants to meet you, also."

Ana's eyes opened wide. "What? Me? Who could that be?"

Toshi was quiet a moment, obviously fearful of her reaction, yet he chose to risk it.

"My father is here and has asked to meet you. Will you come in for a few minutes?"

Coming out of a sound sleep, Ana was caught off guard. She reacted from pure emotion,

"Are you crazy, Toshi? Why would I want to meet your father? The person who considers me of such little value as to banish me from your life? Of course…not! I don't want to meet him! How could you do this to me? I don't understand you! You're either totally insensitive or totally insane!"

Ana pushed the car door open and jumped out, facing him squarely with her anger,

"Take me home…and do it now!"

Toshi tried to calm her down. "Ana, he's a human being…with feelings. And he did not banish you. I'm responsible for my own choices."

Toshi suddenly grabbed Ana's shoulders and held her against his chest, whispering in her ear,

"My father has come because he knows how difficult this decision has been. I want him to meet the only woman I will ever love. I want him to know why the choice has been so hard for me."

Ana began to calm down, but, in turn, pressed her mouth against Toshi's ear and whispered back to him in her most cutting, Gabrelli way,

"Who then will comfort me? I have no loving grandmother or father to share my loneliness."

Toshi moved away from her, ashamed of what he had asked her to do,

"Forgive me, Ana. You're right, of course, and I'm wrong to even suggest such a thing to you. I've been totally insensitive. I admit to being slightly crazy right now. Please forgive me. I'll talk to him, he'll understand. I'll be right back to take you home."

He turned away from her to go back into the house, but Ana suddenly blocked his path.

"Wait, Toshi. I will meet your father, if you have the courage to put me in the same room with him and leave us alone. I will be glad to meet him on my terms!"

Her words surprised Toshi and also frightened him. He wondered what she intended to do. Ana stared at him with her most belligerent gaze, waiting for him to make his decision. Toshi decided to take her at her word.

"Then you shall meet him. I will introduce you and leave you alone with him. He will have the distinct pleasure of confronting the wrath of Gabrelli, and I hope he has the courage to face it and the strength to live through it!"

To Toshi's surprise, Ana burst out laughing. He was completely baffled at her response.

"Pray, tell me, sweet Ana, what is so funny to you in all of this?"

"You are so funny! You have no idea what you're talking about. You have never even come close to witnessing the 'wrath of Gabrelli'! But perhaps your father will. I'm ready, let's do it!"

Ana turned to go into the house. But, to her surprise, Toshi grabbed her, pulled her against him, and kissed her so hard she could barely breathe. When he released her, his eyes revealed sparks of anger that she had never seen expressed against her.

"Gabrelli, you are not who you think you are! I know you better that you know yourself. I always have…from the moment we met…and I always will!"

Ana turned back toward him and, with no thought of the consequences, doubled up her fist and hit him so hard on the jaw that he fell against the car and slid to the ground.

Then she shouted at him, "You have only touched the surface of Ana Maria Gabrelli! Lead me to your honorable parent!"

Toshi was so stunned that he couldn't speak for a moment or two. Then he pointed to the house and muttered, "He's in there and I don't intend to join you!"

Holding his swelling jaw, he started laughing and shouted to Ana as she headed toward the house,

"Good luck to my poor 'papa-san.' At last, he will meet his match!"

Toshi decided that he'd be safer to stay where he was. He leaned back against the car and begged the gods he worshipped for some peaceful resolution to this ridiculous dilemma.

CHAPTER 17

"In the midst of love's struggle comes the harsh realization of difference. Where the sacred value of one culture is freedom, the other gives honor to responsibility."
--Ana and Toshiburo

Ana couldn't believe what she had just done to Toshi. She knew she must be on the verge of some kind of emotional collapse to let herself lose all control. But instead of turning back to apologize, she marched onto the front porch of the ancient home, took off her hiking boots, and proceeded into the *genkan*. There, she stopped long enough to slip on the *uwabaki* and entered the large, elegant living room of the Yamamoto estate.

Ishikawa was standing near a small table pouring tea into a cup, undoubtedly to serve the well-dressed man sitting in the low, comfortable chair close by. Ana walked over to the stranger and, in her most "ugly American" manner, introduced herself.

"Yamamoto-san, I presume! I am Ms. Ana Maria Gabrelli. Perhaps your son has mentioned my name to you. I am the brazen American woman who has chosen to fall in love with him!"

Tatsume Yamamoto looked to Ishikawa for a sign of what he should do, then looked back at Ana. He was speechless, but stood with courtesy, rather than force her to look down at him. Before Tatsume could think of a reply to her unexpected announcement, she continued her attack.

"I understand that you have been very concerned about your son with regard to this relationship."

Tatsume stared at her a moment, then suggested, "Could we sit down and talk in a civil manner?"

Ana replied with biting sarcasm, "We could sit down, I suppose, but to talk in a civil manner about love is usually quite difficult. Haven't you found that to be so?"

A smile twitched at the corner of Tatsume's mouth.

"I have found that to be so in every case!"

He motioned her to a chair near him, and they both sat down, facing each other. Ana spoke first.

"Why waste our time trying to be civil? Why not just say what it is we have to say and be done with it?"

"Toshiburo tells me that you are a student of Japanese culture. If so, then you are fully aware that to do as you suggest is not an acceptable option. There are many pathways and many meanings involved in any discussion and, in particular, in the discussion of love."

Tatsume paused a moment and motioned to Ishikawa to leave them. Ishikawa immediately turned and left the room.

Ana felt a sudden rush of anger fill her chest as she watched Ishikawa leave. She spoke without courtesy of concern for Toshi's father.

"Do people always do as you say or respond immediately to a movement of your hand?"

Tatsume looked closely at Ana. He was shocked at her rudeness, yet chose to soften his response.

"Your tongue is sharp, Ms. Gabrelli, and meant to create wounds. Is it because you are in pain that you wish to bring pain to others?"

Ana stared at Tatsume. He did not turn from her gaze, but was captivated by her bright, dark eyes and more captivated by her answer, spoken in a soft whisper.

"You have unveiled my heart, Yamamoto-san."

Tatsume continued speaking to her in a quiet, nearly sweet voice.

"It is only by one's own suffering that one can identify another's pain."

"Tell me, Yamamoto-san, what pain have you suffered that would allow you to understand that which I feel at this moment?"

"You do not obey the rules of kindness or courtesy, Ms. Gabrelli. You push too far into others' hearts."

"I do so because I'm desperate. You've already won this game. I'm the loser. There are no rules that I must follow now."

Tatsume raised his voice to Ana, even though he felt her desperation.

"There is no game between us. My son is not a pawn to be moved about on a game board at my whim...or yours!"

"Isn't that what has happened? You've played him into a corner where he sees no choice, no way to move on his own."

"No, I'll tell you what has happened. My son's destiny was determined a long time ago. He came to us with little hope of life, with an illness that no one could cure. We were told that his heart would not sustain him to adulthood. We could buy him every comfort, but we could not purchase his health.

Toshiburo's health came to him from the heart of a young boy, as a gift. Every day that he lives and breathes is a gift to him. And because of that gift, his life is not his own to spend as he chooses. His life has been spared for a purpose, and that purpose is to offer his intelligence and his strength for the honor of his country.

Now it is time for him to give back that which was given to him, to use his gift for others. But there is a roadblock in his pathway, and that is you, Ms. Gabrelli. You come to him and tell him there is another way he must go. You offer him another direction, to turn away from his obligations and choose the pathway of love.

Tell me, Ms. Gabrelli, is it too late for him? Does he wholly belong to you, now?"

"Does he wholly belong to me? Oh no, Yamamoto-san. He belongs to me not at all. He has chosen to do as his father has commanded."

"I have not, nor would I ever, command my son. The choice is his alone to make!"

"Your unspoken commands are hidden in your kindly-spoken words, 'Make your own choice, Toshiburo,' 'I will stand by you and support you,' 'Your destiny is yours to choose.' Your commands could not be annunciated more clearly. And he has responded to them as you knew he would. He can no longer push against you, for you have so wisely taken away the wall between you. Now he can only offer you his acceptance, rather than his resistance. How adept you are, Yamamoto-san, at the art of turning another's mind to your bidding!"

There was a long silence between them before Tatsume responded. Their eyes locked as if in battle, but his words came in a soft whisper.

"If I were young again, I would fall in love with you, Ms. Gabrelli, as Toshiburo has done. You know too much about hearts and minds. You see too much inside and underneath words. You and I are at an impasse. I want Toshiburo's intelligence, his mind, for his country. You want his heart, his love, for you. How can this dilemma be solved?"

"Toshi has solved it for us; he has given his love to me, and I intend to keep it. Whatever is left is yours."

Tatsume bowed his head and spoke as if in sorrow.

"Then you have destined him to a life of emptiness and heartache. He cannot perform his tasks with any success if you withhold that which he most needs to perform it."

"And what is that?"

"If you take his love with you, then you must fill his heart with your own, or he will not live to perform his duty. He cannot do what is required of him with a cold and empty heart."

The adversaries looked deep into each other's eyes. Ana spoke to Tatsume in an unusually calm voice, as if his words had drained her of anger.

"I see that you love him as much as I."

Then she stood and walked to the window with her back toward Toshi's father. Ana was quiet a moment before she spoke her final words.

"You may be assured, Yamamoto-san, that your son will have all my love to take with him. I shall fill his heart with it. My love will always belong to him wholly, for there will be no other demands upon it."

Ana turned to leave, but Tatsume moved quickly to catch her arm and hold it in a tight grip.

"Thank you, Ana Gabrelli, for loving my son, for giving him beautiful memories that will last a lifetime. I pray that he has loved you as well and that you will take lasting memories of that love with you."

Ana turned away from Tatsume, answering in a voice shaking with emotion, "Yes, Yamamoto-san, he has loved me well and that which I take with me…will last far beyond my lifetime." She left him to ponder her words.

Tatsume Yamamoto, the strong, powerful businessman, fell into a chair close by and began to weep silently. His tears were not only for the broken hearts of these two young lovers, but for the memories this fiery Western woman had called up from his past and the emptiness that still remained within his own heart.

Ana came out of the house to find Toshi sitting on the porch. She sat down beside him and proceeded to lace her hiking boots without speaking. Finally, Toshi broke the silence between them.

"Who won the bout?"

She didn't look up, nor did she answer his sarcastic question. Toshi spoke again.

"You owe me a pair of glasses."

Ana responded with her own sarcasm, "Was the kiss worth it?"

Toshi was quiet for a moment before answering, "A broken jaw and a smashed pair of very expensive glasses? I would say, yes, it was worth every three seconds of it!"

She gave him an angry look.

"You crossed over the line, Toshi. You pushed me too far!"

"And you 'blind-sided' me, Ana. I didn't see any live."

"If you didn't see it, then you know how wrong you were. You don't know me as well as you think you do!"

"And I have the bruises to prove it!"

Toshi carefully touched his swollen, bluish jaw.

Ana looked at him directly for the first time since their argument. She couldn't believe that she had actually hit him so hard. She leaned over and kissed the bruise very gently, then gave him her final blow.

"Just be glad the bruises are on the outside; they'll heal quickly."

Ana started to move away from him to go to the car, but Toshi caught her arm in a grip that felt like a vice to Ana. He stood up, pulling her tightly against him.

"There's an ancient samurai sword hanging on the wall in my living room. Why don't you get it and cut out my heart. Then you would finally be certain that I've suffered enough for loving you!"

His words silenced Ana's anger. She relaxed against him as if finally defeated.

"Take me home, Toshi, before I do any more damage here."

They walked to the car in silence with their arms around each other.

Tatsume Yamamoto stepped out on the porch in search of his son. He saw Toshi and Ana walking toward the car and wondered if they had made peace with each other. He

191

understood their struggle only too well. Ana was beautiful, intelligent, and sensitive, but, more than that, she was very strong. Tatsume wondered if he had seen the last of this woman. Perhaps not.

Ana sat down in the car seat, leaned back, and shut her eyes. She promised herself to gain control, yet she felt as if she were on a roller coaster that was going to stop unexpectedly and throw her out. She wasn't sure where she would land.

What was it that had set her off after feeling so positive after her trip to Kyoto? Ana couldn't even explain it to herself. Was it seeing Toshi in his own environment and realizing how much she loved him and wanted to be with him? Was it the knowledge that there would be another who would be there, sharing that beauty with him? She had told herself many times that she shouldn't go to his home. What happened today had been her own fault for not listening to that inner voice. She had brought it on herself, and everyone else, as well.

When Toshi stopped the car at Ana's door, they were quiet for a few moments. He broke the silence.

"We can't let this be our goodbye, Ana. We can't end our relationship like this."

"No, we won't do that. We both need to relax for a while. Maybe we can talk later tonight. Maybe I'll get my head together by then." She paused a moment, then finished her thought. "I'm not the person you saw a while ago, Toshi. I don't even know that person. Everything was so perfect today with you and me and Ishikawa. I'll always treasure those moments with the three of us together, there on the hillside with so much beauty around us.

But when we came down to the real world, I lost it. All my well-planned resolves from Kyoto just slipped away like dust in the wind. I'm sorry that I hurt you. You didn't deserve such treatment. You've never deserved that. If you feel like it, call me later tonight. I promise to be calmed down by then."

Ana jumped out of the car and ran through the wooden gate. Toshi sat still for a while, as if paralyzed by Ana's words. He didn't know how to help her, nor could he bear to watch her suffer because of his choices. It had been a mistake to invite her to the estate. The day had become a tragedy for all of them, and especially that his father had chosen such a day to visit.

Toshi sat in the car for what seemed like hours, but was only about thirty minutes. He found it impossible to leave Ana in her depressed state of mind. He was worried about her talk with his father and what they had said to each other. There was no way it could have eased the pain in Ana's heart.

Finally, Toshi gathered the courage to get out of the car and try to talk to her. If there were anything he could do to comfort her, he would do it, and if she didn't want to see him, then he would leave, but he had to try. He walked around the house to the back porch. Ana had obviously just stepped out of the shower, for she was sitting on the porch steps drying her hair with a towel. She was dressed in a white, terry cloth bathrobe.

When Ana looked up to see who was coming around the pathway, Toshi saw that her eyes were red from crying. He slipped off his shoes and walked over to sit down on the step behind her. He took the towel from her hands,

"I can at least help you dry your hair, Ana. I don't know what else to do, and I can't leave you with tears in your eyes, especially when I've caused them."

He buried his face in her soft, wet hair and put his arms around her. She turned to kiss him, but he pulled back quickly, whispering, "Go easy. I seem to have run into a brick wall somewhere."

They both laughed as she very gently touched his bruised jaw. They relaxed and gave each other the freedom to be who they were, strangers from two different worlds, but lovers even so.

Later that night, after Toshi returned to his home, he and his father spoke of the future. The purpose of Tatsume's visit had been to plan their meeting with the family of Toshi's promised bride. Because of the wealth of both families, detailed agreements had to be finalized and the date and place of the marriage arranged.

Toshi was quietly agreeable to all that his father requested, except two items, and on those issues, Toshi refused to relent. The marriage could be arranged and announced, but must not take place for at least six months and the Yamamoto estate in Seijo would not be part of any property agreement with the bride's family, nor could it be used by anyone other than himself and Ishikawa until his death.

Tatsume did not understand his son's strong attachment to the Seijo property since Toshi had only lived there for the three years since his return from Oxford. However, he chose not to argue with him on this minor point. Their family estate holdings, apart from this property, were immense enough to satisfy any agreement that would be arranged with the Matsuda family.

In this regard, both father and some agreed that the large, modern home in Shibya, which had only been used for visitors related to Tatsume's business, would become the designated residence of the newlyweds. That house was more suited for entertaining large parties or receiving important guests.

The date that Tatsume had chosen for the final arrangements to be completed and signed was one month from that night. They would meet at the Yamamoto estate in the Kyoto Mountains. This location was chosen so that Sukiyama could be present as the oldest living relative of the Yamamoto family. She would have the honor of giving final approval to the marriage arrangements. After all parties had signed the agreements, Sukiyama would seal the contract with her signature.

As Toshi watched his father write the date of the prenuptial meeting on the official letter to the Matsuda family, he felt as if he were moving in a dream with no control over the ending. A strange calm settled over him, almost as if he had told himself, '*It is done. This part of my life is over. I must begin a whole new life, now.*' Both he and his father signed the letter, then Tatsume poured them each a cup of *sake*. They lifted their glasses to Tatsume's toast: "May you have the wisdom and strength to fulfill your obligations to both family and country!"

They raised their cups and drank, though neither attempted to offer the traditional '*banzai*' ending to the toast. And to Toshi's surprise, his father poured a second cup of *sake* for each of them, asking Toshi to raise his cup one last time. Tatsume put his hand on his son's shoulder and offered a final toast.

"May the memories of your sweet love bring you peace in the lonely hours ahead."

Their eyes met, Toshi's in surprise and Tatsume's filled with a father's tears for his son's loss. When they had shared the toast and set the cups down, Tatsume embraced his son as if he were still his child of long ago. And Toshi spoke words which he could never have believed he would say to his father. "Will you stay with me tonight, father?"

Their work of the evening would set in motion the process of providing Toshiburo Yamamoto the honor and position which Tatsume had always wished for him. Yet, at the same time, honor and position were being purchased at a great price. Tatsume felt the pain in Toshi's heart.

"Let's walk a while in the gardens. The moon is bright and the night is clear."

Father and son stepped out into the moonlight and walked along the rocky pathway without speaking. When they came to the shrine near the hillside, Toshi stepped over the rocks to the altar and lit the candles and incense. There the two men stood, side by side, with their heads bowed before the altar. They offered their supplications to the gods they both worshipped, seeking whatever solace that each required. And for those few moments, their spirits became as one. Much later, they retired to seek their separate rest and to dream their separate dreams.

On Saturday, one week after his father's visit, Toshi knew that the prenuptial letters would be delivered and the marriage arrangements final within the next few weeks. He forced himself to consider the end of his relationship with Ana. No matter how painful that might be, he could not share his love with one woman, while he was promising to marry another.

The time had come to do what had to be done, to say goodbye to Ana. Toshi knew that Ana was making her own plans to leave Japan. And he also knew that he must have the courage to let her go to begin a new life, one that he could not share. He made the decision to approach her with everything that occurred after she left his home the night of his father's visit. But before Toshi could pick up the telephone to call Ana, it rang. He answered it to hear her voice.

"Hi, Tosh."

"Ana, I was just going to the phone to call you."

"Good, then perhaps we can spend a little time together today. I need to talk to you about some things that have come up…about my plans. Do you have time?"

"Of course. When and where would you like to meet? My day is free."

"Let's meet for lunch about 11 o'clock this morning. How about Bertram's near the station? I have some things to pick up down there and it's probably best to talk in a public place. You'll be safer from sudden attack!"

They both laughed as Toshi responded, "At least there will be witnesses if I need to call for police protection. Certainly, I'll be glad to meet you at Bertrum's. Is there anything I should prepare for? A major shock, whatever?"

"Well, since you've asked, yes, you can prepare for a shock and bring your car. We might want to take a drive after we talk or do something for the afternoon. Is that okay?"

Toshi felt his fears rising.

"Of course. I'll be there and I'll try to be prepared."

"'Bye now, see you at eleven."

Toshi set the receiver down very carefully, his mind filled with questions. She sounded so upbeat, as if she had good news to tell him. Yet his wisest judgment told him that was not even a possibility. He would know soon enough.

Ana was shaking when she hung up the telephone, but she knew it was time and she knew what had to be done and done quickly. Some words from an old Western song came to her mind: "You've got to know when to fold up and when to walk away." It was time for her to do both.

Later in the morning, Toshi and Ana were both on time at Bertrum's. They greeted each other at the door with a smile and a light kiss, then walked upstairs into the 'very British' atmosphere.

"I know this is hard to believe, Ana, but I've never been in Bertrum's. When I came back from England, I thought I would come down and try their food, but just never got here. I was so glad to get back to my own peaceful environment and a normal Japanese menu, I had no desire to check it out, though I'm sure I'll enjoy it."

"On my first trip to Japan, I stayed in Seijo and a few times I stopped in here for some real 'meat and potatoes.' You know that's the staple of the Western world. I never could find a good

Italian place, though. I doubt that 'Japanese-Italian' cuisine would ever be good enough for a Gabrelli, anyway."

A courteous waiter guided them to a table near the window overlooking the shopping street. They ordered their meal and drinks, then Ana put her arms on the table and leaned toward Toshi. She moved quickly to their harsh realities.

"I'm leaving Japan in three weeks. I have my ticket and I have my plan. This is it, Toshi. Ito has helped me arrange a part-time job at IEEC in the D.C. area. It pays enough for me to continue my doctorate at Georgetown, where I've already completed my coursework. I have only to enroll for the dissertation process. Everything has fallen into place sooner and much easier than I ever expected. Obviously, the timing is right."

Ana waited for Toshi's response. He picked up his glass and took a drink or two. He couldn't look at her and could barely get his words out.

"All this in a few short days?"

"I talked to Ito the day I returned from Kyoto. He started working on it right away. He mentioned that there were always openings in our D.C. office, and, since they know me there, they seemed quite happy to take me back."

Ana became quiet and more serious as she continued.

"Toshi, I need your help, now. You told me when I called from Kyoto that you would support me. You know we can't be together now."

She grabbed his hand and pleaded with him, "I warned you to prepare for a shock. It's a shock to me, too. One day it's just a possibility, the next it's a reality. Help me with this, Toshi. I have no other choice. It's the least you can do, under the circumstances."

He held onto her hand and tried to answer coherently.

"Please...just give me a minute...I guess...I was wrong. I'm not prepared for this kind of shock. When I think about our time together, it seems that I'm never there for you. I claim to love you and, yet, I'm the one that messes things up for you. I won't do that now, Ana.

You can count on my support. I know that you have to go, to get on with your life and fulfill the goals you've set. You have so much to offer this world, more than you can do here. We both know that."

A part of her was relieved by his response, but part of her still wanted to hear different words. But she knew it wasn't possible and pulled herself together to face what had to be done.

"Thanks, Tosh. I needed you to confirm what I felt was best. It's a big decision, and I knew you would be honest with me. In some ways, it's like a godsend, a way to do what I need to do for myself."

"It's timely, Ana. You deserve the best and I have no doubt that you will be highly successful."

Ana relaxed. He had given her the freedom to move ahead with the plans that must be made for the next chapter of her life. And she knew before she spoke that he could give her nothing else.

The waiter brought their lunch, and the enjoyed the touch of Western cuisine. As they ate, they continued to talk about her plans for leaving Japan, what would happen to her little house, and how Miyuki would make it without her. But Ana did not mention Mishima. She would not mention him to Toshi. Toshi would know only a part of her plan, only the part that included him.

After leaving Bertrum's, they enjoyed a pleasant afternoon shopping for things Ana would need for the trip. When Toshi drove her home, they talked about plans for their final evening together. Ana had already made that decision. She would tell him that they must meet Sunday night, for after she talked with Mishima, she would not see Toshi again. There were not many days left.

"Toshi, I've already confirmed the position with IEEC. After this weekend there won't be much time for us. There are so many arrangements to be made."

"What would you like to do? Shall we go back to the mountains for the weekend, or down to Kyoto for a few days? There are no restrictions; I'll take care of everything."

Ana leaned toward him and spoke with emphasis.

"When I said *soon*, I meant that we must say our good-byes within the next few days. I'll be packing, finishing up at the office, and leaving. If we're going to get together at all, it will have to be this weekend. Can you come to my place one last time? Can you come on Sunday night?"

Toshi leaned his head down in shock. So this was the finale. It had come much too soon. He felt suddenly ill, but he knew he had no right to protest. He had just signed his life away to another woman. And Ana had warned him when she called from Kyoto what had to be done. But he couldn't hold back his feelings.

He whispered a final plea, "It's too soon to be over, to be finished between us. Are you saying that we can't be together after Sunday? Not even allow me to take you to the airport…anything?"

Toshi saw the flash in Ana's eyes. He knew the signs too well. There was no reprieve. She got out of the car without answering him and started to gather her packages from the back seat. Toshi jumped out to help her and they walked, without speaking, to the door. As they set her purchases down in the living room, Toshi broke the silence.

"Forgive me, Ana, your life belongs to you. I'll be here on Sunday night. Just tell me when to come and what you want me to bring."

Ana relaxed and put her arms around him.

"Come when the moon is up and bring the wine. You know I love you, Toshi. This is hard for me, but I can't be part of your life now. I have to find my own."

They said goodbye as they always did, but today their kisses were mixed with tears. When Toshi finally went to the car, he leaned back against the seat to catch his breath. The moment both he and Ana had dreaded had finally come. All the pieces had been put together and the future was upon them.

Now, whatever she offered him, he would accept, for Ana was the most precious gift that life could ever give. He would treasure every moment they had shared, both the good and the bad. Toshi made a promise to himself that their final moments together would be filled with the joy of their love. There was no other way to leave Ana. There was no other way to say goodbye to Ana Maria Gabrelli.

CHAPTER 18

"Let us kiss this rose this one last time, as symbol of a tender love expressed. This love...pure as these soft, white petals. This love...unfulfilled, yet never to be denied."

--Ana and Toshiburo, Farewell

Toshi spent the evening walking through the gardens around his home, attempting to find some peace of mind. Finally, he returned to the house where Ishikawa was waiting for him. The older man knew that all was not well and asked carefully, "What is it, Toshi? What can I do?"

Toshi did not raise his eyes, but proceeded to speak without emotion,

"When I was visiting with my father recently, I didn't realize how true his words were when he told me, 'Your future has come upon you, Toshiburo.' Well, it has come. Ana is leaving Japan. She intends to return to the States within the next week or two. Apparently, she's been offered a position in Washington, D.C. with her company there. But further, she's planning to complete her doctorate at Georgetown University and hopes to obtain a professorship in anthropology.

I certainly can't fault her for wanting to use her intelligence in a challenging way. We all must do that. And, of course, there is no future for the two of us now. Our relationship is all but over."

Ishikawa displayed no outward emotion other than the gentle manner in which he spoke to his friend.

"We both knew that she would have to leave Japan. Even from the beginning, we knew that. Ana could not do otherwise."

"Yes, we knew that." He looked at Ishikawa and asked the question that most troubled his heart. "What should I have done? When I saw her there...at the festival that night? Should I have pretended that I hadn't seen her? Should I have walked on by? Tell me what I should have done, Ishikawa."

"You did what you should have done. You have loved her and will always love her. That is what you should have done and what you will continue to do."

"My actions have brought us both a heartache that will never heal. Ana's tears are like a knife in my heart. I don't know how to live with such a memory."

"Toshiburo, we are all determined to live two lives. One comes to us without our choice, from our family and all the influences that await our first breath. The other life begins when we recognize that we are not totally bound by that which we have been given, when we discover that we can choose for ourselves. Yet, the choices we make are always grounded in those powerful influences from our birth.

You have chosen your own destiny, Toshiburo. You have chosen to fulfill your obligation to family and country as your first line of duty. You were free to make that choice, as free as you could allow yourself to be.

But the influences to which Ana was born are those which uphold the freedom of the individual above all else, above family, above country. Her destiny will always be grounded in that which is most precious to her, a complete independence of spirit."

"Was it, then, our destiny to meet and to love one another as deeply as we have?"

"Perhaps chance brought you together, but destiny has sealed your love, for there was a choice in it. You could each have walked away, and I'm sure you both struggled with what to do. But now, you have chosen different directions.

And, my dear friend, you need not carry Ana's burden. You are no more responsible for this heartache than she. No one can force love into another's heart, nor can anyone or anything force it out. You have both made that choice of your own free will.

Your relationship may end, but when we walked on the hillsides together, I saw in your eyes and in hers the depth of feeling that you have for each other. There can be no ending to such a love!"

Ishikawa walked to the stand beside Toshi's desk. There he poured them each a cup of *sake* and handed one to his friend.

"To what shall we drink tonight, Toshiburo?"

Toshi stood beside Ishikawa. As they raised their cups, the younger man smiled at his mentor and offered the toast. "To a love that will never end."

When they set their cups down, Ishikawa placed his huge arms around the slender frame of his friend to offer comfort and strength. Tonight, Ishikawa would watch over Toshi as he slept, for that fragile heart might need special care.

Ishikawa's counsel helped Toshi to clear his mind and to understand that both he and Ana must now face the results of their separate decisions. While Ana chose to accept the challenges of a new life, he chose to embrace the responsibilities of the old.

Toshi knew that the joy he and Ana shared together would long outweigh the sorrow they would share in parting. And this knowledge allowed him to face the last few hours with his lover determined to create a sweet memory that would last a lifetime for both of them.

On Sunday evening, when Toshi arrived at Ana's door, the sky was dark except for the moon rising over the city. She opened the door to find him looking very handsome in the black kimono from their Fujiview weekend. He was carry a bottle of champagne and a long, narrow gift box. Ana greeted him with a smile.

"So, we're matching…such great minds we share!" She was wearing the white and gold kimono from the same weekend. He laughed at the coincidence.

"Yes, it appears that we both believe in comfort!"

Ana took the champagne and set it on the counter.

"Well, now that the honored guest has arrived, let's have a party! But, I'm embarrassed. I didn't prepare a gift for my guest."

Toshi bowed politely and spoke with a smile.

"That's the benefit of being the hostess. You aren't required to bring gifts. However, you are required to be very kind to those who do."

Ana laughed and took the gift box while he left his sandals in the hallway. As Toshi walked toward the kitchen counter to pour the champagne, Ana asked, "What can I offer you in return for all of this?"

"I must be truthful, Ana. I've only brought champagne. What's in the box is not really a gift. But I will accept anything you wish to share with me."

She offered him a warm kiss, then laughed and pushed him away.

"Pour the champagne, '*kyuji*' (waiter), and come to the porch with me."

Toshi did as he was told. When he walked onto the porch, Ana was sitting on the futon, leaning against the large, soft pillows from her couch. The lanterns were lit and the atmosphere was filled with a special aura of peace, as if a blessing were being offered them on this last night together. Toshi could not believe they had wasted so much of their time in conflict, when they had been surrounded by such beauty. But he recalled that his actions had contributed to most of those difficult moments.

He handed Ana a glass of champagne and sat down beside her. They raised their glasses, each waiting for the other to offer a toast. Toshi spoke first.

"I raise my glass to the 'Angel Gabrelli,' the only woman I have ever loved and to the joy we have shared together." They touched glasses and took a sip. Then Ana raised her glass to his.

"And to you, my 'sweet samurai.' May our memories never fade."

After the toast, they set their glasses on the table beside the futon and shared their love with the intensity of those who were about to part.

Much later, when the moon was high and bright, Toshi whispered, "I have something very special to share with you, Ana. I'll get us another glass of champagne and then tell you about it."

When Toshi returned with the champagne, Ana was sitting on the rock wall that surrounded the garden pond. The lantern light shone against the gold in her kimono, giving her an almost ethereal glow. He caught his breath at the beauty before his eyes. Ana saw the gift box under his arm and asked with a smile, "Is the gift for me?"

To her surprise, he answered, "No, it is for me to share with you in a very special way."

Toshi handed Ana a glass of champagne and sat down beside her, placing the box on the rock wall. The lovers sipped their drinks in silence, savoring the natural beauty that seemed to enfold them in its power. Toshi felt that the gods were surely blessing them, if only for this last moment.

When they had finished their champagne, Toshi opened the gift box and very carefully lifted out a beautiful, long-stemmed white rose. He held the flower gently in his hand and began to speak in a voice filled with emotion.

"Ana Maria, I want to tell you a story that was told to me many years ago by my grandmother, and I have never forgotten it. It was told for a purpose. You will know the purpose. The story is called, "The Legend of the Rose," and it goes like this.

Many, many years ago, a young samurai had completed his long, arduous training and was preparing to take his place in the world. Before he went, he knelt before his elderly mentor and asked him the two most important questions in the life of a samurai.

'O wise one, tell me, how will I find the purpose for my life? And how will I know my true love?'

The sage samurai looked down at the young man kneeling before him, so innocent, so hopeful, and offered him this wise counsel.

'Your life purpose will not be hard to find, for you have been trained well and are prepared to offer your total energies for those causes which are just and true. But, my young friend, I must give you a warning about your search for true love.'

Then the sage samurai turned and plucked a pure, white rose from the bush behind him. He held it gently in his hand and continued his admonition.

'This rose is a symbol of the innocence and purity of true love. As a samurai, you must beware, lest you share it foolishly or without careful thought, for you can only share this rose once in a lifetime. When the soft, white petals of the rose touch your lips and the lips of your lover, you will be bound to one another for eternity. You will never be free to offer that love to another.'

Then the sage samurai handed the delicate rose to the innocent, young man and smiled sweetly as he continued his counsel.

'As long as your heart is true, this rose will remain as fresh and beautiful as it is today, and your love for one another will never face. But if you share this gift foolishly, the rose will shrivel and die. So, too, will your heart, for it will become cold to the needs of those around you.

And, my young friend, this is the final warning: if your heart loses the power to love, you will never be able to determine that which is just and true. You will be destined to wander aimlessly, searching for what can never be restored. There is no shame so great as that of a samurai who has lost the power to love and, as a result, the very purpose of his life.'

Ana and her own 'samurai' sat for a long time without speaking. Both were touched by the message of the simple legend. Finally, Toshi lifted the rose to his lips and kissed it, then turned to Ana and asked, "Will you kiss the rose for me, Ana?"

She laid her head against his shoulder and, covering his hand with hers, brought the rose to her lips. Toshi felt her tears against his hand as she kissed the pure, white flower. He whispered to her, "I have found my true love, Ana. I have given you the power over my heart forever. I know that whatever is required of me, the memory of our love will give me the wisdom to determine that which is just and true and the strength to perform my obligations with honor."

Ana could not speak. Toshi set the rose down on the gift box very gently. Then he took her hand and they offered their love to each other for the last time. No barriers could come between them now, for they had accepted their inevitable parting. They were fully aware that the love they shared was true, its power would never fade from their hearts, its promise was eternal.

The dawn was breaking when Toshi woke to Ana's whisper.

"It's over, Toshi. It's over now."

He did not protest, as he thought he might. The beginning of this love affair had been his choice, the ending was hers. Toshi prepared to leave and, as he did so, he placed the rose back in the box and explained to her, "I must keep the rose, Ana. It's all I will ever have of us."

Ana did not protest, for she knew that he had already given her a gift far more valuable than the rose and one that would enrich her life for as long as she lived. She put her arms around him one last time.

"Thank you, Yamamoto-san, for all that we have shared. You have given me more than you will ever know."

Toshi was touched by Ana's words and knew that he would carry them in his heart as he went into the barren places of life.

He dared to ask one last question, whispering it against her soft, dark curls.

"Will you ever forgive me for what I've done to us?"

She answered as only 'Gabrelli' could, with honesty.

"I have forgiven you…for your innocence."

Toshi smiled, understanding very well what she meant. He touched her face as he walked out the door. Ana waited a moment, hoping that he might turn back for one last embrace, but he did not look back. She shut the door and leaned against it, whispering through her tears, "It's over, Ana. It's over now."

But Ana knew that this love affair would never be over, for she carried within her body the most precious gift a lover can give. The future. It was time to prepare for that future, and Ana knew exactly what she must do.

■■■

When she arrived at the office on Monday morning, Ana's first concern was to visit with Mishima. She left a message on his telephone to stop by her office before his next appointment. Later, when Mishima walked into Ana's office to find out what was happening, she felt a rush of emotion. Perhaps fear or anxiety, she wasn't sure which, but she knew that she had to ignore it and move forward with her plans.

"Mishi, I need to talk with you about something rather personal. Could we have an early dinner tonight, after our planning sessions, just you and I? If you pick the place, I'll pay the bill. It's rather important."

"Of course, Ana. You don't have to beg me to have dinner with you, and you certainly don't have to pay the bill. It's always my pleasure, you know that."

Ana smiled at his kindness. "Thanks, Mishi. Come by my office after work then, and let's go down to the Ginza. We can stop at our favorite *ton-katsu* place on our way out of the city."

"I'll be there and ready for dinner!"

"Oh, by the way, don't mention this to Yuki. I'll take care of that if it comes up. I don't want her to feel left out, but this is just between you and me, Mishi. It's private."

Mishima stopped and looked at her, somewhat surprised, but she merely smiled. He assumed it had something to do with

Toshi and his upcoming appointment to the embassy. It was now public knowledge, though everyone at the office was afraid to mention it in Ana's presence. Perhaps she needed his shoulder to cry on, and if so, he would willingly offer it.

Miyuki stopped by Ana's office after word, as usual, but Ana was relieved to know that she and Sato had plans for the evening. While they were talking, Mishima came in. Ana volunteered Miyuki's information.

"Guess who's going to dinner…with 'the Sato' tonight?"

Mishima raised his eyebrows, "You mean this is getting serious, Yuki? I think you did this a few times last week, too. What's up? Now tell us the truth!"

"Oh yeah, there comes a time when a woman has to accept the fact that her prince just isn't going to be coming by on that white horse thing. And, in that case, frogs start looking real good!"

They laughed at her, but both friends knew that Miyuki enjoyed being with Sato and certainly thought of him as more than a frog.

"Well, have a good time. Mishi and I will be thinking about you and sending out positive vibes. Be sure to let us know how things turn out now and then."

"Yeah, yeah, yeah…as if you cared. I know what you think of Sato, but you two go ahead and talk about me all evening. I'll fill you in later. You know, the truth is, he's not as wild in private as he acts in public. He's actually very respectful of me!"

They all laughed at that one, even Miyuki. Then they went their separate ways, promising to check in later to see how everyone's evening turned out.

When Miyuki left, Ana turned to Mishima.

"Well, shall we get on with it? Let's go eat!"

Mishima laughed innocently. "Let's do it!"

Little did Mishima know that he was about to face the most difficult moment of his life. One which would cause him his deepest sorrow, yet offer him his greatest joy.

CHAPTER 19

"Friends…redefining a relationship. Friends…seeing each other in a new light. Friends…offering their lives and their love to one another…as a gift."
--Ana and Mishima

The *ton-katsu* restaurant was fairly quiet at the five o'clock hour. The dinner rush came later when the huge downtown offices closed. Ana was glad they had arrived early, for she and Mishima could have a private corner to themselves near the back of the restaurant. They ordered drinks and their usual meal, then she lifted her glass for a toast to move into the serious side of their discussion. She was very nervous, but was also ready to test her own courage and the strength of Mishima's friendship.

Ana offered the toast, "Here's to good friends!"

Mishima raised his glass to hers and smiled as they sipped their drinks. Ana moved quickly to the purpose for their visit before she could lose her courage.

"Mishi, you are one of my two best friends. We've been through good and bad together for a lot of years. You've always been there when I needed you…and I need you now."

Ana felt her tears coming and swallowed hard so she could continue, but she couldn't keep her voice from shaking.

"This is where I'm at, Mishi. I'm in the middle of a bad time and you are the only one I know who can help me through it. But first, I want to say this…you have to be honest with me now! Please don't say anything to me just because you think I want to hear it. I don't need any cover-ups. I'm going to tell you some hard truths about myself and it's up to you to decide how you want to respond."

Mishima knew from Ana's words that this was serious. He stopped drinking and leaned back against the booth, as if he were bracing himself for a blow. Ana delivered it and it was as painful to Mishima as if she had struck him.

"I'm returning to the States before the end of this month, Mishi." She swallowed hard and finished. "I'm going to have Toshi's child."

Mishima couldn't control his shocked reaction.

"O my god, Ana! My god, how could you have let this happen?"

Ana looked directly at Mishima. His eyes were closed and he appeared to be in pain. She touched his hand and whispered, "Don't say anything, Mishi. This was a conscious choice and mine alone. Toshi doesn't know, nor will he ever know! You're the only person I've told and the only one I'll ever tell, unless I'm forced to a different decision than the one I'm considering."

Mishi recovered enough to ask in a voice shaking with emotion, "And what is the decision you're considering, Ana?"

"Toshi has accepted the assignment to the embassy. He has also chosen to move ahead with a marriage that was arranged by his family years ago. Our relationship is over.

I can give him up, Mishi, but I will not give up my child, nor will I use this as a threat to force Toshi to stay with me. He's made his decision and I've made mine. His choice has canceled any claim he might ever have on this child."

Mishima could barely speak.

"How then, can I help you, Ana? I don't understand. If you wanted to make a different choice, I know people who could help you in a moment. But, if you're determined to go ahead with this, what can I do?"

Ana looked down, afraid to meet his gaze. She could hardly believe that she was going to say these words to this kind friend, but knew that she must. There were other choices, but none better. She barely whispered her answer, "You can offer us…your love…and your name."

Her words, spoken so quietly, reverberated through both their hearts like clanging bells. Ana was afraid to look at Mishima. She could only wait for his response. She closed her eyes and leaned back against the booth, waiting for whatever might come.

When Mishima spoke, she knew he was crying.

"O, Ana, how you break my heart! You know how much I love you and always have since the moment we met. There's nothing I would ever refuse you. Whatever you ask of me, whatever you want…it's yours."

Ana let her own tears come then. They were tears of relief and thanksgiving for the love of this dear friend. She spoke through the tears.

"I want you to be my husband, Mishi, the father of my child. You are the one person I've always loved for your kindness and friendship. I promise to love you as your wife."

Mishima took her hands in his and looked into her eyes. She met his gaze as he spoke.

"Ana, I know you too well. I know your heart and it doesn't belong to me. It never has and it never will. How can you say you'll love me as my wife? Please don't tell me something that you can never do. Be honest with me about this. What will happen to me, if he comes back to you? Will I be left alone again?"

"You have to trust my words, Mishi, they're all I have to offer you. I'm entrusting my life and the life of my child to you. You will be the only father this child will ever know and I will be your loving and faithful wife. Nothing will ever change that...do you understand?

Even if he came back to me tomorrow and begged me to stay with him...I would never do so. I'm making you a promise and nothing will change it, Mishi!"

Ana paused to allow Mishima to consider the promise she had just made to him, then spoke with strength.

"Don't think that I have no other options or that I come to you in desperation. I'm not afraid to care for my child alone. That's not an unusual lifestyle in my world. But, the truth is, I want you to be with us, Mishi. I know you will love us both and be the father my child should have.

There's nothing more I can say. And you must feel free to make your own choice, but we're going back to the States. If you choose to come with us, I'd really like to be married here with your family and our friends."

Mishima put his head in his hands and sat quietly for a long time. After a while, he reached out and took Ana's hands in his own, pressing them against his forehead to cover the tears coming from his eyes. He spoke haltingly through the tears. "Ana...I will give you my life...and all my love. I will do anything you ask of me...but I beg of you...please don't ever ask me to leave you."

Ana took a deep breath of relief and answered, "Mishi, I promise you, I will never do that!"

With great relief, Ana pulled his hands to her lips and kissed them.

"Thank you, Mishi, for your gift to us!"

The friends cried and laughed together and dried their tears and finally relaxed enough to enjoy their dinner. They both chose to put away their fears and sorrow. An atmosphere of excitement came between them now as they talked of plans for a wedding and for their future.

On the way home, Ana and Mishima were both quiet, thinking their own thoughts. He was afraid that he could never claim Ana's heart, afraid that her love for Toshi would always stand between them. She was thankful for Mishima who would do for her what the one she most loved could not do. Ana promised herself that she would never hurt this dear friend, that she would give him all the love the Toshi could not accept.

When Mishima walked with Ana to the door, he seemed to be struggling with something he wanted to say, but couldn't express. She encouraged him to speak the words.

"What is it, Mishi? Just say it, it's okay."

"Are you...going to see him again?"

She answered without hesitation, "The relationship is over. I will not see him again and he will not attempt to see me. Believe me, Mishima, it's finished."

He relaxed then and allowed himself to think of Ana as the woman who would soon become his wife. His dreams that began so long ago seemed to be coming true, but in such a strange way.

Ana kissed her dear friend goodnight and reminded him, "We have lots of plans to make. Think about the wedding and what we should do. Let's talk later tonight."

She called Mishima later in the evening to begin their planning. Mishima knew of a small Christian chapel near his family's home in Yokohama where they could be married with both Christian and Buddhist priests assisting. He would arrange the location and they could have a small gathering of friends at the home afterwards.

Mishima was especially happy when Ana suggested a short honeymoon trip to the Japan Sea as a beginning for their new life together. The more they talked of the wedding, the more excited they both became. As Mishima felt the excitement from Ana, he allowed himself to believe her words, that she would be a loving and faithful wife to him.

After they said goodnight and went to their separate dreams, Ana thanked God for Mishima and for his loving, humble spirit. Mishima's dreams were filled with the joy of loving Ana as he had always hoped, but never imagined, could be possible.

Over the next few days, everything moved quickly for Ana and Mishima. They included Ito in their plans immediately, for they needed his help to arrange employment for Mishima. Just a few days after Ito made the call, Mishima was assured of a position at the same IEEC office where Ana would be.

The couple moved quickly to confirm their wedding date and reserve the chapel in Yokohama. His parents were ecstatic, as they had known Ana for years and thought of her as one of the family already. While Mishima and his parents planned the wedding, Ana made reservations at a resort on the Japan Sea and for their flight to the States. Everything was fitting together like a giant puzzle.

Ana's head was spinning with the many plans that had to be made for just a simple wedding and a getaway to another land. An important part of that plan included her sister, Valentina. Val was very happy for Ana and Mishima. She had become well-acquainted with Mishima during his college years at Georgetown. He and Miyuki were much like Val's family, having spent so much time in her home as Ana's good friends. Val agreed to find a temporary home for them in the Washington area. They could decide later where they wanted to live permanently.

The only major hitch in all their planning came as a surprise to Ana, from her dearest friend, Miyuki. Ana and Mishima had asked her and Sato to stand up with them at the wedding, and Ana was paying for Miyuki's dress and the trip to Yokohama. In the midst of all this, Miyuki had said nothing except to affirm their decision and to happily participate in it.

Every came apart at the office party for the wedding couple just a few days before they were to be married and leave for the States. After all the speeches, the thanks, the farewells, and good luck greetings for the future, Ito asked them to give their toasts to each other. Mishima stood with his arm tightly around Ana, and, struggling with tears of happiness, gave his toast.

"To Ana, the woman I have loved from the first moment we met and now will be honored to call 'my wife.'"

The crowd clapped and cheered and shouted their 'banzai's.' Then Ana offered her toast to Mishima.

"And to Mishi, my dear, dear friend and now to be my sweet husband."

To everyone's joy, Ana leaned over and kissed Mishima with more passion than either of them expected. Mishima pretended to faint and fell into a nearby chair. Everyone went wild then, teasing and shouting, "More, more!"

While their friends were gathering around Mishima to congratulate him, Miyuki came up behind Ana, grabbed her arm and pulled her into a corner. Miyuki had been drinking and appeared to be very angry. She shouted her questions at Ana.

"What do you think you're doing? Have you lost every brain in your head? I don't even know who you are anymore! Just how many lives do you intend to wreck during your most recent tour of Japan?"

Ana tried to pull her hand away, but Miyuki held her grip. Ana tried to calm her friend.

"Don't interfere with things you know nothing about, Yuki!"

"You don't love him! It's a game with you!"

"You're very wrong on that point. I love Mishi."

"As a friend, you love him, sure! But not as a lover, not as a husband. He knows how much you loved Toshi. What will you do to him? Love him a while and then walk into someone else's arms?"

"Yuki, what's so wrong with what Mishi and I are doing? We've been a part of each other's lives, now we're simply extending our relationship to include marriage and family. What's so wrong in that? Am I taking him from you? Is that it?"

"Ana, I can't talk to you!"

"Of course not, you're drunk. You can't even think, let alone talk. Leave us alone, Yuki. I thought you, of all people, would support us. Are you my friend, or not?"

"O god, Ana, I've been through hell with you and Toshi. Wasn't I the one who was there when he was breaking your heart? Was that some kind of act you were putting on, pretending to love him? Now I turn around and it's Mishi who's the sweetheart.

Do you even have a heart? Who's next? Maybe Ito or Sato! Just let me know ahead of time so I can celebrate with you!"

Miyuki turned to leave, her face red with anger. Ana tried to pull her back, but Miyuki shook Ana's hand from her arm and ran from the building. Ana found Mishima and told him she had to leave, that something had happened with Miyuki and she had to talk to her. Mishima saw that Ana was visibly shaken, and put his arm around her to calm her down.

"She's drunk, Ana. You know how crazy she gets when she goes past her limit. She doesn't mean anything she says and I'm sure she won't remember even saying it tomorrow."

"Has she talked to you or said anything about this? Do you think she might have an agenda that I don't know about, with you?"

"She has never, in all our time together, ever expressed an interest in being anything but friends with me. In fact, there were times in college when we tried to be romantic, but it just wasn't there for either of us. She made that very clear to me. That's not it. I assure you, it's the alcohol."

"I have to find her, Mishi. It's too important to me. We can't celebrate without Yuki!"

Mishima looked worried.

"What will you tell her, Ana?"

Ana understood his concern and assured him, "I will assure her of my love for you and for her. Don't ever worry, Mishi, don't ever worry about the other. You are my only confidante in that regard!"

"But, what if she asks you directly? Can you lie to Yuki?"

"I will answer her indirectly and, if necessary, I will lie! Does that convince you?"

"Ana, please…we're in this together. If you must talk to Yuki, then do so. I trust you completely. If you need me to help with this, you'll call me, won't you?"

"Of course, Mishi. I'm sorry. We'll work it out."

Ana began to relax then. They were partners in a sacred deception and both were assured that neither would ever break that trust.

When Miyuki left the building, she ran to the nearest subway that took her to her downtown apartment. She was totally

214

shocked by what was happening and was aware that she had gone far beyond her limit of alcohol and was out of control because of it. But she had too many questions and was certain that Ana was not going to answer any of them. As Miyuki stepped into the apartment, she decided to go to the one source who hadn't spoken yet, the Honorable Yamamoto-san.

Miyuki dialed the telephone number she had from the night with Ana at the New Otani. Ishikawa answered the telephone almost immediately and, though she was shaking inside from fear, Miyuki tried to sound calm and controlled,

"Ishikawa-san, this is Miyuki Kitada. Ana Gabrelli is a good friend of mine and Yamamoto-san and I are acquainted through the intercultural seminars given by my company some weeks ago. I would like very much to speak with him or have him call me, if possible. It's in regard to Ana's welfare. I'm concerned about her and need to ask his advice."

Ishikawa was quiet a moment, then replied, "Yamamoto-san is not in the house right now, but is on the grounds. I will give him your message. What number should he call?"

Miyuki gave him her telephone number and hung up. She sat down, trying to collect her thoughts so that she could talk to Toshi if he should call back. She suddenly had no idea what to say. Within a few moments, her telephone rang and Toshi was on the line. He spoke to Miyuki as a friend, "Miyuki, I'm sorry that I wasn't in the house when you called. I'm concerned with your statement about Ana's welfare. Please tell me what does that mean? What has happened?"

Miyuki caught her breath and for a few seconds thought about hanging up. She was beginning to come down from her alcohol high, and she wondered if she should have interfered in this private affair. But she moved ahead.

"Please forgive me for intruding on your privacy, but I'm so confused about what's happening with Ana. She hasn't shared anything with me and we've always been so close..."

Toshi interrupted her, "Is Ana alright?"

"Things are so mixed up. I don't know if she's alright, but we've just had a 'going away and getting married' party for her and Mishima. They're being married next week in Yokohama, then they're returning to the States. Ana won't talk to me. I don't understand what's happening. I don't know where to turn for the truth! Do you know what's happened? Can you help me?"

Toshi felt as if someone had struck him very hard in the chest. He could barely breathe, but he knew that Ana's life was no longer any business of his, and he also knew better than to become involved in her private affairs. He was finally able to organize his thoughts enough to answer.

"Miyuki, I'm very sorry that Ana failed to tell you what has happened between her and me. Our relationship is over. I would never presume to tell you something that I felt was private between Ana and myself, but it seems that so much has changed that you should, at least, know this.

The decision to part was mine, not Ana's. My future plans will be made public this week. I think you might already know what that means. I've received an appointment to the embassy and my marriage arrangements have been finalized."

Miyuki drew in her breath.

"Oh my god, that explains everything! I was just so shocked that Ana didn't confide in me after all we've been through together. I beg your pardon, Yamamoto-san, please forgive me for approaching you with such personal matters."

Miyuki's voice faded away into tears. She had no idea how to end the conversation. Toshi tried to calm her.

"Yuki, listen to me for a moment. Ana and I love each other very much, but we have different goals and directions for our lives. We parted with deep respect for one another.

What Ana has chosen to do now is what she feels is best for herself and her future. I'm sure that she and Mishima care for each other very much and will support each other in all their endeavors. I encourage you to celebrate with them and give Ana the friendship she deserves."

"Oh, I'm so ashamed! I understand everything now. Please forgive me for disturbing you at your home."

"Don't worry about that, Miyuki. You and I are friends, too. We've been through some things together and I want you to feel free to talk to me anytime and for any reason you wish. We'll always share a mutual love and concern for Ana."

"Thank you, Yamamoto-san, for straightening me out. I'll be fine, now. And I will support Ana and Mishi. They've always been close and I know they'll have a good life together. And I wish you good luck in your new responsibilities, too."

"I appreciate your calling me, Yuki, and I might offer a word of counsel. I've heard it said that best friends make the best partners in marriage. I know that Ana and Mishima will love and respect each other always. So…farewell, for now."

Toshi had left the door open for Miyuki to call again. She was glad for that and for his kindness in spite of her great discourtesy to this gentleman who would soon be a figure of political power in her country.

Miyuki was calm now and sorry that she had attacked Ana. She understood what had happened, but still felt a twinge of hurt that neither Mishima nor Ana had confided in her. She felt alone and separated from her close friends for the first time in all the years they had been together. Now it appeared that she was on the outside.

When the telephone rang, Miyuki was certain it would be Ana and knew how she must respond.

"This is Yuki."

It was quiet a moment, then Ana spoke, "We have to talk. I must explain what's happening. Can we get together?"

"Come to my place, Ana. Just the two of us. Do you have time now?"

"Yes. I have to be back at my house in a couple of hours, but I'll stop on my way out to Seijo."

"Please hurry!"

Miyuki was anxious to apologize and make peace with her dearest friend. She realized now that Toshi had left Ana with a broken heart and that she had added to Ana's suffering. She was so ashamed. As soon as Ana arrived, Miyuki pulled her into the apartment and put her arms around her.

"Oh Ana, please forgive me. I'm so sorry I spoke harshly to you. I can't believe I said those things to my best friend!"

"It's okay, Yuki. Things happened so fast. I had to make some hard choices and was afraid of involving you. Probably because I knew you wouldn't agree with my decisions."

"Ana, there's something even worse that I've done tonight. I know you'll be very angry and have every right to hate me. I did the only thing I knew. I had to find out what was happening. I called Toshi."

Ana was so shocked that she couldn't even reply. She sat down in one of Yuki's soft chairs and, holding her hands against her head as if in pain, spoke quietly, but without anger.

"Oh, Yuki, how could you do such a thing?"

"He told me that you and were no longer involved in a relationship. Couldn't you have told me that?"

"It was hard for me to tell anyone."

"But you told Ito and Mishima. One was finding you a job and the other was planning your wedding!"

Ana shook her head in despair.

"All I can say is this, I'm sorry that I hurt you. It's true, I was thinking only of myself and no one else. But I can't talk about it to you or anyone. That's just the way it is!"

"So you're taking Mishi with you? Are you actually afraid to go alone? Aren't you the strong, independent 'Gabrelli' I've known for so many years?"

"Sometimes people find a point of weakness. I guess I found mine. Mishi was there and I needed him. I can't explain it, except to say that this is what I want and need. We've always loved each other and we will be good to each other. What more can anyone ask than that?"

Miyuki was quiet for a long time, looking into Ana's dark eyes and trying to fathom what she saw there. Finally, she decided to make peace and let Ana go. She could not penetrate her friend's strong inner defenses.

Ana broke the silence between them.

"Please come to Yokohama with us, Yuki. Share our wedding celebration and be happy for us. How can we make it without you? I want you to be there to support me in this most important moment of my life!"

Miyuki knelt down in front of Ana and laid her head in her lap. She put her arms around Ana's waist and whispered, "Of course, I'll be with you. We'll celebrate your new life. Yours and Mishi's together. I love you both and always will! What would my life have been without you two? Now I know we'll always be together!"

Miyuki jumped up and ran into the kitchen, pulled down a bottle of wine from her cupboard, and turned to Ana.

"Let's celebrate…for all of us! Maybe I'll even find a sweetheart. I have to admit, Sato is beginning to look good to me."

They laughed together and drank their wine, making toasts to everyone they knew. Then, after their mini-celebration, Ana took her leave to pack for the weekend wedding. As she rode home on the train, she thought to herself, '*I wonder what Toshi said to Miyuki about our relationship.*'

But Ana would never ask Miyuki. All that was in the past now. The love affair was over. A marriage was about to begin.

CHAPTER 20

*A wedding...a promise...a gift of love, offered without
reservation. Yet, a final farewell must be said:*
"Sayonara...my sweet samurai!"
     --Ana and Toshiburo

When Ana arrived at her house from Miyuki's, she completed
her final packing. She had already shipped most everything to
her sister, Val, so all that was left were two large suitcases of
personal things and the clothes for the wedding trip. Since Sato
had offered to drive his van to Yokohama, she and Mishima
would send their wedding clothes and suitcases with him. They
would drive Mishima's car down and leave it there for his parents
to keep. They planned to buy a better car as soon as they arrived
in the States.

With everything happening so fast, Ana felt as if she were
walking in a dream, as if she were someone else watching things
happen to Ana Gabrelli from a distance. And 'Ana' would be
married tomorrow. The wedding dress hanging on the door
brought her back to reality. It was going to happen and, by her
own choices, she had created this moment. As she reflected on
those choices, Ana could think of nothing that was within her
own power that she would have changed.

The dress she chose for the wedding was simple, yet elegant.
The white taffeta, strapless gown with a full three-quarter length
skirt came with a white chiffon, long-sleeved overlay that gave it
a very dressy look. And she could use the dress, with or without
the overlay, for many occasions. Mishima's wedding suit was a
pale, gray silk.

The Matsamuras had given them both black pearl jewelry as
wedding gifts. His was a tie tack with matching cuff links. Hers
was a three-strand necklace with three-pearl cluster earrings.
They were quite beautiful. Mishima had wanted to give Ana a
diamond to go with her wedding ring, but she refused. She had
never cared about 'sparkling things,' but she loved the wide, gold
wedding bands they chose. Ana also insisted that they share the
expense of the rings, since he and his parents were providing so
much for the wedding.

Everything seemed to be in order for the beginning of this new chapter in Ana's life. She walked out onto the porch and stood listening to the garden sounds, enjoying the peaceful atmosphere around her. She shed some tears for the memories that still haunted this little place. How precious those memories would always be to her, but they must be relegated to the past, now. The telephone interrupted her reverie.

"Hey, Ana, are you ready for the big weekend?"

Mishima's question was somewhat hesitant, as if he feared she might say 'no.'

She responded cheerfully, "I'm more than ready. Let's do it!"

"This is it, then. I'll pick you up at 8 o'clock tomorrow morning and we'll be on our way."

"And how about you, the trembling bridegroom. Will you make it through all this?"

He laughed as if she were surely kidding.

"I've only been dreaming of this day for the past ten years and certain that it would never happen. You can be sure I will make it!"

"Then, my 'soon-to-be-husband,' we'd better try to get some sleep and I'll see you in the morning."

Ana's voice softened as she told him goodnight, for she was thankful for Mishima, more than she could ever express.

"Goodnight, 'sweet prince of a guy.'"

Mishima was touched by her sweet words. He felt as if Ana had thrown him a kiss, and he needed that. He was more afraid of the future than she, for he was too aware of the depth of Ana's love for Yamamoto. Mishima questioned her ability to release the past and embrace the future so quickly. Though he wanted to open his heart to her and say, 'Goodnight, my dearest, dearest love,' he could only reply, "Goodnight, Ana. Tomorrow will be the happiest day of my life…and I promise to be there on time!"

Ana hung up the telephone and took one last look around. Everything seemed in order and ready for tomorrow's event, so she dragged the futon onto the porch and laid down for the night. Through the next few hours, Ana tried everything she knew, except alcohol or drugs, to go to sleep, but it wasn't going to happen. Her mind was filled with Toshi and she realized, too late, that she should have spent this last night with Miyuki. They could have laughed and talked and drunk wine together until they'd fallen asleep with their craziness.

By two o'clock in the morning, Ana knew what she had to do and she did it. She dialed the number. Of course, Ishikawa answered.

She asked quickly, before she lost her courage, "Ishikawa, is Toshi awake by any chance?"

"I believe that he is, but, if not, I'll wake him immediately. Are you alright?"

She laughed, "I'm sure you know the answer to that question."

"Yes, Ana, I know it. Wait just a moment. He will want to speak with you."

"I haven't much courage left, I think you should hurry."

"Please don't hang up. He'll be right here."

Within a few moments, she heard Toshi pick up the phone.

"I wasn't asleep, Ana. I know from Miyuki what's happening and that you'll be leaving tomorrow. I've spent the night worrying about you, but was afraid to call for fear you wouldn't want to hear my voice. Tell me what you want me to do. Do you want me to come there, to be with you tonight?"

"No, no, it's too late for that! I just wanted to hear your voice. I'm packing and getting ready to begin this new life, but I'm having trouble erasing some memories that are haunting me."

She couldn't stop her tears. Though Ana's tears broke his heart, Toshi knew that he must control his own emotions in order to comfort her.

"We have beautiful memories, Ana, please don't try to erase them. Neither of us can go into the future without the memory of our love for each other."

"Is it just a memory, Toshi? Is it just something left over from the past to recall now and then?"

He didn't answer for a while, then he tried to speak coherently.

"Don't say those words to me, Ana. You know the answer as well as I. I'm only a few minutes away. Please, let me be with you this last time. We need to help each other through this night."

"No, we can't do that! I'm sorry, Tosh, I shouldn't have called you. It's just that I…I just needed to know that you're there, that you won't forget, that's all."

"Do you really believe there is any way I could forget the 'Angel Gabrelli' who swooped down from some heavenly kingdom and knocked me off my feet? The memories we share are the most precious gifts we have given each other, Ana. They are with us always. So keep them in a safe place and don't be afraid to go there when you're lonely. I'll meet you there anytime you choose. We'll be there to comfort each other."

Ana was quiet for a few moments, thankful for his loving words. There was nothing more she could say. Everything had been said except a final goodbye.

"Sayonara, Yamamoto-san, and thank you for your kind words. I'll miss you, but I'm sure we'll be seeing each other often, in our 'safe place.'"

She hung up the telephone quickly and laid back on the floor. Ana couldn't bear to hear him say goodbye. She was certain that Toshi would not call her back, but there were some final thoughts she had to share with him. And, only when they were expressed would she find the courage she needed to go, with a free heart, into the future.

Ana found some stationery in one of the boxes she had left in the cupboard. She sat down on the floor and wrote the words that had to be shared, as much for her own comfort as for his. When she had finished, Ana knew that Toshi would treasure this last communication from the one he loved, for the words came directly from her heart.

She prepared the envelope and walked outside to put it in the outgoing mail box. The wedding would be over when Toshi received it. And it was best that way. When she came back to the little house, her heart was free and she was ready to look forward to the life ahead. And had chosen that life of her own accord, and she knew that it would be good.

In spite of her emotional night, Ana was awake early the next morning. Mishima came exactly on time with Sato's van. They loaded everything and within a short time they arrived at the Matsamura home near Yokohama. Ana had visited Mishima's family on several occasions over the past few years and knew them as kind, loving people, who had always welcomed her with open arms. Now, they could welcome her as one of their own family.

The Matsamura family lived on a large truck farm outside of Yokohama. The property had been in their family for many years and had provided them an excellent living. The beautiful, old house was now used for guests and would be the center of the wedding celebration. But the family lived in a lovely, modern home where Mishima had grown up. It was totally Westernized, and even the furniture was 'Early American' style.

Junichi and Yoko Matsamura were a modern Japanese couple who had the money to travel and to enjoy all the comforts of life, and so they did both. They had worked hard during their early years to expand their farm which now produced the huge peaches, pears, and strawberries that were found in grocery stores throughout Japan. The Matsamura's employed many farm workers and were, indeed, successful entrepreneurs.

Mishima and his older brother, Akira, were the beneficiaries of their parents' hard word and subsequent wealth. Because Akira had chosen to remain as a partner with his parents on the farm, it was understood that the farm would be his. But his parents provided well for Mishima in every other way and he and his brother were good friends.

Everything fell into place for the weekend wedding. Ana thought to herself at one point, '*It's almost as if this were meant to be!*' She found it easier with each passing moment to catch the spirit of joy from their friends and Mishima's family, and from Mishima himself. Ana could hardly resist this circle of love and responded with her own loving spirit.

The wedding took place in the early afternoon on Saturday. The small, Christian chapel was set on a wooded hillside near Yokohama, overlooking a small bay that led to the Pacific Ocean. The day was bright and sunny with a slight breeze that touched the many tiny bells hanging throughout the chapel. Their movements gave a soft musical background to the ceremony, as if in joyful accompaniment.

The bride and groom were stunning in their wedding finery. Mishima, dark and handsome, with Ana's arm on his, was beaming with happiness. Ana wore the white dress, choosing not to wear a veil, nor to carry flowers. But Yoko had given her a row of white apple blossoms to hold her long curls back from her face.

Before they walked into the church, Mishima looked at Ana and spoke from his overflowing heart.

"The flowers look like a halo above the face of an angel. This is the happiest day of my life, Ana. You are my angel and I pray that I can bring you the happiness you deserve."

She whispered her thanks to him, "Thank you for those sweet words, Mishi. Your love is a gift that I treasure."

But she recalled Toshi's words to her, just a few hours ago: *'How could I forget the Angel Gabrelli?'* Ana held tighter to Mishima's arm. Miyuki and Sato walked behind them, Sato in a dark gray suit and Miyuki in a pink, cocktail-length chiffon.

Both priests spoke in Japanese, yet the ceremony and vows were in the Western style. Ana and Mishima made their promises to each other and exchanged rings, then knelt together to be served the wedding sacrament by the Catholic priest. After the sacrament, the Buddhist priest confirmed their marriage with a special blessing.

When the couple stood, they turned to their friends and gave each other a sweet wedding kiss. Of course, this resulted in a standing ovation among many cheers and much clapping. Then they walked to the chapel door and happily greeted their guests as everyone left for the wedding party at the Matsamura home. After the guests were gone and they were alone, Mishima took Ana's hand and guided her back into the chapel. She could tell that he was struggling for words. Mishima sat down on the arm of a pew and pulled her close to him. Looking into her eyes, he asked the questions that troubled his heart.

"Ana, can we be truthful here in this place? I must ask you just this one time, before we begin our life together as husband and wife. Can you ever truly love me without thinking of him? Will his presence always stand between us? Please don't betray me with lies, not now. I need to know your true feelings, whether or not they're what I want to hear."

The intensity of Mishima's love for her brought tears to Ana's eyes. She looked at him and, in some ways, saw him for the first time. Before this day, he had been her confidante and friend. They knew each other inside out. Mishima would know if she lied to him. But at this moment, she was looking at him as her husband, the man she had promised to love and to cherish.

And beyond that, he was the man who had chosen, of his own free will, to love and care for her child.

Mishima was a beautiful young man, strong and sturdy in build with wide, black eyes that flashed with fun or anger. He loved people of every age and he loved laughter and parties. She had seen him in every setting and had found him to be true to himself and his friends. She spoke from her heart.

"Mishi, I made a promise to you today. When I said those words, I meant them. There was no one but you and I before the altar, and there will never be anyone standing between us unless your fears put him there.

When I asked you to come with me, I let him go. Now, I'm asking you to let him go as well. If you don't, he'll remain a shadow over us. He is the past, Mishi, and we are the present and the future. This is our time, just yours and mine and our child's, who we will share as partners and parents."

Ana's own words seemed to open her heart to a new dimension of love for Mishima that she had never felt before. She put her arms around him and kissed him like a bride sharing her love with her husband for the first time. When she pulled away, they smiled at each other and Ana whispered to Mishima, "I do love you, Mishi. Now…let's go party!"

Mishima smiled and returned her kiss, still somewhat afraid of expressing his true feelings for the woman he had loved for so long.

The bride and groom endured much teasing as they walked in late to their own party. The guests were already eating and drinking and having a great time doing both. When the couple arrived, they received many toasts and loud cheers. And in the midst of the celebration, they cut their wedding cake and everyone enjoyed the afternoon.

Since the couple were flying back to the States right away, their wedding gifts were in the form of money. Mishima's parents had been more than generous, offering the finances for their wedding party and also a large sum of money to help them purchase a home in the States. Val and Roger had sent greetings, but promised that their family party would come later, when the newly-weds arrived in the States. Ana and Mishima were well-provided for by friends and relatives.

Much later in the afternoon when everything was quiet at the Matsamura home, Ana and Mishima said their warm and tearful farewells to Mishima's family and all their friends. Miyuki and Sato were taking them to the airport in Yokohama where they would fly to a resort on the Japan Sea for three days, then depart out of Tokyo for the States. Ana and Mishima would not see this loving group for a very long time.

The honeymoon couple caught everyone's eye as they registered in the lobby of the seaside resort. They were each as beautiful as the other. Mishima's muscular build and dark Oriental good looks and Ana's dark eyes and black, curly hair gave them the appearance of being very special people. They walked with their arms around each other, laughing and talking together. Everywhere they went, people responded to them with smiles and greetings.

Finally, Mishima turned to Ana, "Do we have a sign on our backs that says 'These two people just got married and are now on their honeymoon!'?"

"I don't think we need a sign. We're the only ones here who are so brazen as to put our arms around each other and kiss in public. That says a lot!"

"I love all this attention…maybe they'll start asking for our autographs."

Mishima leaned over, right in front of an elderly couple, and gave Ana a long, passionate kiss. The woman pretended to cover her eyes, but couldn't help but watch. They all laughed together. Mishima had rented a small cottage close to the sea and some distance away from the resort crowds. Here, they could sit on their tiny porch and watch the waves rush in or do down to the water for a swim. The cottages were built so they seemed to have their own private space along the shore.

After checking in and getting settled in their cottage, the couple changed into casual clothes and walked along the seashore. Mishi put on his white jeans over his swimming trunks, grabbed his red t-shirt and went out on the porch to wait for Ana. She had fun dressing in the wild outfit she bought for this special occasion. It was a long, multi-colored, wrap-around skirt over a hot pink bikini. She was celebrating two happy events: her marriage and her first experience with the sea.

When she met her husband at the door, Mishima feigned shock at what he saw.

"Oh my god, are you really going out in public like this, with only one weak bodyguard? I'll be mauled and left for dead!"

She laughed and asked, "So, you like it?"

"I won't even attempt to answer that foolish question! Let's risk it."

He took her hand and they walked down to the beach where Mishima swam while Ana sunned on the blanket. When he came out of the water, they strolled arm-in-arm in the sand and the surf. They watched as the sun began to go down and the sunset reflected across the waves. After a while, when the sun was gone, they sat on the blanket watching the moon rise. They talked about their perfect day, the beautiful chapel, and all the love that their friends and family had shared with them.

The happiness of their day and the beauty of the night filled them both with a sense of peace. After a while, Ana turned to Mishima.

"Let's go back to the cottage, Mishi."

They folded up the blanket and walked arm-in-arm to their tiny 'house by the sea.' As they stepped onto the little porch, Ana turned around to look at the moon shining over the water. She spoke in an awed whisper, "It's so beautiful."

Mishi was touched as well.

"An appropriate ending to a beautiful wedding day."

Ana turned to her dear friend and husband, offering him a warm kiss. They walked into the cottage arm-in-arm.

When Ana came into the bedroom after showering and changing into her nightgown, she found that Mishi had opened the shoji doors. The moonlight and sea air made it seem as if they were still on the beach. He was sitting up against a pillow with his arms behind his head, looking at the sea. Ana walked around the futon to his side and sat down, facing him.

She whispered, "You know I love you, Mishi."

She laid her head on his chest and put her arms around him. Mishima pushed Ana's wet hair back and kissed her lightly on the cheek. But he whispered words that chilled Ana's heart.

"Ana, you were more right than I. I don't understand it after such a beautiful day, but I'm the one who's haunted by ghosts.

It's hard for me to put away my fears. I know how much I've loved you for so long. And because of that, I understand only too well how you have loved him. That kind of love can't easily be forgotten or replaced by another. Maybe we both need more time."

Ana was stunned by Mishi's words and pulled back from him. She touched his lips with her fingers, as if to silence him.

"I understand what you're saying and perhaps you do need more time, Mishi, but I don't. My ghosts were exorcised in the chapel this afternoon when I gave you my promise. I meant it. And you made a promise, too. Everything was perfect for us today."

Ana leaned down and whispered, "They say timing is everything, Mishi. Don't take too much time."

She gave him a quick kiss on the cheek, then rose and walked into the sitting room to leave her husband with his own tormented thoughts. Ana understood what Mishima was saying, but she also knew that they had to be close of they would lose everything they had hoped for their future.

After a while, Mishima came out of the bedroom to find Ana sitting in a soft chair, looking at the sea. He knelt down in front of her and whispered, "You must teach me how to love you, Ana. All I know is what I feel. I'm only afraid that I can never replace the happiness he has taken from you."

Ana breathed a sigh of relief.

"You just did, Mishi. We're okay now. We'll be okay!"

The promises they had made before the altar that day were sealed by their expressions of love to each other. The joy they shared in those first moments as husband and wife gave Mishima the courage to overcome his fears of loving Ana, and gave Ana the strength to put her memories away in a safe place.

• •

On the afternoon of Ana's wedding, Ishikawa walked out to the garden where Toshi was resting. He placed his hand on his young friend's shoulder.

"You may want to read this."

Ishikawa handed Toshi a small envelope addressed to him. Though Ishikawa had never seen Ana's handwriting, he somehow knew that the letter was from her. Toshi took the letter and turned it over in his hand. He gave it back to Ishikawa.

"I'm afraid to open it. This is not a good time."

"Then I shall read it to you. She wanted you to have it today or it would not have come today."

Toshi whispered, "This is Ana's wedding day, Ishikawa. If you must torture me further, then do so. You're the one who will have to pick up the pieces of my heart and put them back together!"

Ishikawa opened the envelope. When he saw the first few words written on the page, he felt his own heart breaking. He knew that Toshi was right.

"I will put the letter away, Toshi, and when you feel strong enough you may want to read it...or you may not."

"No, Ishikawa, you're right. I need to hear it now. After all, I'm the one who brought this day about. She shouldn't have to carry all the burden of it. Will you read it to me? I don't think I could look at the words."

Ishikawa read the first few words silently, then handed the letter to Toshi as if it had burned his hand.

"These words were meant only for you. I cannot read them." But Ishikawa stayed close by to comfort his friend.

Toshi held the paper in a trembling hand and forced himself to read Ana's message from her heart to his:

> To my Sweet Samurai,
> "If you ask me to love you, I will do as you say.
> If you ask me to leave you, I will turn and walk away.
> There is only one thing you must not ask me to do.
> You must never ask me to empty my heart of you.
>
> For you are my sunlight, my bright evening star.
> You are my lover, my sweet gentle friend.
> You are the one who has set my heart free.
> You are all that there is, or ever shall be, for me."
>
> Your 'Angel Gabrelli'

The garden was filled with a deafening silence. Toshi leaned over as if in terrible pain and, holding his head in his hands, muttered, "My god, O my god, what have I done to us?"

Ishikawa put his hand on his friend's shoulder and gripped it hard. He answered Toshi's plea in a firm, strong voice.

"You and Ana have both done what you had to do, and that is the end of it!"

For a while it was quiet in the garden, then Toshi whispered the truth that he would face for the rest of his life.

"No, Ishikawa, for the first time since we met, I must contradict your judgment. Though Ana and I must each do what we have to do, it will never be over between us. There will never be an end to it...and I will carry her pain in my heart, even through eternity, for I have caused it!"

CHAPTER 21

"With the anticipation of new life…a new love blooms."
--Ana, Mishima, and Mikoto

In the weeks following their wedding, Ana and Mishima were busy with the many adjustments required in a marriage relationship. However, this new dimension of commitment was a much smoother transition than usual because of their many years of close friendship.

Ana's gratitude for Mishima's sacrificial love allowed her to share more openly with him, being aware of his fears. As she supported Mishima in his new roles as husband and father to the child they were expecting, he became stronger and more self-assured. This inner strength allowed Mishima greater freedom to express his own hopes and dreams, and to become an equal partner in the marriage.

The newly-married couple entered quickly into their respective roles at the IEEC office in Washington. Ana's part-time position gave her the opportunity to move ahead with completion of her Ph.D. at Georgetown. Within a few weeks of their arrival in the States, her dissertation proposal was approved and Ana was hard at work on the writing.

The Matsamura's most pressing concern now was housing. They were comfortable in the small apartment that Val had found for them near Georgetown, but they were both anxious to find a permanent home before the baby arrived. Mishima was especially concerned that they have a place that would reflect both his and Ana's lifestyles. For this reason, he took over the home search project. Ana was perfectly comfortable with that for she knew that Mishima would do nothing without her consent.

For several weeks, Mishima used every spare minute in search of the location for their new home…and he found it. Rather than purchasing a lot for building as they had planned, he found an old country inn sitting against a small range of rocky hills in Virginia, southwest of Washington, D.C. The inn was located within ten miles of a rather quaint little country village and the freeway system still made it possible to drive to their city offices in reasonable time.

Ana and Mishima went out to Virginia on a Saturday morning for a serious look at the property. Leaving the interstate, they drove along a two-lane highway for a while to a turn-off that looked like a private drive with beautiful landscaping of huge rocks and evergreens on each side. A rustic wooden sign directed travelers to follow this road to "The Village of Rocky Hills."

Mishi turned to Ana with a smile of excitement.

"This is it, just down the road on the left is our possible new home! Watch for it now, there are lots of trees along here, but there's a sign you can't miss."

In just a few minutes, Ana saw the sign near a driveway, "The Inn at Rocky Hills." She was impressed. The inn was a large stone and wood structure that appeared to be very old. The front of the building was nearly hidden behind an overgrowth of birch and evergreens.

Mishima drove into the driveway and parked, then he and Ana walked along a rock pathway to the front door. He unlocked the door and they stepped into a rather small entrance area that must have served as an office for the inn. A double glass door opened into several larger rooms, each with a stone fireplace, a large kitchen-dining room and onto a screened porch. Ana could see there was an upstairs and an unfinished addition at one end of the house.

Her first comment was surprise. "Mishi, there are so many rooms! It looks like far more than we would ever need. We've both been living in such small quarters for so long, what would we do with all this?"

But he was so excited, that he began to tell Ana his dreams for their home.

"Honestly, Ana, when I drove up to this place, I saw everything exactly as I dreamed it could be. It's a very sturdy structure and it's built on levels that move back nearly against the rocky hillsides. We could open up the rooms by removing some walls, building large windows, and creating spacious living areas. In the back is a place for a large deck, and we could add porches on the second floor.

And back along the hillside there's a place around the small stream where we could have a Japanese garden. I can see so much possibility here for a beautiful home that would be worth a great deal of money in the future. I've already asked the real estate agent about the price and it seems unbelievably low. She's had it on her hands for so long, that she'll deal with us on most any reasonable terms. I don't think we would have to use even half the money from my parents for the purchase, so we could use the extra to remodel. What do you think, truthfully, now?"

"I think it looks like a major headache and I'm working on two major ones already. But if you're prepared to take it on and think we can afford it, you're the one with the dream. I'd say, 'go for it!'"

They walked to the back of the house where there was a small porch and beyond that the yard stretched back to a stream running down from the steep hills. There were birch and evergreen trees growing along both sides of the little stream. After they had walked all around the property, Mishima was still excited.

"I don't want to do anything you wouldn't approve of, Ana, but if you really mean it…to go ahead, I think we should do it! Are you sure you'll be okay with that? It's our home, you know, not just mine."

"Go ahead, Mishi. I'm sure we'd love it here, especially if you really can do all those wonderful things you're dreaming about. It will be a beautiful home, I'm sure!"

Mishima called the agent as soon as they got back to the city to check on the details of the purchase. All evening they could talk of nothing but the possibility of owning a country inn. By the time they went to bed that night, Ana knew that the house would be theirs.

The arrangements for the purchase were completed quickly and the remodeling began. At first, Ana spent time with Mishima on the planning. But, at one point, she had to let it go. She was working hard to complete her dissertation before the baby came and also working her part-time job at IEEC. Ana trusted Mishima totally with the remodeling project. He had the dream and understood the structural design, almost by instinct.

During the months that Mishima was so busy with his job and the house project, he was gone most of the time. It was then that Ana allowed herself moments of quiet reflection. There were times when she felt that perhaps she was living a lie in the marriage. But she truly loved Mishima in a very special way. Ana also knew that in order to face the future without the one she most loved, she must enter that safe place of memories and dwell there, now and then. And that is what she did, without guilt.

Ana could not deny herself the pleasure of those memories, for she found strength in them. It was Yamamoto, after all, who had opened her heart to the meaning of love. It was Yamamoto who had given her the most precious gift that life could offer, the child who would soon be born. Often, after Ana's journey into the past, she found release in the tears that came with the memories. And then, as if she were cleansed of the pain, she felt stronger and more able to share her love freely with the one who loved her with his whole heart.

On the afternoon of their six-month wedding anniversary, Mishima called Ana at her office.

"Ana, happy anniversary on our first six months! I'll pick you up early today, about 3 o'clock. We're going to celebrate at our new home. I'm so excited. You're going to love it!"

For the last few months, Ana had not even gone out to "Rock Hills," the name they decided to use for their country home. Mishima was totally immersed in the project and she had never seen him so happy. She was convinced that he should become an architect or a major real estate builder, for he seemed to have a natural feel for everything involved in such projects.

She was caught up in his happy mood.

"I can hardly wait to see what you've done out there! Just remember, don't surprise me too much; I may burst with joy!" They both laughed at the reference to her pregnancy.

"No way would I do anything so drastic!"

"Remember, Mishi, I know you're excited, but please, no parties yet. I want to wait until the baby comes and we have some furniture, at least a table in the kitchen."

"No major parties, maybe just a minor one. I'll see you at three o'clock."

At three o'clock sharp, Mishima drove up to Ana's college office and walked in the door. She was just picking up her bag and some books to take home for the weekend, even though she was certain she wouldn't spend much time on her studies. More than likely, she and Mishima would spend their time daydreaming about what to put in their new home. She hurried out the door and ran into her husband's arms. He gave her a warm kiss.

"It's a happy day, Ana!"

"I'm ready for the unveiling, let's go!"

When they drove into the driveway of their home, the first thing Ana noticed was the new sign. It was built of gray, rustic wood and stone. The name carved into the wood was simply, "Rock Hills" with the address in smaller letters beneath the name. Then she saw that the whole front of the house had been refurbished. The original rock had been polished clean and was surrounded with new gray siding that matched the sign.

The trees and bushes around the front had been trimmed and new plantings added to make it look like a small park. The house could barely be seen from the road and only by entering the private drive could one follow the rock pathway to the front door. They walked up to the door where Mishima stopped.

"I have a very special gift for you, Ana."

He handed her a large, gold key that was made especially for this occasion. The words, "Rock Hills" were engraved on one side, and on the other was, "The Matsamura Home" and the address. She kissed the key and her husband and unlocked the door.

"Thank you, Mishi, for this amazing gift!"

Ana walked into the beauty that Mishima had created. She didn't recognize anything from their first visit. Walls had been rearranged so that all the rooms were spacious and all had been painted off-white. Every room was filled with light from huge windows and glass doors that led to the deck and allowed nature to participate fully in the design of the home. The kitchen and dining room floors were covered with a rusty-beige ceramic tile, but every other room was carpeted in a soft, beige burbur.

Ana was nearly breathless at the transformation. The house was like new.

"Mishi, it's beautiful! I can hardly believe this. It was so dark and depressing before. You've let all the light and beauty inside. We won't need much furniture here."

"That's the way I designed it, as simple as possible, and a part of the natural setting around it."

They walked through every downstairs room, the living room, family room, a small bedroom, the dining area, and the kitchen. Ana noticed that the stone fireplace in the family room had been refurbished like the front of the house to look like new. Then they went out onto the screened porch off the kitchen where Ana could see how the other parts of the house had been changed.

Mishima had built a huge open deck across most of the back yard. Surrounding the deck was new landscaping of varied plants and flowers. Ana looked up at the house and saw that it was now a three-level home. Two stairways led from the deck to a narrow porch that spanned the upper levels of the house. One to the second floor, the other to a level slightly higher than the second, but built at the end of the house, close to the hillside.

Ana expressed her surprise at the changes,

"I'm totally amazed at what you've done! How could you even imagine all this?"

Mishima took her hand and led her from the deck and back toward the hills. To enter this area they walked across a small wooden bridge that spanned the rocky stream. Here, among the trees and rocks, was a small Japanese garden with many new plantings of evergreens and flowers. And in the midst of the garden was a small Shinto shrine. Ana could hardly believe what she saw.

"I feel as if I'm on the grounds of a huge estate somewhere in Japan. You have definitely outdone yourself, Mishi! You know what this means, don't you?"

"No, what does it mean?" He looked surprised and somewhat anxious.

"It means that you must change your profession immediately! You have a great gift and it should be used. Can you imagine how many people in the city would love to come home to this at night…and would pay dearly for it?"

"I appreciate your confidence in me, my sweet wife, and maybe someday I will do what you suggest, who knows? But for now, I'm going to be one of those city people who love to come home to this!"

They walked arm-in-arm back toward the house. Mishima got a blanket and some pillows from the car and laid them on the wooden deck, then he went into the kitchen and brought out the dinner that had been delivered earlier in the day. First, came the wine and a special toast to their new home. Mishima held his glass to Ana's.

"This is for you, Ana. This is your new home."

Ana shook her head in protest, "No, Mishi, everything here is for us and you've worked a true miracle!"

He smiled at the woman he loved.

"You are my miracle, Ana! I love you so much and promise to give my life and my love to our sweet babe."

Mishima kissed his wife, his heart overflowing with the joy he felt in bringing such happiness to the one he loved. His joy was increased by the response she gave to his gift.

"Mishi, thank you for what you've done for us. I promise to love you always for your sweetness." Mishima chose to believe her.

They completed their toast and shard a carry-out Chinese meal on their very own new wooden deck. It was the perfect way to celebrate their half-year anniversary. After they finished dinner, Mishima turned to Ana.

"There's something I want you to see, Ana, if you don't mind staying out here for a while. It's really beautiful when the sun begins to go down behind these rocky hills."

They shared another glass of wine and waited for the sunset.

Suddenly, Mishima asked Ana a question that took her by surprise.

"Now that we know we'll have a son, may I have the honor of giving him a name?"

"Mishi, you surprise me! I haven't even thought about it, a name, I mean. We've got some time, I hope. Why do you ask me that?"

"I've been thinking about it for a long time. For some reason, it's very important to me. There's something I've never told you...or Yuki, or anyone for that matter. But I feel so strongly about it. I was born a twin, but my brother died at birth, and I survived. When I was young, I used to wonder if his death allowed me to live. I was always afraid to ask my mother and she could never speak of it. One day I found out from my father that my brother's name was Mikoto. If he had lived, we would have been "Miko" and "Mishi." If you agree, I would like to name our son Mikoto Toshiburo Matsamura."

Ana was shocked into silence. After a while, she whispered a question.

"Why would you suggest such a name, Mishima? Why would you use Yamamoto's name?"

He was silent for a moment, then spoke in an unsteady voice.

"Because I believe that it's only right that a son should bear his father's name."

Ana got up and walked around the deck, trying to control her sudden urge to cry. Mishima's innocence and honesty had touched her deeply. Never would she have chosen to do what Mishima suggested. She knew that it was not for her that he included the "Toshiburo." His Japanese background would not let him refuse the right of this child to bear at least a part of the name that should have been his. Mishima's feelings were for their child, not for her, and for that she was grateful. After a while, she came back and sat down beside him.

"Mishi, you can give our child whatever name you wish. You've earned that right. Just be certain that you know this: I would never have chosen to name him after Toshi. Not even if I had been alone, without you. As far as I'm concerned, Yamamoto gave up all his parental rights long ago."

Mishima put his arms around Ana and let her cry. He could not fathom her thoughts or her emotions. All he knew was that he loved her and would surely love the child that would be theirs.

He leaned down and placed his hands gently on Ana's stomach where the babe lay resting. He kissed her there and said, "Welcome to the family, Miko."

They laughed as Ana put her arms around her husband.

"Thank you for a beautiful name for our son. Thank you for all the gifts you've given me, and especially your love. I do love you, Mishi."

As the sun went down behind the hills and the darkness began to seep into the valley, the garden lights came on automatically. Ana saw that Mishima had arranged the lighting so they could walk anywhere around the house and through the garden area on a lighted path. And since the home was somewhat isolated in its location, the lights not only created a beautiful setting, but provided safety, as well.

"Mishi, you're a genius. This is truly a wonderful place. I believe you've thought of everything! When can we move in?"

"It's ready for us. We have so few possessions, we could move in tomorrow if you wish."

"Let's move in tomorrow, then!"

After a special telephone call they decided to make, the happy pair ended a perfect day with love and light hearts, in each other's arms.

■■

When Miyuki returned to her office from a business lunch at the Otani Hotel, she heard her telephone ringing. It wasn't quite 1 o'clock and she wanted a break from business before she started her afternoon duties, so she considered whether or not to answer it, but finally gave in and picked it up.

"Miyuki Kitada speaking, may I help you?"

To her utter amazement, she heard voices from America on the line.

"Hi Yuki, it's Ana and Mishi! We had to call you and tell you our good news!"

"Oh my god, you've had your baby! Tell me, tell me!"

Mishima answered, "No, that's not it. That won't happen for a while yet, but…Ana, tell her…"

"Yuki, we're sitting on the deck of our beautiful new home in Virginia. We just finished our first meal here and we're enjoying the moonlight and the gardens. When can you come see us?"

"You crazy people! I'm so jealous. You know there's no way I can come and you know why. Because you left me with all this work. There's a big, gaping hole here without you two. But I promise to come when your little baby is born, so I'll see everything then. Send me pictures of your house, every room, so I can pretend I'm there with you."

Mishima took the phone from Ana.

"And another thing, Yuki, we know that we'll have a little boy and you can call him by his own name now! We've decided to name him Mikoto Toshiburo Matsamura, 'Miko' for short.

240

Mikoto was the name of my twin brother who died at our birth and I've always wanted to give my first son his name."

Miyuki was quiet for a moment. She was shocked that they had chosen to add 'Toshiburo' to the baby's name. But her questions would be only for Ana, at another time when they were alone.

"The name is beautiful. So, how's our little 'Miko' doing, by the way? Are you taking good care of him, Ana? Or are you dragging him here and there, doing much more than you should? Knowing you, he'll be dead tired when he arrives."

They laughed at Yuki's comments and Ana answered, "He's fine and I'm fine. Mishi is keeping me out of the house project, so all I'm doing now is reading, writing, and some part-time work at IEEC. I'm going to quit the IEEC job, though, as soon as Miko makes his appearance. My kind husband says we do not need the money, and he wants me to rest up for moving and motherhood and being a professor."

"Yeah, I see you're cutting down to just three major projects now. Good for you, Ana. By the way, Ito has promised that as soon as Miko arrives, I'm on the plane to your place! So keep me posted, okay?"

Ana answered, "You'll be the first to know, we promise! Now we'd better let you get back to all that work we left for you. Take care of yourself, Yuki, and have some fun now and then."

"Oh yeah, I'm filling in your 'after-work' spaces with Sato now. We do all kinds of fun things like go to dinner and I carry him home. And go to the theater and I carry him home, and stuff like that. Great fun, you know, hanging out with an alcoholic."

Mishima laughed at her.

"I know you, Yuki. You wouldn't do any of that if you didn't care about him. Sato has his good side."

"I'll keep looking for it. Well, 'bye now to you guys and keep me posted with all your good news. See all three of you soon, I hope!"

Ana took the phone for a final goodbye.

"Tell everyone hello for us and we'll be calling. Yuki, we love you and miss you!"

Miyuki was excited after hearing from her friends and knowing things were going so well for them. She questioned using Toshi's name for their baby and wondered how that came about. Surely, Ana wouldn't do such a thing to Mishima. Miyuki wanted to get on the plane and go see her friends tonight, she missed them both so much.

Later that evening, Miyuki called Sato to tell him about Ana and Mishima and Miko. He was happy for them and asked if she wanted to go out and celebrate. Miyuki thought about it a couple of minutes, then decided, *'What the heck! I need to lift a glass to the happy trio and who can do that better than Sato?!'* They arranged a time and place to meet. Then she changed into more relaxing clothes and went to meet the only man in her life.

Much to Miyuki's surprise, Sato stayed sober all evening, just drinking enough to feel good and to talk about their friends and their good news and old times. She actually enjoyed being with him when he was able to converse on an adult level. And when he drove her home that night, she was shocked when he walked her to the apartment door and wasn't even stumbling.

Miyuki had a strange thought. *'I think this guy is as lonely as I am. It's true, we're two desperate people. Could this be the beginning of something more than friendship?'*

Miyuki asked Sato to come in and, of course, he said, "Yes!"

CHAPTER 22

*"A precious gift…preserved for all time stirs memory of a
garden night."*
--Toshiburo and Miyuki

Only a few days after her telephone visit with Ana and
Mishima, Miyuki received a message that shocked and surprised
her. A gray parchment envelope was hand-delivered directly to
her by special messenger. Miyuki signed her name to verify that
she had received it personally, then turned it over and over in her
hand, wondering what in the world was inside. In the center of
the envelope was a gold, official seal of the Department of State
for the Japanese government.

Inside the envelope was a card of the same color as the
envelope printed in gold ink. She read the words:

"Ms. Miyuki Kitada is invited to a private luncheon at the
Akasaka Prince Hotel 1:00 p.m., Tuesday. RSVP – Department
of State- The Honorable Toshiburo Matsushita Yamamoto"

Miyuki was speechless. Toshi's timing was uncanny as she
had just talked to Ana and Mishima a few days ago. She
wondered what in the world this meant. Surely, Toshi would not
use his official influence for private matters. Perhaps it had to do
with the IEEC programs. She hoped that was so. Miyuki picked
up the telephone and called the number printed at the bottom of
the invitation.

A pleasant young man answered with the official title of
Toshi's office. Miyuki identified herself, and the young man
asked her to please wait while he checked the file. He was back
in a moment.

"Yes, thank you for calling. The Ambassador will be
expecting you. A government escort will arrive at your office at
1:30 p.m. to transport you to the appointment. If you have
further questions, please let me know and I will relay them to the
Ambassador."

Miyuki hesitated. Since she had no experience with official,
private audiences with 'Honorable' people, she asked, "Will the
gentleman come to my private office, or should I meet him in the
lobby at the specific time?"

"Oh, he will come to your office to make certain that you are properly escorted to the meeting. Is there anything else you wish to know?"

Miyuki wanted to say, 'Yes, why am I being asked to a private meeting with the Ambassador?', but she didn't. All she could do was to wing it and hope that she didn't make any major *faux pas* in the process.

"No, I'll be ready at the designated time and thank you very much."

Miyuki had spent enough time in the States to be totally liberated from the official structures of the upper elitist society in Japan. She realized there was strict protocol and, because of her role at IEEC, decided to review the process with Ito. He was somewhat confused also. All he could do was to give Miyuki his best advice.

"Just be cautious regarding anything you say that might involve IEEC. This may simply be a way that Yamamoto can share personal information with you without drawing attention to your relationship. Since his appointment to the embassy staff, I'm sure he's under constant scrutiny, and anyone seen with him may also be a target for special concern. Go easy and watch what you say or do. It's possible that anything said there will be recorded."

"Oh, gee, thanks, friend! I needed that. What I really need is a crash course on how to speak in sign language or code. Now I'm upset. Why didn't he just call me on the phone like a normal person?"

"Most likely, because he's no longer a 'normal person.' He's a target now because he represents official government. Relax, enjoy, and be aware of his new position."

On Tuesday, Miyuki dressed with great care. She arranged her hair in a severe fashion, pulled into a tight roll up the back. Then she donned her classiest black, silk business suit with a high-necked jacket and a long, tight skirt with side slits. She wore simple, yet elegant, jewelry, a half-moon sterling silver pin with tiny diamond studs and earrings to match.

To clarify the message that this was a 'business lunch,' Miyuki carried her dove-gray leather brief case with shoulder strap, gloves, and shoes to match. When she looked at herself in the mirror, she couldn't help but ask, 'Now, why in the world can't I snag a rich, powerful businessman?!' She was, indeed, a stunning woman.

Of course, Miyuki's entrance to the Center the next morning caused a major uproar. Everyone trailed in and out of her office, just to have a look and make huge compliments, while asking many questions. But she refused to reveal her secret and merely commented, "So, I've got a luncheon date. It happens, you know!"

When the time arrived, a handsome, young gentleman was directed to her office. He introduced himself as an assistant on Ambassador Yamamoto's private staff and invited her to join him for the appointment at the Akasaka Prince Hotel. He handed her his official credential card to ease any concern she might have. She accepted it with a smile and a nod. Then he bowed graciously, motioned her to walk ahead of him, and they left for this surprising rendezvous.

When they arrived at the hotel, Miyuki was escorted through a set of doorways and up a wide, softly-carpeted stairway to a private reception area. Her escort stepped to a door on one side of the hall and knocked. Another gentleman opened the door and accepted the invitation from the young man, then bowed politely and invited her into the room. The escort left them alone.

Miyuki found herself standing in a beautiful, private dining room containing two soft, plush chairs placed beside a round, black lacquer table, next to a large window. On the table was a centerpiece of white chrysanthemums and two lovely settings of fine crystal, china, and silver. She noticed another door inside the room. She had a strong impression that she was standing in a place where a very rich Japanese businessman might bring his *geisha* for a private rendezvous. It reminded her of the wild night with Ana at the Otani Hotel. She was uneasy in the setting.

The attendant pulled out one of the soft chairs, smiled, and motioned for her to take a seat. He poured wine into the two glasses, then walked to the inside door and knocked. Then he turned and left the room by the door which Miyuki had entered. All was quiet for a moment. Miyuki smiled to herself. She had always wondered about this 'other life,' and here she was in the middle of it. She thought, *'This might be exciting, enjoying all the amenities of wealth and privilege, behind closed and secret doors.'*

For a moment, she indulged a fantasy of having a secret liaison with a rich and handsome lover. To her surprise, a distinguished gentleman, dressed in a traditional Japanese kimono, suddenly appeared from the inner door and greeted her with a stiff bow.

"Good afternoon, Ms. Kitada. We haven't met, though I feel that I know you very well through your friend, Ms. Ana Gabrelli. I am Sano Ishikawa. Yamamoto-san will be here presently."

So this was the famous companion of Toshi's that Ana often mentioned. She responded with a smile, "I'm very happy to know you, Ishikawa-san. Ana has often spoken to me of your kindness."

He did not change expression, but bowed and turned to open the inner door. Toshiburo Yamamoto walked through the door into the room. Miyuki was surprised at his appearance. He was, in every way, the newly-appointed Ambassador for Japan with assignment to the United States. His hair was much shorter and carefully trimmed. He was dressed in a white silk shirt, black tie, and a perfectly-cut black business suit. Toshi had become the 'distinguished gentleman' of high rank. He bowed politely to Miyuki, but smiled and winked as he spoke.

"Nothing stays the same in this world, does it, Miyuki? You blink your eyes and a long-haired, liberal-minded guitar player becomes a stiff, conservative, government employee!"

His casual, friendly approach set her at ease. Miyuki gazed at him, trying to convince herself that this perfectly-groomed gentleman was the sensitive, intellectual professor to whom her dearest friend had given her heart. She found it impossible to hold back a rush of tears. Miyuki fumbled in her bag, but Toshi quickly handed her a beautifully-embroidered, white silk handkerchief. As he did so, he touched her hand.

"Thank you for coming. I was afraid you might refuse, under the circumstances."

Miyuki shook her head.

"I would never refuse to see you, Yamamoto-san." She struggled to regain her composure.

"I've asked Ishikawa to be here with us because I don't want anyone to misinterpret our meeting. I'm aware that everything I do from now on will be closely scrutinized. In fact, I'm not even certain which of the gentlemen you've met this afternoon are bodyguards or secret police. This is a definite change of lifestyle for me."

Miyuki laughed at his understatement.

"Yes, I would say it is a major change!"

"Do you mind Ishikawa's presence with us?" Toshi was concerned with her comfort and she appreciated his kindness.

"Of course, not. He's one of your family, and I'm sure he's seen all kinds of people cry."

Toshi bowed his head and answered quietly, "Yes, especially over the last few months." Then he looked up at her and changed the atmosphere. "But now, I'd like to invite you to join me for a light lunch. There is a reason I've invited you here, but let's relax a bit first."

Ishikawa seated both her and Toshi very formally and attended their luncheon table. The two friends shared a lovely lunch together. They talked of Toshi's new role and the changing demands he faced as a member of Japan's diplomatic corps. Neither mentioned his approaching marriage and, not until Ishikawa had cleared the table and poured them each a final glass of wine, did Toshi broach the subject of their meeting.

"I want to ask a favor of you, Miyuki. I have a special gift for Ana that is much too precious to trust with anyone but you. I thought perhaps you might be visiting her sometime in the near future and could take it to her."

Miyuki looked at him in shock.

"Oh Yamamoto-san, please don't ask me to do that! I can't do that."

Toshi reacted quickly, reaching out to touch her hand.

"No, no, Miyuki! It's not what you think. It's just a simple gift, a memento of the past for Ana to take into the future. If you can find it in your heart to do this, you can be assured that we will both find peace with the choices we've made."

"But what about Mishi? He's her husband now and my dear friend. I don't want to do anything that will hurt him."

"Please don't misunderstand. I know that our love affair is over and I'm not trying to keep it alive in any way. I'm glad that Ana chose to go with Mishima. He will love her and be a good father to their children and support her in achieving all of her dreams. But if he should have a question, Ana will know what to say to him.

I've accepted the fact that we must live our separate lives, but the gift will bring peace to her heart, the peace that she deserves now. And it will help my own struggle, as well, to know that Ana will have this precious memento of the past."

Miyuki looked away from him. She stared out the window, trying to collect her thoughts and to find an answer for this unexpected dilemma. After a while, she turned back to Toshi, still unable to give him the commitment he desired, but at least a possibility.

"There may be times when a special gift can mend some of the brokenness when a relationship is ended. If that is the purpose of this gift, then perhaps I can deliver it."

Toshi sighed with relief and bent his head as he whispered, "Thank you, Miyuki. We will both be grateful for your kindness."

He got up and left the room for a moment. When he returned, he was carrying a small, black airport bag. He handed it to Miyuki. To her surprise, it was very light. He smiled, "I'm entrusting my heart to you."

Miyuki felt as if she were actually holding his heart in her hands. She was afraid of the fragile package, afraid that it might contain a force that could destroy the world, or at least the lives of three precious people.

Toshi sensed her continuing fears.

"I promise you that it will be all right. Ana will thank you for your kindness. She needs this with her, Miyuki. It will give her strength during difficult times."

Miyuki sat holding the bag for a few moments. She was about to leave, when she realized that there must be complete honesty between them. There were things this honorable gentleman should know and she was the only one who could tell him. She spoke slowly and carefully, aware of the impact her words would carry. She could not meet his steady gaze.

"I feel compelled to tell you some things that might change your mind about this gift. Ana called me just a few days ago. She and Mishi were celebrating their six-month anniversary and the completion of their new home in Virginia. She sounded very happy and excited about her new life…and about the child they are expecting."

Miyuki's voice broke as she completed the last sentence. Toshi stood frozen, as if he had been turned to stone, then leaned forward to brace himself against the back of the chair.

His voice trembled as he responded to her words.

"Please…don't misunderstand me, Miyuki. I wish your dear friends every happiness and I celebrate the joy they find together. Whatever pain I suffer is of my own making."

They were silent for a few moments as the distinguished Ambassador attempted to regain his composure. He asked hesitantly, "When…are they expecting their child?"

Miyuki felt a tremor run through her whole body at his question. His words and the manner in which they were spoken revealed more than she ever wanted to know. She answered with the same hesitancy that he had asked.

"They…didn't give a certain date, only sometime within the next few months."

Miyuki refused to consider the repercussions of her next statements, but she was compelled to speak.

"They already know it's a little boy and Mishima has chosen a name for him. He wants to call him Mikoto after his own twin brother who died at birth. He has given him the full name of Mikoto Toshiburo Matsamura."

Miyuki's heart moved into her throat as she said the words. She could barely breathe and looked away from Toshi. He responded with a question, obviously shocked.

"My god, Miyuki, doesn't it seem a generous concession to name one's child after his wife's former lover?"

She found his question easy to answer.

"Mishima has a generous heart."

Their eyes locked for a moment. Miyuki knew that she must leave now. She had no answers for any further questions, not even for her own.

Toshi brought their afternoon to an end with a deep sigh.

"I will leave the gift with you in this way. I trust you to know when, or if ever, there will be a time to share it with Ana.

And if you decide that the time is never right to do so, then I offer it to you as a token of friendship for moments past. When was it? Long ago in another age, perhaps? If you wish, you have my permission to display it in your home as a gift from the Ambassador in return for a pleasant rendezvous at the Akasaka Prince Hotel."

They smiled at each other and the tension eased between them. Toshi stepped close to Miyuki and kissed her hand in a formal, yet tender, manner. As he pulled back from her, he whispered, "I feel as if I am waking from a beautiful dream and now must face the realities of my existence. I fear that it will be a harsh awakening."

Miyuki started to speak a word of comfort and farewell, but Toshi had turned and disappeared through the inner door. Their 'rendezvous' was over. Ishikawa walked with her to the front entrance of the hotel. As he helped her into the limousine, he asked where she would like to go.

"I can't go back to work, now. Please ask him to take me to my home."

Miyuki handed Ishikawa a card which he gave to the driver. As he turned back to her, their eyes met. In an unprecedented act, Ishikawa touched her hand and spoke, with tear-filled eyes, "She is very much missed."

Miyuki looked back as the car drove away. Ishikawa was standing like an ancient samurai at the castle gate, watching her leave. His hand was barely raised in farewell. She knew it was his message of love to Ana. Miyuki let her tears come then, for Ana's heartache and for the burden of sorrow that the Honorable Ambassador Toshiburo Yamamoto would carry for the rest of his life.

On the way home, Miyuki thought about the gift that had been delivered into her hands, a precious gift from one lover to another. Toshi had commissioned her to make the choice of when or whether it would be delivered. She was certain that it would not be delivered soon, and it was even more likely that it never would be.

By the time she had arrived at her apartment, Miyuki had made two firm decisions. One, that she would not give the gift to Ana as long as she and Mishima were together. And, two, that life was too short to live it alone. She no longer cared about perfection. Miyuki wanted the warmth of a lover's arms around her and she didn't even care if *sake* were his first love. She was ready to take whatever he would give and enjoy the good moments in between the 'not-so-good.'

She ran into the bedroom, tossed off all the sleek clothes required of her secret mission to the Ambassador, grabbed the phone, and dialed.

He answered and she asked, "Hey, Sato, what in the world are you doing tonight?" She laughed at his response and replied, "Well, let's do it together!"

Just a few weeks later, Miyuki called Ana with her own good news. She and Sato were married and living in his grandparents' big house in Seijo. The grandparents' health had required that they move to Kyoto with Sato's parents.

"Now, when you bring your family to visit, you can stay in our little house on the hillside and we'll celebrate the good old days!"

Ana and Mishima gave Miyuki their blessings and condolences, and congratulated Sato on his wise decision. They laughed together, remembering Sato's crazy antics at all their parties. When Miyuki hung up the telephone, she turned to her handsome husband and said, "Just stay as wild and crazy, and even as drunk as you have to, but promise that you will love me forever!"

Sato answered in his usual flippant way, "My darling wife, I promise to do all of the above!"

Miyuki knew that he would keep each of his promises. But she would love him,
no matter what, for she knew that beneath his craziness there was a heart of gold that would never break her own.

Later that night, when all was quiet and Sato sound asleep, Miyuki got up and walked to the back of the house. She stepped out onto the porch deck to look at the little house where Ana had lived for such a short time. Her thoughts turned to the secret gift that now rested on the top shelf of her closet, hidden behind many boxes.

She whispered to herself in the darkness, "Someday, someday perhaps I will open it, and then I will know what to do. But for now, it will rest in that secret place and will not disrupt the happiness of my dearest friends."

END OF BOOK ONE

Book Two

Can the Power of the Moon Heal Promises Broken?

CHAPTER 23

"In the quiet of evening, memories crowd the mind. One night of sorrow and lives are changed. Then comes the message... 'Shall we meet again this one last time?'"
--Ana and Toshiburo

The house was dark when Ana drove into the driveway. This caused her some concern, for Miko was always there to greet her on Friday nights. This was their special time together after a busy week of varied activities for both of them. Then Ana remembered that her son was staying at his college apartment in the city. He and his friends had made plans to celebrate their spring break together.

Though their home appeared to be isolated, surrounded as it was by trees and the wooded hills, neighbors were close by. Ana had never minded being here alone. She loved the atmosphere of privacy and had never had reason to be afraid.

Tonight, she ate a light supper, then went out in the porch to relax among the beauties of nature. In the quiet evening, Ana's thoughts turned to Mishima. He was the one who had made this moment possible. He had known how to create an atmosphere of harmony with nature that seemed to carry over into their lives. Whenever she entered this lovely home, Ana felt as if she were being wrapped in a mantle of peace. The spirit of Rock Hills was a gift from her husband for which she would always be grateful.

Even more than the beautiful home they shared, Ana's love for Mishima was grounded in his unconditional acceptance of her son. The moment he had named their unborn child, a bond of love seemed to connect him with Miko that even Ana could not fathom. She honored her husband for that tender love and had always been certain that the choice she made was the correct one.

At each point of their child's development, Mishima had been fully involved in his activities. He led the Scout troop and helped coach the soccer teams from the time Miko was old enough to participate in these activities. And as their son grew, so did Mishima's responsibilities in these volunteer projects. Those years were, indeed, happy and busy times for father and son.

Ana participated in certain parts of Miko's development, but was, more often than not, on the sidelines. She had never felt left out, only gratified that Mishima felt free to give his love and his time to their child, and Ana had never failed to express her appreciation to him. In every way, she affirmed his role as a loving husband and father.

Tonight, her memories took Ana to a moment just two years ago, on this very date, when the peace of their home had been shattered. The anniversary of Miko's high school graduation would be remembered as the most tragic night of their lives as a family.

Miko had been an 'early bird' graduate from high school at sixteen and was to receive special honors at the graduation ceremonies, including scholarships for academics and soccer from Georgetown University. He had his father to thank for the athletic awards, for Mishima had been his special coach at home, as well as on the athletic field.

All of Miko's close friends and their parents were coming to the Matsamura home for a combined celebration after the ceremonies. Everything was ready for the party and it was time to leave for the village, but Mishima had not yet arrived from work. Ana and Miko finally left without him. They knew he would come directly to the high school at this late hour.

To everyone's shock, Mishima did not attend his son's graduation. After the ceremonies, Ana and Miko hurried back to Rock Hills to prepare for the big party, but still no Mishima. Ana recalled how angry Miko was, and how apprehensive she had been. She knew that her husband would never miss this night by choice. She had calmed her son's anger with possible excuses, and they went ahead with the celebration.

During the party, Ana called several of Mishima's colleagues at the office who might have word of him or some knowledge of his plans. They all expressed surprise and told her how excited Mishima had been about the graduation and Miko's special honors. By the time the party was over, Miko was so upset that he didn't even want to see his father. He chose to go home with friends for an overnight graduation bash.

Tonight, Ana recalled the very moment when their lives had suddenly changed. She had been awakened by lights in her

256

driveway at 3 a.m. At first, she was relieved that Mishima was finally home, but, instead of the garage door opening, Ana heard the front doorbell ringing. She knew then that her fears would be realized. She opened the door to red, flashing lights and the kind faces of two State patrolmen.

Ana verified the identification materials she was shown. She recalled that, of everything handed to her, the pain in her heart was deepest when she saw the twisted, blackened house key with the inscriptions, "Rock Hills," and "The Matsamura Home." She would always remember the words of the patrolman that were spoken in such a gentle voice.

"I'm sorry, Mrs. Matsamura, to tell you that your husband has been killed in an automobile accident just a few miles from here. It appears that he was driving far beyond the speed limit when he took the curve onto Rocky Hills Drive. His car evidently went out of control and crashed into the rocks alongside the road. The medical report is…that he died instantly."

Ana had done all that was required of her, and not until much later that day had she found the courage to tell her son. The restructuring of their lives had been forced upon them. Miko hardly knew who he was without his father, and Ana realized that she could not fill all of those empty spaces for him. The two of them had to begin a totally new relationship.

Part of that experience of becoming acquainted was the journey they took to Japan. Miko wanted his father's ashes buried in their hillside shrine, but Ana discouraged this. She reminded him that, at some time in the future, this might not be their home. Ana explained to Miko that his father loved Rock Hills and his spirit would always be present there. However, she also knew that Mishima's final wish would be to rest in the land of his birth. Miko agreed to go with her to Yokohama.

There, Mishima's ashes were laid to rest in a beautiful garden that surrounded his parents' private shrine on a hillside near their home. After the ceremony, Miko agreed that it was the best decision to bring his father back to this special place.

When Ana asked her son if he wanted to go with her to Tokyo, he chose to stay with the Matsamuras. He was excited about the trip they planned with him and his cousins to Mt.

Fujiyama and Kyoto. When they returned, he would meet his mother in Tokyo for their flight back to the States.

Ana knew that Miko needed this connection with the family of the father he had loved so dearly. Yet, she longed to show her son the beautiful Seijo estate that Toshi loved, and walk with him in the place that might have been their home. But those secret desires were kept locked away in her heart. This was not the time to open such doors to the past. Miko needed no further complications to his life now, nor did she.

Ana was happy to see Miyuki and Sato, but chose not to stay with them in Seijo. She didn't feel strong enough to be so close to the little house behind theirs and to face the memories that were still lurking there. Miyuki understood, so they met at the Otani Hotel in downtown Tokyo, where Ana was staying. They spent hours talking and laughing about old times and especially their crazy night at the hotel when Toshi hadn't shown up.

Besides some shopping and sightseeing, Ana visited the few friends still left at IEEC. Ito took her to lunch one day and they caught up on each other's lives. He was as warm as ever and gave her much sympathy. Before they parted, he asked the question she expected.

"Have you ever seen him there, Ana? Has your path ever crossed with the Ambassador's?"

Ito had seemed surprised that she could respond so calmly.

"No, I have never had the occasion to meet him."

She did not mention, however, that she had followed Toshi's diplomatic career very closely since he had been assigned to the Embassy in Washington. The relationship between the United States and Japan was, after all, of significant importance to her professional role at the university.

Just a few days before Ana and Miko returned to the States, Sato planned a night out for him and Miko. He was anxious to introduce his young friend to the night life on the Ginza. With much trepidation, Ana agreed. So, after many motherly warnings, the men set out on their night of 'fun and games.' Miyuki came down to spend the night with Ana at the hotel, so they could enjoy their own kind of good times.

The women ordered a fancy meal with champagne and delicious desserts and celebrated their years of friendship by recounting the affairs of both their hearts. They talked and ate and laughed and cried for several hours before Miyuki dropped her bombshell.

"There's something I have to tell you, Ana. I think it's time, even though I know you'll be upset with me. I have something that belongs to you."

Miyuki walked over to the couch where she had set her overnight bag when she came in. She opened the bag and lifted out a rather large package wrapped in beautiful gold gift paper with a huge gold bow. Holding it very carefully, Miyuki set the package on the floor between her and Ana.

Ana asked, "What is this, Yuki? I didn't come bearing gifts."

"Nor did I. This gift is not from me. I'll tell you about it, but you must promise not to be angry with me. I used my best judgment at the time, and I still believe that I was right. However, you may not agree."

"For heaven's sake, Yuki, you've certainly aroused my curiosity!"

"Just be patient! There's a story that goes with this, and I want to tell it exactly as it occurred."

Miyuki began her narrative. "After you and Mishi had gone to the States and Toshi had been appointed to the embassy position here in Tokyo, I received an invitation to meet him for lunch at the Akasaka Prince Hotel.

I struggled over whether I should go or not, but finally decided to accept the invitation, more from curiosity than anything. So, I was graciously escorted from my office to the hotel and into a very plush, and private, dining room on an upper floor. Ishikawa and Toshi met me there. I won't explain everything, just to say that I felt like someone's highly favored geisha. Everything was quite secretive.

Anyway, after a very elegant luncheon and a few glasses of wine, Toshi asked me to deliver this package to you. He wanted you to have it as a wedding gift, but I couldn't do it, Ana. I told him it would be unfair to Mishima. At first, he was upset, but after we talked a while, he understood my feelings.

Finally, he told me to use my best judgment and to deliver it whenever I felt it was best, or not to deliver it at all. He even gave me permission to keep it as a gift from him for our friendship and the good times we had all shared together.

But I couldn't open it, Ana. I decided that it would never be delivered at all, unless you and Mishi should part. I knew, I just knew, that whatever is in this box Mishi should never see, nor ever know about. I didn't want him hurt, Ana. He loved you too much for that."

Miyuki pushed the box very carefully toward Ana, as if it might be loaded with explosives. For a while, Ana stared at it without moving. Then she looked at her friend.

Miyuki smiled, "Go ahead, what can it hurt now?"

Ana picked up the box slowly and carefully began to unwrap it. At one point, she stopped to reassure her friend,

"Whatever it is, Yuki, I know that you made the right decision. This innocent package might very well have ruined at least two lives."

They looked at each other. Both had tears in their eyes. Ana took several deep breaths and laid the box back on the floor. Then she reached down and pulled the last bit of paper from the gift. When she saw what was inside, she whispered, "Oh my god…my god."

She put her head in her hands and began to cry. Miyuki was shocked to silence at Ana's reaction.

Finally, Ana spoke through her tears. "You were right, Yuki, I could never have received this gift with Mishi at my side. But now, it helps me know that there was some truth to our relationship. That Toshi did love me, in spite of the choices he made."

Ana lifted the large, oblong glass case out of its wrappings and set on the floor for Miyuki to see. Inside, attached to a soft bed of black velvet, was a beautiful ceramic rose. Its delicate white petals, green leaves, and thorny stems were so perfectly designed, that it was hard to believe it wasn't real.

"Oh, Ana, it's an amazing work of art! I can almost smell its sweet scent."

Ana opened the envelope attached to the back of the box and found "The Legend of the Rose" written in Toshi's own artistic script. It was addressed to "The Angel Gabrelli" and signed, "Your Samurai, Always."

Very calmly, Ana read the legend to Miyuki. When she finished, there was silence in the room. Finally, Miyuki went to Ana and, with their arms around each other, they cried together. When their tears were dry, they decided to drown the sorrows of the past with the rest of their dinner champagne and get on with life.

Ana wrapped the gift very carefully and returned it to the airport bag. She would not be afraid to display its beauty, even though it might haunt her, for this precious gift finally confirmed the depth of love which she and Toshi had shared. Now, perhaps she could find peace with those memories. Perhaps she could finally lay them to rest.

After their return to the States, Miko began to recover from the loss of his father and was ready to spend more time with his friends and plan for the new challenges of college life. One evening he came into his mother's room to talk a while before he went out with his friends.

"This summer has been a real challenge for me, mother. I just want to thank you for helping me come through this and move on with my life. I love my grandparents. They were so good to me, and my cousins were great, too. Michiko is such a beauty, isn't she? If we weren't related, I'd be in love. But we'll be good friends and write a lot. And now, I'm ready to get back on track."

As Miko started to leave the room, he noticed the sculpture on the mantel of his mother's fireplace. He couldn't help exclaim, "Wow, that's beautiful! Did you get it this summer? I haven't seen it before."

He went over to look more closely at the delicate, white rose.

"Yuki and I found it. It's perfect, isn't it?"

"It's a true work of art, and it looks so real!"

"It's not only lovely, but there's a very special meaning attached to it. Perhaps when you're older and ready to fall in love, I'll tell you the story. And I might even consider giving it to you and your bride as a gift on your wedding day."

Her son gave Ana a questioning look. "There's a story behind it?"

"Yes, but it can only be told to those in love. So you'll have to let me know when that happens and then I'll tell you the 'Legend of the Rose.'"

Miko laughed at his mother.

"But how will you know if I'm not just pretending to be in love, so you'll tell me the story?"

She gave her son an authoritative gaze. "Don't ever underestimate your mother's power. You are your father's son, and I was always able to read every thought that crossed his mind, or his heart. Believe me, I will know!"

"Mothers are too powerful. I'm out of here!"

After Miko left, Ana smiled to herself. Her words were true. She had known the mind and heart of Yamamoto as well as she knew her own. And she knew the same of his sweet son.

Over the next several months, Ana and Miko adjusted to the loss of their husband and father. Ana was busy with her teaching at Georgetown and continued to find challenge in it. She had a handsome, intelligent son who was achieving his own academic goals. And she loved coming home to the quiet atmosphere that Mishima had designed for them.

Though he was only eighteen, Miko decided at the end of his sophomore year in college to leave the dormitory and live on his own. His mother helped him find a small apartment near the university where he would be close to classes and college activities. And Miko was developing a relationship with one of his high school girlfriends who was attending Georgetown, so he did not spend much time at Rock Hills.

Ana respected Miko's choices and did not intend to dictate his private life, for he had, many times over, proven his ability to make wise decisions. Their relationship since Mishima's death had developed into one of close friendship and mutual trust. She knew that her son had been given a strong foundation of love and wise counsel regarding his role as a responsible young man. And, as hard as those long ago choices had been for her, Ana was thankful for the decisions made in the past that had provided Miko with this foundation.

On the second anniversary of Mishima's death, Ana felt a contentment in her life that she had never experienced before. She lay back against the soft cushions of the deck chair, listening to the pleasant sounds of nature that surrounded her as she reflected on the events of the past few months.

She whispered to herself, "My life is filled with challenge and with contentment. There seems to be nothing more that I could want than what I have."

The words had barely passed her lips when Ana was pulled from her reverie by the sound of the front doorbell. Her heart jumped. No one in this area would come to the front door of her house in the evening, or, for that matter, even in the daytime. They would know it was never used.

Ana's 'trip into the past' left her with a sense of foreboding and her immediate concern was Miko. Without further thought, she rushed to the front door. But, to her surprise, she faced a young Japanese man in messenger uniform. He was smiling courteously. Ana spoke rather harshly to him, wanting to leave the impression that his presence was not welcome.

"Yes, what do you want?"

The young man continued to smile as he answered, "Excuse me, please, ma'am. I am delivering this information by personal messenger to Mr. Mishima Matsamura and Dr. Ana Gaberli Matsamura. Is this their residence?"

And had to smile at the mispronunciation of her name. It happened so often. She clarified it for him. "Yes, I am Dr. Ana Gabrelli Matsamura. What may I do for you?"

The young man bowed many times, apologizing profusely for the interruption.

"Please accept my apologies for delivering this important message so late in the evening. I did contact your office at Georgetown University, but you had already left for the day. Your secretary directed me to your home and told me that it would be all right to come here. Please forgive this intrusion!"

The very embarrassed young man handed Ana an envelope and a card to sign, indicating that she had received it. She took his pen and signed the card then, turning the envelope over, asked, "Are you from the Japanese Embassy? Do you know what this is about?"

"Yes, I am from the Japanese Embassy, but no, I do not know what this is about. I am only the messenger who is sent to deliver the message."

Ana offered him a kind smile then, attempting to relieve his embarrassment. She realized that he was exactly who he said he was, a simple messenger. She apologized, "I didn't mean to be so harsh. It's very seldom that anyone comes to my door, and especially in the evening. I hope you understand my concern."

"Oh, yes, and I beg your pardon if I have upset you."

The young man bowed again as he turned to go.

Ana shut the door behind him and, not knowing what to think about this strange interruption in the night, sat down on the couch and very carefully opened the envelope. A smaller, light blue, textured envelope with the official seal of the Japanese Embassy fell into her lap. The names were written in a familiar script in the center of the envelope. She asked her question out loud, "What in the world is this?"

Ana opened the envelope carefully to find a blue card with these words embossed in gold:

"You and your family are cordially invited to attend a reception in honor of the retiring Japanese Ambassador to the United States, Toshiburo Matsushita Yamamoto, in recognition of his years of outstanding service accorded the mission of cementing relationships between our two nations.

The reception will be held at the Japanese Embassy and hosted by:

> *The President of the United States*
> *The United States Ambassador to Japan*
> *The Japanese Ambassador to the United States, newly* appointed"

A smaller RSVP card and envelope were enclosed for the names of those who would be attending with her.

Ana read the card over several times, then tossed it on the coffee table with a sigh. She spoke aloud to the empty room.

"So now this. Nearly twenty years later, and now this."

Ana wandered through the house and out onto the patio. She sat down on the stone wall facing the Japanese garden and felt the crush of memories. Tonight she had come home, anxious to enjoy the quietness of this peaceful home, but all she had done was go back to the painful places in her life. And now, she was faced with the most poignant of all, an invitation to see

264

Yamamoto, to talk to him, to meet his wife and family. How could she face that? Yet, how could she refuse?

The night was long and Ana's wakefulness lasted until morning. The invitation had to be answered. A decision must be made. It was evident that Toshi wanted her to come or her name would not have been among the invited, nor would she have received a hand-delivered message. He was returning to Japan and he wanted to see her…this one last time. How could she refuse?

Now Ana knew for certain that Toshi was aware of her presence here, her role at the university, even where her home was located. All of these things touched her deeply and frightened her as well. Never, in all of these years, had either of them attempted to contact the other. It was almost as if fate had determined this moment, for now she was without defenses. There was no Mishima to stand between them, and Miko no longer needed her protection. But the ambassador did not know these things. He had sent the invitation innocently, only to say a final farewell.

Ana struggled with the rush of emotion that filled her mind and heart by this surprising message. Finally, she accepted the fact that there was no choice at all. She had to see him. And she would take Miko with her to face this 'sweet samurai' with his past. Ana chose to ignore the consequences. It was time that all their truth was told.

Ana knew that Miko would be sleeping late on the weekend, so waited until nearly noon to make the call. He answered in a groggy voice, "Uh, hello, mother. What's going on? I'm doing my Saturday thing…sleeping in."

"Sorry to bother you, but I have some information that might interest you. We, that is, you and I, have been invited to a little party. I believe the card says something like, 'a reception hosted by the President of the United States.'"

All was quiet on the other end of the line, then Miko came alive.

"Cut it out! That's an underhanded way to wake me up before noon on Saturday!"

"Oh yes, another thing. It also says on this very impressive, officially-sealed invitation that we will be greeting the Japanese

Ambassador to the United States on his retirement from service. And, we will be meeting the newly-appointed Ambassador from Japan. Are you at all interested in attending this tiny, insignificant *soiree*? There's an RSVP required."

"What a question...!"

Ana didn't let Miko finish his sentence before she added, "Oh, just for your information, the retiring Japanese Ambassador is a former friend of your father's and mine. When we were working in Japan, our IEEC staff presented some seminars for his classes at Tokyo University. We all became acquainted and had some good times together. I'm surprised, though, that he still remembers after all these years. Well, what is it...yes or no?"

"If you're going and I'm invited, then I'm going! Put me on the list and give me the date so I can mark my calendar. By the way, is there any possibility that Suzi could be included? She would love it."

Ana could think of no reason to refuse his request.

"Of course, but you must both agree to follow my instructions on dress and protocol. I'm sure Suzi will enjoy a bit of pomp and circumstance. It will be very exciting, no doubt!"

"I promise that we'll do everything you say. And, by the way, might I add a personal note. You must have been very good friends of this mystery ambassador to receive an invitation from the President. I'm duly impressed!"

"And well you should be. After all, twenty years ago I was younger and much more impressive."

"In more ways than one, I'm sure. This could prove to be a very interesting evening. I can hardly wait."

"You will have to practice your manners, beginning with great respect for your parent and elder."

They laughed together before hanging up. Ana's mind began to whirl with the many plans that would have to be made. And among them, the approach she would make to the Honorable Ambassador Toshiburo Matsushita Yamamoto, his wife, and family.

As the day of the embassy reception came closer, Ana became increasingly nervous. She found herself reliving the experiences that she and Toshi had shared, both good and bad. Her nights were restless and she longed for the moment to come and to end. At times, Ana nearly convinced herself to find an excuse for not attending. She would send Miko and Suzi in her place. But, finally, she couldn't resist the pull of her heart to meet this long-ago lover face-to-face for this one last time.

Two days before the reception, Ana received a surprising telephone call at her university office. The caller identified himself as a member of the private staff for Ambassador Yamamoto. He spoke formally to Ana, "Dr. Matsamura, I am calling on behalf of Ambassador Yamamoto regarding the embassy reception. He would like to offer you and your family private transportation to the reception on Saturday. A member of our staff would be most happy to come to your home and transport you to the embassy. If you wish this courtesy, would you please give me your address and directions to your home?"

Ana was speechless for a moment. How pleasant it would be to have someone drive them into the city. She thought to herself, '*Why not?*'

"We would be most happy for such kindness…and please relay our thanks to the Ambassador."

She proceeded to give the staff officer Miko's address and telephone number in Georgetown. Ana would never expect them to drive all the way to Rock Hills. After the arrangements had been made with her caller, she began to feel somewhat relieved of tension and her spirits lifted.

When Ana called Miko to let him know about the special limo that would be picking them up at his apartment for the reception, he chuckled.

"Now tell me you were 'just friends' with the ambassador! A special limo service? My mind is filled with suspicion and I can only say, I'm very anxious to meet this honorable gentleman."

"I hate to discourage you, but the 'honorable gentleman' of which you speak is married and has, I'm sure, several beautiful children. Goodness, I had no idea that my son had become such a romantic!"

"If so, I must come by it naturally, and I don't mean from my father."

"And, if so, it most surely *is* from your father!"
And she meant it literally.

CHAPTER 24

"In the silence of a garden night, love, more than memory, confessed. Now, comes the question… 'Why?' There are no answers. There is only the hope of forgiveness."
--Ana and Toshiburo

Ana drove to Miko's apartment early in the afternoon of the embassy reception, so they would all have plenty of time to get ready. The weekend before, they completed their final shopping and everyone was happy with the results. Ana spared no expense on their clothes for the evening, for she was fairly certain that this would be the most auspicious occasion in which they would ever participate.

Miko was handsome in his casual-cut, black tuxedo and gray-striped vest worn with a white, banded-collar shirt and white satin neck bow. Suzi chose a fitted, black silk, strapless gown with side slits from mid-calf. Her red-gold hair was pulled back in a tight roll with long curly strands on the sides. A pair of dangling, black crystal earrings was her only jewelry.

Ana had struggled over her dress for the evening. First, she thought conservative black would be best, but then decided that she didn't want to be conservative. What she wanted was color to give her courage for this very special occasion. She found the dress that suited her taste perfectly. It was a pale pink, taffeta gown with a full skirt and narrow boat-collar that extended across her upper arms like sleeves.

When Ana put on the gown, with her diamond necklace and earrings, she knew it was the right choice. She didn't even mind the gray streaks so evident in her black hair when pulled back with the diamond hair clips. Nor did she attempt to cover the crinkling lines around her large, dark eyes. Ana felt strong and beautiful and ready for whatever the evening might bring.

The embassy limousine stopped at the apartment building exactly on time. Miko was waiting in the front hallway and buzzed Ana and Suzi to come down. Everything went as planned. When they arrived at the embassy, their driver escorted them into the front lobby where they were met by a young Japanese man in formal dress. He looked at the card in his hand and asked, "Are you Dr. Ana Gabrelli Matsamura?"

She replied, "Yes, and this is Mikoto Toshiburo Matsamura and Suzannah Morgan Randolph."

The young man bowed very low to her, then offered Ana his arm as he escorted them into the formal, reception room. Ana felt an increasing nervous tension as they approached the receiving line for the honored guests. The young escort was very kind and assured them that he would be with them throughout the evening to make certain that their needs were met. Not until they were very close to the honorees, did Ana catch a glimpse of Toshi. He was smiling and shaking the hand of a guest. The first sight of him, after nearly twenty years, was a shock to her. He was even thinner than in his youth, and his black hair was now silver-gray, but the gentle smile remained the same.

Ana turned to their escort with a question, "Isn't Ambassador Yamamoto's family present this evening?" She had noticed that Toshi stood alone between the President and another Japanese gentleman that she assumed was the new Japanese ambassador.

The young man replied in a whisper, "The Ambassador is divorced and has no children."

She offered a quick apology.

"I'm so sorry. I didn't know. It's been many years since we met."

Ana felt a heavy sadness for this gentle man who had obviously been denied the pleasure of a loving family.

Their escort proceeded with the introductions by presenting them to the American Ambassador to Japan and his wife, who greeted them politely. They visited for a few moments until the American Ambassador turned to introduce them to the President of the United States and his wife as, "Dr. Ana Gabrelli Matsamura, professor of anthropology and Japan studies at Georgetown University and friend of Ambassador Yamamoto; her son, Mikoto Toshiburo Matsamura; and their friend, Ms. Suzannah Morgan Randolph."

Ana glanced quickly at Toshi when the names were read, but he did not turn his head toward them. Ambassador Yamamoto seemed to be deep in conversation with another guest. The President and First Lady were very gracious and, to Ana's surprise, asked how she and the ambassador had met. Ana smiled as she responded to the unexpected question.

"When Ambassador Yamamoto was a professor at Tokyo University, nearly twenty years ago, I was a member of a team of educators who presented intercultural seminars to his classes. We shared an interest in understanding the uniqueness of the many different cultures of the world."

The President and his wife visited with the three of them for a few moments. Then the President touched Ambassador Yamamoto's arm and Toshi turned toward Ana at his words, "Ambassador Yamamoto, I believe you are acquainted with Dr. Matsamura, a professor of anthropology at Georgetown University. She will introduce her guests to you."

Toshi smiled and reached out to take Ana's hand. To her surprise and pleasure, Toshi kissed her hand in the courteous manner of the French. It was then that she saw her grandfather's gold watch in its place, where she had always imagined it would be. She wanted very much to lift it out of his vest pocket, to open it and read the inscription again. Ana knew that Toshi had surely treasured this gift and had, no doubt, lived by its challenge, "To be honorable, is to be successful."

Toshi greeted Ana with the familiar smile and twinkle in his eye, "Thank you very much for coming this evening, Dr. Matsamura. This will be my last tour of duty in the United States…and I was somewhat worried that we might miss seeing each other altogether."

He asked his question then.

"But, I had expected to greet your husband as well. Is Mishima not with you?"

Ana ignored the question and turned quickly to introduce Miko and Suzi. Her heart was pounding with apprehension as she did so, yet her voice was calm.

"Ambassador Yamamoto, please let me introduce you to my son, Mikoto Toshiburo Matsamura, and to our close friend, Suzannah Morgan Randolph. They're both students of International Studies at Georgetown."

The Ambassador did not change expression, but greeted Miko and Suzi graciously, then turned back to Ana. In a rather hesitant manner, he asked again, "And, your husband?"

She finally answered the question, "Mishima was killed in an automobile accident two years ago. Mikoto and I have been alone since then."

Toshi appeared visibly shaken by the news and responded with obvious concern.

"I'm so sorry to hear this, Ana, for you and your son."

He turned and spoke directly to Miko, "I knew your father in Tokyo. He was a very fine man. I know it must be difficult to have lost his companionship."

Miko was surprised at the Ambassador's apparent concern.

"Thank you, Ambassador Yamamoto. I appreciate your kindness. My father and I were close and I do miss him, very much."

"Your obvious respect for your father speaks well of his love for you."

The ambassador and the young man exchanged smiles, then Toshi turned to Suzi.

"I'm glad to know that you and Mikoto have chosen to learn more about the world in which we live. I do hope that you can keep it safe for the future."

The Ambassador smiled and offered a surprising suggestion to the young couple.

"If you're interested, I would like to invite the two of you for a private tour of the embassy after the formalities of the evening are completed. After all, you both may be a part of this lifestyle one day."

Toshi looked intently at Miko and added, "And since you and I share the same name, perhaps you will be destined to follow the same path that I have chosen."

Everyone but Ana laughed at the Ambassador's teasing comment. She was glad that Toshi didn't have the courage to look to her for a response. But Miko answered with enthusiasm, "I certainly hope my name has predestined me for such a path! It is, after all, the career I'm attempting to follow."

Miko and Suzi were pleasantly surprised at the Ambassador's gracious manner. Suzi responded to his invitation.

"We would consider it a great honor to have a private tour of the embassy!"

"Then I will arrange it, if you're not in a hurry to leave."

271

Toshi looked to Ana for approval. She was glad that he had offered such a kind invitation to the young couple, but was still somewhat in shock from his words to Miko, "…since you and I share the same name." But she remained calm.

"Thank you so much, Ambassador Yamamoto. We're certainly in no hurry."

He turned to Miko and Suzi. "Then that is what we will do. I will let your escort know our plans and he will be happy to show you what life is like behind these secret doors. And while you two enjoy the tour, perhaps Dr. Matsamura and I can renew our friendship from those long ago Tokyo days."

Toshi turned back to Ana with a question in his eyes. She answered it with enthusiasm, "Of course, Ambassador, I would love to spend a few moments sharing the events of our lives during these past years."

"Then I will be most happy to meet you in the garden after the ceremonies are complete. There will be refreshments and music there."

Toshi bowed to each of them as he made their introductions to the gentleman who would take his place as the new Japanese Ambassador to the United States.

After they left the receiving line, their guide was at Ana's elbow to direct them into the dining area where they were seated at a table near the dais. Ana was glad they were close enough to observe Toshi without being in his direct gaze. She was having difficulty remaining calm as it was. Their brief, courteous exchange had left her with many questions. Hopefully, those questions would be answered later in the evening.

Following the elegant meat, the formal presentation of honors to Toshi was impressive. The President awarded him a special medal of honor, citing his outstanding efforts to maintain positive relations between their two countries. Other statements of respect for Ambassador Yamamoto were offered by the United States Ambassador to Japan and the incoming Japanese Ambassador.

Toshi gave only a brief response, stating the joys and challenges he had experienced while working closely with the officials of the United States, especially the President. He offered thanks for their cooperation and friendship. The last part of his statement was filled with emotion.

"I will recall these years as the most demanding, yet, in many ways, the most rewarding of my life. I am only sorry that they must be shortened by circumstances that are beyond my control."

He bowed deeply to the officials on the dais and to the audience and spoke his final words.

"I have appreciated this opportunity to know each of you as friends and as colleagues in the task which we have been called to perform, that of maintaining peaceful relations among the nations of this world. I am honored by your kindness to me. And now, I must say 'sayonara' to each of you, and to this beautiful country."

Toshi was visibly moved by the immediate standing ovation. He bowed over and over again to the audience and was not ashamed to wipe tears from his eyes. Ana felt his sadness at leaving this role which he seemed to have so successfully filled. Her tears for him now were mixed with the tears she shed for her own loss when he had chosen this path.

As Toshi stepped back to take his seat, Ana saw a quick movement behind him. It was Ishikawa. Standing in the shadows in the rear of the dais, he had been watching over his friend as always. Now he stepped forward and handed something to Toshi. Apparently, it was medication, for she watched as Toshi put his hand to his mouth and took a quick drink of water. No one would have noticed the movements unless they were watching carefully. She had noticed and now had further questions.

The formal part of the evening was over. Everyone began to move around, talking to one another, greeting the honored guests and walking into the gardens for music and refreshments. Ana encouraged her young escort to go ahead with the embassy tour for Miko and Suzi. She wanted to be alone to think her own thoughts and to contemplate all that had occurred during the evening.

After the young people left, Ana followed the other guests to the beautiful embassy gardens. There, musicians were playing the *koto* and *samisen* and champagne and Japanese delicacies were being served from elegant tables along the walkway. The surroundings were pleasant reminders of her days in Japan and Ana found herself revisiting the events of those years as a student and as an employee at IEEC.

Many guests stopped her along the way to introduce themselves and to share friendly conversation. She enjoyed the opportunity to speak in the Japanese language with several others as she followed the lighted pathways through the garden. After a while, Ana took a glass of wine from one of the refreshment tables and found a shaded alcove where she could sit down and relax. The evening had been exciting as well as stressful in many ways.

Sitting alone on the stone bench, the wine, the music, and the garden setting took her back to the little house in Seijo. Ana felt as if she were being enfolded in a soft, warm blanket of memory. She leaned back against the bench and closed her eyes, but did not sleep. After a while, a familiar voice interrupted her meditation.

"Are you enjoying the beauty here?"

Ana slowly opened her eyes. Toshi smiled and sat down beside her. She had transported herself completely into another world, but his voice brought her quickly back to reality.

"Yes, very much. The gardens, the music, everything is so peaceful. And your guests are very courteous. I've enjoyed the opportunity to use my Japanese language skills now and then. The whole evening has been very exciting, Yamamoto-san. Thank you so much for the honor of sharing this special moment in your life."

"I am honored that you chose to accept the invitation, Ana. It's hard to believe that we've been so close to one another all these years without ever crossing paths. How strange that seems now."

"Yes, but we were walking in different directions. There was no way that our paths could cross."

All was quiet. Ana had a sudden fear that they were treading on dangerous ground. And when Toshi spoke again, those fears became reality. His words cracked the façade of peace between them.

"Perhaps, after all, the pathways we chose were not the ones we should have chosen."

Ana felt a sudden, unreasonable anger rising inside her chest. She couldn't believe that he could still turn her emotions on and off with a word. She whispered, "Please don't do this, Toshi. What's done is done. Don't ruin this beautiful evening."

But he refused the warning.

"There was nothing beautiful about this evening except your presence…and that of your son."

Ana responded with care, trying to restore the atmosphere of casual friendship between them.

"I thought we could share a peaceful moment here in this setting or I wouldn't have come."

Toshi leaned forward on the bench and put his head in his hands. Ana could feel the heaviness of his spirit and knew that they were going to hurt each other. There was nothing she could do but wait and let it happen.

Finally, he whispered the words that she most feared, "Why did you do it, Ana? Why didn't you tell me about Mikoto? Did you really believe that I would turn my back on you when you needed me most? If you had been honest with me, nothing could have torn us apart, nothing!"

She gripped the edge of the stone bench. Her heart was pounding in her ears. What was he saying to her? Didn't he know the meaning of those words? Ana swallowed hard to keep from venting years of anger upon his head. Instead, she spoke very quietly, but the words were meant to hurt him as he had just hurt her.

"Why should I have told you, Toshi? My love was not enough for you. Why would I trust that the love of our child would be enough? Do you think that I would've threatened you to stay with me? If so, then you've never understood how much I loved you!"

Toshi felt her accusations against him like the thrust of a knife blade in his heart. He could barely speak in his own defense.

"I gave you my heart, Ana."

She answered with an unbridled cruelty, "Yes, and I gave it a name…Mikoto Toshiburo Matsamura!"

He leaned back against the bench and sighed as if he were in terrible pain. Ana felt his struggle, but chose not to help him. He had to face his own ghosts. There was a dreadful silence between them until, at last, she heard him speaking as if from a far distance.

"My god, my god, Ana. I haven't the strength to withstand your sword thrusts. There is nothing left of me, now!"

Ana couldn't speak. She had no words of comfort to offer him and wanted only to run from his presence or to kneel and beg forgiveness for hurting him when there was no reason to do so. Everything was behind them now. They had no future, so why had he insisted on bringing the past and all its struggles into the present. She was shocked when she heard his next words. They were spoken as if there had been no heated exchange between them at all. He had chosen the pathway of peace as he had been taught so well to do.

"Mikoto is a beautiful young man. I can tell that he is intelligent and perceptive like his mother. You have raised him well, Ana."

She glanced at him, wondering where he was going with this sudden change of mood, but she gratefully followed his lead into calmer waters.

"He has an excellent heritage, and has been fortunate to have a loving father who taught him to respect others and himself. The three of us have had a good life and a happy one together."

Ana didn't want to hurt him further with the reference to Mishima. She only wanted him to know that Miko had been well-loved and well-taught by a kind father.

Toshi turned to her with a half-smile, speaking with his usual kindness.

"And what of his mother? What did she teach him?"

She met his gaze and answered as quietly as he had asked, "She taught him to love others with an open heart and to forgive them quickly when they err."

There was silence between them for a few moments, then Toshi asked the question that was most troubling to him.

"Will you ever forgive the one who so grievously erred against you?"

She looked away from him, touched by the intense burden of guilt that he still carried in his soul and sorry that she had added to it with her bitter words. After a long silence, she turned to face him. With a sudden rush of emotion, Ana put her hand on his in a gesture of love and concern.

"You have nothing to be forgiven for, nor do I. We each did what we had to do at the moment. Your decision was guided by a deep sense of responsibility to your family and your country, mine by a dream of love. You walked away with your memories locked inside your heart, but I'm different from you, Toshi. Memories were not enough for me. I couldn't go alone. I couldn't go without something of you."

There was a long silence between them. After a while, Toshi took her hand gently in his own. He pressed it to his lips for just an instant, then released it as he spoke.

"Thank you, Gabrelli, for your attempt to free my soul from its burden of guilt. But tonight, when I looked into the face of your son and saw my own image reflected there, I felt all my strength crumble into dust.

In that instant, I knew that not only did I turn my back on the woman I loved, but I denied my own son his father, and myself the joy of knowing our child. There will never be a healing for such wounds, wounds that I deliberately inflicted upon us all!

I cannot believe that I so totally misunderstood what Suki-ma said to me so long ago. She tried to tell me that I must always choose the honorable and responsible path. I have chosen neither. I chose the path that brought honor only to myself. I gave my own responsibilities to another.

Thank god for Mishima and his humble heart! Tonight you and Mikoto have brought me face-to-face with the pride that has filled my own life. There is no recovery from the terrible mistakes I have made. None of us will ever recover from them!"

Ana realized then how serious Toshi's illness had become. There was a weakness in him that frightened her. She remembered earlier tonight on the dais when Ishikawa had given him what appeared to be medication. She tried to ease his suffering with her words, "I didn't bring Miko here to hurt you, Toshi. I brought him as a gift. I wanted you to meet him and know what a beautiful son we have and for him to meet you as well. He will know someday that you're his father. Perhaps he may know that now, in the same way that you recognized him."

"When the invitation was sent, I only wanted to see you, Ana, just once before returning to Japan. I knew that I would not be back here again. I fully expected to greet you and Mishima and your son. Miyuki had told me about Mikoto, but she failed to tell me about Mishima's death."

There was a silence between them for a moment, then Ana chose to move away from the atmosphere of sorrow that had surrounded them.

She asked very gently, "Were you surprised that I came?"

"That would be a major understatement! I saw you when you walked in. You are still the most beautiful woman I have ever seen. It took all my diplomatic training to remain calm."

"But you looked so controlled when I walked up to you. As if I were just another guest."

"Didn't you feel my hand shaking when I touched yours?"

Ana laughed and whispered, "No, I thought it was mine that was trembling. And, Toshi, I want to thank you for something very special."

"I can't imagine what thanks I could ever deserve from you, Ana. What was so special?

Ana reached across and ran her fingertips along the gold chain of her great-grandfather's watch. She pulled the watch from his vest pocket and held it in her hands.

"For remembering this gift and wearing it for me tonight."

Ana opened it to read the inscription as Toshi repeated the words, "'*To be honorable is to be successful.*' I have never failed to wear it through all these years. The watch has become a part of me, that part which reminds me of your presence and your love. But, as yet, I have not lived up to its challenge."

Ana closed the watch carefully and placed it back in his vest pocket as she whispered, "You have always been an honorable man, Yamamoto-san. I could never have loved you if you were anything less, nor would I have given you this gift. Every choice you've made in your whole life has been based on the honor you hold for others. I may be angry at you for our differences and for what I've suffered because of them, but I have, and always will, respect you as a man of honor."

Ana's kind words brought a much-needed peace between them. To seal that peace, they shared a gentle kiss. For a few moments, they both imagined that they were sitting on the quiet porch of Ana's little house in Seijo. The memory was sweet, but it was interrupted by a voice from nearby.

"Yamamoto-san, most of the guests are gone and the young people have returned from their tour of the embassy. It is time for the evening to be over."

Ana recognized Ishikawa's voice and rose to greet him. He held out his huge arms to embrace her. She had always felt safe and protected when Ishikawa was near. How glad she was that Toshi still had this kind friend to watch over him.

Toshi and Ana followed Ishikawa into the embassy. They did not speak, but they both felt that a semblance of peace had come between them. Ana knew that she had, at least, tried to ease his guilt and let him know that the love they had shared so long ago was still there in her heart.

After everyone said their thank-yous and goodnights, Miko and Suzi walked out to the embassy limousine with their driver. But Toshi held Ana back a moment, guiding her to a quiet alcove near the entrance.

"Thank you for coming, Ana, for your gift of Mikoto, and your offer of forgiveness. Nothing is more precious to me. Do you think that it would be possible for us to spend an evening together before my departure for Japan next week…just for a final 'goodbye'?"

"Of course, I would love it. Please call me when you know what day you'll be free. I'd like to invite you to our Virginia home and to hear about your amazing adventures in the world of international diplomacy."

They moved easily into each other's arms, as if there had never been a separation between them, and their tender 'goodnight' held promise of one last moment together.

CHAPTER 25

"Two broken hearts now healed by love, and peace, at last, comes as a gift. Yet, also, comes the promise of a final parting!"
        --Ana and Toshiburo

The hour was late when the partygoers finally returned to Miko's apartment. Ana stayed overnight so she could sleep late and take her time getting back to Rock Hills. Though her thoughts were spinning from the evening with Toshi, Ana was soon sound asleep. But her dreams were of the past and mixed with images that disturbed her rest.

When morning finally came, Ana was awake far too early, still restless from her night dreams. She blamed it on the bed, but knew otherwise. The emotional evening with Toshi had stirred so many memories of long ago. Now, for a while, she would have to deal with them again. She wanted to see him before he left for Japan, but had no idea how they would even face a final parting now that their love for each other had been so tenderly renewed.

Questions began to plague her about that meeting. *'Should I ask him to our house? Should I risk opening the wounds even further than we have already done? Or should I say a final goodbye on the telephone, hang up and leave it at that?'*

In the midst of these disturbing thoughts, Ana heard a soft knock on the bedroom door and Miko's voice, "Mother, are you awake?"

"Yes, and dressed. Come on in, Miko."

He was barely awake, but came in and sat down on the bed.

"What a woman! It's seven o'clock on Sunday morning and you're ready for a major trip. I can hardly open my eyes."

"I'm sorry if I woke you when I took my shower, but I really was trying to be quiet."

"No, no, you didn't wake me. The telephone did."

Miko's demeanor suddenly changed. He became solemn.

"What is it, Miko? Are you upset about something? About last night? You can talk to me about anything, you know that."

280

Miko took her hand as he answered, "No, no, it was nothing about me. It's about the Ambassador. The call was from Mr. Ishikawa. He wanted you to know that he's at the Georgetown hospital with Mr. Yamamoto. The Ambassador has had a serious heart attack, and Mr. Ishikawa asked if you could come."

Ana turned pale, as if the life had been drained from her body.

"Oh my god! I knew last night that something was terribly wrong. What does Ishikawa want me to do? Did he say what I should do?"

Miko was surprised at his mother's reaction to the news about the ambassador.

"He asked if you would call him back right away. I have the number. If you can come, he'll send someone for you. Why is it so important that you go, Mother? What can you do?"

Ana calmed down for Miko's sake.

"Yamamoto and I were good friends in Tokyo. He was very kind to me and now I can return that favor. Ishikawa obviously believes that I can relate to the Ambassador as a friend from our younger days. A personal touch is often important when people are very ill. I'll call him back immediately."

Miko gave her the number and watched his mother closely as she made the call. The embassy secretary answered and told her that a car would be sent for her and should be there within thirty minutes. She didn't take time to ask about Toshi; she would know soon enough.

When Ana hung up the phone, she touched Miko's hand.

"They're sending a car for me. I'll see if there is anything I can do to help and let you know how things are going later in the day."

At the hospital entrance, a staff assistant led Ana to a private reception room for family members. Ishikawa met them there. Though his expression did not change, there was a tremor in his voice.

"Thank you so much for coming, Ana, your presence will mean everything to him."

She was suddenly frightened by the apparent seriousness of Toshi's condition. She couldn't help asking, "Have I done this to him, Ishikawa? We had some difficult moments last night. Neither of us has recovered from our parting and, of course, I said things that should never have been said. The whole evening was painful for him, leaving his appointment, leaving the States, and then my presence…and Miko's. We should never have come!"

She collapsed against Ishikawa. He gripped her shoulders and pushed her away from him to look into her eyes.

"Toshiburo has been ill since the day he was born. His life has been prolonged by many different methods. That has been my only purpose for being with him, to help him live as long as possible. We have been very successful in our struggles and had hoped that he could return to his home in Seijo, but we did not leave soon enough.

You did not cause this. On the contrary, your presence is his only hope for even a little more time. I have done everything that I can do. You are the only one who can bring him comfort and strength now when he needs it most."

"I'm not convinced that our conversation last night didn't cause this."

"You may accept the blame, if you wish, but no matter what the cause of his collapse, I am certain that your presence will be the only reason that he will fight for life. Please come with me to talk with his doctor, then you must go to Toshiburo."

He took Ana's arm and they walked together into a private medical office where Ishikawa guided her to a soft couch.

"I must be with Toshiburo now, but rest here until the doctor returns. He will tell you what is happening and what you should do."

Ana closed her eyes and began to talk to herself, hoping to gather courage for what might be ahead. *I must be positive now. I must find the strength somewhere inside of me to be his lifeline, to help him believe that he can live and that there is a reason to do so. I owe him that for all that we've meant to each other.'*

When the doctor entered the room, he saw a beautiful, dark-haired woman sitting with closed eyes and her head resting on the back of the couch in his outer office. She seemed to be sound asleep. Dr. Dominic Donatelli stopped to stare at her. This was not the person he had expected to find. He had been told that Mrs. Matsamura, a friend from Toshi's Tokyo University days, would be waiting to speak to him about his patient. Dominic sat down across the room wondering what connection there was between his patient and this beautiful 'mystery' woman.

Ana slowly opened her eyes to face the direct gaze of eyes as wide and dark as her own. She smiled and asked, "Are you Ambassador Yamamoto's doctor?"

He returned the smile and had the distinct feeling that this woman was drawing him into some secret place where he had never been before. Dominic spoke to break the spell that her eyes and smile had cast on him.

"Yes, I'm Dominic Donatelli, Ambassador Yamamoto's personal physician and a heart specialist here at the hospital. The Ambassador had been a patient of mine for some time. And you are…Mrs. Matsamura?"

His gaze seemed to indicate further questions. Ana explained before he could ask, "Please, I use my maiden name, Ana Gabrelli. My husband is deceased. He and I were close friends of the Ambassador when we were young and all living in Tokyo. Presently, I'm a professor of anthropology at Georgetown University and was at the embassy reception last night. The Ambassador seemed to be fine when we left him, though he appeared to be somewhat tired from the stress of the evening.

But, please, let me know how he is and what I can do for him. We were very close friends and he has no family here."

Dominic felt her deep concern, and he felt much, much more. He hesitated, trying to choose his words carefully. He could tell that she was fearful of her friend's condition.

"Mr. Ishikawa has informed me that I should speak to you as one of the family. He believes that your presence will help the Ambassador gain strength to fight for his life. Unfortunately, Mrs. Matsamura…"

Ana interrupted him.

"Please call me Ana. I think we should be less formal under the circumstances."

Dominic smiled at her wisdom.

"And when you feel comfortable to do so, I hope you'll call me Dominic. We'll be together for a while and I'm hoping to see a positive result of our different types of care. But I've been asked to be frank with you, so I must do that.

Mrs. Mat…Ana, we must face the fact that there is no hope for Toshiburo's recovery. His heart will not sustain more than a few months of life at the most. And that is more than likely an unrealistic estimate. He may not live through this day."

Dominic stopped and moved his chair closer to her, covering her tightly clasped hands with his own.

"Those of us who care for Toshiburo can create an atmosphere that will encourage him to fight through these crucial moments. And, perhaps, even allow a somewhat normal life for a short time. If we are successful in our cooperative efforts, I would consider that a miracle for which we could all celebrate!"

Ana stared at him, listening intently to every word. She was trying to control the fear that struck her heart at the thought of Toshi's approaching death. When the doctor finished his explanation, she laid her head back against the couch and shut her eyes again. Then she spoke with him in a hushed voice, "I cannot even fathom life without Toshiburo Yamamoto, without knowing that he lives and breathes somewhere in this world. I cannot even imagine the meaning of the words you've spoken to me. Surely, this won't happen to us now!"

Dominic saw her tears and moved to offer comfort, but she stopped him.

"No, no, I'm alright! It's just that I choose not to believe you. I have to believe that we can work a miracle, you and I."

"I don't know what you consider a miracle, Ms. Gabrelli, but I would consider it one if my patient could live through this day!"

"That's not enough for me. Please, let me see him now. I know what I must do and you know what you must do."

The power of Ana Gabrelli's spirit filled the room and Dominic's heart. He began to believe that with this woman's help it could very well be possible that his patient might live beyond all expectations. Dominic rose and held out his hand to Ana. The intensity of these few moments together drew them into a mutual embrace, as if they were making a pact to give all of their combined strength for one purpose…to save the life of Toshiburo Matsushita Yamamoto.

When Ana entered the hospital room with the doctor, she stopped to catch her breath at the sight which met her eyes. Dominic gripped her arm as they walked toward Toshi. He was so pale that he looked almost 'ethereal,' like a spirit caught between this world and the next. His eyes were closed and there seemed to be no strength in him.

Tubes of every kind were flowing in and out of Toshi's body. One machine was essentially breathing for him by forcing oxygen into his lungs and out again. Ana went to him immediately and turning to the doctor for a nod of permission, pulled a chair close to his bed. She grasped Toshi's hand, hoping that he could feel her presence. Then she put her face gently against his cheek and began whispering to him.

"It's Ana and I'm here with you, Tosh. We're going to come through this together and then I'm going to take you to my home in the Virginia hills where you'll find beauty and peace and strength. Just blink your eyes or squeeze my hand, something to let me know you hear me.

Please, Tosh, you mustn't leave us yet. We need some time just for the three of us, you and me and Miko. Promise me that you will do this for us. Promise me that you will do what I ask of you now."

Over and over, Ana whispered her plea to Toshi, lightly touching his arms and hands and face. Ishikawa came into the room after a while to relieve her, but she refused to move from Toshi's side.

"When he makes the promise I need, then you can take my place."

She had been with Toshi for nearly an hour when Ana felt a slight response. Toshi didn't open his eyes, but his slender fingers closed on her own. She pressed her lips against his hand and lifted her head to smile at Ishikawa.

"He has made a promise to me. He has promised to do what I ask of him. He'll give us some time."

Ishikawa walked across the room to Ana and gripped her shoulder. He saw Toshi's fingers holding hers.

"You are right, Ana. He will come back to us. He will come back for a while."

Ana whispered, "Just a little time is all I ask. And then, I'll leave it up to him."

Over the next few weeks, Dominic, Ana, and Ishikawa worked together to perform the miracle that would allow their patient and friend continued life. Dominic took little credit for Toshi's recovery of strength. All the doctor could do for his patient was to administer medication to stimulate his heart for continued life and to provide oxygen for continued breath. Dominic recognized that it was Ana's powerful presence that gave Toshi the desire to remain involved in the struggle for life.

At the end of Toshi's fourth week in the hospital, Ana came into his room to find him sitting up in bed and Dominic standing beside him. He was no longer plugged in to any type of medical device. Dominic gave Ana a huge smile and announced, "Behold! We have a new patient today!"

"Who has worked this miracle? Was it you, Dr. Donatelli?"

She walked around the bed and sat down beside Toshi to give him a very gentle 'welcome back' kiss. He accepted it with a smile. The doctor answered her question.

"What can I say? Perhaps my amazing medical brain is finally kicking in, or perhaps Ishikawa has found the drug that science has been searching for, or there's always a third possibility..."

"And what is that, dear doctor, sir?"

Ana looked askance at the doctor as he answered, "It could very well have been the constant attention of the gracious and beautiful Ms. Gabrelli. Whichever you choose, or all of the above, The Honorable Ambassador is back among us."

Toshi smiled and added, "I choose number three with the hope that this treatment will continue to be prescribed on an hourly basis."

Ana kissed him again and answered, "You can be certain it shall be or we will have to fire your personal physician! By the way, doctor, will you allow me a moment alone with your prize patient?"

The doctor answered with a teasing smile, "Now Ms. Gabrelli, please don't undo what we've all worked so hard to achieve. Go easy, now."

Ana laughed and gave him a warning look, "Go away, Dominic, and leave us alone!"

As Dominic left the room, he looked back to offer a final word of advice.

"Have a good visit, but don't hurt my patient. I'll give you fifteen minutes and I'm back."

Ana picked up one of the small pillows from Toshi's bed and threw it at Dominic. He ducked, but caught it, answering as he left the room, "There are those in the medical world who have great respect for my amazing intelligence!"

Ana waved the good doctor away and sat down on the bed beside Toshi. She became very serious as she asked, "Do you remember the promise you made to me?"

He looked at her with a smile.

"This is not a major quiz, is it? I'm not sure where you want me to go with this."

She laughed and started over.

"Okay, I'll give you some free points for having been 'out of this world' for a while. The day after the reception, when I came here to see you, I sat beside you and held your hand. You promised that you would come stay with Miko and me at our home in Virginia. Do you remember? You promised that you would do whatever I ask of you, now."

"I'm sorry, Ana, I don't remember anything since the reception. When I came to my senses a few days ago, I hardly even knew where I was. If I made promises to you, I will do my very best to keep them, but you must not even imagine that I will ever be well again. I am alive today and I have hope for tomorrow, but I can promise you nothing beyond that."

"That's all I'm asking. But you see, you gave away the best years of your life to someone you didn't love. Now, I'm asking you to give these last few moments to the ones you do love. I want this time with you, Toshi. And I want it for Miko, so he can know his father. You made the promise and I intend to claim it. Sorry, but you have no choice. When you leave here, Toshi, you must leave with me!"

Ana laughed and gave Toshi a kiss on the cheek, then turned quickly and left the room. She did not look back, but ran down the hall into the elevator. To say those words to Toshi were hard. She had to exert all the strength she could muster to overpower his fears, knowing that her own fears were tearing her apart. The thought of losing him, of knowing that he would soon be leaving her forever was so painful that she could see nothing but darkness ahead.

As she prepared to leave the hospital for the night, Ana made an important stop. She went to the flower shop and ordered a special arrangement, wrote a note on the card, and asked the florist, "Would you please take these flowers to Toshiburo Yamamoto's room? It's very important that he have them right away!"

The florist promised that she would have them in his room as soon as the arrangement was ready. Ana smiled as she read the card, for the words were as much for herself as for the one she loved. She would be all right, now. She would have the strength to do what needed to be done.

Toshi was stunned by Ana's final words to him and by the manner in which they were spoken. He could tell that she hadn't lost her Gabrelli spirit. And there was no way to resist her, for everything she said was true. He had broken trust with the woman he loved. Toshi couldn't even imagine how he could have made such a choice, but he knew that it was time to make amends for it. And what disturbed him most was the fact that, once again, he would be leaving her. He would be hurting Ana this one last time in a most terrible way.

Dominic came in soon after Ana had gone. He was surprised that she had followed his instructions.

"I was sure Ms. Gabrelli would be here tormenting you in one way or another. She is definitely a woman to be reckoned with."

Toshi smiled in agreement. "You have never spoken truer words."

Dominic watched Toshi's reactions carefully to make certain that the heart monitor recorded no signs of stress. So far, he seemed to be holding his own without the varied machines that had kept him alive for the past few weeks. From this point, he might only have to use the monitor at night and some periodic oxygen, as needed.

The doctor sat down beside his patient with a desire to talk openly with him.

"You seem a bit solemn, Toshi. Tell me how you're feeling."

Toshi sighed and responded truthfully, "My physical body is feeling as well as I could expect, but my spirit is troubled."

"In my profession, we're wise enough to be concerned with the effect of the spirit upon the body. Do you want to talk about it?"

"Yes, I realize that talking about it is all I can do at this point. I'm not afraid of death, Dominic, although I've struggled with it all my life as if I were. But now that it's upon me, I'm more trouble by involving others in the process. This journey has been a long and tiring one, and I'm certain that the ending will not be pleasant for those who much suffer...by watching the suffering of another.

There's something very important that I want to ask of you, but I cannot phrase the words. In my own culture, there would be no problem with it. But I know that there are restrictions here. Do you understand what I'm asking of you?"

"Yes, I understand perfectly and you need not discuss it further, Toshi. As your doctor, I can tell you that your wishes will be followed. You can trust that as a promise."

"Then I won't be hesitant to fulfill my promise to Ana, to be with her and Miko until this is over."

Toshi reached out his hand to Dominic. The doctor gripped the slender fingers of his patient to whom he had issued a death decree, and they shared in a solemn oath. Dominic spoke it aloud.

"When you tell me that the time has come, I will fulfill my promise to you with neither hesitation, nor remorse."

Toshi smiled at his doctor and friend.

"Whatever Ana wants from me now, whatever I am able to give, I can offer her knowing that you will be there for both of us."

As Dominic turned to leave, an orderly came into the room with a lovely *ikebana* arrangement of slender, purple Japanese iris. In the center, shining like a ray of sunlight, was one perfect white rose.

"This is for you, Mr. Yamamoto."

The young man set the arrangement on a small table under the window where Toshi could view it from his bed. Then he handed Toshi the envelope that had been attached to the flowers. Toshi turned the envelope over. He was almost afraid of the power that might emanate from the words on the card, for he knew it was from Ana.

He whispered to Dominic, "I need to be alone for a while, Dominic."

The doctor understood and responded quickly, "I'll go now, but I'll be back in a few hours to make certain things are set for the night. After all, we're anxious to get you out of this sterile environment and into a place of comfort where you can relax and recover your strength."

"I don't know how to thank you for saving my life and giving me a few added moments on this splendid planet. Perhaps during the time that is left, I can make up for some mistakes I've made in the past."

"Don't be hard on yourself, Toshi. You need all the strength you can muster to enjoy the time you speak of. And, who knows, perhaps those moments will turn into hours or days or months. The human body and human spirit can sometimes work wonders of their own when they are put to the test."

Toshi had to laugh at the indication of miracles occurring at this point in his illness.

"I promise you that I will be happy with just a few extra moments. I wouldn't dare consider anything beyond that. I believe that you and Ana have much in common. You are incurable dreamers."

"I couldn't be in this profession for long if I didn't leave a space for a few dreams now and then, could I? I face too many harsh realities all day long, every day. And, my friend, where would this world be without dreamers?"

Toshi answered in a mere whisper, "We would surely all be in hell. And thank you for reminding me of that fact."

The two friends laughed at the difference between them and the need for that difference. On his way out the door, Dominic put his hand on Toshi's arm and smiled, "Read your card and enjoy your dreams tonight!"

When the doctor had gone, Toshi looked at the envelope in his hand. He wondered what final message Ana was sending him after their conversation. He pulled out the card and read the simple words, written so carefully in Ana's script:

"To my 'Sweet Samurai,' Now is our forever. Your only love."

Toshi felt a sudden pain strike his heart. He wasn't certain whether it was from the joy of knowing that Ana could still love him, or from the bittersweet knowledge that their 'forever' would be for such a short time. He prayed to all the Buddha's he knew and to all the Shinto gods that there might be a "time after time" in some mysterious realm of existence where their love could be fulfilled as it should have been so long ago.

Much later in the evening, before he received the medication that would allow him to rest for the night, Toshi asked Ishikawa, "Would you please bring me the white rose from the flower arrangement by the window?"

Ishikawa did as Toshi asked. Toshi held the rose gently in his hand.

"Tell me the Legend again, Ishikawa."

Ishikawa sat beside his friend and told him "The Legend of the Rose." When Ishikawa finished, Toshi smiled at him and whispered, "I kiss the rose for Ana."

He pressed the white petals against his lips and held them there for a moment, then handed the flower to Ishikawa. His friend placed the rose carefully in the arrangement and watched over his friend through the night.

The strong, stoic 'samurai' was not ashamed of the tears he shed for the only person he had ever loved. He had promised long ago to be with this dear friend and care for him wherever the pathway should lead. Ishikawa knew that their journey together into that mysterious, eternal realm would soon begin.

CHAPTER 26

"Faced with the reality of a life, like sand, slipping away
as if caught in the ebb and flow of the tide, how does one
break the power of that eternal flow?"
--Toshiburo

Toshi continued to gain strength over the next few weeks and
was finally able to maintain a daily routine with minimal artificial
assistance. Upon Dr. Donatelli's recommendation, the team of
heart specialists approved the decision to allow his patient to be
moved from the hospital to Ana's home in Virginia. In order to
facilitate the process, Dominic visited the home where he and
Ana worked out an acceptable plan for Toshi's care.

At the hospital exit interview, the specialists were honest in
their statements to Toshi. They told him that there was little they
could do except make certain that he was provided with a
comfortable environment and the necessary medications to
sustain life for as long as possible. Their predictions were that he
would be fortunate to enjoy more than six months of life ahead.

Toshi accepted their statements graciously.

"Thank you very much for your kindness and professional
treatment during my recent struggle. You have prolonged my life
and I do appreciate that. I am well aware of my future, or, should
I say, the lack of it, but I want to assure you that I intend to make
these last moments of value, not only for myself, but for those
with whom I share them."

Toshi was relieved that Dominic had chosen to remain as his
primary specialist. The doctor assured his patient that he would
be making routine visits to the Virginia home, as well as
treatment in emergencies and encouraged Ishikawa to call him
immediately should there be any concern for Toshi's health.

At three o'clock the next afternoon, Toshi, Ishikawa, and
Dominic went by ambulance to Rock Hills. The driver was a
hospital technician who would set up the medical equipment
being transported with them.

On the way to Rock Hills, Dominic watched Toshi carefully
for any signs of stress from the trip, but everything went well.
The doctor and his special patient also had a chance to visit on

the way. Dominic was interested in Toshi's relationship with Ana and took this opportunity to ask, "I have a question for you, Toshi. How is it that a Japanese ambassador is so closely acquainted with a dark-eyed professor at Georgetown University?"

Toshi caught the twinkle in Dominic's eye and laughed as he replied, "I've been waiting for your question, doctor. And I can answer in a few words. We met long ago when we were young. Our paths crossed for a few short moments, but with Ana Gabrelli that is enough to last a lifetime! And now, twenty years later, our paths cross once more and it is as if there were no years in between."

"Then it truly was a love affair?"

Toshi hesitated before answering, "We loved each other and will always do so. But then, as now, the barriers between us remain insurmountable."

Toshi looked intently at Dominic as he continued, "Her presence is a powerful force, wouldn't you agree?"

The men smiled at each other as if sharing some secret knowledge between them. Dominic answered very quietly, "Yes, I would agree."

Neither spoke further of the subject, and Dominic vowed to lay aside the stirrings in his heart in respect for this gentle man who had become a friend.

Ana was well-prepared for her guests. She arranged the large family room on the first floor to serve as Toshi's bedroom and put up several Japanese folding screens to separate that part of the room from the lounge area near the fireplace. The bedroom off the family room was set up for Ishikawa. Both of these rooms had large sliding doors that opened onto the rear deck with views of the rocky hills and the gardens.

Another adjustment Ana made was to hire a young Japanese woman to do the cooking and housekeeping for them. Ana knew that Ishikawa and Toshi would appreciate having their beloved Japanese cuisine as often as possible. And, relieved of these responsibilities, she could spend all the time necessary with Toshi. Ana's mind was at ease, for she had done everything in her power to make her home comfortable for Toshi and Ishikawa, as well as for herself.

By noon, the medical equipment was arranged and everyone sat by the fireplace in Toshi's room to relax. Ana looked at Dominic with a question.

"Well, what does the good doctor think of the arrangement here? Will it be acceptable for your patient?"

"Ana, you have a beautiful home that can certainly provide a restful and inspiring environment. One feels a part of nature in this place. I'm sure that this, in itself, will help our patient recover strength. Did you say your husband designed it?"

"Yes, this is his dream home. He designed the renovation of this old place and watched over every board, brick, and nail that went into it. I'll give you a tour before you go back."

Just then a young Japanese woman walked into the room with a bottle of wine and glasses for a special toast. Ana proceeded to introduce her to everyone present.

"You must meet Yoshiko Yasutaka, our 'angelic visitor' who has come to stay with us and who will cure our ills and bring us much joy with her delicious Japanese cuisine."

Toshi caught Ana's eye and gave her an appreciative wink and a smile. Then Toshiko served the wine to the group and they waited to see who would give the toast. Dominic quickly took the lead.

"Let's raise our glasses to offer a blessing on this house, its hostess, and all who dwell herein. May there be peace and healing in this place."

Everyone was moved by Dominic's words and the spirit in which they were spoken. They drew close together to touch their glasses against Toshi's and drank the wine.

Ana responded to the doctor's words.

"I believe that toast says everything. Thank you, Dominic, for your blessing on us all."

While Dominic and the medical technicians made a final check of the 'life-preserving' equipment, Ana walked over and knelt down in front of Toshi who was sitting in one of the soft chairs by the fireplace.

She whispered to him, "Are you ready for this, Tosh? Are you ready for the second Gabrelli chapter in your life?"

He covered her hand with his and leaned over to whisper so no one else could hear, "I'd better be ready, Ana, for by all predictions, it will be the last chapter of my life."

Ana blinked as if he'd struck her and pulled back in shock. She couldn't stop the sudden tears. Toshi quickly put his arms around her.

"Forgive me, Ana, you didn't deserve that! Please be patient with me. I can't explain my feelings. It's as if…my life is like sand flowing through my fingers and I'm watching it, but can't catch it or stop it from slipping away. We may not be able to do this, Ana. You have to be honest with me, now. If you can't do it, we mustn't even try. I don't want to hurt you any more than I already have, but it seems that there is no other way this can be done."

"You've hurt me before and I've lived through it. I'll be honest with you, but have made me a promise…to do whatever I ask. Can you trust me enough to fulfill it?"

Ana waited for his answer. Toshi smiled and gave her what she needed.

"I have promised to trust you and to do whatever you ask of me, and I will do my best to keep that promise. So, now I'm totally at 'Gabrelli's' mercy and frightened at the prospect!"

"And, I am now requesting a demonstration of your trust. Kiss me, Toshi, to make amends for hurting me."

Dominic and Ishikawa had noticed the scene by the fireplace and both were concerned. They had seen Ana's shock and her quick tears. As they completed the arrangements for Toshi, Ishikawa touched Dominic's arm.

"They will be alright. I am here to watch over them. I will be here for Ana as well as for Toshi."

Dominic smiled, "Ishikawa, I trust you to know what's needed for both of them. You know how to contact me, any time of day or night."

Ishikawa nodded in assent, but did not speak, nor did he return Dominic's smile. Dominic walked over to talk with Ana and Toshi.

"I think everything's in order for your stay at this beautiful resort, Toshi. But I must steal Ana for a moment. She's promised me a tour of Rock Hills."

Dominic took Ana's hand and helped her up from the floor where she'd been sitting beside Toshi. She began the tour, "You'll be surprised at the space we have here. From the front, it looks like an ordinary home, but it is anything but that!"

Ana led Dominic through Toshi's room to the front hallway and up the stairs. They entered a study-sitting room between two large bedrooms and a room for the Japanese bath. From the study were sliding doors opening onto a porch with steps down to the deck.

"This is Miko's world. He still keeps many of his things there and comes out now and then on the weekends. Sometimes he brings friends with him. It's nice for them to get away from campus and the city whenever they want. My world is on the next level."

The hallway took them up a shorter flight of stairs to Ana's suite that included a sitting room, a study, her bedroom, and bath. Everything was off-white with beautiful Japanese artwork on the walls. Large ceramic pots and plants were in corners and beside the huge fireplace in the sitting room. The sliding doors from this room opened onto a porch with stairs to the first floor deck.

"This is unbelievable, Ana! You have so much privacy and so much space. This looks like an architect's dream home!"

"Mishima had a special gift for design and really should have been an architect. I encouraged him to do it and he intended to get more formal training after Miko entered college, but his death came too soon.

He wouldn't have done it earlier because he was practically a 'full-time dad.' He did all the things for our son that mothers usually do, plus everything that dad's do! I don't think it was a sacrifice for him, at all. He loved every minute of it."

"You can tell he loved his family to have created such a beautiful home for you."

Ana answered very quietly, remembering the depth of love that Mishima had shared with the woman who loved another man and with the child who was not his own.

"Mishima was a very special person. This home is, indeed, a monument to his love."

Ana looked at Dominic and smiled, "There's more!"

Ana enjoyed showing Dominic every inch of her home, the gardens, and the shrine. He continued to be enthralled with the beauties of Rock Hills. As they came back to the house, he commented, "I can't imagine a more perfect place for Toshi to be than in these beautiful and peaceful surroundings."

Ana smiled, "Thank you, Dominic. I'm very happy that he's been given some time to be here with Miko and me...and that you'll be watching over him and all of us!

Now, let's go enjoy a famous 'Yoshiko' meal. I don't know if you like Japanese food or not, but you will love *her* Japanese food!"

Toshi chose to join the group in the kitchen for his first taste of Japanese food since the embassy reception. Ishikawa pushed the wheelchair to the table and they all enjoyed Yoshiko's *sukiyaki*. Ana was glad to see that Toshi was able to eat a portion of the healthful and delicious food. Everyone complimented Yoshiko graciously, to which she responded with many bows and *arigatos*.

After dinner, the hospital crew prepared to leave and, while Ishikawa took charge of Toshi's care, Ana walked outside with Dominic. As he opened the door to step into the ambulance, Ana suddenly grabbed his arm. Dominic turned immediately and put his arms around her. He knew that she needed his strength. Ana whispered her question, "Am I strong enough to do this, Dominic?"

Dominic answered without hesitation, "I have no doubt at all, Ana. You're strong enough to do whatever you have to do. And Ishikawa and I are here to support you. Among all of us, don't you think we can bring Toshi the comfort and strength he needs?"

"Yes, I know we can. Thanks, Donatelli. We'll make it...all of us, together."

He smiled and let Ana go to the one she had obviously loved for so long. Dominic kept his own feelings in reserve. If there were ever a time for them to be expressed, they would be waiting for her, but for now, they must remain unspoken.

Ana returned to the house with added strength from Dominic's support. She knocked on Toshi's door to say goodnight and make sure he was comfortable. When Ishikawa opened the door and welcomed her in, Ana saw that everything was in place for Toshi's first night at Rock Hills. The fireplace was lit and gave warmth to the room and Toshi was sitting by the fire, resting in one of her large, soft chairs.

She whispered, "It was so quiet in here I thought you might both be sound asleep. May I come in and say goodnight?"

They welcomed her, of course. Ana sat down on the rug beside Toshi and leaned against his chair. She asked him, "What do you think of my home?"

"This is a beautiful and peaceful setting. I feel very comfortable here."

Then she asked hesitantly, "Wouldn't you rather be in your beautiful mountain home in Seijo?"

Toshi did not hesitate to answer, "No, Ana, this is my home, now. Your presence makes it complete. There's a calming spirit here. Mishima was a master artist with his design."

"Yes, he planned it carefully to include the beauties of the natural world."

They sat quietly for a while, each thinking their own thoughts about the unusual day they had just spent.

Toshi finally broke the silence.

"This home is a blessing, Ana. Thank you for sharing it."

Ana sat up and put her arms around him, "I think we should say goodnight now. You've had quite a day."

He smiled and accepted her goodnight kiss. Ana felt his mouth soft and warm against hers. She tasted the sweetness of his love and, for a moment, her heart was lightened. Toshi kept his arms around her as he whispered, "Ana, you are life's most precious gift to me."

Toshi's response confirmed her decision to bring him here, though it had been against his better judgment. Ana knew that he needed her now, even as much as she needed him. For a few moments, the lovers held each other and let their tears mingle with their kisses. Then Ana pulled away with a whisper, "Goodnight, Toshi, sleep well and wake up refreshed for a new day at Rock Hills."

She left him then, hoping he would rest through the night. She was certain that she would not. When she was finally relaxed and ready for sleep, Ana poured herself a glass of wine and sat down by her large window facing the hillside. She wondered what Mishima would think if he knew that the one he most feared was sharing the home that he had built with such loving hands for him, Ana, and Miko.

In a way, it didn't seem fair to her husband's memory and all that he had done for her. But in another way, it seemed that it was destined to end like this for her and Mishima and Toshi. Their lives had been intimately entwined for many years, and now it would end here in this place of beauty.

Ana knew that when everything was finished, she could never live in this house again. In all of this beauty, there would be too much sadness to remember. When Toshi left her this time, she would leave the past behind and not look back.

After Ana had gone upstairs, Toshi and Ishikawa continued to sit by the warm fire. Both were silent, contemplating the change in their lives.

Toshi finally broke the silence.

"You are the better half of me, Ishikawa. Tell me what do you see ahead for us?"

"We will find joy and peace here. We will be strengthened and, when the time comes, we will walk the pathway required of us."

"Are you going with me?"

"Yes, I will be with you wherever you go."

"You need not take this journey, my dear friend. You will be free when I am gone."

"When you were a small child, I was asked to come and share my wisdom and strength with you. I made a promise that no matter where you went, I would never leave you alone. There is nothing you can say that will stop me from fulfilling that promise."

"I did not choose this path, Ishikawa, and you need not do so. You can make a different choice. This is not required of you."

"It is my choice; therefore, it is required of me."

"You have loved me too much."

"No, that is not true. I have not loved you enough to heal your heart. That was my charge and my promise. I have failed both."

Toshi wanted to protest Ishikawa's self-defacing words, but knew that he must not do so. Ishikawa would make his own decision. Later that night, with Ishikawa watching carefully over his dear friend, Toshi slept well.

In his dreams, he saw a young man, vibrant and filled with love for the beautiful young woman walking beside him. The pair stopped at the edge of Lake Kawaguchi. There they could see the glory of Mt. Fujiyama reflected on the waters of the lake.

Suddenly, the young man let go of his partner's hand, smiled and said to her, "I'm going to cross to the other side, now. When you're ready, I'll be waiting for you."

The young woman started to follow her partner, but stopped and waved at him, "I can't go just yet. Watch for me. I'll be there."

The young man was soon out of sight. There was no sorrow there, for she saw in the quiet, crystal waters of the lake a reflection of her young lover standing peacefully on the face of the sacred mountain. She turned and walked away.

When Toshi awoke the next morning, for the first time in many weeks, he felt refreshed. As he watched the dawn come through the windows, he recalled his dream of the night before and was filled with a spirit of peace. He did not ask why this fate was his. That was a simple matter. He had been born with a physical defect that would one day end his life. His questions had to do with the future, but he knew that only by stepping into that future, would he know what awaited him there.

After his dream in the night, Toshi knew that whatever time was left for him must be shared with the one he loved. Ana's gift to him in his suffering had been renewed life. His gift to her now must be continued hope and assurance. Their gift to each other had already been given in days past, their eternal love and their son, Miko.

Over the next few days, Toshi and Ishikawa adjusted to a new lifestyle at Ana's home. The beauty and comfort surrounding them allowed Toshi to relax and gain strength. The restful silence granted him relief from the intense activity of the hospital. This, in itself, contributed to his renewed determination to live each day to its fullest.

Each afternoon, when Ana returned from her college classes, she and Toshi spent time together walking in the gardens and becoming reacquainted with each other. Toshi wanted to know how Ana had spent each moment of her life since their last goodbyes in Seijo, yet she was afraid to speak of it. He was afraid of the pain it would cause them both.

One evening, after they had taken a short walk through the garden, Ana turned to Toshi with a question.

"Why don't you ask me the questions that are in your heart?"

Toshi looked at her in surprise, "And what are those questions, Ana? Perhaps you know them better than I."

He waited, fearing that she knew him too well.

"About Mishima and Miko and our life together."

Toshi answered the only way he could, with the truth.

"I don't want to hurt you, Ana. I'm afraid of your tears. They break my heart and it's too broken as it is."

"I've heard it said that tears can be healing, that sometimes they can heal the brokenness between two hearts."

Toshi knew that Ana needed to talk to him. She needed to tell him everything that he was afraid to hear. They walked onto the deck and sat down in the soft chairs. He was silent for a moment, then he spoke with care.

"Of course, I want to know everything, every moment of your life since we parted, but I will leave it with you this way. You decide what you can speak of and when you feel it should be said. I trust you to know when that time should be."

Ana knew by his carefully-worded statement that Toshi was afraid of the past. But, at least, he had given her the freedom to share with him when she felt he was ready to hear it. And that was all she needed. She would know the time to speak.

Toshi broke the silence between them with his own question.

"There is something from the past that I want to know, Ana. A long time ago, I sent you a gift, through Miyuki. Did you ever receive it?"

Ana smiled as she thought of the night she opened the present.

"Yes, I received it, but in a very strange way. Not at all what you would have expected. Before I tell you about it, I want your promise that you will not be angry with Yuki. She told me that when you gave it to her, you gave her permission to use her own judgment about when to deliver it."

"I couldn't be angry with Miyuki, not even if she refused to deliver it at all. I gave her that choice."

Ana's voice softened as she spoke to him. "The rose is so beautiful, Toshi, and I thank you for it. When I opened it, I knew that Yuki had made the right decision. It didn't belong in this house with Mishima. Surely you knew its power. It is a touching symbol of our love for each other. It was as if you had sent me your heart."

Toshi whispered, "Before my precious 'Suki-ma' died, she gave me the ceramic rose and instructed me to send it to you. She knew that my decision had broken your heart as well as my own. The rose was her last gift from her 'samurai' lover, and it was delivered to her on the day of her wedding to my Grandfather Yamamoto. She had often told me the legend that I shared with you at Seijo, but I didn't know she had the rose until I opened the box and read her message inside. Sometimes I think that Suki-ma died of our broken hearts."

Ana put her arms around Toshi. "I'm sorry that I didn't get to meet your Suki-ma. I would have loved her. Yuki gave me the gift just two years ago, after Mishi's death. She and I were at a hotel in Tokyo the night before I was to return to the States. Miko was staying for the summer with the Matsamuras.

When I opened it, I nearly fainted. I was expecting a wedding gift of some kind, like a tea set or a ceramic vase. Yuki knew when she saw what it was and when I read the legend to her that she had done the right thing not to deliver it to me sooner. And I agreed.

If you ever have the strength to come up to the third level of this house, it's on my mantel there. I look at it every night before I go to sleep and every morning when I wake up. It's so beautiful and so thoughtful of you and your grandmother. Knowing it was hers, makes it all the more precious."

After a while, Toshi spoke.

"And while we are looking back, I must thank you for the gift you gave me on the night before your wedding. When I received your letter, only the knowledge that you and Mishima were already married, kept me from going to Yokohama. Your sweet words have filled the empty places in my heart all through those years. I have never deserved your love, Ana. You knew that from the beginning. And I still don't know why you offer it.

But that love gives me the courage now to accept whatever life still has for us, to risk being here with you in Mishima's house. There's a certain irony in this whole situation that frightens and humbles me. I find that being here, in this beautiful place, is surely a gift from Mishima, as well as from you."

Ana felt her inner strength slipping away at his words.

"One minute I feel so strong and know that I'll be able to help you through this. And the next, I can't bear to think of what's ahead. I really want to curse some god somewhere. Things aren't working out well for us, Tosh. They're not working out well at all! Who do we curse for this?"

To Ana's surprise, Toshi responded with a slight smile.

"When I was young, I often thought of cursing the gods for my illness, but I didn't know which one had done this to me. When they told me it was inherited, I thought of cursing my parents for creating this weak heart inside of my chest. But neither of them have ever suffered such a problem.

After Suki-ma told me her love story, I even thought of the romantic tale that her lover left because he was dying of heart disease and didn't want to break her heart as well. And I was the one targeted to inherit it. There are many options, I suppose, if we want to curse someone!"

Ana had to laugh then, knowing that he was teasing her.

"I've got a better idea! Let's stop wasting our precious energy cursing unknown gods and relatives, and use it only to love each other and make every day a good one!"

"I fully agree."

They chose to use their precious energy by sharing their love with each other until Ishikawa, like a watchful parent, disturbed their respite from reality.

CHAPTER 27

"Father and son, long separated, discover a bond beyond friendship. Years lost, fade away in the power of the moon."
--Toshiburo and Mikoto

While college classes were in session during the school year, Ana and Miko had a standing Wednesday luncheon date to catch up on each other's activities. This week, Ana brought up the subject of the Ambassador's presence in their home.

"Miko, do you think it was the right thing...to offer our home to the ambassador during his illness?"

He looked at his mother in surprise.

"Of course, I think it's a wonderful thing to do! After all, you were friends in the past and he needed help. We've got that big house out there with rooms we don't even use. Besides, I wouldn't mind having the chance to talk international politics with a 'pro' when he's feeling better."

"Well, I was a little concerned since I didn't consult you about the arrangement. I'm glad you approve and, since you mentioned it, I'm certain Yamamoto would enjoy sharing his diplomatic experiences with a young man who's considering that career direction. And besides, it could be good therapy to get his mind off his health."

"You don't think it would upset him? I mean, there's obviously a lot of stress in his position. He may not want to discuss it again. You know how that happens, sometimes, 'when it's over, it's over.'"

"I think he'd be honored that you would consider him a mentor. We all need someone to look up to us once in a while. He's a fine person, Miko, and I'm sure he'd be open to discuss any concern you might have about your future career."

"I may be out this weekend, then. I don't know what Suzi's plans are, but if I don't have any conflicts, I'll be out sometime on Saturday."

"Great, you'll brighten our day! Invite Suzi to stay over, too. There's plenty of room here!"

Ana was excited about the weekend. She knew Toshi would be very happy to see Miko. Not only would it give him an opportunity to share his experiences in the diplomatic world, he could become better acquainted with his son. She chose not to mention the visit, however, in case Miko wasn't able to make it. A surprise would be much better than a disappointment.

When the weekend arrived, so did Miko. It was late Saturday afternoon when he walked out to the deck and found Toshi resting in a soft lounge chair. He walked over to greet their distinguished guest.

"Good afternoon, Ambassador. I just came out from the city for a while. May I disturb you for a few minutes?"

Toshi laughed as he answered, "I *hope* you won't disturb me…but you can certainly visit with me if you wish. Please, sit down and relax." He pointed to the empty lounge chair beside him.

Miko smiled and turned to go back to the kitchen.

"Just a minute and I'll bring us some iced tea."

When he returned, Miko handed the Ambassador a glass of tea and sat down beside him. Toshi opened the conversation, "First of all, please address me informally. I'm not an ambassador any more. I'm just an ordinary citizen of the world, lounging on your lovely porch and totally dependent upon your hospitality. Please call me 'Toshi' as everyone else here does. I prefer it."

"Well…I'll try. But don't get upset if I forget now and then."

They sipped their tea for a while, then Miko finally gathered the courage to explain the reason for his visit.

"I have an ulterior motive for coming out today. Be sure to tell me the truth, now. Do you mind if I pick your brain a little, about the life of an international diplomat? I'm interested in that career and this is the first time I've had a chance to talk to someone who has actually lived it."

Toshi answered with a pleasant smile, "Feel free to ask me anything you like and I'll decide if I'm free to answer."

"Thank you, I really appreciate it. I guess, in general, I'd like to know if you would choose this career again. I mean, has it been a rewarding experience for you?"

305

Toshi looked closely at Miko, trying to decide if his questions were loaded with hidden meaning. He chose to believe this young man was genuinely interested and responded honestly, "You know, of course, that you've started with the most difficult question. I come from a culture which made my choice much simpler than yours might be. I was expected to make this choice, so I did. You, on the other hand, have more freedom to choose.

I would never attempt to advise you, but you've asked an honest question, and I'll give an honest answer. In the first place, to give one's life to this profession demands that one give up every other part of one's life. If I were a young man like you and had been free of all expectations placed upon me, I would not have chosen this profession."

"What? Are you serious?" Miko was stunned by the answer.

"You expected me to answer differently?"

"Well, yes, I did."

Toshi explained, "My inner desires were more academic, much like your mother's. I've always loved the atmosphere of the university classroom. At the time of my appointment, I was a professor of international politics and foreign relations at Tokyo University. That was my first choice of profession and those were the happiest moments of my professional life.

The life of a diplomat is tightly structured and highly competitive. It demands constant awareness of all sides of every issue and requires a strong will. At times, it even requires the willingness to do what one may feel is not 'right' in order to reach agreements among conflicting parties. I often found it debilitating to my inner values to accept one solution when I knew that another was the better way to go.

In the classroom, one can find freedom and the exciting exchange of ideas. There is opportunity to explore all sides of issues and express them in discussion without the need to come to a final conclusion. That is more who I am than who I have become. I gave up the classroom to fulfill the expectations of others."

Miko noticed Toshi's hand shaking as he lifted his glass to drink. He realized that the question had triggered an emotional response from the former ambassador who had recently been celebrated for his great success in the field of international relations.

Miko was shocked to silence. He looked away from Yamamoto for a moment. His question had been a mistake and he blamed his mother for encouraging him to do what his gut feelings had told him not to do.

But Toshi quickly relieved Miko's distress by smiling and asking his own loaded question.

"You asked for the truth, but did you really want it?"

"I'm sorry if my question upset you. Perhaps it was too personal."

"No, Miko, the question was not too personal, but it does upset me to address it. Now I have to face the consequences of what I did not know then. You have the benefit of my experience. However, the young are often skeptical of counsel from their elders. They most often believe that everything will be different for them because they are different persons. And, perhaps, that is so. You must choose your own life direction."

"My mother warned me that if I asked you a question, you would answer it. But, I didn't expect the answer you've given."

"Your mother knows, as do I, that this question is important to you. She and I both value honesty. However, I must add that she is much more blunt and to the point than I. Have you inherited that gift from her?"

"I don't think so. She even frightens me sometimes. Mother tells me that I'm more like my father; I can smile when I want to cry. It's easier for me to avoid confrontation than to participate in it.

You've given me a good lecture on the diplomatic lifestyle, though. I'm thinking now that I should consider my career direction very carefully. I'm not sure if I'm cut out for the type of life you've just described. I really appreciate your honesty, Ambassador...I mean, Toshi."

Toshi smiled and laid his hand on Miko's arm. "Miko, you must not take my words as 'advice' to you. That would be a mistake on your part. I would never presume to give you advice on the future. My words were a simple answer to a question from someone who comes from a very different background than my own."

307

Miko thought a moment about Toshi's comment. "We may have different backgrounds, but I'm not so sure we're that much different from each other. You've given me a lot to think about."

They sat together in silence, drinking their tea and each thinking about what the other had said. After a while, Ana came out on the patio to join them.

"Mmmm, it's so quiet out here. Should I disturb your meditations?"

Toshi answered with a smile, "You could never disturb us. Our meditations, I'm sure, could never be as enjoyable as your presence."

She laid her hand on Toshi's shoulder, and looked at her son as if he were her student and she his professor. "Such poetic words, so well spoken. Miko, are you taking notes on the manner in which the diplomats of this world win over their adversaries and even obtain signatures on peace agreements. You will learn from a master."

There was no way Toshi could resist her baited comments.

"You see, Miko, it takes great diplomatic finesse to remain anywhere close to your mother and maintain a semblance of peace. She follows none of the accepted rules for peacemaking!"

Miko laughed and agreed, "Then I might make it as a diplomat, after all. I've had several years of good training in that exercise."

Ana frowned at them both and sat down to join them.

"I take that as a compliment on my excellent teaching skills. Well, my dear son, have you learned anything of value from our resident diplomat this afternoon?"

"I've learned never to ask a former diplomat if he would ever choose that profession again."

Toshi glanced at Ana. She raised her eyebrows at him.

"Oh, so he told you the truth, then?"

"It was more than the truth; he gave me a warning."

She looked at Toshi accusingly, "You mean you left out all the amazing benefits of such a career…world travel, honor, prestige, public acclaim, awards, medals…shall I go on and on?"

Toshi felt a masked hostility in Ana's comments and reacted to it.

"Those are not benefits, they are bribes."

"Such cynicism! Do I detect a bit of 'it's always easier to look back and be sorry, than it is to look ahead and be wise' attitude?"

Miko saw his mother's eyes flashing the way they had often done when she was angry with him. He knew he was in the midst of a battle, but didn't know why or what it meant. He helplessly waited for the explosion.

As difficult as it was for Toshi, he refused to let Ana bait him into a war of words in front of Miko. He controlled his anger while attempting to calm hers. He replied to her question with a smile, "Miko asked me an honest question. I gave him an honest answer. That is all there was to our discussion."

Ana saw the warning in Toshi's eyes and chose to heed it. She returned his smile, "I'm sorry I disrupted your conversation. I merely came out to tell you that Yoshiko would like to invite you both to dinner. Will you join us?"

Miko jumped up, thankful for a break in the tension.

"I'm ready, let's go eat!"

He left for the kitchen while Toshi stood to walk in with Ana. She took his hand and held him back, "I'm sorry, Tosh, I don't know why I..."

Toshi interrupted her, "Don't ever apologize to me for being who you are! Who you are is the woman I love. Your wild, Italian nature is what gives you the passion that captivates me. You so easily express all the emotions that I can hardly even accept in myself, let alone share with others! You make me whole, Ana. Even when I'm angry with you, I love you for forcing me to feel my own anger!"

Toshi was suddenly moved to express his feelings in a way that surprised them both. He pulled her toward him and kissed her with a passion that he didn't know he still possessed. When they stopped for breath, he spoke, "Look what you've done to me, now! Your spirit is everywhere in this place. I can't seem to resist it."

Ana laughed at him, "You may become a living, breathing human being again."

"I'm not sure I'd know how that feels. I've been dead too long and..."

Ana stopped his sentence with her own passionate kiss.

"That's how it feels…don't you remember?"

As they turned and walked toward the kitchen, Toshi noticed Miko and Yoshiko standing on the kitchen porch looking toward the deck. He realized that he and Ana had not been alone.

"I think we may have become a spectacle. Your son and housekeeper seem to be in shock at this sight. What do we do now?"

"Oh, let's just enjoy being celebrities and go eat dinner!"

The onlookers stared unbelieving at the scene on the deck, then Yoshiko punched Miko on the arm and smiled, "Isn't that sweet?"

"I don't know about sweet, but it certainly is surprising!"

She grabbed his arm and turned him around.

"It's not polite to stare!"

They laughed and both looked back one last time before they went to the kitchen to pour the tea. When Ana and Toshi came in, everything seemed normal. Toshi chose to defer any comments to Ana. And she intended to say nothing. If anyone wanted to ask, she would have an answer. But Yoshiko and Miko were both afraid to say a word and hoped they hadn't been staring.

Yoshiko was the first to break the silence.

"Someone call Ishikawa to dinner. Everything's ready."

Miko moved quickly, "I'll get him."

He was relieved to have an excuse to do something. His mind was still whirling from the conversation with Yamamoto and from the emotional scene he had witnessed between the distinguished Ambassador and his highly-volatile mother. Miko was certain that, for some reason he could not fathom, his mother had instigated everything that had happened. He was definitely confuse.

In spite of the events of the day, everyone enjoyed the delicious meal and joined together to compliment Yoshiko on her wonderful cooking. While they were eating, Miko found himself watching his mother and Toshi, trying to uncover any hidden meanings in their conversation. He was relieved when Suzi called and he was able to leave the room for a while. When he came back, Toshi and Ishikawa were not in the kitchen.

Miko looked at his mother in surprise, "Where did they go?"

310

"Toshi needed to rest. He'll be okay."

But Miko noticed that his mother's concern showed openly on her face. He felt a tremor of fear go through his body. When he was visiting with Toshi, he had forgotten the Ambassador's fragile health.

His mother reminded him, "One moment he seems so strong and the next, so weak. It's easy to forget that the illness is in charge of his life. And it's hard for him to remember, too. He just needs to rest, now."

Ana averted her gaze from her son as she went outside. He followed her and, for a while, they walked through the gardens in silence. Then Miko found the courage to speak.

"Yoshiko and I enjoyed that kiss on the deck. We were just surprised, that's all."

Ana smiled at her son's attempt to uncover the relationship between her and Toshi. She chose to relieve his mind somewhat.

"I'm sure you've concluded that Yamamoto and I have been more than friends in the past."

"I haven't concluded anything, but I suspect it now. It certainly doesn't bother me, if that's what you think. We all have our moments, don't we? In fact, I feel real good about it. You both have excellent taste. It's just that you are such, well, exact opposites that I can't imagine you in a close relationship, at least not for very long."

His mother laughed at Miko's perceptive conclusions, "Well said, my son. And that is exactly why he became the distinguished Ambassador and I chose to marry your father and have a family and career.

"Were you ever sorry about that choice, Mother? You missed a lot of those amazing 'benefits'!"

She laughed at his reference to their conversation with Toshi.

"I wasn't into taking 'bribes'!"

Ana smiled at her son and patted his cheek as if he were still a child.

"You're a bright, young man and totally free to choose your own direction in life. That is, if you are totally free. I keep forgetting about the beautiful, red-haired Suzannah. Has she a word to say about your future?"

"Ah, ha, and now the sly attempt to turn the questioning toward me! I'm an educated man, not your little boy any more. No more mind tricks, Mother! You didn't answer my question. Are you going to satisfy me...or not?"

"With your suspicious and romantic mind, I doubt if anything I said would satisfy you."

"Well, maybe a passionate love affair with sad and tender endings and rose petals thrown over the gurgling falls..."

:"...just before I throw myself over? I caught you. I am still alive and well."

"But only because Mishima rescued you and took you into the sunset to..."

"Rock Hills, Virginia? What a romantic ending! If you were still my little boy, I'd tell you to take a cold shower and go to bed."

"Why do you always get the last word?"

"Because I am much older and much more Italian than you! Go help Yoshiko with the dishes. We'll have a more intelligent conversation when you recover from your romantic illusions."

"Okay, okay, but just let Yoshiko and I know when the next episode in this romance drama will take place. We don't want to miss out on anything!"

Miko turned and ran to the house before his mother could find anything to throw at him. He loved finding a crack in his mother's perfect armor. At last, he could look at Dr. Ana Maria Gabrelli Matsamura as a human being, just like him. Miko jumped with joy all the way to the kitchen.

Sitting on a stone bench in the garden, Ana laughed at Miko's crazy antics. But something disturbed her at the same time. He had almost retold the whole story as it had actually occurred, complete with the rose petals. She felt her past coming too close to her son's future and was fearful of the consequences.

Though Ana had no idea what she would do now, she felt certain that the truth was not an option. She could not even imagine herself telling Miko that his father was not his father, but just a sweet man she had loved in some far distant moment of her youth?

The last few days had drained Ana's energy and put new fears into her mind. She climbed the stairs to her suite and

312

enjoyed the luxury of a hot, soothing shower. After the relaxing shower, she laid down on the bed and fell sound asleep. She did not wake until morning.

Much later that evening, Toshi woke from the rest that his body had required after dinner. He felt his strength returning and was thankful for the special medications that Donatelli had prescribed for him and for the ministrations of Ishikawa. Toshi knew that without these helps he would not be able to continue life, for the pain would be unbearable and the weakness debilitating.

At times like this, Toshi felt a strong sense of guilt for the financial blessings that had been a gift from his father, for only because of those blessings, were the benefits available to him that kept him alive. Toshi did not fail each day to offer prayers to the gods he worshipped for those who suffered without relief, simply for lack of material wealth.

These were the thoughts that troubled his mind as Toshi strolled out onto the deck. The moon was bright and all was quiet. Nature seemed to be inviting him to enjoy the evening and to let her provide her own ministries to his body and spirit. He gladly accepted the invitation.

Toshi walked through the gardens for a while, then stretched out in a soft deck chair where he could look into the face of the moon and gather its rays and wisdom. Ishikawa brought Toshi a glass of sweet wine and returned to the house to allow his friend time for private meditation.

After a while, Toshi realized that there was someone else enjoying the moon with him. Miko was sitting on the steps of his second-floor deck. He spoke to Toshi in a hushed voice, not wanting to break the spell that the moon was casting over their surroundings.

"My father would always say on a night like this, 'What a perfect night for moon-viewing.'"

Toshi replied in the same quiet tone, "And I would agree. Moon-viewing is an important part of our Japanese culture. At my home in Seijo, there is a small house on the mountainside that was built just for that purpose. If I were at my home tonight, I would be there in that little house. I would be kneeling by the open windows, lost in the power of this perfect moon."

Miko moved down the steps to the deck. He pulled a chair close to Toshi, stretched out with his face to the moon, and asked his question, "How does the moon give its power to you?"

"Perhaps everyone would answer that question differently. As a child, I believed that its power was in its light. I knew that if the moon had no light, we wouldn't be able to see it, so it would have no power. I believed that its light was its purpose, to let us see the world around us in a different way. All the colors are muted in the moonlight; we see only dark and light and shadows. Yet, it is all beautiful.

Then I remember how surprised I was when I became older and discovered that the moon had the power to direct the tides of the earth. The consequence of that power is unlimited.

And then, there were times I felt its power reaching into my heart and touching something there, as if to bring life to that which had no life. I can't describe that experience, except to say that when it happens, I feel that I must fall on my knees and bow to the moon's presence inside of me.

What amazing power is in that tiny, silvery ball. I have never fathomed that mystery, for I am not a scientist. I am merely an observer of its beauty and a recipient of its power."

Miko and Toshi sat quietly for a while, each thinking their own thoughts. Miko finally broke the silence.

"We're all so different, everywhere. You see so much in this moonlight because you've been taught to spend time thinking about it. Here, we don't think about the moon, we just enjoy it. When we have a beautiful, moonlit night in these Virginia hills, we think about love. We want to be with our sweetheart and drive out on a quiet hillside by a little lake and say sweet things to each other and make love like crazy! That's what we call moon-viewing on this side of the world. That's the power and the purpose in our moonlight. It's just for love, sweet love!"

They laughed together and Toshi commented, "I can't think of a better purpose or of a stronger power than that. In the end, love is really all there is to life anyway, is it not? What higher purpose is there than to share your life with the one who is dearest to you? And if this beautiful moon inspires you to that purpose, it certainly is powerful. Perhaps our two worlds are not so different, after all."

The two men, from very different worlds and with a generation of age separating them, sat in silence for a long time without comment or movement. They both seemed lost in their own contemplations. Until the younger man asked a question that brought sudden pain to the heart of the elder.

"Is my mother 'dear' to you, Yamamoto-san?"

Toshi seemed frozen by the words Miko had spoken to him. He wanted to walk up the steps to Ana's room and ask her to come down and answer her son's questions. He was too fearful of the results if he should attempt to do so. A thousand different words floated through his mind, but he finally chose a simple truth.

"There was a time, when we were young, that our paths crossed for a moment. But then…we each chose to walk in different directions."

"But you're not the Ambassador tonight, who never answers a question directly. You're a friend who is sharing my home with me. I may be young, and perhaps you'll consider me 'impertinent' to ask such a question, but my mother is very precious to me. I need an answer, not the vague explanations you would give a committee on trade agreements."

The silence between them lasted a long time, but Miko waited patiently for the answer. Toshi finally spoke.

"Miko, you are young and you are, indeed, impertinent. But I understand how precious your mother is to you, as you are to her. The answer to your very personal question is 'Yes. She is dear to me.'"

Miko felt something turn over in his chest. He had expected Toshi's answer, but when he had heard it, he was shocked to silence. They sat a long time in the moonlight before Miko could find the words he wanted to say. He barely whispered them.

"Is there enough power in this moon to inspire you to share your love with the one who is dear to you?"

Toshi responded with kindness.

"There are some questions that cannot be answered simply. They intrude into the private heart of another where there are emotions which dare not be expressed in such harsh, cold form as words. In the matters of the heart, events must evolve of their

315

own accord and whatever occurs will be the best way. I beg your pardon, Miko, but I cannot discuss this with you further."

Miko stood and bowed with respect to this powerful, yet gentle, man whom he was now assured had loved his mother very deeply and still did.

"Goodnight, Yamamoto-san, sleep well. We'll see what events might evolve tomorrow 'of their own accord.'"

Miko expected a rebuke from this gentleman whom he had just spoken to as if he were one of his college friends, but it did not come. Instead, Toshi laughed at him and waved him away with a simple word, "Goodnight, Miko. You are, indeed, your mother's son. The final word must always be yours!"

Miko could not resist a final word.

"How right you are!"

He ran up the stairs quickly so Toshi could not speak a last word. Toshi laughed, even as tears fell from his eyes, for the gentle heart and perceptive mind of his own, sweet son.

CHAPTER 28

*"The brilliance of the moon overpowers the heart with a
longing that can never be fulfilled! O light of heaven's
sky, why do you torture me so?"*
            --Toshiburo and Ishikawa

After Miko left, Toshi sat in the moonlight for a long time
reviewing their conversation. He was touched that his son had
respected him enough to encourage his relationship with Ana.
Yet Toshi felt certain that the obstacles between him and his
former lover were insurmountable and could allow nothing more
than a warm friendship. He finally left the beauty of the night to
take his much-needed rest.

When Toshi entered his room, Ishikawa was waiting.

"You are late, Toshiburo. How did you find the moon?"

"Its brilliance is filled with power, but it has laid a heavy
burden on my heart."

"There is nothing but beauty in the sky tonight, how could
such beauty burden your heart?"

Toshi was quiet a moment, not wanting to speak the truth that
Ishikawa already knew too well.

"With a longing that cannot be fulfilled. I have nothing to
offer her but my weakness and the promise of a final
abandonment. I should never have come here!"

Ishikawa chose his words carefully in response to Toshi's
despair.

"How sorry I am that you have not learned the wisdom of the
moon, my friend. All of your life you have knelt on moonlit
nights and faced the bright rays from the sky. You have given
reverence to the moon, but you have never learned its wisdom.
Even Ana has tried to teach you, but you have not understood.
Now you must learn, Toshiburo, before you break your own heart
as well as hers. For yours will break under its burden of despair
and hers from its emptiness."

"Then teach me, once and for all, Ishikawa. Teach me what I
haven't learned. I don't want to hurt her again, but it seems
inevitable that I will do so."

"The power you felt tonight in the moon's silver rays should not bring a burden to your heart. That power is a gift to you, for the wisdom of the moon is this: 'Love is the power of life. There is no death in it, there is only hope, for love is eternal.'

Look into the face of your son and tell me that love is a burden too heavy to bear. Ana's love for you has brought a gift of eternal joy to all of us. She has understood the meaning of love. She has never been afraid of giving it away. But now her greatest fear is not of loving and losing you, but that you will refuse to accept the gift when you need it most. And this proud refusal on your part will, indeed, break her heart and yours!

If you can give your love to Ana now, without hesitation or fear, it will be the most precious gift that you could offer her. One day your ashes will be scattered across the face of Kawaguchi, but your love will continue to touch the lives of all those with whom you have shared it. Would you condemn Ana to the sorrow of facing your death without the joy of having shared your love fully and freely to the end of your life?

You must seek your own truth, Toshiburo. You must find your own answers to life's dilemma. Tonight the moon has offered you its wisdom, but do you understand it? Will you accept it? Only you can answer those questions."

Without waiting for a reply from his friend, Ishikawa left Toshiburo and walked out into the moonlit night to seek his own peace. But there was no rest, now, for Toshi. He opened the outside doors to let the moonlight disturb his mind and heart until morning.

Toshi recalled that it was he who had finally reached out to Ana. He had sent the invitation to her for the embassy reception. After all those years in the same city, neither of them ever attempting to disturb the other's life, he had made the move toward her.

He began to question his own motives. Was it merely pride that held him away from her now because he had nothing to offer but his weakness and the final struggle? Would there be any hesitation if he had come to her in strength? So many years ago, he left her because of his sense of responsibility. And now, would he walk away because of his pride?

Perhaps, after all, his love for Ana was not strong enough to conquer his own fears. Tonight, Toshi wept for the shame of his own weakness, not the weakness of body, but the weakness of spirit to fulfill the promise he had sensed in the moons bright rays, that life is for living.

The dawn had come when Ishikawa returned from his night on the mountain paths. He found Toshi still dressed and sitting in one of the soft chairs by the fireplace. Ishikawa's fears rose as he went quickly to his friend's side.

"Yamamoto-san, forgive me! I should not have disturbed you with my counsel last night. You have not slept. You must rest now."

Toshi waved Ishikawa away.

"No, no, it's alright. I had to think about many things, to answer questions in my own mind. You were right to speak your thoughts to me. We're friends. We must be honest with each other for there's no time to be otherwise. I thank you for your disturbing words. But now, I must rest, and I need your help to do so."

Ishikawa prepared the medication that would ensure a restful sleep for his dear friend. He made certain that the oxygen and heart monitor were in place, then left him to the rest that the drugs would bring. Toshi would not wake for several hours, but Ishikawa was certain that Toshi's strength would soon return.

Ana woke early and ready for the day. She had slept like a child through the night. As she came into the kitchen to prepare some breakfast, she noticed that Toshi's doors were closed and the blinds drawn. Within minutes, Ishikawa walked into the kitchen and motioned for Ana to come onto the porch with him. She knew that something had happened last night to disturb Toshi. Ishikawa spoke to her.

"Toshiburo had a difficult night, but he is resting now with help from medication. You mustn't worry. He will recover strength later today, after his sleep."

"What happened? Has his heart weakened? You must tell me. Why didn't you wake me?"

"No, no, he was merely sleepless and this weakened him. He will be fine after the rest. You will see."

"Why don't you tell me the truth, Ishikawa?"

"You and Toshiburo are the only ones who must deal with the truth. I cannot tell you his truth."

While Ana and Ishikawa were talking, Miko came down the outdoor stairs from his room. He had heard part of the conversation and was worried now.

"What's going on? Is it Toshi? What's happened?"

Ishikawa answered his questions.

"I was merely telling your mother that Toshiburo is resting today from a difficult night. I assure you, he will be better soon."

"Oh no! I hope it wasn't because of our conversation last night. We talked pretty seriously about some things and we were up late. Have you called Dr. Donatelli? Shouldn't we call him?"

Ishikawa responded soothingly, "You must be calm. Toshiburo has been doing very well, much better than any of us ever expected. It is only natural that he will have some difficult times now and then. If I think the doctor should be called, we will do so. I'm checking his pulse and the monitor often, and he is receiving oxygen and medication. There is no cause for alarm at this point."

Ana felt Miko's concern, but she trusted Ishikawa's wisdom.

"Thank you, Ishikawa. Just keep us posted. If we can do anything to help you, whatever you want, let us know. I think we should all relax now, have a good breakfast, and continue our normal routine."

Ana took Miko's arm and led him into the kitchen. Ishikawa joined them there and they shared a healthy breakfast. When they finished their meal, Miko spoke to his mother in a very distressed voice.

"Mother, I've got to talk to you about last night. Let's go upstairs to your room. I'm afraid that I've upset Mr. Yamamoto. We had a very serious discussion, and I said some things that I shouldn't have. He actually became angry, even though he expressed it in a polite way. But I felt it very strongly."

Ana saw that Miko was quite upset.

"Then let's go right now and talk about it!"

They went out to the deck and up the stairs to Ana's suite. She was concerned about what this late night discussion might have revealed. Though she knew that eventually every truth must be told, she wondered if it had been told in the moonlight without her presence.

Miko started talking the moment they entered his mother's bedroom. He was pacing up and down and almost in tears.

"Mother, I can't believe what I did? I went far beyond the limits of courtesy with Mr. Yamamoto. We were just sitting there, talking about the moonlight and its power. And then he said something about the need to share love with people who are dear to us, and I simply asked him, well, if *you* were dear to him. There are so many signs every day between you two, and then that kiss on the patio yesterday. I wanted to know what he felt for you. It seemed a natural question at the time, but after I asked it, I realized it was a major mistake!"

Ana remained calm so that Miko could relax and tell his tale coherently.

"What made you think it should not have been asked?"

"Because the question invaded his privacy. He was quite upset. We had expressed our personal feelings about the power of the moon and its beauty, and he explained to me the importance of 'moon viewing' in Japanese life. It was a very comfortable conversation, until I asked that question.

He tried to avoid answering directly, but I pushed him and he finally admitted that you are dear to him, but that some questions intrude into the private heart and should never be asked. I knew he was upset because he ended our conversation abruptly."

Ana sat down on the floor in front of the fireplace and was quiet for a long time. Miko walked over and sat down, leaning against the fireplace, facing his mother. He waited for her to speak, and she finally obliged.

"Miko, you are an intelligent young man with a sensitive spirit. You are on your way to discovering your future. I believe that this moment has brought us to the point where we can relate to one another as adult to adult. Would you agree?"

Miko looked at his mother, sensing the change in the atmosphere, and he was worried.

"What do you mean, Mother? I feel like an adult, but sometimes I'm not sure I'm ready to be one. What will be different between us, as adult to adult?"

"I will respect you enough to be open with you about my own life and feelings. I will no longer protect you from knowledge, even though it might hurt you. I will listen to you with the same intensity and openness that I give my peers. You will share with me without worry of being censured by an over-protective parent who wants her son to be perfect.

In other words, we will be honest with each other, without fear of repercussions or cracks in our love. Those are some things that will be different. Do you think you are ready for such a 'relational shift'?"

"Well, the way you put it, it sounds like a *major* shift in some ways, but in other ways it just sounds like we'll continue being friends. I guess that's what I was describing last night with Mr. Yamamoto. Suddenly, I was relating with him 'adult to adult,' but it seemed natural because I have never known him as a parent. I don't know how I would do with a shift between you and me. I'm a little afraid of what I would be giving up."

"Miko, you were giving advice about love relationships to the Ambassador last night. Somehow, I believe that you are quite ready for this new role, and I'm ready to take the step with you, dear son. I respect you very much and, because of who you are, I need to share some information with you that I believe you're ready to hear and to understand."

Ana felt calmer than she had ever expected when she had envisioned this moment in the past, but Miko had set the stage perfectly. She knew it was time. She began speaking the words that would change everything between her and her son.

"Miko, you haven't known Toshiburo Yamamoto as a parent because I've never allowed you to know him in that role. I gave you a wonderful father, Mishima Matsamura, as a gift."

Ana looked directly into Miko's eyes and whispered, "But you were a gift to me from Yamamoto."

She paused to let the words and their meaning sink into his mind. Ana struggled with the tears that wanted to come flowing out of her heart, all the emotion that had been locked away for so long.

"Do you understand what I'm saying, Miko? The Ambassador is your natural father. That's why you've felt close to him and able to share with him without fear. Because you belong to each other."

Ana looked at him, waiting for his response. Miko appeared to be in shock. Finally, he stammered, "I don't...understand what you're saying."

"Then I shall clarify it for you. You are the son of Ana Maria Gabrelli and Toshiburo Matsushita Yamamoto."

Miko jumped up and walked to the window with his back to his mother. He was shaking his head 'no,' as if he wanted to reject the words she had spoken. Then he sat down on the bed and put his head in his hands, as she had seen Toshi do a thousand times.

"I don't understand this, Mother. I don't understand what this means."

"I think you understand it very well. Your mother fell in love with a man who had already been destined for a role that did not include marriage to an American woman. We loved each other very much. I'm sure that you've seen evidence of that love in the past few days. But our futures didn't match. Responsibility to family and country came first for him. My love for him came first for me. It was my own choice to bring you with me when I left him. He was not aware of your presence.

Mishima offered to come with me as your father and my husband. We had loved and respected each other since we were college friends, and we continued to do so as marriage partners. I promised Mishima that you would never know the truth while he was alive. And for that reason, I promised myself that Toshi would never know either.

I didn't tell Toshi that you were his son. I didn't have to. The moment he saw you at the embassy reception, he knew that you belonged to him. The shock of that knowledge and the pain it has caused him, has stolen his future.

Now, my dear son, I've opened the door of adulthood to you. Are you ready to walk inside? Tell me, as one adult to another, what should I have done differently?"

"Oh god, Mother. I don't think I'm ready to be an adult if it means facing this kind of truth!"

"I'm sorry to hurt you, Miko, but how do you think I feel and have felt all these years?"

323

"But what am I to do with this? Do I cry now for losing Mishima as my father? Do I cry for never knowing Yamamoto as my father? Do I cry for my mother for loving a man who could leave her so easily? I don't know what to do with this kind of truth!"

Ana responded to his anguish. "There is one thing you have very wrong, Miko. Yamamoto did not leave me easily. You see the result of his loss. He is far too young to die of a broken heart. I have had you to love and care for, my gift from him. But he has had nothing but emptiness in his own heart."

"But how am I to feel about my father, Mishima? How shall I honor his memory?"

"You feel what you feel! He loved you as his only son. He gave his life to you. How does one feel about a father who will do that? You will love him dearly and honor him for as long as you live. And I will do the same for the love he has given you."

"Then how should I feel about Yamamoto? Am I angry for his leaving your or not acknowledging me, even now, when he knows who I am?"

"What do you want to feel about him? You've already told me that you're comfortable with him, you've shared your heart with him, you respect him, you're concerned about him. What more can you feel for a man you've only just met? That's a good beginning for a friendship, isn't it?"

"Then we are to be 'friends'? When do we become father and son? And how does that happen?"

"That happens whenever you want it to happen. Don't you think he's yearning for that relationship with you? But you must be the one to approach him. He would never impose his feelings on you. He knows that you have your own memories of a loving father. But, I can assure you, if the time should ever come when you choose to share with him in that way, it would be the sweetest moment of his life."

"I know that you still love each other. Now that you've shared your secret with me, I remember little things since the day he came here."

"Yes, I do love him and I hope that you can come to love and respect him also, before he leaves us for the last time."

Miko looked up at his mother.

"Then, he really is going to die? Isn't there some way to save his life…a heart transplant, anything? I don't want this to happen now, just when I begin to understand his kindness to me."

"There's no reprieve from this death sentence. Everything that could be done, has been done. But now, I want to ask you an important question. You told me that you encouraged Yamamoto to renew his relationship with me. How do you feel about that, now?"

Miko was quiet a moment, then he smiled at his mother as he answered her question.

"I meant it when I said that and even more so now! Just because I understand more about your relationship doesn't make you any different from anyone else. You deserve the same happiness that I would want with someone I loved. Especially now, when time is so important."

Ana asked Miko a final question with a tremor in her voice, "If we were to marry now…would you stand beside him and support him as my husband and your father?"

Miko did not hesitate.

"Yes, of course I would! After all, I'm the one who suggested it to Yamamoto last night. It seems ironic, doesn't it, that my 'wise counsel' was being given to my own father?"

Mother and son shared a warm embrace and a few tears. Ana's truth and Miko's acceptance of it had sealed a new and deeper relationship between them. Assured of her son's support, Ana was now ready to face the Honorable Toshiburo Yamamoto with the challenge to fulfill the promise he had made to her.

Ana told Miko of her intentions, "The day that Toshi came here, he promised that he would do anything I asked of him. And I intend to ask, 'Will you be my husband and the father of our son?' There's no reason for us to be afraid of that question, now. The three of us belong to each other and we belong together."

Ana gave her son a final hug and a smile.

"Welcome to the adult world, Mikoto, and to all of the exciting challenges it will bring you!"

He returned the hug and the smile.

"Well, I asked for it and now we're in it together…all the way!"

CHAPTER 29

*"A joyful celebration, yet fears invade the heart with a
knowledge of the loss ahead. Words of comfort from a
friend restore much-needed strength."*
--Ana and Ishikawa

The next morning, Ana was up early and restless from the
events of the night before. After being assured by Ishikawa that
Toshi was sleeping late and had no problems during the night,
she knocked on her son's door.

"Miko, are you awake? Let's go to the village today."

"Come on in. I've been awake for hours and I'm ready to do
just about anything."

His mother was surprised to find him up and dressed for the
day. She let him know about Toshi.

"Ishikawa says Toshi is still asleep, so let's go look for a
present for Suzi's birthday next Saturday. How about it?"

"Wouldn't you rather go to the city?"

"No, no, that's a trip. I think we can find something special
at one of the village shops. Suzi likes pottery, doesn't she?"

"Suzi likes anything that's wrapped in gift paper."

"I'll get a food list from Yoshiko, then let's get out of here!"

Ana didn't dare reveal her concern for Toshi, but she also
knew Ishikawa would be honest with her if there were any reason
to worry. She got the food list from Yoshiko and let her know
that she and Miko would have lunch at the Bread Basket, if there
were any messages for them.

As they drove out of the driveway, Miko commented, "Do
you realize that you and I haven't had a break since way before
the embassy reception? Let's treat ourselves to a whole day to
just relax and enjoy. How about it?"

"That's okay with me! By the way, wouldn't you like to plan
a party for Suzi's birthday next weekend?"

"I was afraid to mention a party with…everything. What do
you think?"

"We can't miss a chance for a birthday bash. It will do us all
good to liven up the routine and besides, I think our Japanese
guests would enjoy a little country culture. We'll introduce them

to the strange ways of the Rocky Hills village folk. If something unforeseen should happen, we can always do a quick switch and have a quiet dinner."

"That's fine with me and I know Suzi will be open for either one. She understands the situation."

"Go ahead and invite your friends, and we'll have something special, one way or the other. I'll order the cake and ice cream while we're here today. We can plan the meal later with Yoshiko."

Ana and Miko wandered through the village shops, looking for just the right gift for Suzi. They saw many interesting works of art, from rustic clay pottery to beautifully-designed alabaster and glass. Of course, mother and son could never agree on the perfect gift for Suzi.

After a couple hours of searching through the art shops, Ana found the perfect piece. It was a delicate alabaster sculpture of a slender young woman reaching upwards in a graceful pose. Her long dress was flowing against her body, as if she were dancing in the wind. The figure was part of the stone from which it was sculpted, so it appeared to be emerging from the rough-hewn rock.

Ana felt that the beauty of the piece was enhanced by its size. From the base of the rock to the tip of the uplifted arms, it was barely ten inches high. Miko was impressed, but wasn't sure whether Suzi would appreciate its value.

"It's beautiful, but I've never seen a piece of art at Suzi's place. She may not be into that sort of thing."

"I love it! In fact, I even think it looks like her. So, whether she's into it or not, she's going to get a piece of it. Now, you go find your own gift."

Ana bought the figure and had it wrapped in shiny gold and silver paper, with huge bows. As they walked through the shops, they both relaxed and enjoyed visiting with friends and catching up on the village news. At one point, Miko stopped to look in the window of an exclusive shop where the owners crafted their own jewelry.

"Let's go in here a minute. I'm thinking of getting Suzi a ring."

As they looked around, Ana noticed a beautiful set of matching wedding bands. The wide, heavy-gold bands had a slightly raised strip of gold across the top filled with tiny diamonds. The rings were simple, but elegant. Ana took one of the owners aside and asked, "If I should be interested in these wedding bands, would it be possible for you to bring them to my home for a special fitting?"

Since Ana was well-known by everyone in the village, there was no hesitation on the owner's part.

"Of course, Ana. I'd be glad to come out whenever we arrange it. Just give me a call. And let me congratulate you on your plans, if that is in order."

"Thank you, but I would appreciate this being kept between you and me. I'm not certain just when the congratulations will be in order. I still have some convincing to do."

Her jeweler friend commented, "Well, perhaps when he sees the ring on your hand, that will be convincing enough."

"I'll call to let you know my progress!"

They laughed together.

Miko looked at some beautiful settings as well, but wasn't excited about anything. But he found what he wanted at another small jewelry shop. It was a pink-cast pearl set in a heavy, gold wrap-around band. As they left the shop, he turned to his mother, saying, "I want you to know that this is not an engagement ring. I've got a whole lot of life to live before I make that kind of commitment."

Ana smiled, with some relief, and assured him, "That decision is yours, Miko. I know you care about Suzi but, in fact, you both have a lot of life to live!"

Miko suggested they have lunch and check in with Ishikawa. He was still worrying about Toshi after their in-depth conversation together the night before. When they left the jewelry shop, mother and son walked the few blocks to the Bread Basket and ordered the special of the day, clam chowder in a bread bowl with a fresh vegetable salad and iced tea. As their meal was being prepared, Miko called Ishikawa.

He came back to the table with a smile.

"Toshi's much better. Yoshiko said he woke up about an hour ago and came out to eat lunch with them in the kitchen. He and Ishikawa were walking around the gardens. What a relief! Now I can relax and enjoy the rest of the day!"

During lunch, Miko and Ana planned Suzi's party. Miko wanted to invite the three couples who were close friends with him and Suzi. He also suggested that, since it would be at Rock Hills, it would be nice to ask Dr. Donatelli to join them. He was practically a member of the family anyway. Ana agreed.

They decided to have a casual picnic meal with birthday cake and presents. Miko suggested some music and dance on the deck so the young people could entertain the 'older folks.'

Ana reacted to his words with a challenge.

"If there's music and dancing, we'll see who the 'older folks' really are in this crowd. Don't count me out just yet!"

By the time the pair had finished their shopping, ordered the things for the party, and picked up Yoshiko's list of groceries, it was nearly 3 o'clock in the afternoon. They had enjoyed their day together and had accomplished what they set out to do. On the way back, Miko reopened the topic of their late night talk.

"I feel like things are getting put together inside of me, Mother, after our visit. Would you mind if I talked with Toshi to let him know that I'm aware of our relationship?"

Ana took several deep breaths. She hadn't expected this.

"Don't misunderstand, Miko. I want everything out in the open as much as you. But Toshi's health is precarious. There's no way to predict how me might respond to this. If I can convince him to accept the idea of our marriage, it would seem natural that would be the time to share everything. Give Toshi and me some time to work things out between us first. Can you do that?"

"I understand what you're saying, Mother, but I'm just afraid that I'll say something accidentally and mess things up!"

"Don't worry. We'll work on it and I'll keep you posted."

During the next few days, Ana and Miko were on the telephone nearly every day making plans for the Saturday party. Toshi seemed to regain strength, but Ana was still very concerned and did her best to keep everything on an even keel, purposely avoiding any topics that might lead to conflict. His sudden weakness the Saturday before had frightened her. And

Dominic had started coming every other day instead of his once a week visit. This raised questions in her mind, as well.

On the day before the party, Ana approached the doctor as he was leaving the house.

"Dominic, is there anything I should know about Toshi's condition? Are there things I should be more careful of or changes we should make here? Your coming more often concerns me."

She laughed, then added quickly, "Not that I don't enjoy seeing you, but…you know what I mean."

"I don't need to cover up with you, Ana. If there were any serious changes, I would let you know. I'm just keeping a closer eye on things since the incident last weekend. The only changes I've made are increasing the oxygen intake to stabilize his breathing and some increased pain medication. That's all for now. The main thing is that he not push his limits. You can always help with that."

Dominic smiled to reassure Ana that no major changes were taking place.

"Besides, I enjoy coming here. It's a beautiful and peaceful environment. The meals are great, the wine is excellent, and the company stimulating. I hope you don't mind if I take advantage of all these side benefits of my job."

"Of course not. I'm just glad there are some benefits in coming all the way out here to watch over one patient."

"He's one very important patient and one very fine human being. I have appreciated knowing him, as well as each of you."

"Well, thanks for your kind words and for relieving my mind. Before you go, why not have a glass of our 'excellent' wine. I want to discuss something else with you."

Dominic sat down on the porch while Ana poured them both a glass of wine.

"Miko wants me to offer you a special invitation to our birthday party for Suzi tomorrow night. I hope you can join us."

"Are you sure you want me to come? Wouldn't the presence of a 'medicine man' be rather intimidating to the group?"

"You're not just a 'medicine man,' you're part of our family and it would make Miko and Suzi very happy. Besides, I need a dance partner. We're going to have music and a 'good old time.' Can you handle that?"

"It's enticing, to say the least. So yes, I'll be very happy to invade your family circle. What should I bring for Suzi?"

"She loves gifts, maybe a jazz CD or some exotic scent or whatever you wish. I'm sure you would have good taste."

They finished their wine and Ana walked out to the car with Dominic. He spoke a final word to her.

"I'll see you tomorrow night, then. And you mustn't worry about Toshi's condition. This is the way it will be, until it's over."

Dominic knew immediately that he had made a major blunder. Ana turned ashen and leaned against him as if she were going to faint. He grabbed her arms and held her.

"I'm sorry, Ana, I'm a doctor. I deal with this every day of my life. Sometimes it makes me cold to others' feelings. Please forgive me."

"I'm not afraid of honesty, Dominic, but surely it can be accompanied by kindness. I'm in a vulnerable position right now. I love this man and I know only too well that I'm going to lose him much too soon."

"Those words should never have been spoken, and I apologize from the bottom of my heart. I would never purposely hurt you or anyone here. You're all very important to me."

She put her hand up to silence him.

"I know what you go through every day, dealing with death and sorrow. It's not your fault. I didn't expect to be so weak or to react so quickly."

Dominic put his arms around her to offer comfort. His strength was like a transfusion of energy and she needed that energy desperately. She was thankful for his understanding heart. He asked, "Are we okay, Ana, you and I?"

"We're okay, Dominic. You're very important to us. We all need your strength and your wisdom…and your kindness."

He smiled as he spoke a final word, "I promise to remember the kindness in the future."

Dominic kissed her cheek as a good friend would do in a difficult moment and turned to leave. As Ana started back to the house, she glanced toward the garden. Ishikawa was standing at the entrance to the shrine, as still as a statue. He was watching

331

her. Ana knew that he had seen her and Dominic together and wondered what he was thinking. She walked toward the shrine. Ishikawa did not move, nor take his eyes from hers.

When Ana was close to him, she asked, "What do you know about life, Ishikawa?"

"I know that it is only a brief moment in the midst of an eternity."

"Is life fair?"

"Fair is not a good word. Life is a gift. All we can do is accept it, however it is offered to us."

"Is there ever time for love?"

"Where there is love, time is not important."

"Are you teaching me, or are you telling me?"

"I would never presume to teach you, Ana."

"Then tell me, Ishikawa, what you have discovered about love?"

"I have found that it is precious and must be tended with great care."

"And when one has tended it and cared for it and it flies away, what does one do?"

"One finds joy in the memory that reaches beyond time and brings everything present once again."

"Do you have a memory of a love that returns to you as if it were present?"

"Why do you insist on probing into my wounded heart?"

"I'm trying to discover how I will live when this is over. I'm trying to find a guide who will understand where I have been and where I must go."

"I am not that guide. My way is not your way."

"You wept with me once, long ago. Will you be here to weep with me again?"

"Yes, I will be here. We share our tears and then I will go my own way."

"That's all I need to know."

"You will find love again, Ana. There is no way that life can stop you from loving."

"When this is over, will life stop you from loving?"

"Why do you ask questions for which you already know the answer?"

Ishikawa turned away from her and walked into the garden and along the rocky hillside. Ana felt some relief from her concerns. Dominic had assured her that Toshi had regained strength during the past week. Ishikawa had assured her that he would be with her through whatever lay ahead. And Miko and Suzi were their salvation. Just being with them, watching them enjoy life and each other was uplifting to everyone.

Saturday brought the promise of a beautiful day. The sun came out to warm the hills and gave a boost to the household as they prepared for the party. Miko and Suzi drove out from the city early in the afternoon to arrange the deck for the big celebration. And Toshi enjoyed watching the preparation from a soft lounge chair while he soaked up the energy of the sunlight.

By five o'clock, everything was ready and the guests had arrived. With the three young couples from the city, Dominic, Ishikawa, Toshi and Ana, Miko and Suzi, and Yoshiko and her husband, Ishiro, they had quite a group. Ana had decided to have the meal catered so Yoshiko and Ishiro could enjoy the party with the rest of them and would only need to take care of the final clean up.

The birthday meal included roast chicken, barbecued beef, baked beans, spicy rice, crunchy potatoes, several different salads, and the final cake and ice cream. The drinks were iced tea and cola and, of course, some special wine for the birthday toast to Suzi.

After everyone filled their plates with food, they sat at a long table arranged on the screened porch by the kitchen. The first and most important order of the evening was Miko's birthday toast. He looked very handsome as he smiled at the beautiful Suzannah.

"Welcome to all of you on this joyful occasion as we celebrate the birthday of the most beautiful, red-haired woman I know, my dear, sweet friend, Suzannah Morgan Randolph."

They all raised their glasses to her and emptied them. Miko gave Suzi a very warm kiss and everyone cheered as Suzi gave him a very warm kiss in return. Ana was sitting across the table from Toshi. They smiled and winked at each other during the exchange of kisses by their son and his sweetheart.

As they began the meal, Miko turned to Toshi, who was sitting next to him.

"My mother hates this food, but it's a typical American meal and I love it. And I also have to warn you that tonight you'll experience a real live Virginia 'country party,' music and all. I hope it won't shock you too much."

Toshi laughed, "You forget, Miko, I spent four years of my college life in the States and the last sixteen years in and out of this country. There is very little that can shock me, least of all a Virginia country party!"

After the meal, they enjoyed the cake and ice cream dessert as Suzi opened her presents. She was very gracious in her thanks to everyone, including Toshi for a gift of very expensive French perfume and Dominic for a book of sonnets by Elizabeth Barrett Browning. But when she opened Ana's gift, Suzi's eyes filled with tears. She was so touched by the beautiful sculpture. Ana felt that it almost made up for Suzi's apparent disappointment with Miko's gift. She had noted Suzi's immediate reaction when she opened the jewelry box and knew that this beautiful, young woman had expected something other than a pearl ring.

Ana recalled Miko's words when he returned from Japan two years ago, "If Michiko were not my cousin, I would be in love with her!" Perhaps there was more to that statement than just a casual observation.

After the gifts were opened, the party adjourned to the deck to continue the celebration. Yoshiko and Ishiro brought the cake, chips, and cold drinks to the deck table for the group to enjoy during the rest of the evening. And then the real party began. The music was country rock and the young people loved it. They knew all the steps, the twirls, and the whirls, and the onlookers enjoyed watching the dancers go crazy with the rhythm.

Later in the evening, Miko asked his mother to dance with to "Saturday Night at the Twist and Shout." She and Mishima had joined their village friends at many parties through the years, so she knew the steps perfectly. They had a great time giving it all their energy. After a few moments, the rest of the dancers just stood back and watched, clapping and cheering them on. When the music stopped, mother and son received a huge ovation. They took their bows, then each of Miko's friends took turns dancing with his mother. Ana finally collapsed into her chair, laughing as she turned to Toshi, "I had hoped you wouldn't have to witness my 'down home country' side. I've lived in these Virginia hills far too long!"

He was laughing at her, "I loved it! I think you were born to dance. Get Dominic on his feet. I'm sure he's more talented than he knows."

She turned and grabbed Dominic's hand, "It's time you embarrassed yourself. I hate to suffer alone."

Dominic gladly accepted the challenge and they started to move with the music. Ana had to agree with Toshi; this man was definitely a dancer. The couple enjoyed a few fast country dances, then Miko played one of his favorite country love songs to slow the pace a bit. When Ana heard the music, she started to leave the dance floor, knowing that the song was meant only for lovers. But Dominic began to move with the music and, before she could pull away, his arm tightened around her. As they danced together, Ana was aware that her partner was singing this love song to her. When the music finally stopped, he whispered, "I've never heard that song before, but the words are very touching."

Ana didn't respond to his comment, but remarked casually, "Thanks for the dance, Dominic. You have great talent."

"It takes a dancer to know one. We should do this again some time." He didn't release her hand until Suzannah came over and pulled him back to the dance floor.

Ana was relieved to sit down. She put her arm around Toshi and asked, "Wouldn't you say that they make a beautiful couple?"

He was quiet a moment before answering, "I would also say that Dominic and Ana make a beautiful couple."

She looked at him with a dark scowl. He responded with a teasing smile and a plea.

"Don't hurt me now. I was merely commenting on the scenery, nothing else."

"When will you learn to keep your comments to yourself, especially when you know they could lead to violence?"

"I've been missing that flash in your eyes, Ana. I had to give it a test to see if it's still working."

"As long as you're here to turn it on, it will be working."

She was sorry the minute the words were spoken, but Toshi winked and answered with a smile, "Don't count me out, just yet."

Ana leaned over and whispered, "Don't worry about that. There is much more life to be lived here before any of us is counted out."

"If that's a threat, you're frightening me."

"It's not a threat, it's a promise. And you may very well have a reason to be frightened!"

Toshi shook his head and sighed, "No one is safe when Gabrelli is scheming. You will give me warning, I hope, so that I may be prepared with a proper defense."

"When have I ever given you warning about any of my plans?"

Toshi laughed as he answered, "Never!"

"So, why do you think I would start now?"

Ana gave Toshi a quick kiss and jumped up to bid the party guests goodnight.

CHAPTER 30

"Friends...sharing the truth of their hearts. Facing together, with a new dimension of love, that which lies ahead."
      --Ana and Dominic

"Mother and son... sharing the truth of their hearts. Facing together, with a new dimension of love, that which lies ahead."
      --Ana and Mikoto

The morning after the birthday party was quiet at Rock Hills. The young people had gone back to the city for the night and Toshi was sleeping late. Ana, Ishikawa, and Yoshiko were relaxing over a late breakfast when the telephone rang. Yoshiko answered, then handed the receiver to Ana.

"It's Dominic. He's checking to see if everyone is alive and well this morning."

Ana took the receiver, "How is the good doctor after his wild night in the Virginia 'wilderness'?"

"I'm doing fine, but wondered how Toshi made it through the night. Do I need to come out today?"

"No, Ishikawa tells us that Toshi had a restful night and is still sleeping peacefully. Maybe the party was good for him, after all. And since it's such a quiet day here, I wonder if you'd like to meet me for lunch. I need to stop by my office for a while and there are some things I want to discuss with you."

"Sure. I kept the day free in case I needed to come out. Where do you want to meet and what time?"

"Meet me about noon at The Bistro in the Village Center, near the Georgetown campus. Do you know where that is?"

"Yes, I've actually been there a few times. It's a very nice place. So, I'll see you then."

After they hung up, Ana took her leave of Yoshiko and Ishikawa.

"I'm not sure when I'll be back, so don't worry if I'm a bit late. I have some paperwork to take care of at my office and some other errands in the city. Tell Toshi I'll see him later today."

Ana walked into The Bistro just a few minutes after twelve and found Dominic seated in a booth near the back window. She was nervous. There were some very important and private matters she wanted to discuss with him. Ana needed his help and, because of the role he played in their lives, he was the person most likely to offer it. If he refused, she would find her own way.

Dominic stood and held out his hand to Ana as she came toward the booth. His eyes were brighter than usual and expressed concern. As Ana took his hand, he pulled her into a warm embrace. She found herself reluctant to move away from the comfort of his arms.

After they sat down, the waitress brought them each a glass of wine. Dominic smiled at Ana, "I hope it's alright. I took the liberty of ordering our lunch and the wine."

"Whatever you choose, I'm sure it will be fine."

Ana took a sip of wine and a deep breath, then, without further comment, began to share the reason for their visit.

"I might as well tell you everything straight out, Dom. I'm going to have to make some changes in my life and I need to make them now! Living on the edge of disaster is taking its toll on me. I can hardly sleep through the night for fear of what the morning will bring.

Toshi and Ishikawa seem to have ways of facing whatever comes when it comes, but, as much as I try, I can't make peace with the threat hanging over us. I've considered several options and believe I've found the only one that I can live with and still keep my balance. I'm only asking for your opinion and your suggestions, Dom, not your permission."

Ana paused and took another drink of wine. Dominic waited for her to deliver whatever blow must come. She leaned toward him and whispered with a smile, "This is it, Dom. I want to have a wedding in the garden shrine for Toshi and me, and I want it now!"

There was dead silence while Ana waited for his response. Dominic's shock was too apparent. Ana knew immediately that he had hoped for something quite different. He finished his glass of wine and looked out the window without speaking. Ana saw that he was struggling with some deep-seated feelings. Finally, he took a deep breath and, choosing his words very carefully, began to share his thoughts.

"First of all, Ana, I will be honest with you. Last night, when we danced together, I felt something between us that was more than friendship. In my wild, Italian dreams I had hoped you were going to invite me to fill some of your personal needs as a vibrant woman living with the fear of loss. The joke is on me, is it not?"

He laughed without humor. But to his surprise, Ana touched his hand and answered with her own admission.

"I would be lying, Dom, to pretend that I hadn't entertained the thought that you could very well fill my emotional and physical needs. Why deny it?"

He covered her hand with his. "Thank you for the confirmation that I wasn't totally misreading the unspoken messages between us. And please forgive me if I've overstepped the boundaries of this relationship."

"There's nothing to forgive. We're both human and we're alive and well. But our timing is off. I love him, Dom, and there's much more to it than just those simple words. He and I have belonged to each other since the first moment we met. I can't explain it. But now, whatever time is left for us, we need to be together, as husband and wife.

For both our sakes, we need to fill the space between us with our love. Can you help me? As his physician and friend, can you assure him that this is a positive choice, not a destructive one?"

Dominic recognized the depth of this woman's love for the man he had come to honor and respect. He could not refuse her.

"I can certainly assure Toshi that there is nothing destructive in the power of love. That's one force in the universe that doesn't destroy nor debilitate. I'll do whatever I can to encourage him to listen to his heart, which I know holds so much love for you. And, for the benefit of my patient, I can think of no treatment more effective than to share the remainder of his life as the beloved husband of Ana Maria Gabrelli!"

Ana whispered through her sudden tears, "That's all I ask, just to encourage him. Then he'll have to decide what he can do. But we're wasting so much time being separate…when we need to be together. I feel myself slipping into this dark chasm of sorrow, and I don't want to go there, not now when he needs my strength."

Dominic handed Ana his handkerchief, then moved beside her to offer whatever comfort he could.

"Forgive me for not being aware of your feelings, Ana. I should have known that your 'bravado' was a cover for Toshi and for everyone else in the immediate vicinity."

After a while, Ana regained her composure and Dominic moved back to his side of the booth to face her.

"How do you think I should approach him, Dom?"

"You're the only one who can answer that. You'll just have to know the moment and the words. You're good at words. Though, I'll admit, your timing may not always be perfect!"

They both smiled, remembering the many outbursts that Ana was prone to make at most all of the wrong moments.

"Well, I'd better get it right this time. I'll accept any suggestions."

Dominic threw up his hands, "I'm a novice in the affairs of the heart. I've never been successful in that area. Though I have no advice for you, I'll support you in whatever choice you make. I'm also sure that Ishikawa will be there for both of you. He believes very strongly that you and Toshi are star-crossed lovers."

Ana recalled to Dominic, "Ishikawa has always stood by me. He was very kind to me when Toshi chose to go to the embassy and to accept the marriage arranged by his family. He and I have always been 'soul mates' in our love for Yamamoto."

Dominic took Ana's hand in his and asked, "Then, how shall we leave it?"

"I wish I knew. As long as I know that you support me, we'll just play it by ear and hope that one of us will come up with a way to approach the subject. Otherwise, I'm afraid that it will rear its head in some wild 'Gabrelli' way that will blow the whole thing!"

"Perhaps you should just tell him how you're feeling and see what happens. Aren't we always encouraged to go with honesty as the best policy? Besides, I can't imagine Toshi ever refusing you anything. I must admit, I would have no resistance whatever should those loving eyes shine on me in such a way!"

Dominic smiled while Ana gave him a parental look as if her son had said something ridiculous.

"Be good, Donatelli!"

But she took his hand and held it tightly in her own, saying, "Thanks for your support and your kindness. Maybe I'll make it through in one piece after all."

"You'll make it through, Ana. I'll be here for you as a friend who loves you in many different ways."

They smiled at each other as their lunch was set before them. Then the two friends relaxed and spent the next two hours sharing good food and becoming more personally acquainted.

When they parted outside the restaurant, Dominic watched Ana drive away, realizing that he had just promised to help this woman who had stolen his own heart to give her heart to another. He walked back into The Bistro, ordered a double scotch, and for the next hour attempted to recover from a major disappointment.

By the time Ana arrived back at the house, the sun was hidden behind the rocky hills. She was anxious to know how Toshi had weathered the party. She was also nervous about her approach to him now. Ana recalled the day in the hospital when Toshi had promised Ana to do whatever she asked of him. And now, she was ready to claim that promise. With Dominic's encouragement, she felt certain that Toshi could have no reason to refuse her this final request.

Ana walked onto the porch and started to open the door to the kitchen, when Miko came out to meet her. He seemed very upset.

"Mother, where in the world have you been all day?"

She was taken by surprise and had no time to answer before he asked a second question.

"Have you been with Dr. Donatelli?"

She recognized some hidden agenda in his questions and reacted immediately to the insinuations, "What is that question supposed to mean, 'Have you been with Dr. Donatelli?' What does 'been with' mean, and why is that suddenly a problem for you?"

Miko continued to press his mother in a way that felt insulting to her.

"I mean that his answering service has been calling here. They've been paging him all day and found that your name was

341

on his calendar. He's been 'out of range' of the pager and, according to his secretary, there is only one reason he is ever 'out of range'!"

Ana's anger rushed over her like a whirlwind. Her own son was accusing her of who knows what, except that she knew very well "what." She flew into a rage and, unfortunately, did not take time to look around. If she had, she would have been aware that Yoshiko was inside the kitchen and Toshi and Ishikawa were both on the deck, all within a few feet of her and Miko. Everyone in the household could easily hear the confrontation that followed.

Ana was completely out of control and shouted at her son, "How dare you speak to me like that! How dare you suggest such a thing to me! And, even if it were true, what would it matter to you? You have no right to question my life or my lifestyle. What I do with my time is my own affair and mine alone! You've crossed the boundary of propriety, Mikoto, when you treat your mother like a child…without reason!"

Miko stepped back from his mother, shocked at her sudden burst of anger. He had never felt its sting in his life. He tried to apologize, "Mother, please, I'm sorry. I didn't mean what you think."

But his apology only fueled Ana's anger. She raised her hand to quiet his apology.

"Stop right there! You did mean it or you wouldn't have said it. And, tell me, what would you say to me if your suspicions were true? Tell me that!"

On the deck, Toshi started to get up, hoping to calm the situation between Ana and Miko, but Ishikawa caught him by the arm and forced him back down.

"Leave them alone. This is between mother and son. There are times when anger can be a good thing to clear the air where there is misunderstanding and confusion."

Miko backed against the porch wall at the sudden force of his mother's anger.

"Mother, please don't say these things to me. Can't we sit down and talk without so much anger?"

"When have you ever witnessed my anger directed at you, Miko?"

"I've never seen it before and it frightens me. I know I've caused it and I'm sorry. I have no right to question anything you do."

His obvious fear calmed her somewhat, but there was too much hidden emotion that needed to be released. She let it go.

"Miko, you are not the cause of my anger, but you are the reason for it. I have lived so many lies and covered up my own feelings for so long, that this is how everything finally comes out…in tirades against the innocent!"

"Maybe it's time I heard your truth and understood your feelings. You know all of mine!"

Ana laughed at his innocence. "Perhaps it is time. You know a part of it, but you certainly don't know the extent of it. Yes, I was with Donatelli today. So, your intuition was correct, but your insinuations are wrong! I went to him for help, that is all, as a counselor and a friend. Here is my truth, if you want to know it. My sweet, innocent son, you have only known one side of your mother, the side that I allowed you to know. But underneath my strength is a terrible weakness.

Yamamoto is the only man I have ever truly loved and now I must watch him die by inches before my eyes. With him goes my heart and my hope, and I'm afraid of such loss. I'm standing on the edge of a canyon of despair, and I'm afraid I'm going to slip into it and never find my way out!

You see, Miko, how your accusation against me today was the ultimate insult? I couldn't restrain my anger in the midst of my despair and I won't apologize for it. But I do apologize for frightening you with my outrage. You don't deserve that. I'm not angry at you. I'm outraged at the cause of my anger, that life is not perfect and we have to live it as it comes to us!"

Miko accepted his mother's rage, though he hardly understood her explanation.

"My life has been so perfect and I've always believed yours was, too. We seemed to have such a happy life together. Now I discover that underneath all of that were truths that couldn't even be spoken. I keep wanting to believe that there really is such a thing as 'true love' and 'perfect marriage' and everything good around us. I didn't know what I was getting into when I told you I was grown up enough to be friends with my mother."

Ana laughed at him, "So, you discover that friendship means hearing some bad news with the good. Discouraging, isn't it? Do you want to go back and be my innocent little son again and let me be the strong, perfect mother?"

"Even if I did, it's too late for that! I asked for the truth and I got exactly what I asked for. Now I'll have to deal with it, even if I don't understand it."

"How right you are! What's that old saying, 'Be careful what you ask for, you might get it'? Innocence is a wonderful 'state of being,' but it also requires that one remain a child. I beg your pardon, Miko, but I must welcome you to your 'baptism of fire' into the adult world. I only pray that you will be wiser than I!"

"How would you have been wiser, Mother, if you could go back?"

"I would have remained behind the safe, iron gates of St. Mary's Convent in South Boston and never longed to experience another world."

"I don't believe you…you would have missed out on me!"

His words silenced her. She walked over and put her arms around her son. With tears in her eyes, she whispered, "You are worth whatever price I've paid and will continue to pay."

Ana turned from her son and hurried through the front hallway and up the stairs to her room. There, she threw off her outer clothes and laid down on the soft rug by the fireplace. She was wet with perspiration from the emotional scene with Miko.

She mentally reran the tapes of her words to him, recognizing how wrong she had been to blast him with such anger. Yet, she did not feel the need to repent of it, for she had felt the sting of his accusations and knew there was no reason for them.

After a few moments' rest, she jumped into the shower to try and rid herself of the results of this emotional day. The steaming water soon relaxed her body as well as her mind. She began to breathe normally again.

Much later, when she stepped out of the shower, Ana slipped on her terry robe and grabbed a towel to dry her hair. She walked into the bedroom with the towel wrapped around her wet hair to rest a while before dinner. There, she stopped in her tracks. Toshi was sitting in a chair by the fireplace waiting for her. Ana stared at him, speechless. He returned her gaze, but said nothing.

When she spoke, her voice was shaking with an emotion she couldn't identify.

"How did you get up here?"

Toshi's eyes did not waver from hers as he answered, "I simply walked up the steps."

She saw a hint of a smile as he spoke. Ana was concerned that he would waste his energy on a trip to the third floor suite. He had never come there before.

"Was that a good idea?"

"I thought so, or I wouldn't have come."

"Don't you know that this is dangerous territory right now?"

"I have some idea of that. Am I in danger?"

"I guess that depends on why you've come. I suppose it must be important or you wouldn't have climbed so many steps and used so much of your precious energy."

"I've come to make an accusation against you."

Ana stared at him, her eyes wide with apprehension.

"Well, join the club. I can handle a few more accusations today. Of what would you like to accuse me, dear Ambassador, sir?"

He ignored her sarcasm and answered in a quiet, kind voice, "I've come to accuse you of loving too much."

Ana had to swallow to keep her heart in its proper place. She had expected something much more sinister and now was unsure of what was coming. She responded, very close to tears, "I recall a young samurai admitting as much to me some time in the distant past. Is it possible, do you think, to love too much?"

"No, it is not possible."

"Then why do you accuse me?"

"Because you've chosen to give your love to one who is undeserving of such a gift."

"We've both known that for a very long time, haven't we? But it seems, that deserving or not, I made that choice of my own free will. No one forced me to it, least of all the undeserving party."

"Your choice has brought too much heartache to the innocent.

"Who is innocent here? Myself, my son, the one I chose to love? Which one of us is innocent? If I made the choice of my own free will, then I deserve to suffer for it. I'm not innocent.

I'm guilty of bringing whatever pain I suffer upon myself. I knew the risk and I chose to take it with my eyes wide open!"

"No, Ana. I'm the guilty party. You didn't choose the heartache, you only chose to love the wrong man."

They looked at each other a long time without speaking, Ana wondering how to approach him with her question, and Toshi waiting for her to tell him what they must do now to bring peace to their hearts before it was too late.

Ana spoke first, "I assume that you have either heard Miko and me arguing or you have heard about it."

"I was on the deck with Ishikawa. I heard you speaking to your son."

Ana laughed at his understatement, "You mean you heard me *yelling* at my son!"

"Miko did not deserve your anger. It belongs to me."

Ana put her head down, not wanting to meet his steady gaze. She knew the truth in his words, and she was ashamed of her treatment of their son. Finally, she whispered, "Do you want a final chance to clear your name?"

Toshi knew very well where Ana was leading him. She had made her intentions clear in the hospital room, even before they came to Rock Hills. She was asking him now for what he was afraid to give, but knew that he must. He gave his answer.

"I will do whatever you ask of me, Ana, to bring peace to both our hearts. Tell me what you want of me. Tell me what I must do to free my heart of its burden of guilt before it is too late."

"If you mean what you say, your penance is very simple. All you need do is agree to an arranged marriage."

He smiled at her unbelievable optimism and whispered his question, already knowing the answer, "And who will arrange it?"

"I will. And you will stand beside me and promise that you will never leave me again."

"How can I make a promise such as that, when our future is already determined?"

"What were those words we spoke in the Seijo garden? Weren't you the one who asked me to believe in the 'Legend of the Rose'? Weren't you the one who convinced me that there is a love that goes beyond this dimension of time?"

All was quiet for a moment, then Ana heard him whisper the words she had waited a lifetime to hear.

"Ana Maria Gabrelli, will you promise to be my wife, to forgive me for the suffering I have brought upon us both and to offer your love to me with the hope that our love shall extend even beyond time to eternity?"

Ana smiled as she answered, "Yes, I will promise to be your wife, I do forgive you for all that has hurt us, and I promise to love you…even to eternity."

To Toshi's surprise, Ana took him by the hand and led him into her private study. There, on the fireplace mantel, he saw the white ceramic rose lying on its bed of soft velvet. Ana whispered, "Now we can celebrate the true meaning of this gift, at last."

They stayed together for the rest of the afternoon, sharing the sweetness of memories and the joy of a new commitment to love one another in spite of that which threatened their future. They made the conscious choice to believe that their love would be fulfilled and could extend beyond the boundaries of time.

Much later that night, when all was quiet, Ana went to Miko's room. They made their peace and Ana shared with her son the decision that she and Toshi had made, to marry and to enjoy whatever time would be allowed them. When mother and son parted at his door, Ana smiled and touched Miko's soft cheek.

"You're the man you've always wanted to be. I've had to make my own choices and live with them, now it's your turn. Welcome to the adult world Mikoto Toshiburo Matsamura."

Ana laughed as she gave him a goodnight kiss.

"You are so like the father for whom you are named. You have a sweet and loving nature. Don't ever change that as you grow old and wise. And, for heaven's sake, don't adopt your mother's wild ways!"

Miko gave her a hug and promised, "I will do my very best to be nothing like my mother, except to be as strong as you are and to stand up to whatever life offers me. Somehow I'm not sure I have your kind of strength, but I promise to work on it. With your help, of course!"

Mother and son parted with a new dimension of love between them. Since the fateful night of the embassy party, they had shared their fears, their suspicions, their anger, and their final truth…and had come through as friends.

CHAPTER 31

"A promise is agreed between lovers to make their peace,
to share their love, to look beyond the fears...to joy!"
--Ana and Toshiburo

After the emotionally-charged day and evening at the
Matsamura household, the next morning began quietly. Yoshiko
came early to prepare breakfast, but no one was stirring. She
wondered with some fear how the evening had ended with such
an explosive beginning. Yoshiko didn't see Ana, but at 7 o'clock,
she did see the car leaving the driveway. She thought to herself,
"Strange that Ana didn't come in to let me know where she was
going." The mystery worried her even more.

Ana hadn't slept well at all. Too many thoughts were
whirling in her mind. She wondered how to tell Dominic about
the confrontation she had with Miko and the decision she and
Toshi had made. Dominic would certainly have some wry
comments on the timing of both events.

At 6:30 a.m., Ana was wide awake and ready to move. She
jumped up, grabbed her jogging suit, and headed for the village
to run the trails with the early morning group. She and Mishima
had been regular joggers for many years. Since his death,
however, Ana had not rejoined the group, but today she felt the
need to release her emotional tension with some physical exercise.

Ana's decision was a wise one. Her friends welcomed her
with enthusiasm, and she enjoyed the hard run on the trails. Ana
had forgotten how important this exercise was to her mental and
physical health. Afterwards, she and several of her friends
stopped for breakfast at the deli market. They enjoyed a relaxing
visit, laughing and sharing their family news. And, of course, the
presence of an Ambassador in their midst was of great interest.

After breakfast, Ana stopped by the market to pick up fresh
fruits and vegetables for Yoshiko, then wandered through the
shopping areas just for her own enjoyment. As she thought of the
wedding ahead, she felt a sudden burst of excitement that seemed
almost childish in her adult world, but Ana reminded herself,
"Weddings are made for joy and the anticipation of a new
relationship. I'm going to relax and treasure the moment."

She purposely stopped at the jewelers and looked at the gold bands again. The jeweler smiled and asked, "Have you convinced him, yet?"

She smiled in return. "I'll be calling you soon."

Much later in the day, when Ana drove into the Rock Hills driveway, Dominic's car was there. At first, her heart took a fearful leap, but then she remembered that it was nearly 2 p.m., and the doctor was only keeping a previously arranged appointment with Toshi. She brought her market purchases into the kitchen and started putting everything in its place. Yoshiko came rushing in from Toshi's room to speak to her,

"Ana, we've all been so worried! Where have you been? You disappeared and were gone practically all day. We couldn't imagine. Is everything alright?"

Ana appeared shocked at her concern.

"I'm sorry, Yoshiko. I didn't sleep well last night and was filled with an amazing burst of energy early in the morning, so I took off to the village for a jogging run. It turned into a day at the market with my friends. I guess I got carried away and time seemed unimportant. I'm sorry I forgot to call."

"Well, you'd better get in there and relieve everyone's minds. Miko, in particular. He's been going crazy thinking he'd upset you so much yesterday."

Ana dropped what she was doing and hurried into Toshi's room. She walked in with a bright smile and greeting for everyone, "Hello, hello! Good, everyone's here. I have to apologize for not leaving a note for Yoshiko this morning when I went to the village. I drove in early to pick up some things at the market and, honestly, didn't plan to be gone so long."

Miko's face showed great relief at her upbeat entrance.

"Thank heavens! I thought you'd flown away for good. What in the world were you doing all day?"

Ana knew his reason for worry and walked over to give him a quick hug.

"Well, I went to the jogging track first and ran like crazy. It felt great! It's been a long time since I've used my muscles. And then I had a late breakfast with friends. Of course, there was much curiosity regarding our harboring a foreign ambassador. Small towns are great, except when you want privacy! I ended up shopping for Yoshiko and here I am, much later, but feeling much better!"

When Ana turned to greet the others, she noticed Ishikawa watching her intently from the corner of the room. She realized then that they had all been worried. She was sorry for her insensitivity, but had been filled with such energy that she had put aside any negatives from the day before.

She continued with the upbeat attitude, "Well, how about this group? What's the word for the day?"

Ana walked over to Toshi and sat down on the floor next to him. She looked up at Dominic and asked, "Is this a good day for your prize patient?"

Dominic returned the smile and replied, "From all reports, it appears to be one of his best."

Toshi entered the conversation with feigned seriousness, "In diplomatic circles, when one is discussed as an object, one can easily become offended enough to actually declare war on the guilty parties."

Ana laughed and jumped up on her knees, turning directly to Toshi.

"How are you today, Ambassador, sir? Have you recovered from last evening's rather dramatic events?"

"Unfortunately, I've been awake since very early morning and feel neglected that you didn't ask me to go jogging with you. By the way, Ana, do you think this is a good time to inform the present company of the negotiations we completed last night?"

"Absolutely, but wait a minute. I'll be right back."

Ana jumped up and ran to the kitchen. She grabbed Yoshiko's hand and dragged her into Toshi's room. Then she looked at Toshi and announced, "All the important people are here. Now, the Honorable Ambassador has an announcement to make!"

She bowed and gestured to Toshi to take over as they gave each other a knowing smile. Toshi proceeded to speak to the group in his most stilted ambassadorial voice, "I was approached last evening by the proprietress of the Matsamura estate with the following declaration: Either I agree to an arrangement of marriage with said person or I must immediately vacate the premises.

After weighing my options carefully, I have chosen the least troublesome, or should I say the least inconvenient, option. Or, how should I say this to be absolutely correct, Ana?"

"You should say, 'Yes, I will marry you, Ana.' And you should say it with feeling, or you will suffer much more than trouble or inconvenience!"

Toshi replied in a serious manner, "Pray god, that I may be delivered from the wrath of Gabrelli!"

He took Ana's hand in his and kissed it with a display of grave drama. Then he looked at her with a loving smile and asked, "Ana Maria Gabrelli Matsamura, will you do me the great honor of becoming my wife?"

Ana had not expected his tender response to their playful, but serious, game. She was touched by his sweetness and couldn't resist putting her arms around him and responding to his question with a quick kiss on the cheek.

"Yes, I will marry you, Yamamoto-san."

Everyone in the room clapped and cheered. For an instant, Dominic's eyes met hers. They were dark and unsmiling. She read them easily. He would support her as he had promised to do, but he was concerned with the choice they had made. After the congratulations were over, Toshi asked Ana a final question so that everyone could hear.

"Did I get the wording correct on that proposal statement you wrote for me?"

She gave him a scowl and a threat, "Be careful! You're not yet out of danger of banishment!"

Then the questions began. When and where would the marriage take place? And, in each instance, Toshi directed the questions to Ana as the 'wedding coordinator.' They all enjoyed teasing the couple whose happiness was evident in their tender smiles and the manner in which they carefully teased one another.

Miko commandeered Yoshiko to help him bring wine and glasses from the kitchen so they could offer their toast to the happy couple. When everyone's glass was raised, Miko gave the toast.

"To my mother, Ana Matsamura, whom I love and honor. And to the one she loves and honors, Toshiburo Yamamoto.

May they share peace and happiness in their marriage and the support of their family and friends."

Miko looked at Toshi and gave him a warm smile and a tip of his glass. The son especially wanted the father to know that he was welcomed to the family. Miko's special kindness to Toshi was noted with joy and relief by his mother.

After the toast, Miko shook hands with Toshi and kissed his mother, then took his leave.

"I'm meeting Suzi for dinner in the city, so I won't be back tonight. She'll be happy to hear your good news, though. You might call her tomorrow, Mother."

Then Miko leaned over to whisper to Ana, "Is everything okay between us, now?"

She answered without hesitation, "I love you, Miko. You and I will always be okay. Enjoy your evening. We'll have lots of plans to make."

Ana gave him a kiss and sent him on his way, then she and Yoshiko went to the kitchen to put away the market goods. Since everyone had eaten a late breakfast and no lunch, Yoshiko planned dinner earlier than usual, so Ana helped her get things together. Dominic came out to the kitchen and drew Ana aside, "Can we talk a few moments before I leave today?"

"Sure, have dinner with us and we'll visit afterwards. Anything important I should prepare for?"

"Yes, I think it's important. We'll talk later." He walked back into Toshi's room.

As Ana showered and dressed for dinner, her mind was filled with concern. She didn't like the negative vibes Dominic was sending her now, but she was determined that, no matter what was disturbing him, she would not change her mind regarding the wedding. She and Toshi would fulfill their long-ago promise to each other, despite any difficult odds they faced.

Yoshiko used Ana's purchases from the fresh-food market for their simple meal. She broiled the shrimp and served it with stir-fry vegetables, rice, and cabbage salad. Their dessert was sweet, juicy peaches and cream. Everything was delicious.

They all enjoyed the meal together and, to Ana's relief, Dominic and Toshi seemed to be relaxed in their conversation together. Ishikawa was quiet, as usual, but once during the meal, he and Ana locked glances. He gave her an uncharacteristic wink. She smiled and winked back. Ana knew that Toshi had seen their private communication for he reached over and put his hand on her back in a gentle caress. The warmth of his response touched her heart and she thought to herself, '*Perhaps there will be time for us...perhaps there will be just enough time.*'

After dinner, while Ana and Ishikawa helped Yoshiko clean up the kitchen, Dominic and Toshi spent some private time together as doctor and patient. Dominic approached Toshi with his concerns.

"You know that you're entering a difficult phase of your illness, Toshi. Do you really feel able to move ahead with this marriage? Do you believe it's a wise plan, at this point?"

Toshi didn't hesitate with his reply, "You're my doctor, Dominic. If you tell me that this is an impossible choice to make, that it will endanger or shorten my life, then you and Ana and I will have to take your concerns under consideration. Is that what you're telling me?"

Dominic was quiet for a moment. He stood up and walked to the fireplace, not facing Toshi.

"Of course, I can't be certain of what the repercussions will be. I'm only telling you how things will most likely progress so you can make your decision with some knowledge. But, as far as the wedding is concerned, I have other worries."

"Are you worried about Ana?"

"Of course, I'm fully aware that her happiness is in your hands and I need to be honest with you. Ana came to me yesterday in a very disturbed state of mind. I spoke to her as a friend and encouraged her not to be afraid to share her love with you. Inside my heart, I'm convinced that love is a blessing that can neither hurt nor destroy.

But, as your doctor, I must point out that you're the one who must make the final choice, for you're the one taking the risk. In the midst of this fatal illness, how much stress can you handle? How much of your own suffering can you share with her?"

Toshi was quiet as he considered how to respond to Dominic's questions. He knew they were valid and spoken out of a medical context. Finally, he answered in the only way he could, "Ana and I know that we have no future together and we'll both be hurt by the situation we're facing. But, Dominic, we also have to make our peace with each other. And we have been blessed with some time to do that.

When we were young and had all the time in the world, I walked away from Ana's love. I will never make that mistake again. If she's willing to share her love with a dying man, how can I refuse her? If you want to save Ana further sorrow, then you must convince her of the folly of this marriage. I have given my life over to her, now!"

Dominic knew from Toshi's words that it was too late to save Ana, but he also knew that he would be there to support her. He gripped his friend's hand as he spoke.

"I'll be here for both of you in whatever way I'm needed. I have great respect for you and Ana, and I pray that you will find happiness in whatever moments you are allowed to share."

Toshi welcomed Dominic's assurance and friendship.

"Thank you, Dominic. Ana will need you more than I. My fate is sealed and my time short. She is an intelligent, vibrant woman who has a lifetime of love waiting for her. I hope, that when our time together is over, you will encourage her to find it."

The two men shared a firm embrace as the doctor whispered to his patient, "I will support you in any decision, and when the time comes, I will encourage Ana to keep the memory of your love in her heart and move on with her life."

Dominic left Toshi quickly, as he was not a man given to express emotion in the presence of others and he felt the need to do so now. He walked out to the patio and into the garden shrine to be alone. Something from the tender heart of this gentle 'samurai' had touched the strong, independent heart of the doctor.

Dr. Dominic Donatelli was well-acquainted with death and dying. He had always met it with concern for those who suffered, but always from a safe emotional distance. Now, suddenly the carefully-constructed walls around his heart were crumbling. For the first time in his medical career, the doctor found himself vulnerable to a new kind of pain. He was suffering from the loss of a patient whom he had come, without his awareness, to love.

Dominic stayed in the shrine and allowed himself the freedom to release his sorrow in the uncharacteristic form of tears. His tears were shed for the emptiness that this loss would leave within his heart. And, beyond that, for the knowledge of how much more painful this loss would be to the heart of the woman he loved.

Much later in the evening, after Toshi had retired for the night, Dominic and Ana met on the kitchen porch where they would disturb no one with their conversation. They shared a glass of wine and enjoyed the beauty surrounding them. The sounds of the mountain stream flowing nearby, the cicadas, and the deep croaking of frogs were relaxing to both of them after the emotional day.

Ana spoke. "I can read your thoughts, Dominic. I want you to know that there are only two things that would stop me from this marriage. If you were to tell me that it would shorten Toshi's life or hurt him in any way beyond what he already suffers, then I would reconsider."

Dominic was restless. He stood up and paced across the porch, unable to look directly at Ana.

"I can't tell you that your marriage would result in either of those two things. Nothing is certain at this point. But I can tell you that your marriage will bring you even closer to the pain he suffers. Have you thought of the toll it might take on your own strength? He needs your strength. Sometimes, help can be more effectively given if it comes from some distance."

"I don't believe that what you say is any reason to change our plans. Be assured, doctor, that I know what's ahead. But I can no longer stand outside of his struggle and watch it; I have to participate in it with my offering of love and strength. You're his doctor, you can stand apart. But I love him and I can no longer do that."

Dominic smiled at her words, but would never tell her the depth of sorrow that he had just experienced within his own heart. She would not understand that neither could he stand apart, even though he must continue to give the appearance of doing so.

"I understand what you're saying, Ana, and I'll tell you what I told Toshi a few hours ago. I'll be with you through this and offer whatever help is needed for both of you. That's all I can say now."

"Then, Dom, it looks like we're in this together all the way, doesn't it?"

"We're in this together, Ana."

Their eyes met and Dominic's voice shook with emotion as he touched his glass to hers.

"Here's to the culmination of a love affair that has spanned miles and years. May you both find joy in the midst of your greatest challenge."

They both took a sip of wine and set their glasses down to share an embrace. As Dominic turned to leave, Ana touched his cheek gently with her hand, saying, "You are a blessing to us all."

Only his deep love and respect for Toshi gave Dominic the strength to leave Ana without expressing his love for her. Because of the choice that these friends and lovers had made, Dominic knew that he must put aside his own needs. If there were ever to be a relationship between him and Ana, it must be in the future and separate from that which they would face together now.

While Dominic spent the night with his own torment, Ana was planning the wedding for her and Toshi. She consciously chose to think of this special moment as if they were beginning a new life with hope and dreams for their future. She chose to put aside her fears and indulge her dream.

Twenty years ago, because of Toshi's status, they would have been married in the Japanese style with crowds of relatives and friends; with both Buddhist and Christian formal ceremonies; with several changes of clothing, from the traditional Japanese red to Christian white; with a formal dinner and songs and poetry and testimonials from friends.

But Ana knew exactly what she wanted for her and Toshi now. They would be married in Mishima's shrine on the mountainside. She would ask her Catholic priest from the village diocese to perform the ceremony. Everything would be simple and the focus of the ceremony would be their vows with the 'rose.'

After the wedding, Ana would take Toshi down the North Carolina coast to the beautiful Sandcrest Resort for a short honeymoon trip. She knew that the sea air and the unique beauty of the coastal resort would be good for him. It would be a pleasant change from the 'hospital' environment of Rock Hills. But, of course, that would depend on how Toshi and Dominic and Ishikawa felt about it. She would broach the subject tomorrow.

Ana slept that night without sorrow or fear. Her heart was lightened by the hope of a new dimension of commitment between her and her 'sweet samurai.' She felt certain that these last moments together were all that they needed to face the ending of this love affair with the strength and courage that would be required.

CHAPTER 32

*"The celebration...a new commitment made. Two lives
joined together. A love, once lost, is found!"*
--Ana and Toshiburo

The next morning after breakfast, Ana and Toshi talked about
their wedding plans. Toshi was fully accepting of everything that
Ana suggested.

"What you've described is perfect with me. I appreciate the
beauty and simplicity of being married in the garden shrine. And
I will agree to do or say anything your Catholic priest requires to
make the marriage legal and acceptable to your faith. However,
that falls short of a quick baptism!"

They both laughed and she assured him that her priest, Father
Marcus, was a liberal theologian who had no problem uniting an
Italian Catholic in marriage with a Japanese 'Shinto-Buddhist.'
The priest had been good friends of the Matsamura's for years
and fully accepted Mishima's differing beliefs.

When Ana mentioned the wedding bands, Toshi asked her a
direct question.

"Ana, can we face some reality in this regard?"

But as soon as he said the words, Toshi realized they should
not have been spoken. Ana's eyes filled with tears as she
answered, "I know very well that we don't need a wedding, nor
wedding bands, to seal our love for each other. But I need it,
Toshi, only because I'm a dreamer who's been forced to face too
much reality in my life. I love you enough to be with you and to
share whatever is ahead. But I need you to love me enough to
indulge my simple dreams."

Toshi put his arms around Ana and kissed her tears away,
saying, "Ana, I love you enough to indulge you any 'simple
dream,' and I'm aware that without those dreams, I wouldn't be
here. You would have given up on me long ago and I would
have given up as well."

"Then perhaps you can join me in a 'willing suspension of
disbelief' as we move through this life drama together. We'll be
like any ordinary lovers who plan to spend the rest of their lives

together. Is it too much…to think of our marriage as a beginning instead of an ending?"

He smiled at her capacity to look beyond reality, as if there were no death sentence to face, "It's not too much, Ana. There's only one thing that I could never successfully pretend. And that is the suggestion that we are like 'any ordinary lovers.' There has never been anything ordinary about Ana Maria Gabrelli or about her love. And, thank God or Buddha or the stars for that!"

They ended their planning session in each other's arms. Later, Ana moved ahead with all that needed to be done for this very *un*ordinary wedding and for all that was to follow.

Over the next few days, Ana talked with her sister, Val in Boston and with Miyuki in Tokyo to invite them to Rock Hills for the wedding ceremony. To her surprise, Ana had found a simple wedding dress in a village shop and was having it altered to fit, the rings were sized and purchased, Father Marcus had visited at the house to meet Toshi and go over the final arrangements for the service, and Yoshiko had taken over the reception planning.

Dominic spent time with Ana and Toshi planning the trip to Sandcrest. They all agreed that Ishikawa should stay with them and Dominic would check in periodically in case of any unforeseen problems with Toshi's health. Ana had rented a large condo for a month-long stay with the option of extending the time if they should choose.

On Thursday afternoon, before the Saturday wedding, Ana received the call she had been anxiously awaiting. It was Miko.

"Mother, guess who's here."

"I hope it's Yuki and Sato!"

Miyuki grabbed the phone from Miko and started shouting, "We're here! I don't believe we actually made it. When can we come out? We've gotta talk, talk, talk!"

"Tell Miko to pack you up and bring you out here, pronto! You can be here in a couple of hours, more or less, so hurry! We've got plenty of food and drink and we're ready for you!"

Within two hours, their Japanese guests arrived and Miyuki and Ana fell into each other's arms. It had been nearly three years since they had been together in Tokyo after Mishima's death. Now they could celebrate a happy occasion.

Sato finally separated them and gave Ana his usual passionate hug and kiss. She indulged his embrace, making faces at Miyuki behind his back. They had both accepted Sato's weaknesses long ago, recognizing that was who he was and always would be. They loved him in spite of himself, but more especially for loving Miyuki.

Before Ana led them into Toshi's room where Dominic, Ishikawa, and Yoshiko were also waiting to greet the guests, she grabbed Miyuki's shoulders and looked her squarely in the eyes.

"Yuki, I want you to know that this is what I want and it's a very happy time for us. I know how you feel about Toshi, but Yuki…"

Miyuki interrupted her, "Ana, I'm here to celebrate with you. I love you and whomever you choose to love, believe me, I will do my best to love as well. If you can welcome him back, after everything that's happened between you, don't worry about me. I'll welcome him with open arms and kisses and anything else you think is appropriate! You can trust me, Ana."

They hugged again and Ana asked her second question, "Is Sato okay with this? He and Mishi were so close."

"Sato? Sato is constantly drunk with wine and love. He'll probably break Toshi's arm off congratulating him. You know, of course, he always counted on your marrying him after you moved into his house!"

"Oh, sure, we know Sato. I don't think it was marriage he had in mind at all when he gave me the keys to that little house!"

The friends laughed and hugged each other as they went into Toshi's room to meet the others. When they walked in, Toshi stood to greet Miyuki with a smile and a courteous bow. She was surprised at how well he looked. She had expected him to be nearly skin and bones. Though he was thinner than when Miyuki had seem him last on Japanese television, his hair was longer and worn in the same casual style as in his youth. He seemed relaxed in khaki trousers and a soft, beige sweater. She thought he looked much younger than she would have expected.

Miyuki walked over to take Toshi's hand. As she did so, she felt the warmth in his eyes and was drawn to put her arms around him. She whispered in his ear, "Did Ana tell you that I couldn't give her your gift until after Mishi's death?"

He smiled and said simply, "You were wiser than I. Thank you for that."

Ana wondered, as she watched Miyuki and Toshi greeting in such a warm fashion, if perhaps they had met at some time that she wasn't aware. Miyuki had only mentioned the one visit at the Akasaka Prince Hotel. Had there been others? And why did it disturb her now?

Toshi turned to introduce Miyuki and Sato to Dominic and Ishikawa. Though Miyuki had met Ishikawa at the hotel in Tokyo, Sato had never met him before. Everyone visited a while before Yoshiko invited them all to share the lovely dinner she had prepared. Miyuki noted that Toshi and Ishikawa did not join them in the kitchen. She asked Ana, "Does Toshi usually eat alone?"

Ana answered, "This is a pretty stressful week. Dominic felt it would be better for him to preserve as much energy as possible. He may join us tomorrow. We just let the doctor take charge of his activities."

"I'm surprised at how good Toshi looks, even though he's very thin. He appears much stronger than I expected."

"He seems to be doing well. I hope that continues, at least until I get that final 'yes' at the altar!"

They laughed together, though there were tears in their eyes, then joined the group for the evening meal. After dinner, Ana took Miyuki and Sato up to Miko's room where they would be staying until after the wedding. They rested a while, then changed into more comfortable clothes and came downstairs to spend the evening with their friends. Miyuki and Ana had already made plans to spend the late hours in Ana's third-floor suite discussing 'woman things' and the good old times.

The group were all seated on the floor around the fireplace in Toshi's room when the conversation turned to their days in Tokyo. Sato recalled Ana's housewarming party at his little Seijo house and asked Toshi, "Do you still play that mean guitar? That was a fun night we had, and what a surprise when you made the music."

Toshi answered with a smile, "I believe that was my last public concert."

"You were great! I'd love to hear some of that music again." Miko picked up on Sato's request.

"Why not play a few songs for us, tonight? I've got my guitar upstairs. Do you want to try it? I can't play much, but the guitar still works."

Toshi laughed as everyone chimed in.

Sato asked, "How about that, 'Rollin' and Tumblin''? That did us all in!"

"Whoa, that's far out of my league these days! I wouldn't last one round. Besides, I'd probably never make it to the wedding, and I think that's why we're all gathered here."

Miko encouraged him, "Well, something slow and easy, then. If we know it, we'll all sing along."

Toshi finally gave in, "If I can play your guitar, then I'll do a piece or two. We might be able to get through 'Alberta.'"

Miko jumped up to get his guitar. While he was gone, Sato turned to Toshi and asked a point-blank question: "You know, I've wondered over and over again why you didn't marry this beautiful woman the first time you had the chance. Why was that, Toshi?"

Ana looked over at Toshi and smiled as she covered her face with her hands. Everyone in the room seemed to be holding their breath, waiting for his answer. Toshi was quiet, as if he were thinking carefully about what to say. Then he looked directly at Sato and answered his question in very simple words, "I can only account for that by being young and incredibly stupid at the time."

Ana broke in, unable to leave well enough alone.

"I might add at least one other variable to the list. Wasn't there something about 'obligation to family expectations'?"

Toshi glanced at Ana, fearful that she was leading him into troubled waters, but she smiled and, to his relief, went in a different direction.

"I'd like to think that your choice was based on a bit more than stupidity. Could anyone as brilliant as I fall for just another 'stupid guitar player'? I think not!"

Miyuki jumped in, laughing at Ana's statement, "Oh god, everyone look out. 'Gabrelli' is getting wound up. We're gonna have a blow out and no one here will be safe!"

Ana retorted, "Hey, now, is that fair? I may hand out tongue lashings now and then, but I've only struck one adult in my whole life…as I recall."

Toshi couldn't resist adding in a very quiet voice, "And I've got a permanent lump on my jaw to prove it."

Ana laughed and pointed an accusing finger at him, "But, you must admit you did deserve it, now, didn't you?"

Toshi rubbed his jaw as he replied, "I made a purely innocent move."

Ana interrupted him, still smiling, "You kissed me without invitation and insulted me as well!"

Though Toshi and Ana were sparring in fun, Miyuki was wary in case she might need to quickly change the subject. But Toshi was enjoying the exchange with Ana. He knew they both used words like a game and tonight it was a game of love.

He responded to Ana's prodding, "Since when is a kiss an insult?"

Ana looked at him, pretending to be very serious, "Since it became a 'weapon of power.'"

Miyuki's hair began to rise on the back of her neck, but Toshi didn't stop.

"Hey, I was the one who got knocked to the ground. Your fist was much more powerful than my kiss!"

Toshi had walked into Ana's trap and she couldn't resist her final point. She jumped up and gave her future husband a passionate kiss on the mouth. Then she fell to her knees in front of him.

"I don't think so!"

Everyone laughed with relief as Toshi put his arms around Ana and kissed her just as passionately. He gave in, saying, "You win again, Gabrelli!"

Ana laughed and pushed him away.

"It's time for that song you promised."

Miko handed Toshi his guitar and he strummed around until he got the sounds he wanted. Dominic spoke up, "Go ahead and play, 'Alberta.' I remember the words to that one."

Most everyone in the group knew the Clapton song, so they had a good time with several of the slower ones, including "Alberta" and "Layla." Toshi ended their music session with

"Have I Told You Lately That I Love You?" Ana and Toshi, of course, sang the song to each other.

The friends ended their gathering in an atmosphere of warmth and love for each other and for the couple who would finally pledge their vows of marriage. Ishikawa and Yoshiko brought in the champagne and they raised their glasses to Ana and Toshi.

Myuki gave the toast.

"To friends and family, to all our sweet memories and the promise of an old love made new."

They emptied their glasses, then Miyuki and Sato shouted their 'banzai's' and the rest joined in to conclude the evening.

As the group began to leave, Ana grabbed Miyuki's arm, "Do you still want to talk tonight or are you too tired?"

"When have I ever been too tired to talk with you, Ana?"

"Then I'll knock on your door on my way up and you can come to my room. We need to be alone. I'll say goodnight to my 'soon-to-be-husband' and be right up."

The friends hugged and Miyuki went upstairs with Sato. Miko and Suzi said goodnight to everyone as they were on their way to the city and wouldn't be back until the Saturday wedding. Before he left the room, Miko walked over and put his arm around Toshi.

"That music was great! I want you to know that I'm very happy for you and my mother. I know you've made the right choice."

Toshi responded to Miko's kindness, "Thank you very much, Miko. Your acceptance means a great deal to both of us."

After all was quiet again, Ana turned to Toshi and put her arms around him. He seemed very serious and she could tell that he wanted to say something to her. Finally, he asked the question, "You know that you were very wrong tonight, don't you?"

Ana had no idea what he was thinking, but went along, "What was I wrong about?"

"About me."

"What about you? What do you mean?"

"I was very stupid, Ana. The truth is, you fell in love with a very stupid person and you'll just have to face it. You were a poor judge of character and now must suffer the consequences!"

Toshi smiled as he kissed Ana goodnight. His final words were spoken gently and with great love, "I'm ready to place my heart in Gabrelli's hands."

Ana could not resist a whispered warning, "Then, my 'sweet samurai,' fasten your seat belt and prepare for the ride of a lifetime!"

The lovers laughed together as they shared a final goodnight kiss, then Ana left Toshi to his rest and went to spend the night talking of the past and the future with her dearest friend.

On her way to Miyuki's room, Ana stopped by the kitchen to pick up a bottle of wine and two glasses. Miyuki was waiting for Ana's knock and the two friends ran up the stairs to Ana's suite, shut the door behind them, and began to celebrate.

Throughout the night, they recalled every era of their friendship history, starting with the college years at Georgetown, to their first tour of duty with IEEC in Tokyo, to Ana's fateful meeting with Toshi on the night of the O-bon Festival, to Toshi's appointment to the embassy, to Ana and Mishima's wedding, to the advent of their sweet Miko, to Miyuki and Sato's marriage, and up to the moment.

The friends laughed and cried, swore at all men, then promised to love them all forever and tried to think of ways to create the perfect man by dissecting pieces and parts of all the men they had ever known and putting one together just right. Then, near morning, they decided they should just clone Nishiyama and go into business selling their clones to the women of the world.

They agreed that if everyone had an 'Ito Nishiyama,' they would not only become multi-millionaires, but would always be treated with honor and respect, their lover would be true of heart, gentle and kind, intelligent and industrious, and even handsome! Then they looked at each other and shouted in one voice, "What's wrong with us? Why didn't we go after him when we had the chance?"

But Miyuki remembered, "Oh yes, I recall that one of his most endearing qualities was his complete dedication to his wife! That pretty much put an end to our prospect of nailing the perfect man and that's why we ended up in these crazy relationships!"

Then they cried some more and Miyuki proposed an end to their wild night.

"Ana, let's crash before we hurt ourselves. I need some sleep!"

They grabbed pillows and blankets and made a bed on the floor. Before they went to sleep, they hugged each other and promised that they would always be best friends and never again talk about their old lovers or tell anyone about their perfect composite man.

Needless to say, Ana and Miyuki did not wake up with the dawn. In fact, it was nearly noon before anyone had the courage to knock on their door. Sato was chosen for this assignment. He was the least likely to feel the pain of their sudden reaction to sunlight.

When the women finally answered the knock on their door, they were both pretty much wiped out from the wild night. Ana jumped up and ran to the shower, but turned the knob to 'cold,' instead of 'hot.' When Miyuki heard Ana screaming, she screamed, too, and Sato ran for the bathroom door, thinking something terrible had happened to Ana. But Miyuki knocked him down and ran ahead of him to help Ana. By then, Ana had the water regulated. They all ended up shouting at each other and laughing.

Miyuki helped Sato up and warned him, "Be careful whose bathroom door you break down!"

Then Yoshiko came running up the stairs to find Miyuki and Sato sitting on the bed, holding their sides with laughter.

"What's happening up here? We heard the screams and shouts clear in the kitchen!"

Ana came out of the bathroom in her robe with her hair wrapped in a towel, "We're trying to recover from our drunken stupor and I did it the hard way. The water was ice cold! We're okay and we're hurrying. Yuki, get to the showers, we've got things to do today. Sato, to the kitchen. I have to get my clothes on!"

Sato made his own suggestion, "I think I should stay here. You two need a chaperone to make sure you don't injure yourselves permanently!"

Ana pointed him to the door.

"Out, out…now!"

Yoshiko followed him to make sure he didn't turn back.

About thirty minutes later, Ana and Miyuki walked very sedately into the kitchen. Ana had on her sunglasses and Miyuki was begging for coffee. Neither could look at the food on the table.

Ana mumbled, "Please don't wait lunch for us. Go ahead and eat. Just hand us coffee cups and the pot and we'll be alright in a few hours."

She sat down beside Toshi, but hardly knew where she was. He offered an observation, "I believe you've both had enough 'pot' to do for weeks ahead."

Ana pulled up one side of her sunglasses and gave him a glazed, but deadly, look.

"Who said that?"

Toshi laughed and asked, "Ana, do you know what day this is?"

She was quiet a moment, then began to panic.

"O my god! Is it Saturday? Did I miss my own wedding?"

Everyone laughed as she held her aching head. She took off her sunglasses and stared at Toshi. He smiled and waited for the trouble he knew was coming.

She obliged, saying, "You have yet to experience the full extent of Gabrelli's wrath, but I assure you, the moment you least expect it, it will come!"

She grabbed his hand and pressed it against her heart.

"Do you feel that pounding? You frightened me and for that you must sure suffer some dreadful punishment!"

Toshi held his hand against Ana's heart as he leaned over and kissed her. His public display of affection surprised Ana and everyone else. Then he smiled and said to Ana, "This is the day before the day before our wedding. I just wanted you to know that."

Ana leaned over and whispered to him, "You started this, but I want you to know that I will finish it!"

"And when will you do that, sweet Ana?"

"The night after tomorrow night. Be you warned!"

"I am warned and will be ready."

368

She returned his kiss, then looked up and issued an ultimatum to everyone at the table.

"Yuki and I must have coffee now or I shall take off these sunglasses and you will all be totally disintegrated!"

Everyone quickly pushed their own cups and coffee pot toward both the groggy women and watched them drink. The rest of them enjoyed Yoshiko's delicious lunch.

CHAPTER 33

"A wedding in a garden shrine. Late perhaps, but not too late. Two lovers give their hearts to one another, forever intertwined as one."
--Ana and Toshiburo

After lunch, Ana and Toshi sat at the table talking about their final wedding plans. She and Miyuki would go to the village today to pick up the rings, confirm the flower arrangements for the ceremony and the luncheon, and Ana would have her final dress fitting. Yoshiko was handling the wedding luncheon and Miko was taking care of the music.

Toshi smiled at Ana, amazed at her highly-organized planning for such a simple ceremony. He would have been happy to have an informal gathering at the shrine with a word or two from the minister. She knew what he was thinking and responded, "I know this wears you out just thinking about it, but, I promise, all you have to do is walk from your room into the shrine, stand still for a few moments, agree to be my husband in a sentence or two, then walk over to the table and sit down for lunch. Now, isn't that simple enough? If you want, you can skip the lunch!"

Toshi laughed at her, "It's that 'agree to be my husband' sentence that is most frightening! Just what will that require of me?"

"To agree to be my husband merely involves doing everything I ask of you from now on. That can't be too frightening, can it?"

Toshi gave her a look and a smile.

"I think you know my answer to that! As I recall, I have been the recipient of many Gabrelli orders in the past. You will be kind, won't you?"

Ana put her arms around him and whispered, "If I had been strong enough to issue this order long ago, we wouldn't be in this situation, would we?"

"That's hard to say, Ana. I may not have been wise enough to follow it."

"I know your heart too well, Toshi. Wisdom would not have been a factor. You would have been kind enough to follow it. I was the one who made the error in judgment. I didn't trust your kindness, nor your love."

"Do you really think anything we would have done could change this moment? I have far outlived all expectations. We would still be facing the same ending."

"But we would have had time. If I had been strong enough, we would have had time."

"This is the time we have. The past is of no importance. From this moment is what we have. I will stand before your priest and promise to follow every order you give me from that moment on…except one."

Ana looked at him in surprise.

"And what 'one' is that?"

Toshi's eyes suddenly filled with tears as he replied, "I think you know the answer to that question."

He put his arms around her and held her close enough that she could feel his heart beating against her own. Ana pulled away from his embrace and gave him a tender kiss. Then she touched his cheek and whispered, "Yes, I know the answer to that."

Ana rose quickly and left Toshi to think his own thoughts as she prepared for the activities of the day. In spite of the circumstances surrounding them, Ana was determined that she would allow nothing to diminish the joy they would share on their wedding day.

Saturday morning, the caterers came early to set up the canopy and tables for the wedding luncheon. The florist brought large potted bouquets of white chrysanthemums to place along the garden path and around the shrine where the wedding would take place. And, just inside the entrance to the shrine, Father Marcus had placed a small altar on which was laid a purple satin scarf. On the scarf were the gold wedding chalice and the wedding rings. At the front of the altar lay a beautiful white rose with its stem wrapped in long strips of white satin. Everything was ready for this moment, so long delayed.

At eleven o'clock, all was in order. The wedding guests included Dominic and Suzannah, Yoshiko and Ishiro, Ishikawa,

Val and Roger and their three children. Miko's college friends provided the flute, violin, and vocal music.

The wedding party entered the garden as the young woman sang the touching love song, "Evergreen." Father Marcus and Toshi walked side-by-side into the shrine. The priest stepped behind the altar, while Toshi stood in front and turned toward the aisle to await his bride. Though he had lost weight in the last few months, Toshi appeared well and was very handsome in a gray, silk suit with white shirt and gray tie. Ana had given him a white pearl tie tack as a wedding gift. And all the men in the wedding party, including the musicians, wore a white rose in their lapels.

Then, Miko and Miyuki came in together. Miko wore a suit of dark gray with a tiny burgundy stripe and a burgundy silk tie with a gray pearl tie tack. Miyuki wore an Oriental-style, pink satin dress with dangling, gray pearl earrings and her hair pulled back tightly in a roll. Miko took his place on Toshi's right and Miyuki walked to the other side of the altar.

During the last verse of "Evergreen," the bride stepped onto the pathway leading to the shrine. The joy in Ana's heart was evident in her countenance and one could almost hear the fitted dress of white satin with side slits and a straight neckline. Tiny white roses were embroidered along the neckline. Ana pulled her hair back with white, pearl-encrusted combs and wore no jewelry. She carried a bouquet of large, white roses. Her beauty was nearly hypnotic.

As Ana approached the altar, Miyuki took the roses from her arms and Toshi stepped forward to take her hand. There were tears in his eyes as he leaned forward to kiss her cheek and whispered, "The 'Angel Gabrelli' approaches."

Ana smiled and kept a tight grip on his hand. They turned together toward the altar and Father Marcus. The priest gave a short prayer invoking the God's blessing on the purpose of their gathering. Then he offered a personal statement to Toshi and Ana regarding their love for each other and the value of sharing this precious moment with family and friends.

At the end of the statement, Father Marcus picked up the white rose from the altar and spoke to the group.

"Ana and Toshiburo and I would like to share with you "The Legend of the Rose." This is an ancient Japanese legend that was passed down to Toshiburo from his grandmother and has a very special meaning to those who stand before the altar today and, perhaps, to each one of us."

The musicians played softly as Father Marcus read the legend. At its end, the vocalist sang, "The Kiss of the Rose." Then the priest handed Toshi the white rose. Toshi turned to Ana to offer his wedding vow.

"Ana Maria, I have loved you from the first moment I saw you. I didn't know your name, but I gave you my heart. Though our paths have taken us in different directions, I have never stopped loving you, nor will I ever do so. I kiss the rose, Ana, to promise my eternal love to you."

Toshi kissed the white petals and handed the rose to Ana. She took the rose from him and offered her own pledge with a smile, "Toshiburo, I didn't want to love you, but you taught me how to open my heart and let love in. You will be in my heart forever. I kiss the rose as a symbol of my true and eternal love for you."

Toshi place his hand beneath hers and together they laid the rose on the altar. Father Marcus lifted the sacred chalice and spoke to the bride and groom.

"Do you promise, before these witnesses and before your God, to love and honor one another from this moment to eternity?"

They answered together, "We do."

The priest continued, "Then drink of this sacred cup to seal your promise and offer these golden ring to one another as a symbol of your eternal love."

He handed the cup to Toshi. He took a sip of wine and gave it to Ana who did the same. The priest took the chalice from her and set it back on the altar. Toshi and Ana took the rings, in turn, from the priest and slipped them on each other's fingers. They stood, holding hands and facing each other, while the young musicians played and sang a special song that Ana had chosen as her wedding pledge to Toshi. The words and the title were significant to their relationship, "For You For the Rest of My Life."

Father Marcus ended the service with a short prayer of blessing for the newlyweds and the final announcement, given with a smile of approval and joy for them both.

"I now pronounce you husband and wife."

Ana and Toshi shared a wedding kiss and, while the musicians played more celebrative music, their friends came to congratulate them. Then they all adjourned to the luncheon table and to many toasts and cheers. The couple had requested no wedding gifts, only the gift of their guests' presence and support. The joy they had shared with Ana and Toshi was the best gift that could be given.

Much later in the afternoon, Sato and Miyuki departed for a trip to New York City before returning to Tokyo. Miko and Suzi were driving them to D.C. to catch their plane north. Before leaving, Miyuki and Ana had a few minutes alone in Ana's suite. They gave each other a goodbye hug as Ana expressed her happiness, "Yuki, thank you so much for being here. Just to know you have been with me through everything, and especially on this day, the happiest day of my life...will carry me through whatever we have to face ahead."

"I'll be with you whenever you need me, Ana. You are my most precious sister. We're more than sisters. I think we're just one person divided into two."

Ana responded to Yuki's love with tears, saying, "You know, of course, that the next time we meet will be in Tokyo. I only hope that we can prolong that visit."

Miyuki jumped back from Ana and shook her. "

"Hey! This is your wedding day and the happiest day of your life. No slips into dark places, understand? Go have a great time on your honeymoon and waste no energy on anything that hasn't happened yet. At least wait for it to happen before you start suffering it!"

They gave each other a final hug and kiss, then Miyuki and Sato went on their way north, while Ana and Toshi went with Ishikawa to the North Carolina coast for their honeymoon at the Sandcrest Resort. Toshi was happy for the chance to spend some time by the sea, and Ana was glad to relax in a setting with no responsibilities. Ishikawa would be there to care for both their needs.

Dominic stayed after the wedding to be with Toshi until they left for Carolina and had a few moments alone with Ana before the trip.

"I just want to assure you, Ana that Toshi seems to be doing well right now. I'm sure you will have some quality time together by the sea. Your wedding was beautiful. I've never been to a wedding that was so touching and meaningful to everyone present. You two are, indeed, 'star-crossed lovers.'"

Ana gave him a hug. "Thanks, Dom, for those sweet words and all of your support. You're so important to us. I think I'll feel a bit 'uncertain' without your presence with us in Carolina, but we'll keep you posted."

Dominic took her hand and held it tightly, saying, "Listen to me, now. It doesn't matter what time of day or night, if you need me, call. I can be there by private plane in just an hour, that's all I need. But, honestly, I believe Ishikawa will know when the call should be made, so trust his judgment. But if you feel uneasy, I'll be there for you."

He put his arm around her and they walked together to his car. When Dominic opened the door to get in, he turned to Ana and leaned over to kiss her on the cheek.

"You are some woman, Gabrelli! Now go enjoy the beauties of Sandcrest with your 'sweet samurai' and let Ishikawa and I handle the hard stuff."

"Strange, that's exactly what my husband told me not so long ago. Maybe I'll try it."

Within only a few hours, Ana and Toshi found themselves on the terrace of an elegant condo overlooking a wide expanse of green lawns and beautiful landscaping that melted into the sandy beach of the Atlantic Ocean. Their wedding day ended with a lovely meal served on the terrace, complete with a table setting of white chrysanthemums.

When she saw the flowers, Ana couldn't help but comment, "And this is how it all began."

Toshi laughed, "And how it almost ended before it began, as I recall. You were tough on me, Ana."

"I was afraid of you. I knew you would have too much power over me even before I knew who you were."

"I thought it was you who overpowered me! Wasn't it I who was running through the streets of Tokyo trying to touch your hand? And when I did, I didn't ever want to let it go."

Their eyes locked and Toshi knew, too late, that they should not have revisited the past. Ana offered the blow he expected.

"But you did let go, didn't you?"

Toshi faced her with the question that troubled his heart, "Is it because you love me so much, Ana, that you can't resist hurting me?"

She stood up and walked to the edge of the terrace, staring out at the beauty. It was a while before she could answer, and Toshi chose to wait. Ana finally responded to his question.

"Yes, I've always loved you too much. I knew the moment I turned around and faced you in the Tokyo street that I would love you too much and would never know the fulfillment of that love. And, you see, I was right, wasn't I?"

Ana turned from him and walked down the rocky path to the sea. She stood there looking at the waves lapping across the sand and against the huge rocks jutting out from the shore. Her mind flashed back to another life when she had stood with Mishima by the shore of the Japan Sea on the eve of another wedding day. A shadow passed over her heart.

Toshi waited a while before he went to her. There was nothing else to do. He could not let Ana's fears disturb this beautiful day. They had promised each other to 'live for the present moment,' but how could Ana do that? Toshi knew that every time she looked at him, she was faced with the anger she felt for his past choices and with her fears of the future. Ana, as much as she tried, could not live in the present moment. And their love could not exist in any other place. The past was gone and they had no future.

Ana felt Toshi's arms around her and his gentle voice close to her ear, "Where are you, Ana?"

She leaned back against him. "We've lived too many lives, you and I."

Toshi tightened his embrace as he asked, "Is this the life you want to live?"

She answered without hesitation, "Yes, this is the only life I have ever wanted to live."

"Then I suggest we live it. Love me, Ana, and if I die in your arms tonight, I will enter the eternal world with great joy!"

They walked back to the condo and for a while gave their love to each other as husband and wife. The joy they shared together overcame the fears that had troubled both their hearts, even on this beautiful wedding day.

Much later that night, after Ishikawa had completed the necessary preparations that would allow Toshi to sleep peacefully through the night, Ana heard a knock on her door. She jumped up to answer it, expecting Toshi to be there, but it was Ishikawa.

"Toshiburo will sleep well, now. Come walk with me, Ana. It is a beautiful night."

Ana was glad for the chance to be alone with Ishikawa. He always seemed to know when she needed his strength. They walked down the path by the sea before either of them spoke. Ishikawa went first.

"This was a beautiful day for you and Toshiburo. It was a day that we have all hoped would come. Ana, perhaps he has not told you, but I want to tell you. These years that were lost to you and Toshiburo have been torture for both him and me!"

"Perhaps it's too dangerous for us to talk about these things."

"I am talking to you because I sense that you are having trouble laying them to rest. It has always been easy for me to know what you are feeling. And my concern is as much for you as it is for my dear friend. Let me be the one who receives your fears and anger, not him. I am strong and can help you. He must use all his strength to live another day for you."

Ana knew the wisdom of his words and asked him the question she had almost asked of Toshi.

"Was it foolish for us to marry, now? Have we made a terrible mistake?"

"The only mistake either of you has every made was made by Toshiburo. He knows that and it has broken his heart and has shortened his life. His own guilt is a terrible burden for him to bear. I have had to watch his struggle."

"We can't erase the past, can we?"

"No, but you can rid yourself of its power by letting it go, and determining to live only for the day that you face when the morning sun rises."

"Can I let it go…to you?"

"You must let it go to me, for I am the only one who can bear to hear it. I am strong enough to carry your pain, as well as his. I am stronger than your anger or your fears!"

"Shall I give you my burden tonight? You may never sleep again."

"That is of no concern. My concern is that you sleep well, so that you can give your love and your strength to your husband when he needs it most. Give me your burden, Ana, tonight, before any damage is done between the two of you."

They walked far down the shore to a cove where they could sit on the huge trunks of trees washed white by the tides. Ishikawa sat down. Ana stood and paced back and forth in front of him.

"I need to tell you how angry I am because of his weakness and his lack of trust in our love. I was forced to live for sixteen years with a man I loved only as a friend, because of that!"

"How did Toshiburo force you to do that? Wasn't that your choice?"

"What choice did I have? Toshi was leaving me alone, with nothing!"

"But you made the choice to take Miko with you! You made the choice that forced you to live with this man you did not love, isn't that so?"

"Toshi gave our life away, Ishikawa! He gave away our future as if it were nothing. He spoke of 'responsibility to family,' but those words felt like excuses and lies to me. He and I were the family he should have been responsible to, he and I and the children we would have.

When I remember what I suffered because of him, I can't believe that I'm walking down that same path again. It's all the same. I've made the same promise to the same man with the knowledge of the same ending. He will leave me alone again…with nothing."

"What do you consider 'nothing,' Ana? You have renewed your love for each other. You have become a family and your son knows his father. You have the blessing of time together, time you had not expected to ever have. You have this time to share a great happiness!"

"Tainted always with fear of the loss ahead."

"You chose to marry him, to put your fears and anger away and to live as if today is all that matters. Why do you insist on breaking your own vows? You break them every time you allow the past to destroy the beauty of the present!"

Ana fell to her knees before Ishikawa. She bowed her head and pressed her hands against her eyes as she whispered, "I'm not strong enough to face it! I thought I was, until today before the altar. After this beautiful day, how can I give him up again?"

"You have always had the courage to do what had to be done. Your strength has been proven over and over again. And you will be strong now because it is required of you."

Ishikawa stood over her. He reached down and gripped Ana's arms, lifting her to her feet as if his own life depended on her strength. He put his mouth against her ear and spoke in a hoarse whisper, "His pathway is hard. He is suffering great pain, both physical and emotional. Yet, he attempts to cover it up for you. If you have ever loved Toshiburo Yamamoto, if you love him now, then you must care for him tenderly and then you must prepare to let him go. There will continue to be life for you, Ana, and love and joy. I can promise you that."

Ana fell against Ishikawa, devastated by his words. The two friends held each other as if to share whatever energy they both possessed. Then they walked to the seashore and sat down near the surf. Moonlight broke through the night clouds and offered its own power and beauty to their silent meditations. After a long time, Ishikawa spoke.

"I must be with him now and watch over his rest."

He rose to return to his friend, but hesitated. Ana understood what Ishikawa wanted to say to her and quickly assured him, "I'm alright, Ishikawa. You were right. I needed to let go of my anger and be reminded of why I'm here in this beautiful place. Love brought me here and love will sustain me, now."

Ishikawa returned to watch over his friend. Ana stayed by the sea alone. She was calmed by her own words and the truth that she felt as she had spoken them. This was her wedding day, and it had been sweet, as well as bitter. But tonight she had cleaned her heart of the bitterness. Only the sweetness would remain, and she recalled it as she sat alone.

The wedding day had been a surprise to Ana. In all her dreams, she had never envisioned such a moment. Until the night of the embassy reception, she had believed that Toshi's love had been lost to her. But when their hands touched in greeting, Ana knew that their love was as strong as it had ever been.

And now, she had kissed her husband goodnight concerned that he wake in the morning. Her heart ached with love for him and with concern for what he was suffering. How sorry she was that she had ever added her own emotional baggage to his physical pain. Yet, Ana also knew that if she had not shared her feelings with Toshi during these past weeks, he would never have revealed his continuing love for her.

Ana felt a calm assurance filling her heart. She turned from the sea and its pounding surf and walked back toward the quiet resort. As she stepped onto the screened porch, Ana saw the shadow there. He had been watching and waiting. She took his hand and felt the strength flowing into her own.

He whispered into the darkness, "Perhaps his love has come late, Ana, but it has not come too late!"

She smiled and whispered to her dear friend, "No, it is not too late. It has come just in time. Thank you, Ishikawa, I can sleep now."

Ana went to her rest.

CHAPTER 34

*"A moment of joy...a time for lovers to open their hearts,
forgiving the past. A moment of sorrow...fearing the
future, yet finding strength in the pull of the tide to
love...and let go!"*
--Ana and Toshiburo

Ana woke to a soft knock and a whisper at her bedroom door.
"Are you awake, Ana?" It was Ishikawa.

She jumped up quickly, threw on her robe, and hurried to the
door.

"What is it? What's happened?"

Ishikawa smiled and attempted to calm her fears.

"Everything is fine. Your husband is up early and invites you
to join him for breakfast on the terrace, but he doesn't want to
disturb your rest."

Ana leaned against Ishikawa for a moment to recover from
the shock of being awakened out of a sound sleep.

"Of course, I'll join him. What in the world time is it?"

"It's nearly nine o'clock. We've been walking through the
gardens. This is a beautiful place for a quiet rest."

"I guess it's not as early as I thought. Just give me a few
minutes to shower and dress. I'll be there right away."

Ana hurried through her morning shower, brushed her wet
hair, and dressed in a sleeveless cotton vest and slacks. As she
came through the living room doors onto the terrace, she saw
Toshi stretched out on a lounge chair, his hands behind his head,
enjoying the beauty of the day.

She walked over and knelt beside him. Toshi smiled and ran
his fingers through her thick, wet hair as he spoke, "At last, the
Angel Gabrelli graces us with her presence."

As she kissed him good morning, she whispered, "She comes
to pay homage to her 'god' for his gift of love."

Toshi replied quickly, "I'm no god, Gabrelli."

Ana answered with a smile, "And, I'm no angel."

"Ah, but that's where you're wrong. You come to me, at
times, as an 'avenging angel,' haunting my dreams at night and
pressing your sharp sword against my heart for the pain that I

have caused you. And then, you come as a 'comforting angel' who brings memories as vivid as your gentle touch and the sweet words of love we've shared in our few moments together.

All through these years apart, I could not resist your 'angelic presence.' I called you up, not caring which came to me, the sharp sword or the gentle touch. I only knew that I had to have your presence with me or I could not live through another day."

"Have I brought you such pain and bitterness, Toshi? Is it I who has injured your heart and broken it completely?"

"No, sweet Ana, you are innocent. I have done it to myself and to you."

Ana knew the truth of his confession, but also knew that it had come too late to heal the brokenness in either his heart or hers.

She put her arms around him and said, "Let me be your comforting angel, Toshi, for the rest of our time together. There is no vengeance left in me. There is nothing in my heart but love for you."

Toshi smiled at her sweet words which brought some comfort to his heaviness of spirit. Then they shared their wedding breakfast in leisure. Ishikawa did not join them. He left them alone to enjoy whatever peaceful moments they could in this beautiful setting.

During these quiet days by the sea, Toshi and Ana had time to heal some wounds that had separated them emotionally and had caused them both a great deal of pain. As difficult as it was for her, Ana finally admitted to her husband that she had made a grave mistake by leaving him without knowledge of the child they shared. She realized, too late, what a dreadful choice she had made. She had never understood nor trusted the depth of Toshi's love for her.

One evening as they were resting together by the fireplace in the living room, Toshi made a surprising statement to Ana.

"There's something I need to share with you about Sachiko and me. Though it's difficult for me to speak of it, I want you to understand everything as it really was, rather than as you think it might have been."

Ana sighed, not anxious to hear about his life with another woman, "You needn't tell me anything about that part of your life, Tosh. It's not necessary, now."

"But it's important to me that you know the truth so there will be no questions left between us in this regard."

Ana sighed, "Then tell me what you must."

She moved away from him and sat on the floor with her back against the soft couch near the fireplace, facing him. She waited with apprehension for the words that she had hoped would never be spoken.

Toshi began his narrative.

"Our marriage took place about eight months after you and Mishima left Japan. Sachiko and I did all that was expected of us by both families, including the engagement parties and the many layers of receptions. The formal wedding was everything it should have been and more, with both Shinto and Buddhist rites. And, to my surprise, Sachiko requested a short Christian ceremony with a white dress and wedding vows spoken in French. She told me that she had converted to Catholicism while studying in France. I was surprised, for we had never discussed this before, but, of course, I had no objections.

When all the 'after ceremony' celebrations were over, we began our wedding trip. Our first time alone was at a very exclusive resort in the mountains of New Zealand. We were surrounded with amazing natural beauty that touched both our hearts, but in the midst of this glorious setting, the reality of our situation dawned upon us. Our marriage had been arranged and performed to perfection, yet, now we faced the glaring fact that we were husband and wife and that we did not love each other. It became a sad affair.

I offered Sachiko the assurance that I expected nothing of her other than a public commitment, but she took my words as an insult, as if she were unacceptable to me as a wife. The whole situation rendered us both helpless. She was in tears, which I could only interpret as fear and shame, and I was unable to soothe her anguish in any way whatever.

Finally, I begged her forgiveness for allowing the marriage to go forward when we both loved other persons. When she realized that I was as miserable as she, we were able to talk to one another openly and face our mutual problem. She told me then of her love affair and Pere's promise to wait for her as long as necessary.

After all the truth was shared between us, she gladly accepted my suggestion that we be marriage partners for the public only. She promised to do all that was required as the public wife of the Ambassador, and I promised to honor and support her in that role. I also offered her the freedom to be with the one she loved in as discreet a way as possible. I even suggested an immediate annulment, but Sachiko was horrified at the prospect of bringing such shame to her family. She asked, and I agreed, that we continue the marriage for a ten-year period.

It was ironic, was it not? On our wedding night, we spent the whole time making plans for our separation. By the end of the evening, we had sealed our friendship by laughing and crying and drinking and talking about our shared plight. The next day, we were able to enjoy the beauty around us and to continue our wedding trip with some semblance of pleasure.

Though we couldn't love each other as husband and wife, we did care for each other as friends. The only sadness between us was my own loss for which there was no recovery. Sachiko had a gentle heart and tried to comfort me when my sorrow became heavy. In that way, she was a blessing which I missed very much when she was gone. But knowing that she was finally with the one she loved soothed my loneliness. At least one of us was able to retrieve what we had lost.

Of course, the whole situation was a fiasco, yet, in another way, it was a gift. We helped each other fulfill our obligations to both family and country. I assumed it was my destiny to do so, for that is what occurred. And it appears to have been hers as well, to accompany me on a part of that journey."

It was a long time before Ana was able to speak. She could hardly imagine the loneliness that Toshi had suffered, while she had Mishima and Miko to love and care for. She finally broke the silence.

"I saw the two of you, only once, on a television news report when you first took your assignment in Washington, D.C. Your wife was beautiful, and you both seemed so happy. When you turned to wave at the camera, I noticed that you kept one arm around her as if she were a fragile flower that was very precious to you. Now, I understand that, in a special way, she was both.

I have to tell you, Toshi, that I am most thankful that you did not attempt to contact me after Sachiko was gone. Too many things would have been disturbed. You were wise, much wiser than I might have been in the same situation."

He responded as Ana knew he would, "I must assume that everything has occurred according to that which was meant to be."

Though Ana did not accept Toshi's words as her truth, she knew that this firm belief was the only comfort left to him. She would never dispute that belief. Toshi had one last request of Ana, which he was hesitant to make.

"Perhaps, sometime in the future, when everything here is…finished…you might contact Sachiko. I would like for her to know that there was a time when you and I renewed our love for each other…that there was a moment of joy, at last, for her 'sad Ambassador.'"

He laid his head back against the soft chair and shut his eyes. The room was empty of sound, except for the crackling of the wood as it burned and dropped against the fireplace grate. Ana went to him and they comforted each other for their shared sorrow…the loss of what might have been…and the fear of what surely would be.

Because Toshi's health had remained fairly stable at Sandcrest, they stayed beyond their original plan. Near the end of their second month, both Dominic and Ishikawa agreed that the environment of the sun, the sea, and the clear air had obviously been good for their patient. They saw no reason to return to Virginia, at this point.

Dominic flew down each weekend and, on several occasions, brought Miko and Suzi with him. He encouraged Toshi and Ana to remain at Sandcrest as long as they both felt it was a positive experience for everyone concerned. During his visit after their tenth week at Sandcrest, Dominic found time to be alone with Ana. They walked along the beach together, enjoying the sun and beauty of the sea. He finally broached the subject that was disturbing him.

"I think we need to talk about the future, Ana. Toshi is holding his own here in a way I would have never thought possible. But you need to remember that he's on borrowed time."

"Why discuss it, then? It we all know that, why not just accept it and let's enjoy our small miracle?"

"Don't misunderstand me. I just want you to know the truth. His heart is becoming weaker, though his spirit is strong. And, for a while, his spirit has the upper hand. I credit that to you and to the amazing power of love."

"What are you trying to say, doctor?"

Dominic frowned at Ana's defensive attitude which made it difficult to know what she was thinking.

"I believe you know very well what I'm trying to say."

"Yes, and I also know there is no need to say it."

"Are we on the same side here, Ana?"

"I'm not sure. Why not let me live in my little dream world for a while. I'll get knocked out of it sooner or later!"

Dominic and Ana stood, almost like adversaries, he trying to penetrate her emotional armor, she holding it tightly around her heart. He chose to surrender to her stronger need. Looking out toward the sea, he whispered, "Enjoy this beauty, Ana. You and Toshi both deserve every moment of happiness that life offers you."

He left her then to return to the world of reality which he had chosen as a profession, but which had suddenly become a dreadful burden on his heart.

Late one afternoon, near the end of their twelfth week in Carolina, Toshi and Ana were resting on a bench by the sea, enjoying the beauty around them. Toshi asked, "Do you have a problem if we stay here at the resort a while longer?"

Ana was surprised at his question, but said, "I have no problem whatever. It's very comfortable here and my leave of absence at the university is for the whole summer semester. I can even extend it into the fall if I choose. There's nothing that would keep us from staying as long as you want, Toshi."

"There's something very calming about the sea, the clear air, the sun. Somehow, I feel a different kind of energy in this place. Have you felt it?"

"Yes, the sea air clears my mind and I love the beauty that surrounds us. I have no problem with a longer stay, but perhaps we should discuss it with Dominic."

Toshi's reply was casual, almost disinterested, "We can let him know our change of plans. I'm sure he'd like to be informed."

Ana caught Toshi's attitude clearly. He did not intend to ask Dominic's opinion. After all, why should Toshi ask his doctor about such a decision when the only power Dominic had over him was to relieve his pain with medication and to help him breathe until his breath was gone?

It was this thought that disturbed Ana and pushed her to ask, just as casually, "How long would you like to stay?"

Ana knew instinctively what he was thinking. *As long as it takes me to die.* But neither of them spoke such words.

Toshi simply replied, "For a little longer, perhaps a week or two. But if you want to go back, I'll do whatever you feel is best."

Their eyes met for just an instant, then Toshi turned his gaze back toward the sea, waiting for her reply. He did not know that, in that quick glance, Ana had seen something in his eyes that had never been there before. She had seen surrender. Instinctively, she wanted to challenge his attempted deception, but instead, she replied calmly, "We can stay as long as we like. We're not rushed for time." His answer sent a wave of shock across her heart.

"I think…two weeks will be long enough."

He smiled, as if relieved, and reached over to touch her hand.

"Thank you for understanding, Ana."

But she understood too much. It was all she could do to return his smile and reply casually, "I'm going to take a quick run along the beach. It's such a perfect day. Do you mind?"

He laughed at her question, "Of course not! While you run, Ishikawa and I will do some walking around the resort."

Ana went back to the condo to change into her swim suit and tennis shoes for the run. On her way down the beach, she called to Toshi, "Ishikawa's on the patio if you need anything. I'll be back in an hour or two!"

When Ana was out of anyone's hearing she began to shout her anger at the world and at Toshi's decision and her own weakness. She reached the mile marker and ran into the surf to lay down in the cool, wet sand.

The waves, washing gently over her body, seemed to cleanse Ana's spirit. She felt the power of the tide as the water came over her and rolled back out to sea again. She realized that if she were to be washed into it, she could resist for a while, but eventually there would be no recourse. She would have to go wherever it wished to take her.

Ana lay in the sand and the sea for a long time, filled with respect for the natural world that was enticing her to come and share its journey. She began to daydream of the places she might go with those mighty waves, those faraway places she had never seen. She wondered if she would find peace there.

After a while, Ana began to understand what she had seen in Toshi's eyes today. He had fought the tide of illness since the day of his birth, and now he had no resistance to its power and its pull. Not only had he surrendered to it, but there was a longing in him to be released and to go with it, as if it were a friend. Ana wept for her husband and for his terrible struggle and for herself.

While her thoughts were centered on the one she loved, Ana's attention had been drawn from the power of the rushing waves. She suddenly realized that the sand was slipping away from beneath her. She tried to stand but found that she was caught in a riptide that was strong enough to carry everything on the beach out to sea. She rolled over and over, trying to grasp the rocks beneath the sand but found nothing secure enough to hold her grip.

Realizing that she was losing her battle with the sea, Ana cried out for help. Of course, there was no one near. She knew that wasting her energy in a useless struggle was only getting her closer to the dark chasm of water that could become her grave. In the midst of her fears, Ana remembered something she had been taught when she had first learned to swim: *If the tide should pull you out to sea, don't waste your energy fighting against it. Relax and go with the flow. When it rushes back to the beach, you'll have the strength to swim in with it and to find a stronghold.*

Ana forced herself to relax and let her body move out with the tide. As she did so, she felt her strength returning and when the next rush of waves came toward the beach she was able to swim back to a safe place. When she finally crawled onto the dry sand and out of danger from the powerful tide, Ana started laughing and crying and panting for breath. She shouted to the sky or to anyone who might hear, "That was too, too close! You wild waves, you taught me a lesson today that I shall never forget! I'm not ready for your kind of 'peace.'"

After a few moments of rest, Ana recovered her equilibrium and began the long, slow trek back to the condo. Looking out at the rushing waves for which she now had much greater respect, she realized how fortunate she and Toshi really were. They had been given a short space of time to fulfill their promises to each other. But now she must grant him the gift of peace for which he longed. She must let him go. And he had given her these next few days to do so.

By the time Ana reached the condo, it was nearly dark. Ishikawa caught her as she ran from the beach toward the rocky path that led to the porch.

"Ana, where in the world have you been? We were getting ready to call the beach police. It's nearly dark and you've been gone for hours! What has happened? Are you alright?"

Ana was out of breath from the run back and couldn't answer quickly enough for Ishikawa, "I...just...ran. I'm okay!"

"No, you're not okay, you're soaking wet. Did you swim by yourself? You know you can't do that in these waters. Come to the house and I'll get a blanket and some hot tea."

He took her arm, but Ana was so exhausted, she stumbled and fell. She laid down on the grass and tried to explain what had happened. "I'm not hurt. I was just lying in the water, just touching the sea, that's all."

He helped her up and shook his head at her.

"Ana, you are so much trouble. You are always trouble!"

She started laughing at him and couldn't stop. Toshi heard the commotion and came out of the condo. When he reached them, he couldn't believe his eyes. Ana was rolling in the grass, laughing, while Ishikawa was standing over her with his arms on his hips, like a parent with a bad child. He looked at Toshi and started walking toward the house.

"She is too much trouble! You must handle her. I give up!"

Ana looked so ridiculous that Toshi couldn't help laughing. He tried to get her attention, asking, "What have you been doing? You're soaking wet! Have you been in the sea? For heaven's sake, Ana, are you crazy?"

"Yes, I am definitely crazy! I really am sorry that I worried you. I know it's later than I thought, but I started running and got into the rhythm, I guess, and went too far. Then I laid down in the water to cool off and just enjoyed it a while."

Toshi sat down on the grass beside her. Ana finally sat up and tried to be serious.

"I'm sorry, Toshi, I didn't mean to worry anyone."

"You'd better get out of those wet clothes. Ishikawa has dinner waiting for you."

They started to the house, but Ana stopped and put her arms around her husband. She began to kiss him as if she had just found her long-lost love. She whispered, "I don't want dinner. I just want to be with you."

"You are such a crazy Italian, Gabrelli. What is to become of you?"

"Without you, I don't know! Where will I find another 'sweet samurai' to play love songs for me?"

"Did you find a bottle of whiskey floating toward the beach? Is that why you've been gone so long? Or were you drinking with that wild group in the next condo? I never know what to expect from you!"

While he was laughing at her, Ana suddenly crumpled to the grass and began to cry. Toshi was speechless at this sudden rush of emotion. Whatever happened on the beach, she was more than out of control, she was nearly hysterical. He put his arms around her and began to speak in a quiet, calm voice, "Talk to me, Ana. What happened on the beach? What is it, why the tears now?"

She could only shake her head, 'no,' and continue crying. Finally, Ana pulled herself together enough to walk back to the condo with Toshi. They went to his room and sat down by the warm fire where he helped her out of her wet swimsuit and wrapped a blanket tightly around her cold body. She continued to shake and her tears wouldn't stop until Toshi offered her the warmth she most needed. Only his love could calm her now for she had experienced his death. She had already felt him slip away from her into the tide.

Later in the evening, Ishikawa joined them by the fire. He brought Ana some hot soup and tea. She knew that she couldn't tell them everything that had happened on the beach, so she offered a simple explanation of what she had done.

"I ran to the mile marker and needed to cool off, so I laid down in the surf. When I began to feel the power of the waves, I was somewhat fearful, but at the same time I was fascinated. I must have relaxed too much, for I suddenly realized that the tide was pulling me out to sea. That's when I began to panic!

I called for help, but there was no one near. Finally, I forced myself to relax and go with the tide. When it rushed back to shore, I swam in with it. I can assure you, I've learned the hard way that beneath the beauty of the natural world lies an awe-inspiring power. I won't tempt it again!

I'm sorry, Ishikawa, but when I saw you there on the beach and knew I was safe, I just lost it. I couldn't stop laughing for the pure joy of being alive!"

Ishikawa pleaded Ana's forgiveness, "If I had known what you had just been through, I would never have treated you so disrespectfully. Please forgive me."

Toshi added his own apology to Ana, "And I can't believe that I accused you of being crazy when we nearly lost you!"

"Oh, quiet…both of you. I'm okay and I deserve the title of 'crazy,' for sure! What I did was stupid and anyone who ever goes to the ocean knows never to swim alone and certainly should know not to lie down in the sand and wait for the riptide to flow over them.

I think I'd better go to my safe bed and thank all my guardian angels and the gods of the universe for bringing me back alive. I'm worn out!"

Ishikawa left Ana and Toshi alone. For a while, they did not speak, but enjoyed the pleasure of being close. Then Toshi whispered, "Thank god, you came back to us. There is no life without you, Ana. You are my life."

"And you are mine. How will I live without you, Tosh? Tell me that."

"You will live, Ana. You will live and love again because you cannot do otherwise."

Perhaps he was right. Perhaps she would find love again, but tonight she would share her love only with him. They stayed together until very late.

After she left her husband to his rest, Ana couldn't sleep. During the night, she cried and prayed for strength to live through the loss that was ahead. She asked herself, *"Why didn't I let go when the tide was so close to pulling me out?"* But she knew very well why. She had a love of life that would never allow her to make the choice that Toshi was making now.

Ana knew that she would come through the darkness ahead, for she had fought the pull of the tide with all her might, and she had won. She would have the strength to conquer the pain of losing the one she loved. But far into the night, Ana continued to ask herself, *"How will I ever say goodbye to him? How will I ever be able to say goodbye for the last time?"*

When the moon rose high over the sea, two friends sat together on the warm sand, leaning against a huge rock. One whispered to the other, "It will not be long, Ana. I stayed with him after you left tonight. He was sleeping, but I heard his spirit sighing in the darkness. I have heard that sound before. It is a message that the spirit is longing for release, release from the pain that is required for continuing here."

"How will I live through this? How can I ever live without him, now that we've made our peace with one another?"

"You are strong and your spirit is filled with life. And as long as you have memory, his presence will be with you. But you must not attempt to hold him here. There is nothing left now but suffering. You must let him go and free his spirit to move into that other realm. You have made your peace together in order to let him go. I will be here to help you."

The two friends stayed by the sea until dawn broke across the waters. Their tears were shed as if from one broken heart. At last, Ana whispered the words for which Ishikawa had patiently waited.

"I felt the pull of the tide yesterday and its promise of peace was enticing. I know that I must allow Toshi to find the peace for which his body and his spirit are longing. I know that I must let him go. He has chosen to surrender."

"He is only waiting on you, Ana. The time is up to you."

"He asked me tonight for two more weeks. Is it too long? Should I tell him he is free to go now?"

"If he has given you a time, then he knows how much suffering he can endure. Each of us knows our own body. We know the limits of our strength. If he has asked for two more weeks, that is all he needs, but he needs that."

After a long silence, Ana said the words that she would never have believed she could speak, "I will give my husband whatever time he has asked of me…and then I will let him go."

Ishikawa whispered to the wife of his dearest friend, "He will thank you for his release."

CHAPTER 35

"The beauty of the sea calms the spirit, yet the awe-inspiring power of the rushing waves causes one to contemplate the ebb and flow of life. There is a pattern and a purpose in all things, even in death."
--Toshiburo Yamamoto

During the next two weeks, Ana made every effort to create a positive atmosphere for her husband. She and Ishikawa did not speak of what they knew, but surrounded Toshi with their love and support. Together, the three of them enjoyed the beauties of the Carolina coast and the quiet evenings by the fire. Ana loved listening to Toshi tell about his childhood, his grandmother, and his escapades at college. He seemed free now to speak to her of everything he had experienced or dreamed of experiencing.

After Toshi retired each evening, Ana and Ishikawa sat by the sea and talked together. At these times, Ana realized that Ishikawa needed to share with her as much as Toshi did, for he had chosen to go with his dear friend in his own way and in his own time. Ana drew from him the stories of his own life that he had never shared with a living soul.

When she and Ishikawa left each other late in the night, Ana went to her room and wrote as much as she could remember of what both men had told her about their lives. She knew that these stories were precious, not only for her, but for Mikoto and for his children. This was the history that would sustain her and her son in the future.

No word was ever spoken among the three friends at Sandcrest about the ending that was near. And when the day came, Ana and Ishikawa stood together by the sea, watching the sun come up bright and warm against their faces. Ana turned to him and smiled, "Let's make this a beautiful day!"

The friends walked toward the condo to prepare for the last few hours they would share with the one they both loved in equal measure. Ana had called Dominic earlier in the week to let him know what was happening. He would be flying down with Miko within the next hour or so. She knew that Toshi would want to say goodbye to his son.

Ana promised herself that she would be honest with Toshi and also that she would be strong for him. After all, she knew something about strength from the experiences of her life up to now, including the recent contest with the sea. Her foremost concern was her husband's comfort at this difficult moment. And to help with this, she dressed with care for the last few hours they would spend together.

Ana chose the brightest outfit in her closet, as if this were a day of celebration. She put on her pale orange slacks with a matching sleeveless top and lacy blouse, then pulled her hair back with an orange chiffon scarf. Ana found that she was dressing for herself as much as for Toshi, trying to keep her spirits high.

While Ana was preparing for the day, Ishikawa entered Toshi's room to see if he were awake. He found his friend dressed and sitting in a chair by the fireplace, though it wasn't lit. The air was already warm from the sun. The night before, Toshi had refused both the oxygen and the pain medication. Ishikawa did not argue with him at the time, but he decided to talk to him today, for Ana's sake.

Toshi appeared stronger than expected as he greeted Ishikawa, "I was able to rest now and then through the night and feel as well as I could expect after these past few hours on my own. Have you talked with Ana?"

"Yes, she's ready to accept whatever decision you make. But, Toshi, I want you to reconsider one point. For those of us who love you, we understand your desire to be released from the prison in which you have existed for so long. But, for Ana's sake, I hope that you will accept some medication for the pain. Choosing our time of death is a personal matter for each of us, but choosing to suffer pain that is not required hurts everyone. The sorrow of losing you is enough."

Toshi was quiet for a moment before he answered, "I'll see how the next few hours go and promise to consider your suggestion. Have you called Dominic? He'll need to be here soon."

"I've already done that. He and Miko are flying down and will be here by lunchtime. Won't you please let me offer you something to relieve the pain before you begin this day?"

"Let's wait for the doctor. Things are not beyond my ability to handle as yet."

Ana was sitting on the patio drinking a huge cup of hot, black coffee when Ishikawa and Toshi came out to greet her. She searched her husband's face for answers to her questions. He appeared pale and tired, but he smiled as if it were an ordinary day. Ana stood to embrace him, offering a silent prayer that he would gain strength from her energy.

When they sat down to breakfast, Toshi leaned toward his wife with a teasing smile and whispered, "You're as bright and beautiful as the sun, Ana. There are times when I think nature cannot be equaled in its beauty, until I gaze upon 'Gabrelli,' and then I have to admit my error in judgment."

Ana laughed at his teasing comments and addressed Ishikawa.

"All those years of diplomatic negotiation have served him well, wouldn't you say, Ishikawa? He has become an expert at the turn of a phrase. And at turning our attention from the problem at hand."

Toshi smiled and winked at her, continuing to keep their attention elsewhere.

"And how have you found the sea this morning, Ana? Has it become friendlier to you since your frightening experience with the tides? Are you ready to return for a challenge with those mighty waves?"

"It was frightening, I'll certainly admit, but I've been frightened before and don't think for a minute that a little sea water can get Gabrelli down!"

"I would like to believe that there is absolutely nothing that can conquer Gabrelli's spirit. Would I be correct in assuming that?"

Ana knew what Toshi wanted from her. He wanted assurance, without asking directly, that she had accepted his decision and would come through with strength. Her first thought was to crumble at his feet and beg him not to leave her, but instead, she gave him what he needed.

She leaned toward him and spoke quietly, "If my spirit could be conquered, it would have happened long ago. There were times in my life when I faced foes much stronger than the sea and I discovered how much power there can be in the human spirit when it is challenged. I've never forgotten those experiences, nor what I learned from them."

Their eyes locked in a familiar struggle, as she continued, "I learned that there is nothing, absolutely nothing, that life can do to me that can conquer my spirit…unless I choose to surrender it."

Toshi responded quickly to the assurance she had given him that she could withstand the loss ahead. He knew that now was the time to speak the words that had to be spoken. He looked directly at her and whispered, "Forgive me, Ana, but I have chosen to surrender."

She did not flinch, nor did she turn away from his gaze.

"We each have to choose our own path, Toshi. If that is your choice, then I will honor it."

There was nothing more to be said. They had shared the last bit of hard truth that ever needed to be spoken between them. Ana had given Yamamoto the freedom to leave her, as she had given one other time in the past.\

Ishikawa wisely interrupted the tense moment, "You must take some nourishment and enjoy the beauty of the day."

Ishikawa served them a light breakfast, but Toshi chose not to partake of it. Ana knew that it was his choice and did not mention her concern.

After she had eaten, Ana asked her husband, "Do you feel like spending some time by the sea?"

Toshi answered with a smile, as if it were just another day, "Of course, that's why we came here, to share the peace that nature can bring us through her beauty and her power."

Ana grabbed a large beach towel from the porch rail and the pair walked arm-in-arm to a quiet cove near the sea. She laid the towel on the sand so they could relax as they shared their final moments together. She knew they must open their hearts to each other now, for it would be the last time. They sat down and leaned back against the sandy hillside with the warm sun on their faces and the pounding surf in front of them. Ana posed a question to her husband.

"If this moment is all that is left for us, Toshi, what shall we do with it?"

He answered without hesitation, "We must speak only of our love for each other."

"Then speak to me of your love, Toshi, and I'll tell you of mine."

They did not waste time, nor words, but spoke only of that which was in both their hearts. They spoke of the love which they knew from their first moment of greeting so long ago on a hot summer's night in Tokyo. They held each other and allowed their tears to relieve the pain that each had suffered for past mistakes and for the coming loss. Time had been the enemy of these lovers. Only moments had been given them. A few moments in their youth, a moment in a garden shrine, and only a moment now with the sun and the sea. Once again, the promise of separation loomed over them, but from this separation there would be no reprieve.

When they had shared the depth of their love as husband and wife, when they had emptied their hearts of the sorrow that lay ahead, they made their final promises to each other.

"If there is a place in the eternal world where we can meet again, I promise you, Ana, I will wait there for you."

"And, if that is so, Toshi, I will find you."

Later in the morning, they returned to the condo, their hearts at peace. They were both aware of what this day would bring and had accepted that which lay ahead as inevitable.

While Toshi and Ana were together by the sea, Dominic and Miko had arrived by special plane and were waiting at the condo. Dominic was discouraged at Toshi's decision to give up the struggle. Though the doctor knew that it was a fight that could not be won, still he felt there was time left. Before Toshi and Ana had returned, Dominic expressed his discouragement to Ishikawa.

"I'm sorry Toshi made this decision now. I'm sure he could have several more weeks, perhaps months, of quality life with the treatment we're using. But, without the oxygen, there is no chance and no time. How could he do this to Ana?"

Ishikawa answered for his friend, "Toshiburo knows this illness inside out. It came with him to this life and it will finally take his life from him. He has told me that he is tired of the struggle. He has found it too difficult to live on increasing medication that brings shadows to his mind and constant machines to give him breath. He has told me that he is ready to accept whatever fate is designed for him. That is all I know."

"How is Ana handling it?"

"She has accepted Toshi's decision for she knows that this is a choice he must make for himself. But she wants to talk with both of you. There are many things to discuss now and plans to be made."

When Toshi and Ana arrived back at the condo, Dominic met them on the patio. Ana noted his discouragement as the doctor greeted them.

"I came as quickly as I could. We need to visit a while now."

His patient responded quietly, "Yes, you and Ishikawa and I should talk. Please excuse us, Ana."

Dominic finally met her eyes.

"Miko is in the living room, waiting to see you, Ana. I'm sorry about what's happening. We'll visit later."

Ana hurried into the living room. Miko jumped up when she walked in.

"Mother, are you alright? Dominic's pretty upset. He thinks Toshi has given up too soon."

"No one but Toshi knows what 'too soon' is. He knows his own body and what he can handle. Obviously, he's reached the limit of his strength. How can I fight against that?"

"But you've had such a short time together. It doesn't seem fair to you. He seemed so determined to do whatever he could to continue his life."

"The truth is, Miko, I was the one determined for him to live and to have the wedding and to have a few moments together. I didn't give him a choice in those matters. He made promises to me that I've required him to keep. Somehow, I had the mistaken idea that our love could work a miracle. But the miracle hasn't occurred and he's tired of the struggle."

"Do you think Dominic can change his mind?"

"No one will change his mind. He has surrendered to the illness and there's nothing any of us can do. I've accepted it. We'll be all right, Miko."

"I'm sorry, Mother. I wish I could change things and bring you the happiness you deserve. After all these years of loving someone, then to have them leave you just when you start a new life together. It isn't fair. You've lost too much. We've both lost too much, Mishima and now, Toshi."

Ana grabbed her son and gave him a hug as she answered in an unusually upbeat way.

"Hey, we have each other and we have great friends and wonderful memories. What more do we need, anyway? Let's go face what we have to face and get on with life!"

Ana smiled at Miko. He was so much like his own father, tender and gentle and concerned for others. She was happy that he portrayed so many characteristics of Toshiburo Yamamoto. She was only sorry that father and son could not have had more time together, so they might have known each other better and come to love each other more deeply. Though she had been a part of creating this history, she could not change its direction now. That choice was out of her hands.

After a while, Ishikawa and Dominic came out of Toshi's room. Miko asked Dominic if he could talk to Toshi for a moment. The doctor assured him, "Of course, I know he'd like to share a few moments with you. Your mother and I have things to discuss, so we'll take a short break, but you may go in."

As she and Dominic turned to leave, Ana touched Miko's arm, saying, "We'll be back soon. I think Ishikawa has a special meal planned for us all a little later."

Miko very quietly opened the door to Toshi's room and asked, "Can we talk a while, just you and I?"

Toshi smiled and invited him in, "Of course, Miko. Your mother and Dominic are going to spend some time together so we can be alone."

Miko sat down on a chair close to Toshi's bed and reached over to touch his hand. Toshi clasped it in his own. Father and son offered comfort to one another.

The doctor and his patient's wife walked along the stretch of beach where Ana had experienced her struggle with the sea. They sat down on the sand and leaned back against a large tree trunk that had been swept in with the tide.

Ana was the first to speak.

"Did Toshi tell you what happened here?"

Dominic looked at her in surprise.

"No. He didn't. What happened?"

"Perhaps I should call it a cathartic experience now that I look back on it. I'm surprised that Toshi or Ishikawa didn't mention it."

"I guess we were concentrating on how to keep your husband alive when he's refused to accept my counsel. There's nothing I can do now, Ana. No one can live without oxygen and the valves of his heart are all but useless. He may not live through this day and you should be prepared for that."

Dominic was surprised at Ana's calm response.

"I'm prepared for whatever comes. Toshi has asked me to let him go. At first, I thought I couldn't do it, but that's when I came here to this stretch of beach. Quite by accident, or should I say by my own foolishness, I was nearly washed out to sea with the riptide.

I really did believe that I couldn't live without Toshi's presence in my life. I thought that I would rather go with the tide than be without him again. But when the option was offered me, I didn't make that choice. I fought for my life and won the battle!

Toshi has surrendered. He has no fight left in him and wants only to be done with it. He would walk into the sea this very minute, except for his desire to return to Fuji. His longing now is to have his ashes scattered across the waters of Lake Kawaguchi so that he will always be in the shadow of the great mountain.

I respect his desires and I've given him my blessing. But that's not who I am. I will fight for my last breath! So, you see, Toshi and I are both ready for the end of this sweet love affair."

Dominic was quiet for a while, struggling with his own feelings of loss at what was ahead. He finally responded, "Then the decision is made?"

"Yes. It's irrevocable."

"Then you must make sure that I'm with him at the end. His death may not be easy and he asked me, even before we left the hospital, to help him at that moment. I promised that I would be there and would do whatever he needed. If you have problems with that, then you shouldn't be there with us."

"I have no problem with that."

Ana looked at Dominic with no fear, only an honest acceptance of what was to come. Then she left Dominic to think his own thoughts as she returned to be with her husband.

When Miko sat down beside Toshi, he noticed how pale his father was and that he was having trouble breathing. He voiced his concern, "I don't want to tire you, but I just wanted to talk a little while. I'm going back to the city tonight."

"Do you have to go back right away, Miko? I think your mother may need you now."

Miko noticed the softness in Toshi's eyes. He was touched by the love which Toshi expressed to him without speaking of it. Miko looked away so Toshi couldn't see his own tears as he answered, "I'm not sure; maybe I'll stay. I just wish…we could have known each other better. I don't even know the words to say…just that…I feel so close to you."

Toshi smiled at his son, "I've come to love and respect you very much, Miko. You're a fine young man with great goodness of heart, and I feel so fortunate to have known you." Toshi's voice became gentle as he continued, "I'm also glad that we can be honest with each other about our relationship. I would never want to diminish the love you have for your father, Mishima. He deserves that love. And he deserves my respect."

The moment was filled with a heavy sorrow that neither could resist sharing with the other. Miko reached over and took his father's hand, holding it tightly in his own. He didn't know what else to do to show his love and concern.

Toshi touched Miko's soft, black hair as he whispered, "There's something I want to give you, Miko. Something that belongs to you. Would you please bring me the black velvet case from the mantel in the living room?"

Miko looked at him in surprise and, without hesitation, walked into the living room and came back with the case in his hand. Toshi smiled and spoke with a more noticeable shortness of breath, "This was a gift to me from your mother…as I prepared to enter diplomatic service nearly twenty years ago. When she gave it to me, I protested…for I knew it should belong to her son. But, of course, she would not listen. The gift…came to her from your great-grandfather Santino and its history goes back to your Italian ancestors.

I've worn it at every formal occasion that I have ever attended…as a diplomat for my country. And each time I touched it, I thought of her and of her Italian heritage. Now, I can give it to you officially…and thank you for letting me borrow it for a while. This bit of gold has given me strength…and comfort through all these years."

Ana had returned to the condo and started to enter Toshi's room when she saw what was happening between him and Miko. She stopped and quickly turned back to the beach and out of sight. She did not, in any way, want to interrupt this private moment between her husband and their son. They both needed this time to say goodbye, for there might not be another opportunity for them to do so.

When Dominic came along the beach close to the condo, he found Ana leaning against a large piece of driftwood, obviously waiting for him. He was surprised and asked, "What are you doing here? I thought you went back to the house."

"I started to, but I almost interrupted a private moment between Toshi and Miko. I didn't want to break into that."

To Ana's surprise, Dominic took her arm and pulled her against him.

"You'll have to help me with this, Ana. I've been in this business for many years and have always been able to keep my distance, but everything about this case is uniquely different from anything I've ever known. I find myself rendered nearly helpless.

I've come to love and respect my patient to the point of wanting to reject his wished and do everything in my power to keep him alive. And I've come to love and respect my patient's wife and her son to the point of wanting to be a part of their lives for the rest of my own. How do I solve these dilemmas?"

Dominic release her and turned back to face the sea, shocked at his own outburst. Ana hesitated only a moment before answering, "The answer is so simple. Do as your patient tells you and let him go. And keep your friendship with your patient's wife and son and accept whatever follows."

He turned to her with a somewhat cynical burst of laughter, "My god, you're something else, Gabrelli. You've solved all my problems in two seconds and two sentences. If you were on my medical consultant staff, we'd make a fortune!"

"You asked for it, you got it. Now let's go face what we have to face. We'll do this together!"

There was nothing left to do but that. The two friends walked back toward the house to do what had to be done.

A few hours later, Ishikawa prepared a simple meal for the group and served it on trays in the living room where Toshi could be comfortable in a large, soft chair. Dominic lit the fireplace and everyone relaxed in the warmth and pleasant atmosphere surrounding them.

Their dinner was fresh, broiled shrimp on a bed of rice and vegetables with a dessert of warm custard. Though Toshi did not join them in the meal, he was strong enough to share a few comical experiences from his career as a diplomat. They talked of other times in their lives, trips they had taken, good food they had eaten in faraway places, the birthday party for Suzi, and the wedding in the garden.

The evening became a time of sharing and was much like a family reunion. They were all involved in many of the events they discussed. Though this group had gathered for a sorrowful purpose, they were cheered by the companionship of those they loved and respected.

After a while, Dominic noticed that Toshi was showing signs of fatigue. He broke up the gathering by asking Miko about his plans.

"What have you decided, Miko? Are you going back tonight?"

"No, I've decided to stay for the weekend. Should I get reservations?"

"No, you won't need to do that. You and I can bunk on these soft couches here. Of course, I get the biggest one since you're young and agile and can still fold up your legs."

"Then that's what I'll do. I've got my airport bag in the car. I'll get your stuff out, too, Dominic."

Miko left to go to the parking lot near the main building for the bags. Dominic and Ishikawa went with Toshi to his room. Before Toshi left the living room, Ana gave him a kiss and told him to rest well. When she put her arms around him, she could almost feel his slender frame melting beneath her touch. She turned quickly to the tasks that would occupy her mind until Dominic would let her know what to do.

404

Two hours later, the doctor came back to the patio where Ana and Miko were talking and drinking coffee in the moonlight. He walked over and sat down with them. He spoke slowly and with deep emotion.

"You need to know that Toshi will not allow me to administer any further medications for pain, nor the oxygen. He's determined to let his body choose its own path. If there are any final words you wish to share with him, you must do so now. He's suffering a great deal of pain. So, you may do whatever you feel is best...The ending is near."

Mother and son looked at Dominic in stunned silence. Miko gasped, "Oh my god!"

He began to sob like a child. Ana put her arms around her son and whispered in comfort, "It's alright, Miko. He wants to go. It will be a blessing and a release from all the suffering he's endured for so long."

Ana did not cry. She merely stared at Dominic, waiting for his direction. Ishikawa came out to the patio and held out his hand to Ana.

"You must go to him, now. You must not leave him alone."

Ana gave Miko a quick kiss, then walked past Ishikawa and Dominic into Toshi's room. She was calm and felt very strong. Toshi was conscious, but was having trouble breathing. He did not open his eyes when she took his hand. She held it against her cheek, whispering to him,

"I'm here with you, my sweet, sweetheart. I won't leave you. If there is anything you want from me, tell me. Do you want me to lie down with you, to be close to you?"

Toshi answered her in short gasps, "Yes...stay with me...don't leave me."

Ana very carefully lie down beside her husband, putting her arms around him so he could feel her presence and gain strength from it. She touched his silky hair and kissed his cheek as she whispered, "I love you, Tosh. We've had some wonderful times, you and I. Think of all the good times, the beautiful moments we've shared. We've been blessed far more than most. Remember the rose. Our love is forever. It will never end. I promise...that I will never let it end."

Sometime later, the others came in. Ana continued whispering to Toshi, reminding him of their days in Tokyo and their sweet love affair. Now and then, he smiled at things she told him. Dominic said nothing about her presence beside Toshi. He knew that his friend and patient was dying and needed to be with the one he loved.

Miko came over to Toshi and leaned down to whisper to him, "It's Miko. I just want to tell you...that I love you and I'm so glad that we've had some time together."

He put his strong, young hand in Toshi's. Toshi barely gripped Miko's fingers as he whispered to his son, "Thank you, Miko...please remember that...I love you, always."

Toshi released his grip and sighed as his breathing became more difficult. Then Ishikawa stepped close to the bed and put his huge, warm hands on Toshi's head. Toshi smiled at the touch, as if those strong hands were offering him a final rest. He relaxed, though his breathing was spasmodic.

It was then that Dominic looked at Ana and whispered, "He's struggled enough. I'm going to do as he requested, Ana."

She did not question, nor resist. It was Toshi's wish. The time had come to let him go.

Ana put her mouth against her husband's cheek and whispered, "Can you hear me, Tosh?"

He moved his hand in hers as if in reply. She asked a final question.

"Are you leaving me now?"

Ana listened carefully for an answer. The words that were necessary for both of them were spoken in a halting whisper, but clear enough that all could hear.

"I love you, Gabrelli...but it's over. Everything...is over now."

Ana kissed her husband's hand and whispered her love to him, then laid her head on his shoulder and looked at Dominic.

"Do what you must, but I won't leave him until he leaves me."

The doctor moved swiftly with the injection. Ishikawa came close to Toshi and placed his hands on his friend's head one last time, speaking words in a Japanese dialect that Ana did not understand. Toshi smiled and whispered his final words.

"Thank you...for your love and for the gift of peace."

At those words, Dominic placed the needle in Toshi's vein and within seconds, his agony was over. After a lifetime of suffering, Toshiburo Matsushita Yamamoto was finally at rest.

All three friends were quiet for a few moments. Dominic closed Toshi's eyes. Ishikawa helped Ana slip off the bed. They stood together looking at the man who each of them had come to respect and honor. Miko put his arms around his mother. Ana did not cry. No one spoke. Then Dominic took Miko's arm and led him into the living room so that Toshi's beloved wife and dearest friend could share a final moment with the one they had both loved equally, yet in their separate ways.

Ana and Ishikawa, arm-in-arm, offered their silence as a tribute to this 'gentle samurai.' Nearly an hour later, Dominic knocked on the door. The time had come to begin the difficult task of filling the emptiness where once an honorable man had stood.

CHAPTER 36

"Remember…and pay tribute to this precious memory. Then wipe your tears, walk silently away and let your heart be free to love again. For love is all…love is all there is to life."
      --Toshiburo to Ana

Over the next few days many arrangements had to be made related to Toshi's death. Ana called Toshi's father in Kyoto to let him know what had happened. Mr. Yamamoto was deeply saddened to hear of the news, but assured Ana that he had been expecting it and was prepared.

"My son led an honorable and fulfilling life. He has lived far beyond our expectations, and, for that, we are most grateful. Though our hearts are sorrowful to lose him, we are thankful that he was with those he loved. I will take care of the final arrangements here, Ana. I hope that you will plan to attend the formal service in Tokyo."

"Of course, we'll be there. You know, I'm sure, that it was Toshi's wish that his ashes be scattered on the face of Lake Kawaguchi. He wants to rest in the shadow of Fujiyama. I hope you have no objections to this."

"He had spoken of that wish to me even when he was a boy. He didn't believe he would live to manhood. But the gods have been good to him and to us. We will honor his wishes and I pray that we can fulfill them together."

Ana was relieved to hear the note of reconciliation from Toshi's father. After a short silence, Tatsume spoke to her in a voice filled with emotion.

"I loved my son with all my heart. Toshiburo has honored his family, his ancestors, and his country. He has been a loving and dutiful son, and our loss is a great sorrow to his mother and me. My dearest wish now is that there be peace between us. You are his wife, the woman he has always loved. I hope that you will grant me the privilege of greeting you as a member of the Yamamoto family and also…of meeting my grandson."

Ana was shocked at the mention of his 'grandson.' She had no idea that Toshi had told his father about Mikoto. She reacted to Tatsume's statement without thinking.

"What do you mean, Yamamoto-san?"

"No one has told me, not even my own son. But, a few days after your wedding, Toshiburo sent me a photograph of the wedding party. I saw immediately that your son is the image of his father in his youth. Don't you think I would know my own flesh and blood?"

Ana dared not respond to his question. She knew that it would be better to wait until they were together to discuss such sensitive matters.

"We'll all be together in Tokyo. I look forward to seeing you again, Yamamoto-san."

"Thank you for those words, Ana. Now I feel assured that we can make our peace."

"Yes, there can be peace between us now, for we both share the same heartache."

When Ana hung up the phone, she was shaking. The memory of her meeting with Tatsume Yamamoto in Seijo and their emotional confrontation was as vivid as if it were yesterday, for that was the moment when she understood so clearly that Toshi could choose no other pathway than the one planned for him since birth. She felt those same emotions flowing over her now—the anger, the frustration, and the disappointment of losing the one she loved. Only this time it would be an ending.

The next day Ana and Ishikawa walked together by the sea, both searching for the strength to face what lay ahead. Dominic had gone back to the city to make arrangements for Toshiburo's final return to his homeland. And Miko had chosen to go back with the doctor. He knew that his mother needed to share these last few moments with Ishikawa so they could comfort one another and prepare for their own parting.

As the two friends looked out at the beauty surrounding them, Ishikawa turned to Ana.

"Shall we sit down here a moment, Ana? There is something I must give you."

Ishikawa guided Ana to a large flat rock among the pieces of driftwood on the beach. They sat quietly for a while before he continued, "Yamamoto left a final message for you. He asked me to give it to you at some quiet moment when we would be alone. Before we leave this peaceful place, you should have it."

Ishikawa reached inside the wide sash of his kimono and drew out a long envelope of heavy, gray parchment. He placed it in Ana's hand. She held it for a while, caressing the rough texture, somewhat fearful of what might be inside.

Ishikawa touched her hand, "Would you like to be alone?"

The gentle friend was somewhat concerned about leaving her on the beach alone, but he was also aware of the intimacy of this moment between her and the one she had loved.

She smiled, touched by Ishikawa's sensitivity, "Yes, thank you, Ishikawa."

Their eyes met and she saw him glance at the waves rolling in from the sea. Ana understood his concern.

"I'll be alright. I've already had my bout with the sea, and I don't intend to take it on again!"

He smiled, "Then I will leave you. When you're ready, come back to join me for our final meal here…in this sacred place."

He left her then, assured of her strength and safety.

Ana sat quietly, her fingers tracing the letters of her name written in heavy gold ink on the outside of the envelope and her heart pounding in fear of that which rested within. Finally, she opened the envelope and drew out its contents. Inside was a piece of folded parchment with a sheet of gold tissue inside. Ana carefully unfolded the delicate tissue and there, before her eyes, she saw the dried remnants of a white, long-stemmed rose.

She gasped, "Oh Toshi, you've kept the rose all these years! How do I face the ending now?"

Ana took a deep breath and forced herself to read the final message from Yamamoto. She whispered the words to the pounding surf,

"My Angel Gabrelli"
REMEMBER..
one summer's night on Nippon Isle
wild drums of bon-odori
beat to the rhythm of my heart
as your eyes met mine.

We faced our destiny
written long before
as if on ancient scroll.
We became
one heart, one soul.

REMEMBER...
sweet love once lost
by miracle regained.
Our promises exchanged
in a garden shrine.
One moment is enough for us.
So kiss the pure white rose
and lay it down
to rest with me
on quiet Kawaguchi Lake.

REMEMBER...
and pay tribute
to this precious memory.
Then wipe your tears,
walk silently away
and let your heart be free
to love again.
For love is all,
love is all there is
to life.

Your 'Sweet Samurai,' always and forever,
On the eve of my last breath."

Ana folded the parchment carefully, placed it inside the
envelope and put it in her jacket pocket. Then she fell to her
knees in the sand and, for the first time since Toshi's death,
allowed herself the freedom to express the pain in her heart
through the cleansing power of tears.

Much later that evening, Ishikawa walked slowly down the
rocky path to the beach anticipating Ana's return. She sensed his
presence and came toward him. When they met, they put their

411

arms around each other in a gesture of mutual understanding and walked back to the deck to share their final meal in this place which would always be associated with their deepest sorrow.

The two friends sat up very late watching the moonlight shimmering on the waves as they rolled in and out across the sandy beach. Their thoughts were communicated only by a reverent silence between them. To Ana, the silence was a tribute to Yamamoto. What words could be spoken of such a man by the two persons who loved him best?

Ishikawa finally stood, "We should rest now, Ana, for that which is ahead."

Ana smiled at her friend, "I know. We'll need some extra-special strength for this trip."

Ishikawa replied with confidence, "We will have whatever is needed."

They went to their separate rooms to rest for the night and the next morning left the beautiful seaside resort for Ana's home. There they prepared for the final celebration of one precious life.

The Japanese Embassy in Washington called Ana within a few days of Toshi's death to let her know the final schedule for the memorial tribute planned in Tokyo and, also, the travel plans for her and her family. After visiting with the Japanese Ambassador, she called Dominic.

"I'm getting worried about making it through this whole program in one piece. Ishikawa is so certain that we'll be fine, but I think I need some strong support, just in case. Is there any possibility that you could come with us?"

Because Dominic was aware of the unusual burden Ana was carrying, he replied without hesitation, "That's no problem at all. I just need to make the flight arrangements right away. I feel so much a part of your family and a friend to Toshi, that it would be an honor to share this moment with you."

"I would appreciate that very much, Dom, and I know Miko and Ishikawa would also. You're a special friend to all of us. You've given us so much time and energy."

"Then give me the information I need to arrange my flights and I'll get right on it."

"No, no, you don't even need to do that! The Embassy has arranged everything and will have extra seats for any family or friends we might want to bring with us. I'll just call them, if you're certain, and let them know."

"I'm certain, Ana."

Ana called the Embassy as soon as she hung up the telephone with Dominic. Everything was take care of and within a few days, they were on their way to Tokyo.

During the flight, the Embassy personnel reviewed the memorial program with the foursome. Ana and Miko noticed immediately that they had been listed as Toshi's wife, Ana Maria Yamamoto, and son, Mikoto Toshiburo Yamamoto. Neither said anything at the time, but later discussed with Ishikawa and Dominic what they should do. They all agreed that it would be better left as written. Too many complications would be involved to make the corrections at this late date.

Ana explained to Dominic, "Toshi and I decided together that taking his name was not an important matter and, in fact, would only add more complications to our future. Miko was hesitant the one time we discussed the name change. After all, Mishima was the only father he knew until a few months ago. My only concern is if there would be any repercussions with the Matsamura family. We can just hope that if they should hear about it, they would accept our simple explanation."

Ana chose to put this problem of 'protocol' out of her mind as something to be dealt with later and, hopefully, not at all.

The entourage from the States was met at the airport by the Prime Minister's representatives and transported by limousine to the Imperial Hotel. There, they were treated as very important guests of the Japanese government and enjoyed luxurious accommodations. After a final meeting to make certain everyone knew what would occur the next day, the Japanese delegation left the family to their rest. Ana was certain that she would sleep through the night after such a long and tiring trip, but she was wrong. Her eyes simply would not shut.

The memorial service was to be held at 10 o'clock in the main chamber of the Japanese Diet the day after their arrival. On the morning of the service, an official car with Department of State personnel escorted the family from the hotel to a reception room adjacent to the Diet chamber. Here, Ana came face-to-face with Toshiburo's parents. Tatsume Yamamoto bowed respectfully to Ana the moment she entered the room. He spoke to her with unusual warmth and with deep emotion, "I am so sorry that this reunion is marred with sorrow. I would have chosen to welcome you to our family in a much different setting. And to finally meet my grandson."

His eyes filled with tears. Ana felt his heartache and responded by embracing him. Tatsume did not pull away but accepted her kindness with humility. They held each other for a moment while Tatsume gained control of his emotions. Then Ana took his arm and, at the same time, reached for the hand of Toshi's mother to introduce them to their grandson. Mikoto stood quietly by as Ana spoke to Toshi's parents, "This is your grandson, Mikoto Toshiburo."

Tatsume bowed to Miko and immediately embraced him. Though Ana had felt no warmth from Toshi's mother when they had been introduced, she watched in surprise as Kumiko Yamamoto bowed deeply to Miko and grasped his hand tightly in both of her own. When Ana glanced away, she saw Ishikawa watching from close by. Their eyes met for an instant and they gave each other knowing smiles. Ana felt a terrible pain shoot through her heart and suddenly realized she was losing her strong support, as well as her sweet love.

Ana could not imagine life without the presence of Yamamoto, neither could she imagine it without Ishikawa who always knew her mind and heart and acknowledged it with a glance of a smile or a touch of his hand. She wondered where she would find her strength now. At that moment, they were called to attend to the purpose at hand.

The memorial celebration began exactly on time. All guests were present and soft *koto* music was playing when the family and close friends were escorted from a side door into the chamber. As they entered, Ana was relieved to see Miyuki and Sato and Ito Nishyama among the friends who would be seated near the family. After a few moments of silence, the memorial service began.

The Prime Minister of Japan gave the opening statements with an impressive eulogy for Toshiburo Matsushita Yamamoto as a 'distinguished Ambassador, as well as a sensitive and intelligent gentleman.' There were many tears shed in honor of

Toshiburo from all those who would feel his loss. The Prime Minister, himself, was one.

For nearly an hour, distinguished guests from many nations were introduced to read their memorials and offer gifts to the government of Japan in honor of Ambassador Yamamoto. It seemed that he had made an indelible mark on the lives of many government representatives, even beyond his contributions to the political arena in which they had worked together.

Then the Prime Minister stood once more. He became quite emotional as he spoke,

"The loss that we all feel together is deep, yet it cannot be measured against the loss that will be felt by those who loved this distinguished gentleman first and foremost, his family."

He invited Toshi's mother and father and Ana and Miko to come to the platform. There he introduced them to the guests and asked Tatsume to share some thoughts of his son. Tatsume stepped to the microphone and read Toshi's last words in his official capacity as Ambassador. They were in the form of a letter to the people of Japan and the international community which he had served.

Toshi's words were clearly representative of who he was as a person. They revealed a gentle heart and an honest love for his country and its citizens, as well as a desire to promote peace among all nations. Though Tatsume was deeply touched by his son's words, he did not weep, but read with strength and a sense of pride mixed with humility for the life of this honored and honorable man who was his son.

After the reading, the Prime Minister stepped forward and made an announcement that surprised the family and, especially, Ana.

"In honor of the unusual service offered to his country by Ambassador Toshiburo Matsushita Yamamoto, I wish to make the following presentations to his family as a representative of the Japanese government and the people of this nation."

Three young men came forward dressed in the traditional costume of the samurai. They were carrying several objects that were explained by the Prime Minister.

"To his parents, Kumiko and Tatsume Yamamoto, I present the ambassadorial seal from the Japanese Embassy offices of Toshiburo Yamamoto in Washington, D.C.

To his wife, Ana Maria Yamamoto, I present the ceremonial costume of Toshiburo Yamamoto, worn at special gatherings during his term as Ambassador to the United States.

To his son, and only child, Mikoto Toshiburo Yamamoto, I present the ceremonial sword of the ancient samurai as a gift from the Imperial House of which Ambassador Yamamoto was a member by reason of his ancestry."

Each of the recipients was escorted to the platform to receive the presentations and offer their thanks. The Prime Minister stood in the center of the group, Tatsume and Kumiko on one side, Ana and Miko on the other. For a few short moments, the koto music resumed as the young men laid the gifts on a table for display and left the platform.

Then the Prime Minister took Ana's arm and they stepped forward together. At the prior request of the Prime Minister, Ana gave the final tribute to Toshiburo. Her statement was simple and spoken very slowly and distinctly in English.

"In the international tradition of honor for those whom we love and respect, will you stand with me for one final moment of tribute to the memory of the Honorable Ambassador Toshiburo Matsushita Yamamoto. I offer these final words to him from all of us:

"To you, my husband,
To you, our friend,

We wish you well on the journey
you have been called to take.
May you find communion on this pathway
with those who have gone before and
with whom you now will travel.

May you find communion there with those
who have given their lives, as you have done,
*   for others.*

We will keep you always in our memory
for you have loved your country and your family
and have served both with honor.
And you have been well-loved.

Sayonara, sweet samurai.
Go gently now, to your eternal home."

As the koto played in benediction to Ana's words, she began to fall silently to the floor. The Prime Minister had anticipated her weakness and held her upright against his chest while Ishikawa quickly moved to help her from the chamber. Dominic followed them to the reception room where they placed Ana on the couch and the doctor administered smelling salts. Within seconds, she blinked and came back to consciousness.

"I'm sorry. It was just…too much."

Dominic sat down beside Ana to keep her upright so her breathing would get back to normal. She began to complain, "I just want to sleep. I'm so tired. I want to forget where I am and what we're doing here. Just for a while, please let me lie down and go to sleep."

Dominic said nothing, but kept his arms around her, forcing her to sit up and breathe deeply. By then, the others had come back to the room. Miyuki came over to Ana and gave her a hug, trying to lift her spirits.

"Everything was perfect, Ana. This was a beautiful tribute to Yamamoto. Now, let's get you out of here and go back to the hotel to rest!"

"I'm ready for rest, but I'm not sure I can make it to the hotel. I just want to sleep here on this couch if Dominic would get out of my way and let me lie down."

He smiled and gave her no choice, "Sorry, doctor's orders. Keep your head up and your breathing deep."

There was a knock on the door and, to everyone's shock and surprise, the Japanese Prime Minister entered. He bowed graciously to Ana and came over to take her hand.

"I am so sorry for your loss, Mrs. Yamamoto. I know you are overwhelmed by everything here, the formalities, the pressures to do your duty by your husband, and for his memory. I want to

417

encourage you now to return to your hotel and rest from this emotional strain.

Your statement was a fitting close to our tribute for an honorable and courageous man, a stalwart 'samurai.' Will you take my counsel and recover your strength? You must go on with your life. That is the challenge that remains for you, now."

Ana was rendered speechless by the Prime Minister's thoughtfulness. She sensed a genuine concern in his words and his manner.

She responded with gratitude, "Thank you for your kindness, sir. Tomorrow we'll take Yamamoto's ashes to Lake Kawaguchi. It has always been his dearest wish to rest in the shadow of Fujiyama. After that journey, we'll be able to rest. And thank you so much for the beautiful gifts you gave us to remember a beloved man."

The Prime Minister spoke his final words, "I consider it an honor and a pleasure to have met you and your family. I wish you the best for your future. Your husband is, indeed, beloved by many, many people throughout the world. Sayonara, Ana Maria Yamamoto."

He bowed graciously and left the room.

Ana leaned back against Dominic and whispered, "Let's go back to the hotel…now."

Later that night, after Ana had slept for several hours, she was wide awake and needed to talk. Miyuki ordered dinner brought to Ana's room, so the group gathered there for the evening. When the food came, they sat on chairs and the floor, eating and drinking and offering toasts to Toshi. Everyone shared good memories of their son and husband and father and friend.

Tatsume and Kumiko even enjoyed telling their stories about Toshi's childhood and they all seemed free to speak whatever was in their hearts. In the midst of tears and laughter, Kumiko shocked the group to silence with her surprising admission.

"I couldn't love him the way I wanted to because I was afraid. When he was just a baby, they said he would not live to manhood. I knew that he would die before me, that I would have to be here like this one day, mourning my own son. It made me angry that he would go away and never come back. I could not love him like a mother should!"

The bereaved mother began to weep. Ana jumped up and put her arms around the woman who had let her heart turn to stone because of the terrible fear that she would lose her own sweet child. Ana remembered her own fears when Toshi came back into her life. To Ana's surprise, Kumiko responded to Ana's gesture of concern.

"I do not deserve your kindness. Will you ever forgive me for my cold heart, for treating you like an intruder in our lives, for hating you because he loved you?"

"I can forgive you everything, but, most of all, I hope you will forgive yourself and accept the special gift I have brought you."

Kumiko looked at Ana with a question in her eyes. Ana whispered with a smile, "Toshiburo's son, and you are free to love him without fear!"

Kumiko smiled at Ana and kissed her cheek. Everyone had shared a most tender moment of reconciliation. Then Dominic broke the silence.

"Let's drink a final toast to Toshiburo Yamamoto, to our love and admiration for a good man and a respected ambassador for his country!"

They made their toast the finale of a most difficult day and adjourned to go to their rest in preparation for what tomorrow would bring.

Dominic stopped Ana before he left the room.

"Are you certain that I should come with you tomorrow? Please be honest with me, Ana. This will be a very special moment for you and Ishikawa and Toshi's parents. I don't want to intrude on your privacy."

"Alright, Dom, I'll think about it. I'm so thankful for your presence. You've given me the strength to make it through today. You are, indeed, a special gift to all of us."

Ana kissed the good doctor on the cheek as he left, then she climbed in bed, gratefully pulling the soft blankets around her exhausted body. But before sleep came, she whispered into the empty space around her, "Why couldn't I have been strong like your mother? Why didn't I pull away when you took my hand? Now look what you've done. You've left me with nothing but empty space in my heart and I'm very much afraid that it will never be filled again!"

Ana shivered under the warm covers, but finally relaxed and let Dominic's medication do its work. She slept soundly, at last.

CHAPTER 37

"A pure, white rose, a final wish fulfilled...'Let me glide
across the waters of Kawaguchi to rest in the shadow of
my beloved mountain. There, at last, I will be at peace.'"
--Toshiburo's last request

Dominic and Ishikawa were up early the next morning. Both
were concerned about Ana and also Toshi's parents. Dominic
could hardly bear to think of what was ahead for them today. He
could not imagine watching the ashes of someone he loved,
Toshi's last visible remains, scattered through the air,
disappearing like dust in the wind. It would be almost as if Toshi
had never lived at all. When he thought of the impact of that
scene, he became almost physically ill. How could Ana face this
day? He had no choice. He would have to be there with her.

Ishikawa made tea and coffee for anyone who wanted to stop
by the room. He was restless, pacing the floor. Dominic had
never seen Ishikawa display such emotion and finally asked,
"What is it, Ishikawa? What are you so concerned about?"

"You know that I will not be returning with you and Ana and
Miko, don't you?"

"Yes, Ana told me. I understand your ties to Toshi."

"Then, you must go with us today to the lake, for I will not
come back here. You must be with Ana to give her strength as
she returns to her home...for Toshi and me."

His words were so matter-of-fact that Dominic started to
answer as if he had a choice. But he knew it would be up to Ana.

"I've offered to come to the lake this morning, but Ana may
not want me to do so. She's going to let me know this morning
what she thinks about it. I realize it's a very private time for all
of you who were closest to Toshi. I wouldn't want to intrude on
that."

"I will tell her that you must be there. After our time at the
lake today, I will be going back with the family to the Yamamoto
estate. From there, I have my own plans. Ana should not be
alone after Kawaguchi, after we leave Toshi there."

"Won't Miko and Yuki be with her?"

"No, they won't be there. They have chosen not to go to the lake."

"I don't understand. Why the change of plans?"

"Miko does not want to go and his mother has left that choice up to him, as she should. He has lost one father. He does not feel strong enough to face that experience again. It was only two years ago when he and Ana brought Mishima back here to his parents. Miko recalls that as a dreadful moment. He's decided to go to Yokohama to be with the Matsamura family for a while until Ana is ready to return to the States."

"I'm surprised that neither Miko nor Yuki will be there with Ana today. How is she handling that?"

"That's exactly why I encourage you to go with us."

"Then I won't give her a choice in the matter. She may be upset, but I'll tell her that I need to be there, if only for my own peace of mind."

"I am much relieved. Thank you, Dr. Donatelli."

After an early breakfast together, the moment of farewell arrived. The group of mourners walked out into the garden as Sato, Miyuki, and Miko prepared to leave for Yokohama. This was difficult for Miko. He had become very fond of Ishikawa, as if this quiet, gentle man were to be a permanent presence in his life. Ishikawa felt Miko's concern and took his arm, leading him to a quiet place in the garden.

"You are young, Mikoto, and have many choices to make. Do not let anything other than your own heart dictate those choices. That is the extent of knowledge that I have learned in all the years of my life. That is all the wisdom I have to share with you…you, the precious son of my dearest friend."

Though Ishikawa's facial expression did not change from its stoic solemnity, his eyes were soft and warm as they looked at Miko. The younger man asked the question that most concerned him, "Will we ever meet again?"

"I will go with your father in my own way. He and I have lived a good life together, and we will be together again. I am only sorry that you could not have known him better. But the father that you did know, Mishima Matsamura, was a good man. His love was very deep and strong to take you as his own. He deserves your respect and loyalty always."

Miko's eyes filled with tears. It was a hard moment and one which made him feel that he had suddenly grown from youth to manhood. He spoke his last words to Ishikawa.

"Thank you, Ishikawa, for your kind words. I hope that somehow I'll be able to develop the qualities that you possess— wisdom, loyalty, and strength. I'll do my best, I promise you that."

The young man put his arms around the solemn samurai. They gave each other comfort in their different ways, then parted. Miko felt stronger knowing that Ishikawa's wisdom would guide him as he face the difficult decisions waiting in the future.

Ana walked with Miko to Sato's car. She said her goodbyes to Sato and Miyuki, then turned to her son.

"You've made a wise decision, Miko. This is a moment that need only be shared by those who knew Toshi best. I'll see you later in Tokyo at Yuki's place. Go on and don't look back with any sense of guilt, okay?"

Mother and son shared a warm embrace, then Ana sent Miko on his way with a reassuring smile. The three friends left for Yokohama and did not look back.

An hour later, the small group of mourners boarded the hotel yacht that would take them to the middle of Lake Kawaguchi. Because it was very early in the morning, the area was quiet and totally private. No other guests were stirring at this hour. The pilot of the yacht drove them slowly toward their destination. Ana did not comment on Dominic's presence, but felt thankful for his support.

Ishikawa stood very still near the back of the yacht, holding a beautiful, gold teak urn very gently in his arms, as if here actually touching his friend. Ana stood beside him with a slender, white rose in one hand and her arm around Mrs. Yamamoto. Ana could feel the deep sorrow this mother now suffered for the loss of her son. At least Ana had been fortunate to have shared her love with Toshi before his death and to have received his love in return.

The quiet atmosphere on the lake was a blessing to each one of the solemn group. When the yacht came to the center and stopped its engines, there was no other sound. They all stood in silent respect for the son, husband, and friend whom they were leaving there. The young pilot took his cue from Ishikawa to let the yacht move slowly across the surface of the lake as he released the ashes into the water.

Ana was thankful for the calm spirit that settled over her. She did not feel the wrenching pain in her heart that she had expected. And when she gently tossed the pure, white rose onto his ashes, she felt only gratitude for the joy shared with this 'sweet samurai.'

They all stood together, watching the beautiful rose drift slowly out of sight. It was as if Toshi's spirit were being freed from the years of suffering and, at last, would find peace in the shadow of his beloved mountain, Fujiyama. Ana smiled to herself, wondering if she would see his reflection on these waters should she ever return to this place again.

No one spoke on the return to the dock, all keeping their thoughts to themselves. After they left the yacht, Ana and Dominic shook hands with Mr. and Mrs. Yamamoto. Ana embraced both of them and offered a deep-felt thanks to the parents for the gift of their son. Before Mrs. Yamamoto turned to leave, she whispered to Ana, "And thank you for the gift of Mikoto. His father's sweetness lives in him and gives us a link to the future that we would not have had without your loving heart."

The women embraced each other again, but Kumiko quickly pulled away and hurried to the waiting car. Then Ana turned to Ishikawa. They walked together to the other side of the dock where they could be alone. He was the first to speak.

"You will be alright, Ana. You have much life yet to live and much love to share. You must not be afraid of loving again. Only in that way do you honor the memory of the one we both loved so much."

"I don't understand your choice, Ishikawa, but I know you're determined to follow it. I wish you were coming with Miko and me to watch over us and make sure we make wise choices in our future. You always seem to know what should be done."

"I have already told you what to do with your future. Will you follow my counsel, Ana?"

She smiled and they held each other close one last time. As he turned away from her, he offered a final word, "If you take Toshi's love and my wisdom with you, there will be nothing but joy in your future."

Ishikawa gave her a most uncharacteristic smile and a wink. It was as if, for just that moment, Toshi's spirit had spoken through his friend. She laughed at Ishikawa and waved farewell. For just an instant, his eyes locked with hers as they exchanged a message of eternal love. He did not wave back, but turned and walked away. This part of her life was over. Ana hoped that she was prepared to move away from the past and find new direction for her future.

Later that night, Dominic and Ana enjoyed a lovely dinner at Sato and Miyuki's home in Seijo. Ana was aware that her friends were concerned about her emotional state, so she put them at ease by relating the experience of peace that had come to her on the lake that morning. She also told them of the kind words from Kumiko and of Ishikawa's final counsel.

They began to relax then and enjoy being together, sharing good food, wine, and friendship. After a while, Miyuki got wound up and started telling tales of the wild things she and Ana had done during their younger days in college and in Tokyo. Ana was glad that Miyuki felt free to describe their crazy night at the Otani Hotel waiting for Toshi to return from the mountains. Their laughter was healing to the spirits of everyone.

Near the end of the evening, Ana looked at Miyuki and made a statement that was met with stunned silence.

"If you have no objections, Yuki, I'd like to stay in the little house tonight."

Miyuki and Sato both stared at Ana in shock. When Miyuki was finally able to reply, her words were spoken in a mere whisper, "You mean you want to stay there…alone?"

"Yes, I'd really like to do that."

Miyuki tried to remain calm as she phrased her questions to Ana, "Do you really think that's wise, Ana? So soon after…everything?"

"There are some personal reasons why it's important to me, Yuki. You should know them as well as I."

Miyuki suddenly lost control, raising her voice more in fear than anger at her friend.

"Oh, yes, I know those reasons only too well! Wasn't I the one who had to pick up the pieces every time he broke you apart? Why would you want to torture yourself further? Haven't you suffered enough? My god, Ana, why would you even want to see the place again, let alone spend the night there?

Don't you know that those memories are still lurking in every corner of that little place? They're all out there. The soft breezes through the evergreens, the garden scents, the sound of water over rocks, even the echo of his sweet love songs. They're out there waiting to break your heart all over again!"

Miyuki began to cry softly as she finished her tirade. Ana seemed to be in a trance, as if no one were in the room except she and her dear friend. Dominic wanted to leave the room and let the two friends work out their obvious deep-seated feelings. He did not want to intrude on such a private matter. But Sato spoke before Dominic could move. Sato's words were offered to Ana in an unusually calm and gentle way.

"Ana, you've been through such a dreadful experience. Tell us why it's so important now, after everything is over, to walk through those memories again?"

The shock of Miyuki's attack had touched Ana deeply. She understood her friend's concern, but could not back away from what she felt was necessary to put away the past and move into the future. Ana was surprised at Sato's wise question and answered in as calm a voice as it had been asked.

"You're right, of course, Yuki. Yamamoto has been like a ghost that has haunted my life for so long. But I'm not suggesting that I want to conjure up that ghost again. That's not why I want to go out there. On the lake today, I had to face reality. I watched his ashes disappear across the water, but everything was calm and quiet. His soul is at rest and my heart is at peace.

All I need to do now is fold up the memories and put them away. They're like old photo albums or love letters that should be put on a shelf and never opened again. I need to do that so I can get on with my life. You can trust me, Yuki. I promise that you can trust me to be alone there and to finish it!"

Miyuki was still upset, and at Ana's final words she reacted quickly, "What do you mean 'finish it'? Those words frighten me, don't you know that, Ana?"

Miyuki stared fearfully at Ana. Ana realized what Miyuki was thinking and responded with assurance, "Oh Yuki, you know better than anyone else how much I love life. I'm a tough Italian from the South Boston streets, remember? Surely you know I would never hurt you or my own son in such a way!"

Miyuki started to cry and whispered her apologies to Ana. The women put their arms around each other and walked out onto the porch together. Ana continued to reassure her friend that she only wanted to get on with her life, surely not to end it!

Dominic and Sat looked at each other, not knowing how to respond to what was happening between the two women. Sato finally explained to the doctor, "Yuki has been afraid that Ana would come here with a plan to do something other than mend her broken heart. She really thought Ana would go out to the little house and just…well, end everything there. The moment Yuki heard the news of Toshi's death, she cried all night for fear of what Ana would do."

"I'm pretty certain you can be relieved of that fear. I believe what Ana says. She's too tough and she loves life too much."

Sato filled their wine glasses and told Dominic about the first time he met Ana.

"Yuki always accuses me of having designs on Ana and, of course, when I first met her that was true. I offered her my little house, hoping for a lot more, but Ana let me know right away that was a wild dream!

It's true about the relationship between Ana and Toshi. Their love affair was difficult, to say the least. And, in the end, Ana was broken. Yuki could never forgive Toshi, but what I thought was crazy, he'd call her now and then to find out about Ana. And Yuki always told him as if he had a right to know. She never told Ana about it, though."

Dominic sat quietly listening to Sato. There was nothing he could say about the past that did not involve him. But, to his surprise, Sato turned his attention toward him.

"And are you in love with our captivating Italian, as all my good friends and I have been at one time or another?"

Sato enjoyed making Dominic uncomfortable. Dominic took another sip of wine before he answered, "That is a question which I have had little time to consider."

427

Sato's eyes sparkled as he continued to tease the doctor, "It takes very little time to fall in love. How long have you known her?"

Dominic knew that Sat was playing a game of mental chess with him and was moving toward checkmate. He was careful in his reply.

"I was Toshi's heart specialist even before his final heart attack. My concern was for his life and that concern has occupied all my time and energy."

But Sato would not relent and laughed as he continued his teasing game, "How much time does it take to fall in love with a woman? I have found that a split second can change one's life forever. When Ana refused my attentions, I turned around and looked into the wonderful eyes of my Yuki. She smiled and I was hers forever! Love is an amazing gift, is it not, my good doctor?"

"I agree that it is, indeed, a gift. And I hope that one day it may come to me as it has to you, in a split second and forever."

Sato leaned forward in his chair and, with a sly smile, whispered to Dominic, "I suggest that love has already come to you. Now, let's drink to forever."

Sato held his glass to Dominic. The doctor knew he was trapped and hesitated, but slowly smiled and shook his head in defeat at Sato's persistence. They raised their glasses in a silent toast and drank the wine. Then Sato suggested they walk outside to see what was happening with the women. As they did so, Sato made another surprising suggestion to Dominic.

"I think you should ask Ana to show you the little house."

"I couldn't do that, Sato! That's her private place, her past. I would never want to intrude on that part of her life."

"There's always been an enchantment about that place. To see it might help you understand the choices she's made."

Dominic looked directly at his host, trying to decide if he were still playing games with him, but he saw only tenderness in Sato's eyes. Perhaps he would follow his advice. It would depend on how Ana felt when she returned.

After a while, the women came up the path toward Sato and Dominic. They were walking arm-in-arm and talking quietly together. Dominic noticed a dim light had been left on at the front door of the little place. Obviously, Ana was going to stay there tonight. He wondered what he should do.

Sato called to Miyuki, "Is everything alright between you two?"

Miyuki answered her husband with a smile, "We're okay! Ana's going to stay down there, so we came to get some things for the night. We'll be back downstairs in a minute. Let's have a goodnight drink together, okay?"

Sato, of course, agreed with that plan, and they all walked into the house to do just that. After the women had collected Ana's things, they came down to the living room where Sato had prepared the final toast of the evening. He poured the *reishu*, a clear, cool *sake* especially popular in the summer, into four square, wooden cups. They each took a cup and held it up to the new day. Dominic was surprised at the taste.

"I guess I was expecting something much stronger. It's not bad at all…much milder than I thought."

They laughed and Sato replied, "You've just come through your first major intercultural experience and have done very well. Now, we look forward to introducing you to many more exciting moments tomorrow!"

Dominic had no idea why there was such a gleam in Sato's eye, but knew he would find out soon enough. They shared one last cup of *reishu* and the banzai salute to "ten thousand years of happiness." There was a message of hope in this cheerful ending to a most distressing day.

CHAPTER 38

"I shall always remember…the sweet perfume of garden flowers, when love was new and promises were made by moonlight. Sayonara, my sweet samurai."
--Ana's farewell to Seijo

After Sato's final toast of the evening, Ana turned to get her suitcase and go out to the little house for the night. But Dominic picked it up and asked, "Do you mind an intruder for a few moments? I'd like to see your Seijo home."

"Of course, I don't mind. I'd love to show it to you."

Ana was surprised, but also glad, that Dominic was interested. They walked silently down the lighted pathway past the evergreens. When they came to the front door of the house, she took the suitcase from him.

"Stay right here a moment and I'll be right back. You need to see this place at its best, otherwise, it's just one large tatami room with a porch."

Ana stepped inside the house to turn on the gas jet that would light the garden lanterns and, except for one small candle, to turn out the inside lights. She quickly stepped out to light the lanterns around the garden. The flickering light from these lanterns guided them to the small garden area behind the house. Ana took Dominic's hand and led him up the steps onto the porch. She had placed the *zabuton* on opposite sides of the porch so they could relax in comfort and enjoy the garden.

She gave Dominic a polite invitation, "Please sit down and relax in the little garden."

They both sat down on the *zabuton* to enjoy the quietness of the evening. Ana continued, "Now, my friend, look around and tell me what you think of this little place."

Dominic did as she asked. The lanterns flickered against the water in the pond and lighted just enough of the garden to reveal the outlines of bushes, flowers, and trees. He caught the scent of pine mixed with some sweet flower that he couldn't identify. Beyond the trees, the city lights flickered in the far distance and a tiny bit of candlelight shone through the sliding screen doors, allowing a bare glimpse of the woman sitting on the other side of the porch.

Though he appreciated the beauty surrounding him, Dominic began to feel uncomfortable. And he knew why. This was a setting for lovers, and he was an intruder in it.

He could barely whisper a reply to Ana's question, "This is an enchanted cottage. It's a place for lovers."

Ana smiled at the truth of his words. He had understood what she wanted him to know. She spoke quietly, "'Only the gentle may enter here, for this is a place where love dwells.' That's what I thought the first night I spent in this house. Its simple beauty nearly took my breath away. And to think that this is the same house where the wild and crazy Sato had his many love affairs! After I realized that, it was difficult to understand the sweetness of this place."

"Perhaps Sato has a sweet side that we have yet to discover."

"I'm sure that's so. He's very good to Yuki, although he has a difficult time remaining faithful."

"But he's kind and that's important, as you have taught me so well. And especially between lovers."

Ana smiled, remembering her attack against his blunt words one night in Virginia.

"Yes, kindness is a virtue that can cover a multitude of sins. I've had trouble developing it myself. Maybe that's why I notice when others have the same problem as I. Yamamoto was the kind, sweet one. I was the one who shouted and raved."

"Perhaps you underestimate your own qualities, Ana. I have never seen such kindness as that which you offered your husband to the end of his life. There could never be a doubt of your love for him."

Ana was quiet for a while, trying to control the emotions she felt stirring within her heart. Finally, she spoke, "This is very strange, you know. I'm showing you a place where I lived once and where I experienced the joy of loving a very sweet man. But, I can't explain my feelings, except that somehow it seems as if our love affair didn't really happen at all.

We were only together here a few times. And when we met in the States, it was for just a few short months. Perhaps, for the first time since he and I met, I'm facing reality. And that reality is simply this: my life was lived with Matsamura. He was the one who loved me enough to give up everything for me. He loved my son and gave his life to him. That's the real story of my life. Mishima is the one who should have been celebrated, the one I should have mourned, but never could.

So, what do you know about love, Donatelli? Can you explain any of this to me?"

"I would never attempt to explain love to anyone. I know much less about it than you, Ana. I thought I was in love once. We married and found out very soon that we couldn't even live together. We tried, but it was a mistake. We began to dislike each other and, in the end, celebrated more at our divorce than we did at our wedding!

You've experienced love in a greater measure than I could even imagine. You know about loving, Ana. I need to learn from you."

"I guess it comes down to a simple matter. It is or it isn't, and it comes to each of us in different forms. Most often, I'm sure, without warning or reason."

"So, tonight, we revisit a beautiful, peaceful place where love was found once upon a time. Those moments are worth celebrating, are they not?"

"And when it's over, they must be put away."

"Put away, yes, but never forgotten."

"Is it safe, I wonder, to bring out the memories once in a while?"

"You tell me, Ana. Is it safe for you to be here in this place, reliving your life with Yamamoto? I can't advise you about something I've never experienced. I have no memories of love that I would ever wish to relive. You must tell me."

"I think it's safe for a while, but I would never want to stay here, inside the memory. There's too much life yet to live. I learned that lesson on the beach at Sandcrest. I chose to live that day, and I choose to do so now."

Dominic looked across at Ana, wondering if she really believed in the words that she spoke so bravely on the day of her lover's funeral. He asked a question of her.

"Why was it that you really came out to this 'haunted cottage' tonight, Ana?"

She did not flinch, but the answer was spoken in a whisper, "To fold up some memories…and put them away."

"Then, perhaps, I should leave you to that task."

Dominic took one last glance at the peaceful setting around them. If there were ever to be anything beyond friendship between him and Ana Maria Gabrelli, it would not happen here. This was the home of someone else's heart. He did not belong in this place.

Ana did not rise, but spoke to Dominic as he started down the steps.

"Thanks, Donatelli, for your kind presence tonight."

He turned and smiled, "Tomorrow you can show me the beauties of the city in return for my kindness tonight. I am a fast learner, you know."

Dominic left her then to the task of folding up memories and putting them away. He hoped that she would be able to complete that task.

When he walked back to the big house, Sato was still sitting in the living room, drinking *sake*. He smiled and offered Dominic another cup, but was politely refused.

Sato asked, "How is Ana?"

Dominic answered with ease, "She's doing fine. We had a good talk. You have a beautiful little place. I can see how it would be a perfect setting for romance."

"Ah, yes, but those days are over for me. Yuki and I have made an agreement, now. Only our children can use it or our visitors. Those other days are gone forever!"

They both laughed. Dominic wasn't sure who to believe, but he chose to believe Ana. Sato gave Dominic a sideways glance, "But as long as you are here, you are welcome to use it for romantic purposes. You have no sweet wife who holds a rope around your neck!"

Dominic laughed and assured Sato that there was no chance of his using their little house for such purposes. As the two men walked upstairs, Sato directed Dominic to his room for the night and left him with a sigh, "Then you are destined to sleep alone and dream of better nights ahead!"

After Dominic had gone back to the house, Ana sat on the porch for a while, indulging in the pleasure of sweet memories and allowing herself the luxury of a few last tears. But she knew that too much life had happened since she had been in this place. All this was too long ago to be relevant. The garden lanterns flickered as she extinguished their glow. Her life with Toshiburo Yamamoto was over. Ana walked into the little house, laid down on the futon and went sound asleep.

Everyone was up early the next morning and ready to take Dominic on his trip to the city. They decided to leave the car at home so they wouldn't have to worry about parking. And, besides, they wanted their "resident tourist" to experience the excitement of trains, subways, and buses as only the Japanese city could supply. Dominic was ready, but somewhat frightened by the sly smiles from his guides as they set out for Seijo Station.

Dominic's first real entry to the culture of Japanese city life found him packed like a sardine and overlooking the heads of everyone on the morning rush-hour train. His friends laughed at the shock on his face as he stumbled off the train at Shinjuku station and was nearly trampled by thousands of workers rushing to subways or trains for various locations throughout the city.

He begged for mercy, "Isn't there an easier way? Did you see my arm stuck up in the air? There wasn't any place to put it and it doesn't want to come down now. When the train turned, my head actually banged against the top. Is there a taller train?"

Sato showed Dominic no mercy as he grabbed his friend's arm and dragged him to the downtown subway.

"Just be glad you're a foot taller than everyone else! At least you can breathe and look out the windows. The rest of us are so smashed, we can hardly breathe. We accept no complaints from tall tourists."

When they left the subway to walk a few blocks to the IEEC office, Dominic convinced his friends to stop at the small hotel nearby for "rest and recovery." They shared a cup of coffee and a breakfast roll as Yuki and Ana recalled the many hours they had spent with their friends in the coffee shop here. They walked the few blocks to the office building.

Ito Nishyama met them at the door with a bright smile.

"You came early! Maybe I'll put you to work again, Ana. Nothing has been the same since you left us."

Ito took the visitors on a tour of the building and explained to Dominic what was happening there. Ana was impressed with the beautiful new additions and also with the extended programs that were offered for businesses who were expanding to many nations throughout the world. She was gratified that so much more was being done now to improve intercultural understanding than had been the case during her tour of duty.

Before the group left the office, Ito invited them to be his guests for dinner at the very elegant Shibya Steak House near Shinjuku Station. They arranged a time to meet, then took their leave to share more of Tokyo's excitement and beauty with their captive friend. As they left for the next tourist site, Ana assured Dominic, "I promise, we're not torturing you for the fun of it, Dom. It's been a while since I've been here, so I'm as much a tourist as you! And I want to see all I can in these few hours. Believe me, we're all suffering together!"

He laughed at her, "Thanks for the sympathy, Ana, but I don't believe there is any way possible that you could be suffering as much as I!"

But he took back his words of complaint later when they walked through the beautiful Meiji Shrine and sat a few moments in silence beside its ponds covered with delicate pink and white water lilies. They visited several ancient temples throughout the area which impressed Dominic with their unique structures, so different from anything he had ever seen. And he found himself nearly speechless at the beauty of the manicured gardens surrounding each of the temple sites.

Later in the morning, the group returned to downtown Tokyo for a walk along the Ginza. There Sato announced, "And now, my American friend, for the experience of a lifetime—crossing the street at the Ginza!"

At the corner of the wide street, Dominic saw hundreds of people rushing across the diagonal corridors of the huge Ginza shopping street.

Dominic hesitated, "Do we have to do this?"

"Follow Yuki; she's an expert. Don't look back or around when she moves, walk as fast as you can. If you stumble, you're dead!"

They all started laughing as the lights changed and the whole crowd moved like a huge stampede. Miyuki led them safely across, but they had to stop on the other side because Dominic and Sato were doubling over with laughter.

"Okay, you people, I have been living in the city all my life and I've seen crowds, but I've never seen anything like this! Tell me how you live through the day? Does anyone just saunter down the street and enjoy the moment?"

Miyuki laughed at him, "Of course not. This is a busy place, no sauntering allowed! If we need a quiet moment, we visit the beautiful gardens, shrines, and temples everywhere."

For the next few hours, they strolled through the many Ginza shops so Dominic could purchase some mementoes of his fast-track visit to Tokyo.

By the planned dinner hour, the travelers arrived back at Shinjuku where they met Ito for their farewell dinner together. He led them to a small, but very exclusive, restaurant near the Keio Plaza Hotel. When they entered, everyone exchanged their shoes for *uwabaki* and were guided to a private dining room by a young hostess in traditional costume. Here they were seated, Japanese style, around a large, low table.

Dominic knew it must be a very exclusive place, for one whole wall was recessed and a tiny stream of water rolled over a bed of smooth, round rocks. Scroll paintings hung against the recessed wall and around the stream were placed beautiful ceramics and an impressive *ikebana* arrangement.

With their tea and *mizu* soup, they were served an appetizer of small, bite-sized pieces of flavored chicken. Ito told him that they were eating "Drunk Chicken." He explained that the chicken was soaked for many hours in *sake*, then cut into bite-sized pieces and grilled very lightly. The meat melted in their mouths and they all sighed with the pleasure of its taste.

Dominic had to comment, "This tastes like nothing I have ever eaten before. I can't taste the *sake* at all. It's sweet and wonderful!"

Their hostess poured the dinner wine, as a young waiter brought the main course of lightly-battered, deep-fried lobster tails. With it came white rice, small dishes of bright red pickles and a variety of tempura vegetables. Everyone smiled, but no one spoke, as they savored each bite of the delicious meal.

Much later, after they had completed their main course, the hostess returned with their dessert of sweet custard covered with thick plum sauce. When everyone was finished eating, Ito raised his wine glass and they joined in a toast.

"Here's to friends and memories and new challenges ahead for us all."

Sato led the traditional salute for "ten thousand years of happiness." They shouted together with their cups raised, "Banzai, banzai, banzai!"

They emptied their glasses, but instead of smashing them against the wall, they chose to set them down carefully on the table. As they rose to leave, Ito walked over to Ana and put his arm around her.

"We both knew where you were going, Ana, even from the beginning. Was the journey worth the price?"

"For that 'one sweet breath of ecstasy? Yes, Ito, it was worth the price."

"Knowing what you know now, would you pay it again?"

She pulled away from him and looked directly into his kind, loving eyes.

"I would pay it again."

"Then you are more fortunate than most and will have memories enough to sustain you through whatever is ahead."

"Thank you for your friendship, Ito. You were there for me at my most desperate moment. I'll never forget that."

They embraced one another and whispered one last 'sayonara' between friends. Ito left quickly to take care of the costs of dinner, but especially to avoid shedding tears in public. Dominic had been watching this tender goodbye between Ana and Nishyama and knew that it was difficult for her. He walked over and put his arm around her to offer sympathy and his strength.

They walked back to the train station in silence. Even Sato was quiet for a while. But when they entered the train with the late evening crowd, much less of a struggle that morning rush hour, Sato finally had to speak.

"Well, that was some delicious dinner and a great ending to a wild and crazy day!"

They all quietly agreed, each of them thinking ahead to the farewells yet to be spoken.

CHAPTER 39

"The loneliness comes...a burden too heavy to bear. How can I return to that place where love's sweetest moments became love's deepest sorrow?"
--Ana, back to Rock Hills

The morning after the tour of Tokyo, Miko called from Yokohama to let his mother know that everything was on schedule for his arrival in Tokyo. They would pick him up at 10 o'clock this morning at Tokyo Station, share a final lunch with Miyuki and Sato, and then board their flight for the States by 3 o'clock in the afternoon.

Everything went as planned and their final lunch together was a treat for Dominic. They stopped at The Robata, one of Sato's favorite haunts. Here they shared some final moments of reminiscing while watching the skilled chef's grill, cut, and toss tender pieces of steak, chicken, and shrimp onto their plates. Served with fried rice and grilled vegetables, the meal was delicious and a pleasant send-off for the travelers.

At the airport, Ana was honest with Miyuki as they shared their tearful farewells.

"You know, Yuki, everything's over for me here. There's no reason to return, except to see you. And I think you should use some of your husband's vast resources and come visit me in the States from now on."

She whispered so no one else would hear, especially Sato, "And come by yourself, so we can enjoy every minute and not have to share our time with anyone else at all!"

"I'll do it! Sato's such a good guy, he'll let me do anything I want. The only hitch is, it gives him the freedom to do whatever he wants at the same time. I have to weigh the trade-off. But I imagine before too long, it will be worth it."

They laughed and hugged each other one more time, then Ana, Miko, and Dominic boarded the plane and headed for their destination. The trip back was long, but Ana was too exhausted to notice. She slept through most of it. During her rest, Miko and Dominic had time to visit about the future. Miko was concerned about his mother and asked Dominic's opinion.

"Do you think I should encourage her to leave the Virginia house? I really don't want to live out there anymore. My next step after graduation from Georgetown will be Harvard, I hope. I'm working on my grades and special internships in political science and international relations, so there might be a chance I'll be accepted there. And, besides, I like the city. I just feel like a part of my life is over, like I'm growing up and leaving home for good."

"But don't you want a home base, Miko? Aren't your ties to Rock Hills strong enough that you'd like to think of it as a base where you can always return and know that your mother is there and all the good memories? Isn't that important to you?"

"Maybe it's nice to have a 'safe place' that's there for you, but I really don't think I need that. My main concern, though, is my mother. I don't want to encourage her to do something that wouldn't be wise, like selling the place and then being sorry about it later."

"Well, I'm sure your mother won't make any decision just because you encourage it. She's pretty strong about what she does and doesn't want. But it sounds like you have some of that strength, too. You should talk with your mother as openly as you've talked to me. Perhaps you both want the same thing, after all."

Miko looked at Dominic with a hesitant smile.

"You may be right. Now that I've practiced expressing my feelings to you, I just might be brave enough to do the same with my mother...maybe!"

"I understand your fears, but if you weaken, call me and I'll coach you before the face-off!"

They laughed together, both aware of the truth of their comments. Miko promised that he'd call for help at the crucial moment.

The closer they came to their destination, Ana found herself coming back to consciousness and, in so doing, began to feel an increasing nervous tension throughout her body. She recalled that it was the same feeling she had on her first trip to Japan as a young college student, the sensation of entering the unknown without a clue of what was ahead, nor a map to guide her.

She began asking questions of herself, *"What will I do with the rest of my life? Do I want to continue teaching? Do I want to stay in the house in Virginia that Mishima built and where Yamamoto suffered? Was that one sweet moment in the garden shrine enough to allow me to find joy there again?"*

Ana was thankful for Dominic's presence on the trip, for he seemed aware of her fearful contemplations. He drew her back to the present by finding comical and interesting things happening all around them. They spent the rest of the time laughing at the idiosyncrasies of their travel partners and the unique situations that always arose on long journeys with strangers.

Before the trip ended, all three of them had been reduced to sharing tiny bottles of unique types of alcoholic beverages. This, of course, encouraged their senses of humor and allowed them to make it to Washington, D.C. without anyone sinking into deep depression.

As soon as the plane landed, Ana called her house in Virginia to make sure Yoshiko was still there. Ana was much relieved that her good friend had agreed to stay until Ana decided what to do with the next part of her life. At least, she wouldn't have to face the memories alone.

When she came out of the phone booth, Suzi was there with Miko and Dominic. Ana greeted her with a warm hug, "Suzi, I'm so happy to see you! We were all sorry that you couldn't have been with us in Japan. We did have some good times along with the tough parts. You would have enjoyed Tokyo."

Suzi began to cry, "I feel so bad not being there with you and Miko. I was thinking of you every day and worrying about both of you."

Ana responded to her concerns with a comforting smile, saying, "It was hard for all of us, but we're doing fine. We'll be okay. We have to go on, don't we?"

Then Suzi turned to Miko, "I brought the car so I could take all of you wherever you need to go. What are your plans now, for tonight? Are you staying in the city?"

Ana quickly answered for herself, "I've just talked with Yoshiko. She's at the house, so everything is fine there. I'm going to take the fast train down from here and leave my bags with you, Miko. You can bring them out this weekend. There's nothing in them that I'll need for a few days."

Ana could tell that Suzi and Miko wanted to be alone, and should be. She knew that her son needed to share his feelings openly with Suzi as he could not do with his mother for fear of hurting her further. Though Miko was hesitant about letting his mother go to Rock Hills alone, he had the feeling that she wanted it that way.

"If that's okay, mother, I'll stay in town and take care of your bags."

She smiled and patted his cheek, "That's fine. Go ahead and I'll see you this weekend."

Miko gave his mother a hug and, not knowing what else to do, took her luggage tickets and left with Suzi.

Dominic turned to Ana with questions.

"Are you sure you want to rush back there? Why not stay here for a few days. There's plenty of room at my place and we can talk and relax from the tension of all we've been through. I need it as much as you, Ana, to come to some closure on this part of our lives."

Ana sensed Dominic's deep concern for her, as well as his own inner struggle with the whole situation. She wasn't able to look at him as she answered, "I can't do that, Dom. I have to go back and work it out and I have to do it now. But you're welcome to come out with me tonight. We could talk a while after dinner."

Dominic knew better than to accept Ana's invitation. He could tell that she wanted to be alone, whether or not it was best, and he chose not to intrude. He replied with a sense of resignation, "No, but thanks for the invitation. I'd better check in with my continuing responsibilities, as much as I'd like to ignore them for a while. But wait here, and I'll get your train pass and be right back."

He turned and left before Ana could protest. He couldn't tell if he was angry at her choice to move back into the past so quickly, or disappointed that she had refused his offer to help her move into the future. When he returned with the pass, Dominic pulled himself together and was able to be more casual.

"Ana, I want you to feel free to call me anytime, day or night. We've been through too much together to just walk away."

Ana smiled and gave him a farewell hug.

"Thanks so much for everything, Dom. You're a wonderful friend and I'm grateful for everything you've done for us, especially your support in Tokyo. I promise to call."

She was gone and Dominic was certain that Ana had no intention of every calling him. If there were to be a relationship between them in the future, he knew very well that he would have to be the one to make it happen.

Much later that night, sitting alone before the warm fire in his comfortable home, Dominic felt a terrible loneliness that seemed to cover him with a blanket of sorrow. He had never experienced the intense connection with others that he had developed over the past few months at Rock Hills. The doctor realized that he had lost more than a patient; he had lost a friend for whom he had great respect, the companionship of a woman for whom he felt a deep love, and, beyond that, the relationship of a family with whom he had shared both joy and sorrow.

Now, suddenly, he was cut off from them all. Dominic felt helpless in a way that he had never known in his life, as if he were a child, lost in the darkness. He did the only thing he knew to do. He grabbed a bottle of scotch from the cupboard and attempted to ease his disturbing thoughts with the soothing liquid. The last thought that crossed his mind before he allowed himself the freedom to enter a state of oblivion was simply, *"How can I ever help Ana out of her sorrow, when I am mired so deeply in my own?"*

The fears that troubled Dominic's mind when he watched Ana walk away from him that night at the airport were eventually realized. Nearly six weeks after their return from Japan, he received a late-night call from Miko. His young friend was very disturbed.

"Please forgive me for calling so late, but I don't know where else to turn. It's my mother. She's in trouble, but she won't let me help her and I don't know what to do!"

The doctor responded quickly, "Tell me what's happening, Miko. Is your mother ill?"

"I think she is, but she won't listen to me and she won't get help, not even to call you. She's just locking herself away from the world and refusing to face reality or even try to make a new life for herself.

Could you visit with her and try to encourage her to share her feelings with someone? Whenever I'm there, she pretends everything is fine, but I know it's not. She's even talking about returning to the resort in Carolina. I don't think it's healthy to want to relive the past, but she won't listen to me. You know, I'm the son...and mothers always know best!"

"Thank you for calling me, Miko. There are several ways I can help your mother and I'll try them all if I have to. The truth is, I've been very worried about her. She hasn't called me since the night we came back from Tokyo. That, in itself, gives me a good reason to make a visit to Rock Hills."

Miko began to relax. He was certain that Dominic would know what to do and that he could leave his worries safely with him.

"Thanks, Dominic. I know Toshi would be the first to ask for your help if one of us were in trouble. He trusted you completely and I feel like you're part of our family. I just hope you can reach my mother and help her out of this, well, I guess it's depression."

"Don't worry, Miko. Between you and me, surely we can get things put together again. I'll let you know how it goes, but allow me a few days in case your mother gives me her usual trouble."

Miko was relieved after talking to Dominic. He knew their friend would do everything he could. He relaxed and went to sleep. But Dominic was finished sleeping for the night. He got up and fixed himself a snack, then went to the den and began making mental notes to himself.

Ana had seemed so strong and capable of handling Toshi's illness and death, even following the funeral. Her only display of weakness was during the memorial service and that was perfectly normal due to stress and the lack of sleep. He had never seen her evidence anything but normal reactions to the difficult situations she had been through. But Miko was afraid his mother had slipped into a serious depression. As a doctor and friend, he would know when he had seen and talked with Ana.

After a sleepless interval from midnight until dawn, Dominic left a message on his office telephone machine that he would be out of town for the day on a medical emergency and would call in later. Then he showered and dressed in casual clothes, ate a good breakfast to give himself strength for the day, and left for Rock Hills. It would be almost 9 o'clock when he arrived. He was certain Ana would be up and ready for the day by that time.

At exactly 9 o'clock, Dominic drove into Ana's driveway. The morning sun had broken through the clouds to promise a beautiful early fall day. Everything seemed peaceful at the house as Dominic walked across the patio to the kitchen door, but a slight shiver of fear caused him to hesitate, wondering what he might find inside. He rang the doorbell, breathing deeply in anticipation of Ana's presence.

Within a few minutes, Ana opened the back door and the friends greeted each other.

"Dominic! My god, what are you doing here at this hour of the day?"

He smiled and answered casually, "Well, I was in the neighborhood…" They both laughed. Ana took his hand and led him into the house.

"Come on in, I was just cleaning up after breakfast. Have you eaten? Are you hungry?"

"No…I mean, yes." Ana laughed as he tried to get his answers straight.

"Yes, I have eaten, and no, I'm not hungry. But I will take a cup of coffee if you have any handy."

"Of course I have." They went into the kitchen where Ana poured them both a large mug of hot coffee. Her smile was genuine and seemed to light up the whole room.

"Let's go out on the deck and relax a while. Do you have time for a visit?"

"Of course. I'm lonely. Don't you know that's why I came all the way out here?"

Ana didn't answer, but smiled and led him to the deck where they sat down in the soft lounge chairs. Ana lifted her mug toward him.

"Here's to friends!" They enjoyed their coffee and the beauty around them for a few moments. Ana finally broke the silence with a pointed question.

"Tell me, Dom, what are you really doing here, in the neighborhood?"

She watched him carefully as he struggled for an acceptable answer. He chose to keep the atmosphere casual.

"You promised to call, but I haven't heard from you, so I thought to myself, *'This is a beautiful day to visit Ana and find out what's happening in her life.'* Do you mind my intrusion on your privacy?"

Dominic smiled and continued his questions before she could answer, "How are you doing, Ana? What's happening in your life now?"

Ana took a sip or two of coffee, then looked directly at her friend. The bright smile faded from her face as she spoke, "I sense that this is not just a casual conversation, so I'll answer you truthfully. I'm not doing well. I'm not doing well, at all."

Dominic felt his stomach tighten. He wanted to put his arms around Ana and comfort her, but knew that was not an acceptable option. He encouraged her to share her feelings.

"You don't need to cover up with me, Ana. That's why I'm here. I'm worried about you, that's all."

"Are you strong enough to hear the truth, Dom?"

He noticed there were no tears in her eyes and wondered what would follow.

"For God's sake, Ana, if you're strong enough to live it, I'm strong enough to hear it!"

Dominic held his breath for fear that she would refuse to continue, but Ana began to talk to him as he hoped she would, as a friend.

"I thought I was making it so well. But all of a sudden the walls have come tumbling down around me. There seems to be nothing left…inside of me. I'm empty, Dom."

She appeared to be so calm and perfectly controlled, but the sorrow evident in her words was overpowering.

"I find that I don't know how to live without him. Even though we were separated for so many years, the knowledge of his presence gave me strength. I knew where he was. He was

446

close by and it was alright that we couldn't be together. There were times when it was nothing more than hearing his name or reading something about him and the work he was doing. That was enough. I could make it.

But now, I can't believe how different it is. He is…nowhere! I have no reference point, no center. There is nothing inside of me. I am totally empty. Sometimes I feel as if I were dead and the body has only to be buried."

If Ana had wept, shed her tears, he could have put his arms around her and offered comfort. But her eyes were dry. Dominic felt as helpless as Ana felt empty. All he could do was take her hands in his and hold them as tight as he could, hoping she would feel his strength and borrow some of it for her own. Finally, he spoke out of desperation.

"Ana, I don't know what to say to you. There are no words that can fill your emptiness or heal the brokenness in your heart. All I have and all Miko has and all Yuki or Sato or Suzi have…is our love for you. And I don't know how to take that love from our hearts and place it inside yours so you can feel life there again.

But I do know this, that until you open your heart to receive our love, then you render us helpless. You've shut the doors on us, Ana. You haven't asked for our help, you haven't shared your fears with us and until someone asks for help, how can it be given?"

"I understand what you're saying, Dom. But I was so certain that the Gabrelli spirit could withstand whatever life threw in its pathway. I've been hurt before, in some dreadful ways, but there was always a reserve inside of me, a strength that made me fight and come back. Remember, it was me who faced the tide and refused to go with it. I was so certain after that experience that nothing could pull me under. Why now…after everything is finished, when it's all over and done, do I choose to fall apart?"

"You're only now facing the greatest test that any of us face. We're always there when others need us, aren't we? You were there for Yamamoto during his suffering, through the agony of his death, because you loved him enough to be there. But, more than that, he loved you enough to admit his weakness and to allow you to be his strength. He loved you enough to let you be with him at his most desperate hour.

That's the final lesson we must all learn from him. Think about it, Ana. Ask yourself what it means for you. You have two choices now: to open your heart and let those who love you fill it with the hope that you've lost, or to live here alone, clinging to your broken dreams and despair."

There was a deafening silence between the two friends. Ana did not respond to his words. She appeared as if carved out of stone, with no flicker of emotion, staring past Dominic at the rocky hills surrounding them. After a while, Dominic sighed with his own sense of despair. He stood up and reached into his pocket, taking out a small white envelope. He tossed it into Ana's lap and offered his final counsel to her.

"If the latter is your choice, there's something in this envelope that will restore your strength and lift your spirits. If that's what you want, Ana, I offer it willingly as a medical doctor and your friend. But I know that you don't need to rely on chemicals to live a fulfilling life.

You are loved, Ana. I only pray that you will not wait too long to accept the love that will heal your brokenness. The choice is finally yours; no one can make it for you."

Dominic waited for some response. She gave no indication that she had heard him, nor did she move to pick up the envelope in her lap. Her gaze did not leave the hillside. He was drained of energy and felt a terrible emptiness within his heart at Ana's refusal to see what she was doing to herself and to all who loved her.

After a few moments of silence between them, the doctor turned and left Ana without looking back. He could not do more than he had done. He had given her the choice of relying on chemicals to dull the pain of heartache, or of conquering that pain with her own strength. He had to make his own choices now, to discover how to fill the emptiness in his heart without the woman he loved. And he was determined to do so.

CHAPTER 40

"In the midst of despair...a journey to recall that place
'from whence I came,' to uncover the hidden mysteries
which haunt my memory. The promise of new life is
restored!"
      --Ana's Journey

Over the next few months, Dominic hoped against hope that
Ana would call, but the call did not come. He finally decided
that he had waited long enough for what was not going to happen.
He knew that those closest to Ana would have to be the ones to
help her now, for he had offered his counsel and his love. It was
all he knew to give and she had refused both.

Dominic found that the excitement he had experienced for
many years in his medical practice had diminished. He recalled
speaking so courageously to Ana of how she must break through
her walls of fear to heal the emptiness in her heart. Now he was
challenged to listen to his own words. He wanted a new direction
in his life and he found it.

By accident of fate, he wasn't sure which, Dominic received
an out-of-the-blue offer to accept a position at Boston University
Medical School as professor of cardiac medicine and head of the
cardiology department. He would be teaching students how to do
what he had been doing for many years. He was a highly-skilled
cardiologist and came to the university with acclaim.

Before he left Washington, D.C., Dominic sold his practice
and wrote a letter to his closest friends and colleagues, letting
them know of the new position. His letter contained his Boston
address, telephone numbers, and an invitation to contact him
should any of them be in the area. Included on that list were Ana
Maria Gabrelli and her son, Mikoto. Though very disappointed,
Dominic was not surprised when no reply or note of
congratulations came from either of them.

At the same time that Dominic was moving into a new phase
of professional life, Ana was slowly moving out of her difficult
period of mourning. Dominic's visit had helped her see more
clearly where she was headed and realize that her independent
spirit was too precious to sacrifice in a moment of weakness. His

wise counsel had given Ana the strength to begin the healing process. As part of that healing, she had chosen to take a leave of absence from Georgetown to enjoy some travel that she had longed to do for years.

Several weeks after the journey to Japan, Ana had received a letter from Tatsume Yamamoto letting her know of certain financial arrangements Toshi had made for her and Mikoto. They were to receive an inheritance from the Yamamoto estate. She had been more shocked than surprised when the letter and legal papers arrived, but was gratified that Toshi's father was willing that his son's wishes be fulfilled.

Now, because of the gift, Ana could well-afford an extended trip without depending on academic or personal contacts for her accommodations. She arranged her travel through an agency and was completely independent to do whatever she wished. This kind of freedom was new to her and added to the excitement of the journey.

Before Ana left on her travels through Europe and Great Britain, she considered calling Dominic to let him know her plans. But they had not contacted each other after his visit to Rock Hills during her period of depression, and she knew how difficult those moments had been for him. He had placed his heart in her hands and been refused.

Ana was not ready to renew that relationship and decided it was better to let the silence remain between them. Perhaps, when she returned to the States, she might feel differently. But, for now, she wanted to be free from any relationships that were reminders of the most traumatic moments of her life.

So Ana went on a journey to create new memories, those that would be life-giving. Because of who she was, a student of intercultural learning, she could not travel just to "see" a place. She and her travel agent planned carefully so that she could remain in each locale for six to eight weeks and live among the people of that area.

This meant that she did not stay with the tourists in expensive hotels, but chose "homestays" with ordinary families. What she most wanted was a personal discovery of those who call themselves by different names, speak different languages, and live according to different customs than she had known. She planned, at some time in the future, to write about these travels from the perspective of an itinerant anthropologist.

The change of scene, meeting people, and sharing the unique qualities of each cultural setting was exhilarating. Ana's mind was open for new horizons and, in the process, her heart began to heal. She found many opportunities to develop intimate relationships along the way, but she had no desire to go beyond the moment. She met people, learned about them as persons, enjoyed their presence, and said farewell with ease.

While enjoying the personal contacts with those of various cultures, Ana shared the excitement and beauty of their homelands. With her new-found friends, she rode the gondolas in Venice, worshipped in the Basilica and the great cathedrals of Rome, attended the bullfights in Spain, skied in the Alps, floated down the Danube, listened to the glorious music in Vienna, and found excitement around every corner in Paris. Yet, in spite of the many opportunities offered her, there was no romance, nor any desire for it.

There were only two special moments that Ana planned on her journey related to her and Toshi. She had obtained addresses and telephone numbers from Tatsume Yamamoto for Sachiko Yamamoto Sassone in Paris and three of Toshi's special comrades from Oxford in England. Before leaving the States, she sent letters of introduction to each of them, including her itinerary. This turned out to be a very pleasant experience in each instance.

Sachiko and Pere' Sassone, with their two beautiful children, Genevieve and Armand, met Ana at the Paris train station on her way north to London. These were the last two destinations before returning to the States. There was an immediate connection between her and Sachiko. The moment they met, they embraced and shed tears of consolation together.

Ana spent the day and overnight with the Sassone family.

After the children had gone to bed, she and Sachiko had some moments alone. Sachiko was the first to speak of their shared heartache.

"I am so happy and so sad for you. My heart is torn that you could not have been together and shared the years that I shared with Toshiburo. You had such a short time and in his weakest hours."

But Ana also sought to comfort Sachiko, saying, "And you lost those years as well. They were stolen from the one you loved…by our need to do the 'right and responsible' thing."

"As you know, however, I had no choice. It was my parents' wish and I had to follow it. Toshiburo was the one who set me free. I am so thankful for his kindness and understanding."

"There is something I wanted to tell you in person, rather than in my letter. I don't know if he ever had a chance to contact you after his resignation from the embassy and the terrible illness before his death. But Toshi and I have a son. His name is Mikoto Toshiburo and he will be twenty years old on his next birthday."

There was a shocked silence between them before Sachiko could respond to Ana's revelation.

"No, I did not know that. Did Toshiburo know during our marriage?"

"He did not know about our child until I brought him to Toshi's final reception at the embassy two years ago. I didn't even have to tell him, for there is such a strong resemblance between the two, that Toshi recognized him immediately. He was very angry and distraught that I hadn't been honest with him.

But, you see, there was so much unspoken between us. His concern with doing the right thing in fulfilling his obligations to his arranged marriage and to his expected role in the State government. I couldn't tell him…for fear of what he might or might not do. I gave him no opportunity to make the choice."

Sachiko put her head in her hands and wept, "Oh, fate is so cruel at times! You see, if you had told him, he would never have married me. He would have honored his responsibility to you, first and foremost. And I would have been freed from my obligation as well. You would have had your lifetime together as it should have been!"

Ana put her arms around Sachiko and they wept together for a few moments, but then Ana started laughing. Sachiko looked up at her with a question, "What can be funny in all this sadness?"

"It's funny because between the four of us, we were all caught in the traps of our cultural expectations. Yet, each one of us knew better, didn't we? We knew that all we would have had to do was tell the absolute truth and we would have been set free from those expectations and would have found the joy in life that eluded us!"

Sachiko began to smile and said, "I know you're right, Ana. If I had told Toshi of my love for Pere' before the marriage, he would never have allowed me to give him up for a loveless marriage. He would have taken the responsibility upon himself and set me free. And if you had told him of your child, he would never have let you go alone! I hope we've all learned something from this strange mix-up of love and responsibility and freedom and cultural expectations!"

"I'm sure we have, but, of course, much too late to make up for what we've all lost. Thank heavens, you had a lover who was willing to wait for you. And now the two of you share the happiness that each of us deserved. I celebrate for you and Pere'!"

"Are you bitter, Ana, towards Toshi…towards me?"

"I think that you struck the real truth, Sachiko, when you placed the first blame on my own failure to be honest. That was the beginning of the fiasco, when I didn't trust Toshi's love enough to be truthful with him when it mattered most. Perhaps that's the main 'cultural value' we can teach our 'intercultural' children—to honor the truth and not be afraid of its consequences. In this case, the truth would have brought joy to all of us."

They ended their moments of honesty in each other's arms as friends who had discovered a tie between them that would last a lifetime. Sachiko offered their home as a base for Mikoto should he fulfill his dream of attending Oxford.

"He will be like my young brother, for his father was more a father to me than a husband, and I can honor Toshiburo's memory by honoring his son."

Ana left for England with much to think about from her visits with Sachiko and Pere'. She felt, somehow, that whatever had occurred in the past was, in a way, as Toshi said, "It seems to have been meant to be for that is what occurred."

When Ana arrived in England, two of Toshi's British roommates took her on a tour of the University and showed her where they had all studied and lived for their years at Oxford. They offered to be her guides on visits to Scotland and Ireland as well. They had a great time together, and she experienced life from the British view.

Ana was surprised to find that she was not saddened when these new friends shared their stories of Toshi's life and loves and their wild school days together. She enjoyed their tales and discovered that she was thinking of Toshi as a person she had known and loved, but who was no longer a part of the present. And, in the process, the pain in her heart was eased.

During these months of travel, Ana made the firm decision to begin a totally new life, including a new professional direction. She had no idea what she would do, but she no longer wanted to teach. She felt the need to relax from the "busyness" that had consumed her life for so many years and also to leave Rock Hills, and all its memories, behind.

Ana made two major decisions. She sent a Letter of Resignation to Georgetown, effective immediately. It was postmarked in Paris. And she wrote to her sister, Val, asking her to start looking for a house in Boston with windows and trees and flowers and privacy…for "Ana's New Life"! It was postmarked in London.

At the end of her year-long journey of healing, Ana was ready for a totally new beginning. Her heart was no longer empty, but filled with the excitement of new directions and the hope of new relationships ahead. When she stepped off the plane in Boston, Val and Roger were waiting for her. After their initial greetings with many hugs and kisses, Val broke the news.

"I have found the house for you! And, if you don't buy it immediately, I intend to borrow the money from you to buy it myself. Ana, it's great! And it's everything you asked for…you're going to love it!"

Ana was excited and ready, "When can I see it? I don't want to go back to Virginia for anything, except to move out. And I may not even go back for that if I can get Miko to do it for me."

Val hadn't expected such immediate enthusiasm, so she backed down a bit.

"Now, you know, I do have several options if you don't like it. I wouldn't leave you with just one choice. But this was so much fun. I got to walk through some of the most gorgeous places in the city. Imagine me telling a real estate agent, 'Money is no object.' It was great!"

"Val, I've had the most wonderful experience. I feel like a whole new person and I'm filled with some kind of amazing energy. I'll tell you everything later tonight, but can we go to this gorgeous place first? Then, if I see one little thing wrong with it, we'll look at the others. You've aroused my curiosity and I won't be able to do anything until I see it. I'm absolutely ready for the next big step in my life."

"Well, we've got all afternoon and evening. Rog can take the luggage to our house and we'll grab a taxi and find a place for an early lunch. While we order lunch, I'll call the real estate agent and we'll go see the place, by golly!"

"I'm ready…take me to my castle!"

After the sisters ate a quick meal at a nearby café, Ana left a message on Miko's answering machine to let him know she was in Boston at Val's place and 'okay.' Val contacted the realtor and everything was arranged for the women to see the house. They hailed a taxi and were on their way.

They drove far across the city. Val explained that the home was one of many being built on the grounds of an old estate. As the taxi came close to their destination, Ana saw beauty all around her. The open green spaces covered rolling hills with trees and lush shrubbery. There were large, new homes being built on the hillsides, though they were not visible from the road.

They entered a long driveway lined with trees and stopped at a locked gate where the guard confirmed their entrance form a real estate listing. The anxious visitors were allowed to enter the very private and luxurious housing development. Driving through the area for a while, they came to a smaller, locked gate where Val used a keycard to open the gate.

They drove directly onto a circle drive in front of a large, white stucco house with a red tile roof, surrounded by many trees and flowers. Ana and Val walked up the wide stone steps to the double front doors. Here Val opened the real estate lock with the key card and the sisters entered the front door that led to a flagstone entryway.

Val led Ana up the wide carpeted steps into a huge open living area. The first thing Ana saw was the white marble fireplace and windows all across the back and side of the house. She also noticed that the white walls had generous open spaces for art work. The room could be filled with large, soft furniture and bright colors would add warmth to the whole area.

Wherever they went throughout the house, Ana felt it was perfection, as if designed just for her. Doors opening off the living area onto the rear patio showed plantings of bushes, flowers, and evergreens. The spacious upstairs included two large bedrooms and attached baths, with a huge den with a large marble fireplace, and a deck overlooking the back of the house and the grounds.

The women walked through the house, both sighing and commenting on the beauty and the possibilities for Ana's new home. Val served as the real estate agent, telling Ana several other good points beside the beauty of the house. The fact that it was a private, locked and guarded entrance was a plus. And all the maintenance was provided. Also, the new owner could choose from different house designs if this one did not meet their specifications. In addition, the owner could decorate as they wished.

After the sisters had walked through the whole house and onto the patio and decks, they went back to the living room and stood together by the fireplace, surveying the beauty all around them. Ana turned to Val and gave her a big hug.

"Thanks, sis, for my new home and my new life!"

They called the agent immediately. Ana had no qualms whatsoever at her quick decision. Only once before in her life had she ever felt so certain about anything. She loved the house and felt that it belonged to the "new" Ana.

Over the next few days, Ana completed all the necessary steps for the purchase of the home and for the move. The house sale was finalized with the papers signed and the money exchanged. When Miko called, he and his mother had a long talk about her trip, the new house, and whether or not he and Suzi wanted Rock Hills. Ana was shocked to hear her son answer, "No, Mother. I don't want the house. I guess I feel the same way you do. It's like…that part of my life is over and I want to start a new one. If I'm accepted at Harvard, I'll move up to Cambridge near you. If I'm accepted at Oxford, I'll be in England. And, by the way, Suzi and I aren't together anymore."

"What? What's happened between you after all this time?"

"We're starting to go in different directions. I don't want to be married. I'm too young, and she's too anxious to be connected to someone. And, besides, there's someone else I care about anyway."

Ana stopped the direction of the conversation.

"Miko, whatever you do with your private life belongs to you. I don't want to know about your romances until you think it's something serious and I should know. It sounds to me like you've got your head on straight and want your education before anything else. And I fully support that. You'll have a whole lifetime for love."

"Well, we'll talk later, but go ahead with the sale of our house; I don't want to go back there and that's final."

"Okay, we'll do it. So, start packing up out there and I'll be down soon to do the same. This is it, then…we're starting a whole new life. Are you ready?"

"With you, Mother, I have to be ready for anything, don't I?"

"Oh, yeah!"

"There's just one more thing, much more important that the house or Suzi or my education. How are you? I mean, the truth. Was the trip what you wanted it to be? Are you a new woman, from inside out?"

"Yes, Miko. I promise you, I've come through the haze. The trip was a blessing in many ways and I've found the courage to begin a whole new lifestyle. I'm leaving the 'old stuff' behind and I'm ready to enjoy whatever lies ahead. How about that?"

"Alright, then! I can sleep now and know you're back among the living and ready for whatever comes next!"

They ended their conversation on a positive note. Ana felt no sadness about Suzi. She and Miko seemed to have come to a mutual understanding, and she was touched by her son's concern for his mother's welfare. He was a sensitive, gentle boy like his father. For this, Ana would always be grateful. She knew that his nature might allow him to be hurt from time to time, but he would never easily hurt another.

There was only one other touchy subject which she would bring up with Miko this weekend at the Virginia house. Ana had decided to legally drop Mishima's name. She felt it was important to her personal identity to start this new life as "herself," with no strings to the past.

Perhaps others would not understand this decision, but Ana no longer cared what others thought. She would be who she was, Ana Maria Gabrelli. At last, she had found a new sense of strength and power from within herself. And she made a firm that never, in any case whatever, would she give away her personal identity again.

Over the next few weeks, Ana stayed with Val through the process of the house purchase and its decoration. Val guided Ana to a decorator and, between the three of them, they finished the home to Ana's complete satisfaction. When all of the furniture and artwork were in place, Ana and Val took a final walk-through. The transformation from the stark white emptiness to a strikingly beautiful and comfortable home amazed them all.

The effect Ana had hoped to achieve was accomplished perfectly. She placed an over-stuffed, white sofa and matching chairs in the living area to add a feeling of warmth and comfort to the home. The stark, white walls were complemented by bright orange, teal, and fuchsia accents in soft floor pillows and filmy drapes. As a final touch, she chose a large, modern painting to hang over the fireplace that accented the bright colors used throughout the house.

In the formal dining area, she chose a rectangle glass table with curved, antique brass legs. The cushioned brass chairs were covered in the same bright colors used throughout the living room. The hanging light fixture over the dining table was the same antique brass as the table and chairs with candle lamps.

A glassed-in extension to the kitchen provided a place for casual dining with a lovely view of the landscaped grounds. Here, Ana placed a round, white wooden table with matching chairs and soft cushions, using the bright accent colors again.

At the other end of the living area were glass doors opening onto a large patio. Ana knew she would spend time in this quiet setting, so she was careful to make it as comfortable as possible. The green, wrought-iron furniture with soft multi-colored cushions was perfect for relaxing among the beauties of nature, and the tiny pond with cycled water gave the impression of a stream running through the patio. Ana couldn't resist a touch from her little house in Seijo, so she added the Japanese lanterns around the pond to give soft light to the garden.

Ana's most valuable mementoes from Japan were arranged artistically in the den off the living room. Here, she installed *shoji* doors as a touch of the Orient to the house. Among other treasures in the den was an ancient scroll which was a gift from Tatsume Yamamoto in memory of his son. The scroll depicted a samurai warrior in formal costume with features evident in the faces of both Toshi and Mikoto.

According to Tatsume, this was purported to be the portrait of an ancestor of Sukiyama's family, though his name was not known. However, Ana knew that this ancestor was, no doubt, Sukiyama's lover, the father of Tatsume, the grandfather of Toshi and Mikoto's great-grandfather.

Beneath this scroll, on a black teak stand, Ana had placed Toshi's wedding gift to her, the white ceramic rose. Within its glass case were several precious items. A tiny gold case which held both her and Toshi's wedding rings, a parchment envelope containing the "Legend of the Samurai and the Rose," written in Toshi's hand, Toshi's last words to Ana before his death, and the poem she had written to Toshi the night before her marriage to Mishima.

Ishikawa had given this envelope to Ana on their final day at Sandcrest. He told her that Toshi had carried this precious message close to his heart since the moment he had received it. When she had opened the well-worn envelope, inside were the remains of the rose they both had kissed on the night they parted that first time, so many years ago.

Other pieces of treasured art were arranged throughout the room, representing gifts from Toshi's many friends around the world, as well as from Japan. Ana had given Toshi's ceremonial robes to Miko to keep with the samurai sword they had been presented by the Prime Minister at Toshi's memorial. These things belonged to his son. She had no desire to remember that particular day. She wanted only those mementoes that came from Yamamoto's heart.

After Val and Ana had looked everything over carefully, they sat down on the steps to the front door. Val commented, "I think we've done it! What do you think?"

"You're a miracle worker, Val! You found my home for me and I'll be forever grateful. Everything is perfect."

"Do you want me to stay with you? It's so big. Won't you be lonely here, tonight?"

"No, Val. This is the moment when I embrace the present and the future, and I say a final farewell to the past. And I need to do that alone. You understand, don't you?"

Val put her arms around her younger sister and gave her a warm hug and a kiss on the cheek.

"This is it, my courageous sister. A new life for a new woman! And, if this house is any indication of that new life, it looks promising."

When Val left Ana alone in the house, she did not worry about her younger sister. Val felt the energy of new life in Ana's words and in everything that she saw around her. After Val left, Ana checked the locks and touched the automatic light switch in the living room to bring the lights down very low. She went upstairs and changed into a loose-fitting, filmy nightgown to relax and enjoy this private moment of transition.

Later that night, Ana sat on the soft cushions of the patio couch, her feet tucked under her, holding a glass of sweet wine and listening to the sounds all around her. There was the familiar lantern light, the water over rocks, the scent of nearby flowering bushes, but other than that, everything was new. The setting was one she had chosen and designed for her new life, not to relive the old.

Ana walked through the kitchen to the large windows that overlooked the surrounding hillsides. She could see street lanterns glowing across the landscape leading to other homes that were not visible to her. She felt an overflow of joy inside her heart. She strolled back into the living room and sat down on one of the soft, multi-colored cushions by the fireplace. She spoke out loud, to herself, "I can't believe this has finally happened. My heart is free of fear at last! I'm surrounded by beauty which I have chosen for myself. I feel so excited, as if my life were just beginning. I'm proud of myself for coming through the pain and out the other side…to the joy!"

Ana started laughing with the pure happiness of one who had achieved a great success. And she had. Ana had come through the sorrow of a dreadful loss to experience a triumph of the spirit. She walked around the living room touching the soft furniture, the bright cushions, the artwork, the shiny glass table. Then she stopped in front of the fireplace and lifted her glass to offer a toast to her new life.

"Here's to memories laid to rest and to dreams not yet fulfilled."

Ana drank the last drop of wine, then turned and flung the glass into the fireplace. She laughed and threw up her arms and danced around the huge living room, shouting to herself and the empty room, "Look out…Gabrelli is back…and ready to take on the world!"

CHAPTER 41

*"A message received from a friend, a heart touched
alive...with joy!"*
        --Ana and Dominic

The first week in her new home had ended for Ana. Val and
Roger came out one evening for supper to see the final decorating
job. Roger was impressed with the beauty of the house.

"Wow! I always knew you had it in you, Ana. This is great!
I love all the bright colors. It looks like you and, it looks like
you're ready for a whole new life!" He gave Ana a warm hug
and a kiss on the cheek.

"We're proud of what you've done, sis. For coming through
the tough times with a blast! By the way, have you met any of
your neighbors? You never know what might be out
there...waiting for you!"

"I haven't met them and, what's more, I don't intend to! As
far as I'm concerned, I live alone on this gigantic estate where
only my invited guests may enter!"

She laughed, but Roger and Val knew she was very serious.
Roger couldn't help reacting to her challenge.

"You mean we can't just drop by for pizza and beer on a
Saturday night?"

"Ha! No such food is served here and my television does not
have the Saturday night fights."

"Oh, so now Gabrelli becomes a snob. I knew it would
happen as soon as I saw that guard at the gate. We poor relatives
will have to stand outside, begging for entrance. Will you let us
in, Ana, and feed the hungry?"

"You're in trouble, Roger, but I suppose I could fix you a
corner in the basement with everything you need...a big, old,
raggedy chair and an icebox full of your favorite...so there!"

Val punched Roger, "See, I told you riches wouldn't change
her."

They enjoyed their evening together celebrating Ana's new
home and her new life. As they parted, Val asked her sister a
question that caused Ana some serious thought later that night.

462

"Ana, I know you pretty well. Are you going to be happy out here in this huge house all alone? Since you won't be teaching, you'll lose contact with young people. That's been your whole life for so many years. It's a big change."

"I feel so comfortable with everything right now, but you may be right. I may need to expand my social life…later."

Val gave her sister a hug and smiled as she left, "Take your time, sweetheart, and enjoy the moment."

Ana thought about Val's question as she climbed into bed. Maybe she should consider contacting some of her former students who might be in the area. Perhaps they might need a place to bunk for a while. Or even one of the visiting women professors at Boston University or Harvard. She had a whole lower floor that was empty and very private. In that way, she could keep her association with the academic world somewhat alive. But Ana grew tired at the thought and felt in no hurry to follow through with it.

Near the end of Ana's third week in her new home, Miko drove up to Boston for a weekend with his mother. When he walked into the house, he was stunned at what he saw. He looked all around and then looked at his mother.

"Is this the mother I know? All these bright colors and this modern elegance? Have you been hiding your real self all these years?"

Ana gave him a big hug and laughed, "Perhaps I have. This is the first place I've ever lived that I chose for myself. The Seijo house was Sato's and Rock Hills was Mishima's. Perhaps this is the real me, after all!"

"I do believe this is the real you. Your wild streak finally comes out in all these fabulous colors. I love it, but I'm afraid to touch anything. This is definitely a showplace. Where can I slouch around and mess up the room?"

"I've got a whole basement, just for slouchy people like you and Roger. I'll let you two design that part of the house. Especially if you do come up here for school, you'll need a weekend getaway from dorm life."

"Weekend getaway? I may be a permanent resident if I can have the whole lower floor!"

Ana shoved him off the couch.

"I allow no permanent residents except me in this house! You've been living away from home too long to ever be comfortable in my space again. But I will give you weekend privileges, with special rules, of course."

"Mothers never change...rules, rules, rules!"

"Poor child, you have had such a hard life, haven't you?"

Miko gave his mother a surprise hug.

"No, I haven't. I've had a wonderful life and wonderful parents and everything I could wish for, and that includes my mother's happiness."

Then Miko smiled and whispered to his mother, "Okay, enough of that. When do we eat?"

Ana fed her constantly-hungry son. After everything was cleaned up from their noon meal, Miko brought in his suitcases for the weekend stay. He had one suitcase filled with his mother's mail that had piled up while she was gone on her trip. Ana had given Miko strict orders to send all business correspondence to her lawyer and financial advisor, but to keep personal mail separate. She did not want to deal with any of it until she had returned to the States.

Miko dumped the whole suitcase on the floor in front of the fireplace and they both sat down to open the many cards and letters of sympathy that had come to Ana from her friends and associates in the Virginia community, the university, and Japan. Near the bottom of the stack, Ana found a letter that totally surprised her. The envelope was dated six months ago and had a Boston postmark. The return address was Boston University Medical School, but there was no name. She handed it to Miko.

"Are you considering a medical career?"

He looked at her in surprise, then realized she was serious.

"No, Mother, that's one career that hasn't yet crossed my mind, though just about everything else has!"

"Well, what could this be?"

Miko turned it over in his hand, "If it's from one of your students asking for a reference to the medical school, it's too late, now!"

"I'll bet that's it. Guess I'd better open it and find out for sure."

Ana ripped open the envelope and found a typed message inside. To her surprise, it was from Dominic.

"Listen to this, Miko. It's from Donatelli."

She read the letter out loud:

"Dear Ana and Miko,

I'm writing to my close friends to let you know that my life has undergone some major changes. A few months ago, I accepted a position as professor of cardiac medicine at the Boston University Medical School. This has brought new challenge to my life as I'm finding the classroom a totally different experience than I've ever known. The personal contact and interchange with students is an exciting and positive change for me.

Since I don't have a permanent home in the Boston area yet, my address is my university office. I would love to hear from both of you to know what new challenges await you.

I realize that sometimes when people make a major change in life, they may wish to move on and not look back to former relationships. This may be the case with you, however, not so for me. If you have any interest in renewing our friendship, on whatever level, I would love to meet and exchange experiences. Perhaps you might come to the Boston area to visit your family from time to time. If so, please feel free to call me at the number on my letterhead and perhaps we can get together.

Your friend always,
Dominic Donatelli"

Miko was as surprised as Ana.

"I wondered what happened to him. He hasn't called me since you left for your trip. I suppose he thought that we'd received his message and just didn't care to answer. Did he know about your trip?"

"No, Miko. To be very honest with you, Dominic came to see me one evening at the house and we ended up in a major...you might say, confrontation. As a result of that, I decided that I needed to find some new directions for my life. I didn't let him know when I left for the trip and haven't contacted him since that night."

Miko was upset about what had happened.

"If I had only known that letter was from him, I'd have called to let him know you were out of the country. I feel terrible about it. We should call him today! I think we should, at least, let him know why we didn't answer."

Ana hesitated before commenting, "Why not let me write him a note, Miko. He may have written us off by now. Who knows what can happen in a few months' time? And besides, I'm sure he's so busy that a call might not even get to him."

"I suppose you're right. But let me have his address. I want to write to him on my own and let him know what's happening in my life. Then, whichever one of us hears from him first, let the other know."

"That's fine with me."

After the busy weekend with Miko, Ana finally had time to think about the letter to Dominic. She was concerned that he might not want to hear from her after such a long silence between them. After all, when they last talked he was angry and she was in a total state of depression. She wondered how things were with him, now. But Ana knew that with the many changes in her life, if she and Dominic chose to renew their relationship, it would be on completely different terms. Now, she could enjoy knowing him as a person apart from their past.

Ana had talked herself into responding to the message and leaving the answer up to him. She wrote her belated reply in an upbeat, friendly mood.

A few days later, Ana's letter arrived on Dr. Donatelli's desk. His secretary noted the name "Ana Gabrelli" at the heading of the return address and took it to him immediately. Jan Martinez had been with Dominic for years and knew all there was to know about his private and professional life. In many ways, she was like family and his only confidante and counselor. He trusted her completely. Jan knew that this would be the most important letter that he could receive.

Dominic was in consultation with a student when Jan knocked on the door. He didn't hesitate to answer her knock. They had a long-time agreement that only very important matters should allow any interruption when his office door was closed. When he opened the door, Jan smiled and thrust the letter into his hand. Dominic excused himself to his student and stepped out to talk to his secretary.

Jan whispered to him, "It's from Ana Gabrelli and the address is Boston."

Dominic looked the envelope over quickly and commented, "My god! I don't believe it, after all these months. I wonder what's going on with her. And why the Boston address?"

"She must be visiting her family. Now, don't dare forget to let me know what's happening!"

Dominic laughed and gave her a hug.

"After everything you've been through with me, I would never do that! As soon as I read this, good or bad, you'll be the first to know."

"Well, hurry. I need to know if you'll need a glass of wine with cheese or black coffee with lots of aspirin!"

As soon as Dominic's student sessions were completed, he opened the letter from Ana, took a deep breath, and began to read.

"Dear Dominic,

I was very happy to receive your note today, even though it was dated some time ago. I want to offer you congratulations on your new position! It sounds like a completely different lifestyle for you and I wish you success in this new challenge. I've also found some new challenges since we last met.

Shortly after our visit at the house in Virginia, I decided to take a journey. For the past year, I've been traveling in Europe and Great Britain and only returned a few weeks ago. Within these few months, there have been many changes in my life.

(Miko just brought my personal mail to me this weekend. I instructed him to save it until I returned. Thus, my late reply to you!)

The most important change is this: I've relocated to Boston. After returning from my journey, I felt the need to redefine myself as a person and to restructure my life. My first step was to resign my position at Georgetown. The second step was the decision to move to Boston. Miko is hoping to be accepted at Harvard next fall and, if this works out, he'll have a place to spend his weekends. Besides, I'll be closer to my sister and her family.

For some reason, this seems important to me now. I've purchased a home here and have just moved in. (Rock Hills is in process of being sold.) So, you see, we have lots of catching up to do. Why not share all of our news over a quiet dinner at my new house? If you have an evening free in the next week or two, please call me at the enclosed number. I'd love to hear from you.
    Best regards,
    Ana Maria Gabrelli"

    As soon as Dominic's sessions were finished, he hurried back to his office. He dropped into the chair opposite Jan's desk and gave her a very warm smile. She saw his black eyes sparkling and knew it was going to be good news.

    Dominic whispered, "I don't believe what's happened, Jan!"

    "Don't just sit there, tell me!"

    "This woman has been out of the country for a whole year and…has just moved to Boston! She's decided to leave Virginia, she's selling the house and she asked me to call her and come over for dinner some night so we can catch up on all our news. What should I do? Should I call her now, or should I wait a while? What's the protocol when there's been such a long silence between us?"

    Jan gave him a completely disgusted look, "Are you nuts? Get on that phone, now!"

    She pointed her finger toward his office as if he were a stupid child whose mother had to tell him what to do. He followed her command.

    Ana answered the phone as she always did, "This is Ana Gabrelli."

    Dominic's heart jumped into his throat at the sound of her voice. He nearly choked on his answer.

    "Ana…this is Dominic. My god, Ana, I can't believe your letter, after so long!"

    He could hear a definite note of happiness in her reply which caused him to breathe a sigh of relief.

    "Dom, I'm glad to hear your voice! I was surprised at your good news, too. You'll make a wonderful professor and I'm sure all your students will love you!

Please forgive me for being so late responding to your letter. I left Miko with instructions to keep all the personal mail unopened until I returned. My plan was to become totally immersed in the experiences abroad, so I was living with families and learning as much as possible about different ways of life there. I just didn't want to even think about anything else during that time.

I'm sorry that I missed your letter, though, and hope you haven't mistaken my silence for something other than it was."

"I do understand, Ana, and it's a relief to know that travel was the only reason you hadn't responded. Of course, I was very worried about that. I've just this minute received your note and am surprised at your news. A bit shocked, even, that you've moved up to Boston. I'm glad you're here!"

"We have so much to talk about with all these changes in our lives. When can you come to my house for dinner? How's your schedule this week?"

"This week Saturday is good. That's a quiet night for me now that I'm no longer the surgeon on call."

"Let's do it Saturday, then."

"Now, where do you live, and how do I get there?"

"Goodness, I could never give you directions. I hardly know where I live myself. This house is in a maze. But I'll fax you the directions. And come early, at least by 5 o'clock, or you'll get lost out here in the dark. There are many twists and turns."

"I'll be there by 5. And thank you very much, Ana, for your message and the chance to get caught up on the last few months of our lives. I'm handing the phone to Jan, and she'll give you the fax number. And besides, she'll be happy to hear your voice. She knows I'll stop being such a grouch now that Ana's back in town."

Ana laughed at his foolishness. After Jan gave the fax number to Ana and hung up, Dominic walked out to her desk and fell into the chair beside her with a broad smile and a dazed look on his face.

"Get wine and cheese, Jan. I've just received a message from an angel!"

Jan reached over and tapped him on the shoulder.

"Just be careful that this angel doesn't clip your wings!"

469

Dominic moaned his answer, "She already has. And I'll need all the 'Hail Mary's' you can muster for this poor, lost soul."

Though they laughed together, Dominic's heart rate increased substantially. He knew there would be no rest until he'd seen Ana and discovered what was happening with her and how she was facing the transition since Toshi's death. And, more than that, whether or not there would ever be a place for him in her life beyond friendship.

Saturday could not come soon enough for Dominic. His mind was in a whirl. He was afraid to see Ana and afraid not to. She had sounded happy and strong on the telephone, as if she'd come through the deep sorrow that had settled over her when they were last together. He worried about the first moment when they would meet, what he should say or do. Dominic knew Ana well enough to be fully aware that however he presented himself to her, it must be carefully done.

Ana, on the other hand, had different concerns. Being with Dominic would be a major test of her new-found strength. She would know when they met whether or not she had put away the ghosts of the past and was ready for new relationships. As Saturday approached, Ana became uneasy. She began to wonder if perhaps this whole thing was a major mistake.

On Friday night, Val called to see how things were going for the "big night" at Ana's place.

"Hey, is everything ready for the first major 'male moment' for who knows how long?"

Val always had a way of putting things in perspective that made them seem natural, harmless, and fun. Ana relaxed at her sister's teasing question.

"I'm actually having some fun with this. I've got your cookbook out, studying it, hoping there is a 'never-fail' guarantee with this complicated recipe you've suggested. Other than that, I'm just worrying about how to talk to a man who's just coming by for dinner. Do you even have an inkling of how long it's been since I've had this experience?"

"Yeah, I'd have the same problem. Just pretend that you're an expert on romance and Italian cuisine and how can you fail? The secret is always in your sauce…and your self-esteem. Just give it all you've got, and let the old chips fall…wherever!"

"In the first place, I'm not ready for the romance thing, but I would like to make it with the Italian cuisine. I've been cooking rice and veggies for so long, I don't think boiling this Shrimp Capellini will do it."

"Oh, by the way, dear sister. Let me remind you that you will be spending an evening with a tall, dark, handsome Italian. Now, if you're not ready for the 'romance thing,' why don't you just call him and cancel this meeting. You're a disgrace to the blood that flows through your veins! Will you please take my advice…relax and enjoy. You're just lucky you found that letter."

"Okay, okay, I'll do my best to uphold the honor of my name. Now, tell me the secret of the capellini!"

Val proceeded to give Ana her step-by-step lesson in gourmet Italian cooking.

CHAPTER 42

"Renewing a friendship broken by sorrow. New life heals
the wounds of the past, bringing hope for the future!"
--Ana and Dominic

Saturday evening arrived and, of course, Ana was prepared. She decided that Dominic deserved the very best for all that he had done for her and Toshi, so she went all-out. Beyond her efforts to create a gourmet meal for her Italian friend, Ana added some special touches to her home. She ordered several large bouquets of multi-colored wild flowers to place near the entry, beside the fireplace and on the glassed-in area off the kitchen where she would serve their dinner.

For the dinner setting, Ana created her own style of beauty with lime green place mats and bright orange napkins, as contrast to the white table and dishes. Just for fun, she added a crystal bowl of orange poppies as a centerpiece. Ana loved the atmosphere the "hot colors" gave to the room. They were an expression of the joy she felt entering this new phase of life.

Except for cooking the shrimp capellini, the most difficult part of Ana's evening preparations had been what to wear for this rather intimate evening with her friend. Val finally had to drag her sister to a dress shop where they found a simple, black dress with a square neckline and short, puffy sleeves. The material was a soft cotton knit with buttons down the front and a flare at mid-calf. Ana chose black since the house was already filled with bright colors and, if she happened to spill the capellini, it wouldn't show. Her practical side won out.

Ana was surprised at the excitement she felt as the time for Dominic's arrival drew closer. She admitted, with pleasure, that her home was beautiful. Not only was the addition of the wild flowers impressive, but she had placed candles of many shapes and sizes around the fireplace and on the glass dining room table.

After the candles were lit and the lights turned down, it was evident that Ana had created an intensely romantic setting. She thought to herself, "Perhaps I'm ready for a new lifestyle, after all, in more ways than one." She decided to take Val's advice and enjoy the moment for whatever it might bring.

The guard rang Ana at exactly 5 o'clock to announce the arrival of her guest. At the words, "Mr. Donatelli is here," she felt a sudden tightness in her chest and had to take a few deep breaths to calm down. She went to the door and opened it.

Dominic had parked his car in the circle drive and was walking toward Ana, wondering how to greet his hostess, but she quickly solved his dilemma. She walked out to meet him with a warm smile and a welcoming embrace. He accepted both with relief and pleasure. She took his hand and led him up the steps into the house. When they walked inside, Dominic couldn't help reacting to what he saw all around him.

"Ana, this is a beautiful home!"

He turned to give her a housewarming gift, a bottle of champagne wrapped in gold foil.

"And you, a most beautiful hostess. I believe this gift fits the occasion very well. This is a true celebration."

Ana accepted the champagne with a smile, unwrapping it as she walked to the kitchen to put it on ice.

"Ah, only the best for such a special evening. Thank you, Dom, we'll enjoy this together."

When she turned back to him, Dominic was standing in the center of the living room, looking around at her home. He could hardly believe what he saw. The flowers, the candles, the bright colors, and soft, comfortable furniture were dazzling.

Ana came toward him, "Well, what do you think? Is this the 'real' me or the 'new' me?"

Dominic was silent for a few moments, walking around the room, looking at everything, touching the furniture and the petals of the flowers to see if they were real. Ana waited for his response. Finally, he answered, "In every place I've been with you, Ana, Rock Hills, the resort in Carolina, and the little house in Seijo, you've always fit perfectly into the setting. But this," he held out his hand as he turned to look at the beauty surrounding them, "this time you've created the setting to fit you. I've never been in a home that matched so perfectly with the personality of its owner. This is the 'real you,' Ana. Everything here is warm and bright and beautiful!"

Ana felt the emotional impact of Dominic's words. She suddenly knew, without a shadow of a doubt, that he was in love with her. She reminded herself to go with care, for she had felt her own heart stirring as he spoke. She responded to his compliments with a smile and a slight bow.

"I thank you, sir, for those generous words."

Dominic continued to walk around the room.

"I can't even imagine anyone but Ana Gabrelli placing a bouquet of fragile, wild flowers beneath a huge, bold painting such as this."

He pointed to the modern art piece hanging above the mantel, "And setting candles of every size and shape around a marble fireplace or beneath a crystal chandelier? This whole room is filled with contrast, elegance alongside the commonplace, but it comes together as…perfection. My god, Ana, for the first time since we met, I believe you've expressed yourself openly! Walking into this house tonight is like stepping inside your soul.

We'd better open the champagne and make a toast to this beauty and to the one who created it!"

Ana laughed to cover her embarrassment at his profuse compliments.

"I do believe we could use a drink or two after that amazing speech! But I thank you for it, Dom."

They walked out to the kitchen where she provided the glasses and he poured the champagne. Then he took her hand and led her back to the living room where they stood in front of the flickering candles around the fireplace. Dominic raised his glass to her.

"To Ana Maria Gabrelli, may this home always radiate the beauty that is you and the joy that should always be yours."

They touched glasses and took a sip of champagne. Then, Ana introduced her own toast.

"The first night I stayed here, I made a toast just to myself. I wanted to hear the words spoken out loud. But tonight I want to make that same toast in your presence, Dom, so there will always be someone to remind me that I mean what I say."

Dominic filled their glasses again and waited for Ana's toast. Her voice shook as she said the words, "Here's to memories laid to rest and…to dreams not yet fulfilled."

Their eyes met and they smiled at each other as their glasses touched. When they finished the drinks, Dominic took the glasses and set them on the mantel, then turned to Ana and put his arms around her. His warmth and strength were offered as one who understood where she had been and where she needed to go. Ana felt his love for her and appreciated it, though she didn't know if she could return it in the way that he most desired.

Ana finally pulled away from Dominic's embrace and led him to the dinner table in the kitchen.

"Now comes the test of whether or not I'm ready for life without Yoshiko. I actually cooked this meal myself, though I had to keep Val on the phone through most of it. Shall we give it a try?"

Ana couldn't believe that everything turned out as she and Val had planned. The shrimp capellini was flavored to perfection, the bread was tasty and hot, the Italian vegetables were just barely crunchy, and the key lime pie was a pleasure to behold, as well as to taste. Dominic gave her the compliment she deserved.

"I'm sorry, Ana, but I had no idea you could even cook. Everything was delicious…totally incredible!"

"Well, you don't need to be quite so surprised at my amazing talents. But, thank you, anyway."

"Is this part of the 'new you' program? Cooking?"

"A little here and a little there. But, believe me, I'm not planning on getting carried away with this. I have other things in mind for my future."

"And what might those other things be, Ana?"

She laughed as she began cleaning off the table, "Actually, I haven't thought of them yet. I just know that one of them will not be cooking!"

"Well, I've just completed a major change in my life, so, perhaps I can help you with the process. It takes guts and, of course, some planning and some opportunity."

"Well, there's one thing I've learned over the past few years—I have the guts. And, recently, I made some plans and carried them out to my complete satisfaction. My trip to Europe, leaving Rock Hills, the move to Boston and this house. How am I doing, so far, doctor?"

Though Ana smiled, there was a flash of defiance in her eyes. Dominic saw that her spirit was back as strong as ever. She was ready to take on anything or anyone that would threaten to tame it. He would never be so foolish as to make such an attempt.

"You're doing great, Ana!"

She laughed at him, "You're still afraid of me, aren't you?"

"Should I be?"

"Probably. Sometimes I even frighten myself."

"You don't frighten me, Ana, but you never cease to amaze me. And I refuse to qualify that statement. Let's do the dishes."

When the table was cleared and everything put away in its place, Dominic poured them another glass of champagne and Ana led him to the patio. They sat down on the soft-cushioned chairs and sipped their drinks in the quiet beauty there. Dominic was surprised that the surroundings of the garden were so close to that of Seijo. He could hear the stream nearby, the garden lanterns were flickering in the shadows of the pines, and he even caught the sweet scent of flowers on the evening breeze.

He felt a chill from under his heart, as if he had walked across someone's grave. He began to wonder just how serious Ana really was about laying memories to rest. It seemed that she had created a monument to the place where she and her lover had spent their sweetest moments. He was afraid to speak for fear that he would say all the wrong things. But Ana spoke first.

"I can read your thoughts, Dom. Actually, this is the first time I've ever been out here in the evening for any length of time. During the day, everything is different. The colors are bright, the furniture modern, the flagstone shines in the sunlight. Even the flowers and trees seem to give off a different aroma. Until this very moment, I'd never thought of the past here in this place. I wonder, if you hadn't been with me tonight, whether I would have thought of it now."

"What do you mean? I don't understand what you're saying."

"Only that you believe I'm fooling myself. You believe that I've created this setting to relive memories, rather than to let them go."

"Did you, Ana?"

"When I bought this house, I went into every room. I sat inside each of them and thought to myself, *'What do I want to feel when I'm here?'* And then, I chose to decorate those spaces according to my feelings. Never once did I say to myself, '*What do I want to remember when I'm here?*'

I'll admit that when I came out here to the garden, I did recall things that I love. I love the sound of water over rocks, the scent of trees and flowers around me, and the candlelight. I've always loved those things, and I wanted to recreate them here for their beauty and their presence. But not for the memories that might be associated with them. If that had been the case, I would never sit in this garden again. I'm not so masochistic as to create a space where either myself of my friends would experience pain."

Dominic was silenced by her words. It was evident that she believed what she said. But he wasn't sure whether or not he did.

"Do you really think it's possible to recreate a particular setting without reliving the memories that are associated with it?"

Ana considered his question for a few moments before replying, "Yes, I know it is. I've done it! I've never once thought of reliving those memories here. You're the one who brought them to this garden tonight. I was sitting here with you, enjoying the beauty around us, the joy of being together, and renewing our friendship.

But you've placed your own feelings inside my heart. I don't come to this garden to relive the past. I come here to enjoy the beauty of this new home, this new beginning. And I resent what you've done to our moments here."

Dominic was shocked at Ana's accusation. He was afraid to answer her or to even attempt to calm her anger. He was further surprised when she stood and took his hand, saying, "Come with me, Dom. I want to show you something that was given to me after Toshi's death. It has helped me through the pain of losing him and has finally given me the courage to begin a new life without him."

Ana led Dominic into the room off the living area which was entered through a sliding shoji door. When she switched on the light, he saw a beautiful tatami room that contained Oriental treasures of pottery, ancient scroll paintings, and folding screens. He turned to Ana, but she answered his unspoken question before he could form the words.

"No, this is not a shrine. These are gifts from Toshi's family and friends. They're far too precious and too beautiful to hide away in a closet or give to a museum. I come here to meditate and find peace for each day. I don't come here to worship the past, nor even to call it up in memory. And this is why."

Ana walked to a beautiful teak table and opened the glass case that contained the white ceramic rose from Toshi. She took out a parchment envelope that held the final words Toshi had written to her before his death. She handed it to Dominic.

"Please read this and don't be afraid of its tenderness. These words have given me the freedom to find new life."

Ana led Dominic to a soft, low chair near the sliding door that opened onto the garden. She switched on the lamp close by and left him alone. Then she went into the living room, wondering how Dominic would respond to what he read.

After a while, Ana walked back into the tatami room to find that Dominic had returned to the garden. The envelope was lying on the chair. Ana wasn't sure what she should do. Perhaps he wanted to be alone. She put the envelope back into the case before she stepped outside. There she saw him sitting in a patio chair with his head back and his eyes closed. Ana sat down in a chair next to him, waiting for some clue to his feelings. He felt her presence and finally spoke in a whisper, "I feel as if I had entered a place where I don't belong. You shouldn't have given me the letter, Ana. It was between you and Yamamoto. I know how much you loved him and what his death has cost you. I feel like an intruder in the private places of your heart."

Though Dominic's words were tender, they revealed a mistaken belief that she had not changed. Ana spoke to his misconception.

"When you and I stood on the yacht together at Lake Kawaguchi and watched his ashes move across the water, I left the rose there, at his request, as a symbol of my willingness to love again. But I wasn't ready to accept the loss. I didn't understand the full meaning of the promise we had made when we were young.

He tried to explain that the rose was a symbol of the love we shared that must continue to be shared with others, or it would have no value. He wanted me to know that there is never an end to loving.

It's taken time, but I'm no longer bound by memories, nor am I afraid of them. I recall how it was the last time you saw me. But I'm not that person now, nor will I ever be again. I'm alive, and I'm discovering the joy of each new day. My heart is free, Dom."

Dominic began to sense a new beauty in the night. He could still hear the sound of water over rocks and he caught the same sweet scent of the garden flowers. But they no longer frightened him. He realized that this moment had no relationship to the past. Everything here tonight was new. And Toshiburo Yamamoto, the one he had most feared and yet had come to love and respect, had given him the freedom to love Ana. Dominic had never expected such a gift.

Much later in the evening, after Dominic and Ana had talked about their many experiences since they had last met, Ana looked at him and spoke very seriously, "There's something I must return to you, Dominic, to ease my mind and to finally close a chapter of our shared past."

Dominic was concerned. He had no idea what she meant to do. Ana left him for a few moments to go upstairs. When she returned, he had walked back into the living room and stood by the fireplace, wondering what further revelations Ana had for him tonight. She went to him and took him by the hand, placing a small white envelope in his palm. He looked down and knew immediately what it was.

Their eyes met in a smile of mutual understanding. Ana put her arms around her friend and whispered, "Your faith in me was all I needed, Dom. I want you to know that I have never opened this envelope."

Dominic's heart was filled with new hope for their future together. His questions echoed that hope.

"Tell me again, Ana, what was that toast you made the first night you spent here in your new home?"

Ana laughed and went to the kitchen to get them each another glass of champagne. When she returned, they raised their glasses as she repeated the words of her toast.

"Here's to memories laid to rest and to dreams not yet fulfilled."

They drank their champagne, then Dominic gave Ana a questioning look as he held up his empty glass and turned to the fireplace.

"Is such wild, Italian behavior allowed here?"

Ana laughed and led the way. They smashed their fine crystal glasses against the inner wall of her beautiful, marble fireplace. The evening ended with laughter and the joy of renewed friendship.

Perhaps this night would be the beginning of a dream that might one day be fulfilled for Ana and Dominic. Perhaps these friends would become lovers and the promise found in the "Legend of the Rose" would be theirs. For the truth in the promise is this: Love is eternal and can never die as long as it continues to be shared with another's heart.

"Remember…love is all, love is all there is…to life!"

Sayonara.

So be it.

THE END

About the Author

Lois E. Taylor Braby is a woman who has lived many lives. Thus, she enjoys telling the story related to one of those lives in the genre of fiction. She has completed two Master's degrees, one in Sociology/Anthropology and the other in Counseling, both from Iowa State University in Ames, Iowa. Ms. Braby has traveled to Japan on two occasions. On her first journey, she went as an "itinerant anthropologist" for a three-month term to complete cultural studies for her Master's degree. She was so fascinated with the people and culture of Japan that she longed to return. Later, she was given an opportunity for a one-year study-teaching program at the Nihon Intercultural Center in the Osaka area. On this second journey, she was able to immerse herself in the culture, to become more acquainted with the Japanese people on an in-depth level, and to enjoy more extensive travel throughout the country.

Ms. Braby views the concerns of the protagonist in this novel as representing her own struggle in returning to her homeland while caring deeply for the culture of the Orient. After her second journey to Japan, she realized that she would probably never have this opportunity again. Her own love affair was with the Japanese people and the culture of this tiny isle. She has portrayed that special love in the struggles of her protagonists to fulfill their promises to one another while trapped in the chains of cultural expectations.

Following her return to the states, Ms. Braby taught sociology and anthropology and served as Career Counselor and Director of Intercultural Programs at a small private college in Iowa. Later she worked as a child abuse counselor for the state of Iowa and author of youth learning materials for a religious organization. She has retired from many years of study, teaching, writing and counseling and has chosen to author this simple love story. She considers this enterprise a catharsis to assist her finding peace with, and finally "putting away," those most precious moments of living among and caring deeply for persons in a culture so uniquely different from her own.